THE CROSSROADS SAGA, BOOK FOUR

ETERNITY

Angel,
Thank you for all
your support & friendship.
Hugs! Mary Ting

MARY TING

Editor: Maxine Bringenberg
Formatting by Inkstain Interior Book Designing

wander or seek, we will all find our family in Eternity. Together As One!"

—Elliot, EllieSewSweet

"Eternity is such a fitting name for the last book of this series. With the amazing characters, story line and worlds that author Mary Ting has blessed us with, this series will stay with ME for an Eternity."

—Mindy, Books Complete Me

"This book brought me together with old friends I had not seen for a while. I love the Crossroads Saga series and the emotional roller coaster it has taken me on. You realize with love and perseverance all things are possible. Eternity is the last book in the series and I don't want to say goodbye so I think I'll just say "see you when I see you.""

—Vanessa, Fairiechick's Fantasy Book Reader

DEDICATION

As the Crossroads Saga comes to a conclusion, I have mixed emotions. I'm so happy and proud that I have written four books and a novella to this saga, but at the same time I'm so heartbroken that it's over. As you all know, I started writing Crossroads as a way to heal from the loss of my grandmother, and I feel like I'm finally letting her go. Though I know she'll always be in my heart and her memories are what will keep her alive, it's still difficult.

I want to thank all my family, friends, and my amazing fans who have given their endless support. I couldn't have done this without all your love I've received from emails, Tweets, and Facebook. And for sure, I've made many friends around the world, where friendship knows no boundaries.

My little prayer for you all...may God keep you always, safe and warm. May your life be fulfilled with all that it has to offer, making dreams come true. May your heart always be filled with joy, laughter, and love. If darkness ever finds you, may your light be strong enough to let love, hope, and faith guide you out. And may you always be true to yourself and shine your light and do for others, even if they don't do for you. May your heart be pure and stay forever young.

Extra thanks to Angie Edwards, who helps me run the official page (Crossroads book); Janie Iturralde, Crossroads Saga Beyond; Mejeani Le Grange, Make Crossroads A Movie; Venna Dowrick, Between & Crossroads Saga Eternity; Amber Hulsey-Lee, Crossroads Saga; and Christi Valencia, Crossroads Saga Fans. I love you all to pieces.

Also to my new friend Kitty Bower, country singer and song-writer, who has written a song for Crossroads Saga called Michael's

Whispers. Check it out on YouTube. Thank you Kitty, for being such a sweetheart and for loving and spreading the word about the Crossroads Saga. You are an amazing friend and an angel.

Extra Extra thanks to Mary's Angels—my street team—extra thanks to the admins—Janie Iturralde, Elliot McMahon, and Jacque Talento. Your eagerness to get my books out there is amazing. Extra times a million to Elliot McMahon and Janie Iturralde for all your time and for all you do to help me get the word out about all my books. Your dedication, time, and friendship are much appreciated. I would be lost without you both. Angel hugs!!!

Thank you to all the wonderful bloggers who help support authors, who have been with me from the begging of my writing journey. Now you've all become my forever friends.

PROLOGUE

SWALLOWED BY COMPLETE DARKNESS, CLAUDIA was unaware of where she stood. Afraid to move, she dared not take a step or make the smallest sound. Her mind told her she was dreaming, but her heart was dreadfully frightened. Something evil, stealthy was coming; she could sense it, inching toward her. Feeling her pulse race, she tried to summon her bow, but to no avail.

Suddenly, a dim light appeared, radiating brighter as it approached her, but then it stopped. What she saw beyond the light shocked her. It was worse than the darkness. She would rather be in an abyss of darkness than to see Michael like this...shirtless, he wore only a pair of jeans, and an angelic golden cuff bound his hands in front.

"Michael," Claudia cried softly, her heart was in torment.

Michael didn't acknowledge her. He continued to gaze down to his bare feet, his head hung low, seeming too ashamed to make eye contact, either that, or he was unaware of her presence.

Cautiously, she took several steps to approach him. Since only God's first angels or their descendants could release the cuff, being one of the descendants, she knew she could do it. "Lucian," Claudia commanded.

Nothing happened.

Strange. "Lucian," she said again, louder and with more force in her tone...but nothing. Frustrated, she decided to ask him questions and go from there.

"Michael," she called softly. "What happened?" Carefully pacing toward him, he didn't even look up at the sound of her voice, the voice he should have known as well as the sound of his own beating heart. Placing her hand on his shoulder, she spoke again. "Michael. I'm here. Who did this to you?"

Surprisingly, his body was icy cold. With a harsh gasp, she wrapped her arms around him to give him warmth and comfort. But when she heard a growling sound like a wild beast would make, she backed away.

Michael set his eyes on her for the first time. They were burning red. His brows were angled in a slant, pinching in the center. The look on his hostile face made Claudia back away even more.

"No, no, no. Michael, it's me. This isn't you," she said desperately as her hand covered her mouth in agonized shock. What was she supposed to do now? She couldn't release the cuffs and she couldn't summon her bow; not that she would shoot him, but at least she would have something to defend herself if he tried to...oh God...no! She couldn't believe she was having these thoughts.

There was no time to think anymore. Michael flashed his wings so fast it startled her, and made her run several feet away from him. His wings were no longer pure white. Streaks of black slithered out from his back. If the change continued at that rate, they would become completely black. Not only that, he now had a different face, a face she had never seen before.

Claudia blinked at this phenomenon, as terrifying shivers shot through her veins. "Where's Michael? I won't let you take him from me!" she shouted. "I'm not going to hurt you." But he continued to come for her as if to harm her. And surprisingly, the golden cuffs were no longer on his wrists. They were simply gone.

She ran away from him as fast her legs would allow, but he was faster. Oddly, she couldn't move with her usual angel speed. With nowhere to go, she had no choice but to surrender.

Not knowing what to do without hurting Michael—though this being's face clearly showed it was someone else—she did what only she could do...she summoned her light. With her hands extended, they glowed the moment they made contact with his beautiful chest. The burst of light shot out so brightly it conquered the darkness.

CHAPTER 1

ICHAEL'S FIST WAS TUCKED UNDER his chin while his elbow rested on the pillow. Brushing Claudia's cheek with his hand, he tried to awaken her. "Claudia...Claudia...wake up."

"No, no, no...I won't let you," Claudia rambled, shaking her head from side to side. Though her eyes were closed, her facial muscles were tight.

"Claudia, my love, wake up." Michael sat upright when she didn't respond to his touch. Claudia had dozed off while they were resting, and as always, Michael had watched her sleep. It was the perfect opportunity to memorize the beauty of her face. Claudia was the reason for his happiness. Her laugher, her smile, her love was what made his heart beat blissfully, fulfilling it with love and hope. But his worry intensified when her words became louder.

"No! I won't let you!"

Wanting to attempt to wake her again, he sat on the edge of the bed and tenderly rubbed her arms to comfort her. "Claudia."

Without warning she bellowed, "Nooo!" Bolting upright, she placed her hands on Michael's shirtless chest. After feeling the blazing heat from her hands, neither his feet nor his hands touched the floor as Michael flew across the room, as if he had been hit with a massive punch. When he landed with a loud thud, Claudia shot her eyes open.

"Michael!" Claudia called.

Stunned, Michael didn't answer at first. After he pulled himself up to his feet, he stood there looking frazzled while raking his hair back.

"Michael...what happened?" Claudia looked flustered.

"I'm alright. Remind me never to get you mad," he said lightly, chuckling.

Claudia ran toward him and wrapped her arms around his neck. "I'm so sorry. Did I do this to you?" Her eyes caught his, demanding an answer.

"You were having a nightmare. Do you remember what you were dreaming about?"

She shook her head, displaying a look of concern.

He brushed her cheeks. "No need to worry, my love. It was just a dream."

She frowned. "Funny thing...I can't remember what I dreamt about, but I remember how I felt."

"I'll make you forget." Michael twitched his brows playfully, then crushed her lips with his. Teasingly, his sweet kisses trailed down her neck, then lower to the base of her breast. Effortlessly, he scooped her up in his arms and carried her back to bed. While he continued his soft kisses to her lips, he pulled her tightly to his chest. Needing to feel more of her, his hand on her back lifted the white lingerie to feel her warm flesh. Gliding his hand lower to her thigh, he straddled her over his hips and ran his hand seductively across her smooth leg. Then he let go.

"FEELING BETTER NOW?" HE SMIRKED, and gazed lovingly into her eyes.

She gasped softly from the pleasurable tingles that erupted throughout her body from his touch but still lingered when he let go. Feeling light headed, she couldn't remember his question and managed to mumble a few words. "Ahhh...what?"

"It worked." He gave a smug grin.

Releasing a light sigh onto his chest, Claudia nuzzled into him and tried to overcome the heated combustion that Michael purposely hadn't finished. "You are bad."

Michael let out a triumphant chuckle. "For you, I'll be anything. I can be really naughty."

She ran her hand gingerly up his firm chest and softly kissed her way up, making Michael quiver from her touch. "I can play the same game, you know?"

"Oh...I know you can," he moaned.

"And you shouldn't start what you can't finish," she pouted.

Michael captured her hands that were trailing over his shoulders and kissed them. "Who said I was finished? I'm just getting started. To be continued...later. So...what would you like to do today?"

"Can we go to the bookstore?"

"Sure. Afterward, I need to take care of something."

Surprised, Claudia pulled her hands back and rested them on his chest again. "What kind of 'something' do you need to take care of?" Her tone was filled with curiosity, playfully teasing him with her fingers.

Michael gripped her hand again, covering over it with his into a ball. "Something...I'll show you tonight."

Claudia sulked. "Hmm...you're going to have me guessing all day trying to figure out what you're up to?"

"That's the plan." He brushed his lips on her knuckles.

"You're cruel," she glared.

"So I've been told by our dear friend Davin."

Claudia's eyes beamed with happiness with the thought of her alkin friends—Davin, Caleb, and Vivian. "Fine. Before we go to the bookstore, I'd like to eat."

"Sure. I'll make you something." Michael kissed Claudia on her cheek, walked to the edge, and dropped down into the kitchen.

Even now, she was awestruck by the marvelous home Michael had built for them. Five layers of wooden platforms, each at least the size of a room, tiered upward and anchored to the surrounding trees for stability. And each room had a breathtaking view.

Claudia looked out the window and gazed through the endless beauty of evergreen trees, wild flowers, and the stream that seemed to flow without end. Beyond this view, she could see the mountain peaks that seemed so small. Inhaling a deep breath, the smell of nature filled her lungs with the purest of air. It reminded her of Island of Eden, and she wondered how Austin was doing.

Though she missed his friendship, she knew his reasons for keeping his distance from her. It was the only way to let her go. Austin was now one of the Twelve, so he had his hands full with other things. How proud she was of him, and hoped that someday she'd get to see him again.

She also recalled the terrible incident when Aliah, one of God deadliest first angels—who was supposedly dead—almost took Austin's life. He had cleverly taken Callum's body and soul. Callum had been one of the one hundred Earth angels called the curators, who each represented a state or a country. After his death, Holly had been selected to fill his position.

Claudia never wanted to think about "what ifs," but she couldn't help it sometimes, especially after the terrible nightmare she didn't want to share with Michael. They'd come so far and had overcome so many obstacles to find their own version of happily ever after that she would do anything to keep it that way.

She had died once to kill Aliah. She had felt she had no choice in order to save humanity and everyone she loved, but if something were ever to happen to Michael...well...she didn't want to think such negative thoughts.

Thankfully, the Twelve had allowed them to stay in their special place, where the two of them could reside without any interference from the Twelve unless they needed Michael and Claudia's help. Their situation was not something the Twelve granted easily...in fact, this was the first time. Regardless, Michael and Claudia felt blessed they could almost live like humans did. They cherished the time together, but her dreams haunted her.

This was the third time she'd dreamt this dream, and it was always the same—light illuminating out of her hands and having no recollection of what the dream was about. The only thing she could remember was how it made her feel—heartbroken, afraid beyond anything she could imagine, and a terrible feeling of loss.

What did her dream mean? Perhaps it was nothing, or post-traumatic stress. She brushed the thought off when Michael plopped back into bed and wrapped his wings around her like a soft goose down blanket, giving her a sense of comfort and love.

"Time to eat, my love." Wrapping his arms around her waist, he nibbled the side of her neck.

"It smells so good. Are you going to eat with me?" she asked, enjoying his caress as her thoughts became incoherent. Not only that, the smell of fresh mangos, avocados, and chicken salad tickled her nose, making her stomach churn with hunger.

"If you want me to, but maybe I should eat you first." He turned Claudia so fast she was now facing him. His eyes were filled with desire, seductively pulling her in while his lips moved slowly to hers.

Claudia pushed him away playfully just as his lips touched hers. "A girl's gotta play hard to get. I can be bad too." She giggled and jumped down to the first floor, moving with lightning bolt speed. Michael never saw it coming.

"SO YOU WANT TO PLAY hard to get. You know I'll go to the ends of the world to find you." He sprang after her, but there was no sign of her. Strange. He was certain she'd jumped down to the first level.

"Catch me if you can." Her voice echoed nearby as she ran from tree to tree, distancing herself from their home.

Michael tried to follow her steps, but he was unable to catch her, always a step behind. "Oh...you're good." Moving with the speed at which only angels could move, he bolted to the surroundings of their home, but Claudia was nowhere to be found. "Claudia, your food will get cold. No more running."

No answer.

"Claudia. I'm not running after you anymore. Show yourself. I give up."

No answer.

"I'm serious now. Please...show yourself." Michael started to panic. There was nothing evil living there...he was sure of it. Even the butterfly crystal necklace he had made for her was as clear as day. It would have turned black if danger was nearby. He had just seen it on her when they lay in bed. He would never have considered this place for their home if he felt there was even a slight chance evil could find its way there.

Hearing no reply from her, Michael's heart pounded and fear pricked every inch of him. Desperately, he searched until he saw her lying on the ground with her eyes closed. Worried, he bent low, felt her pulse, and placed his hands on her cheeks. "Claudia." He lightly shook her, but she didn't move. Michael didn't know what to do, so he scooped her body into his arms and carried her to their bed.

Sitting on the edge of the bed, Michael glued his eyes on her, making sure she was taking in air. He thought about many options, but decided to wait. Raking his hair back, he recalled how he had almost lost his love and how broken he had been without her. She was his light, his purpose for living, his everything and more. Seeing her helpless like this brought back the dreadful memories of waiting to see if she would recover from the death crystal she had inflicted on herself to save the world, and that alone made his heart race even faster.

Though he had forgiven himself for selectively suppressing her memories instead of erasing them as ordered by the Twelve, he couldn't help feeling guilty, especially when those memories rushed through unwillingly. As strong and powerful as she was, she looked so pale and frail.

Day turned to night. Running out of patience, his thoughts wandered with terrible thoughts. Margaret and Agnes were the two he trusted most besides Katherine, but he didn't want to come across Austin, so he decided it was best to take her to Halo City.

After making up his mind, he closed his wings gingerly around her, carried her across the vast sea of puffy clouds, and entered a place he had known for many years: a place that was once his home, a place he held dear to his heart, a place where it all began.

CHAPTER 2

When Michael entered, Philip, Agnes, and Margaret rushed to greet him with alarmed expressions on their faces when they saw Claudia's legs and arms dangling in Michael's arms.

"What happened?" Philip's tone raised with concern.

"I don't know...she ran...I chased...I mean...she didn't run from me per se." Michael had a difficult time trying to explain their playfulness since it was personal and private. "She wandered off by herself and I found her. It happened earlier today. Since she didn't awaken, I thought it was best to bring her here. I didn't know what else to do, especially since she's been through so much."

"You did the right thing by bringing her here. Take her to my room and I'll examine her," Agnes directed.

Michael followed her down the hall, past the main room where the meetings were held, then through another hall. After placing her on the bed, he was instructed to leave. Though he was hesitant, he knew he had no choice, so he told Agnes he would look for Alexa Rose and wait by the fountain.

AFTER MICHAEL LEFT THE ROOM, Agnes placed her hands several inches above Claudia's head and allowed her light to emanate. Starting from there, she slowly glided them downward without any physical contact. Hovering downward, past her chest to her stomach, Agnes halted in absolute astonishment.

MEANWHILE, CLAUDIA WAS SLOWLY PEELING her eyelids open. Stunned to see Agnes, she focused and began to ask questions. "Agnes? Why am I here, and where is Michael?" Claudia's mind reeled with terrible thoughts. Seeing herself at Halo City made her question whether Michael and her being together had been a dream. If it was, she didn't want to wake up.

"Michael is fine. He's waiting for you at the fountain. I asked him to step outside. Do you remember anything that happened?"

Now that her mind was at ease and she knew Michael was fine, she answered. "I remember running and...I must have fainted and...." She paused, blinking her eyes with wonder. "I think...I'm not sure, but I think I know the reason why now." With everything that had been happening, she couldn't remember her menstrual cycle. Claudia knew she was late, but she thought it was due to stress and anxiety. With all the changes in her body, she didn't know what was "normal" any more.

"Does Michael know?" Agnes asked nonchalantly.

Claudia's eyes grew wide and her cheeks flushed. Bewildered to think that Agnes knew, she ignored her question to ask her own. "You know?"

"Yes. I could feel a life inside you. And if I'm not mistaken... there are two."

Claudia gulped down a nervous lump of uncertainty, astounded by the reality of Agnes's words that confirmed her suspicions. She'd hoped to have a normal life with Michael, if that was even possible, but to have two miracles inside her was unbelievable. "I knew something was different because I felt different, but I wasn't sure what it was. And I've been so hungry, more than usual. I know how this happens, but I'm just...just a little shocked...actually hugely shocked."

"We don't talk about what humans would call 'the birds and the bees.' Alkins and venators know that creating a life is forbidden, and there is a good reason for that; however, I know what you're thinking. Austin is Katherine's child. So you know, even angels are not perfect. Things in life happen for a good reason, and I for one am glad Austin was born. It wouldn't be the same without him as well as all the others that were created forbiddingly, especially you, Claudia. Just so you know, I can't wait to see your miracles being born." Agnes lit a heartfelt warm smile.

"Thank you." Claudia returned the smile. She didn't know if she should be feeling happy or ashamed. Regardless of Agnes's words, it was forbidden. Those who would be against it would frown upon Michael and her.

"I've never been pregnant so I don't have any words for guidance," Agnes continued. "You should speak to Katherine. One thing for sure, you fainted because you needed nourishment. They're taking your energy. You must eat to support them. From what I understand, your pregnancy will be fast, only three months. You'll be showing real soon."

Though there was never a doubt in Claudia's mind she would give birth to the two precious babies growing inside her, she felt overjoyed that she had Agnes's blessing. "I will talk to Katherine about it. Please don't tell anyone just yet."

"I will keep silent, but I'm most certain they will be just as happy as I am...well, some of us at least. I won't be able to hold your secret too long. You'll be showing soon enough. Having Michael's and your genes, they will be strong and healthy. So...I'm guessing Michael doesn't have a clue."

"No...he doesn't. I myself just found out today." For unknown reasons Claudia became extremely worried. This issue had never been brought up for obvious reasons. What if Michael didn't embrace her pregnancy? Would he look at her differently? "What would you like for me to say? He is very worried about you."

"I know." Claudia glued her eyes to the bed, then back up to look Agnes squarely in her eyes. "Please tell him it was due to lack of eating...I guess." That wasn't exactly a lie, and it was somewhat true. "I would like to tell him when we're alone, if that's okay with you."

"Sure, I understand."

"Thank you."

"Before I get Michael, you have to promise me that you'll come back for a checkup. You don't need to come often...most likely twice, a month from now, and the day of the birth."

"Yes, I promise."

"Good. I'll go get him now."

Claudia lay back with mixed emotions. She wanted to scream out loud and rejoice over her pregnancy, but she couldn't. Though she was thrilled to carry the lives they had created by love, one question was on her mind...were they ready? Having children before she got married would have never happened in her human life, but her life was different now. It was a life she accepted and cherished because of Michael, but still a life in which she'd had no choice because of her special soul.

Her thoughts were broken when she felt a light breeze tingling her skin, knowing who had caused it. Michael appeared, standing by the entrance with both of his arms crossed like he was trying to hold himself together. He looked so dashing, utterly taking her breath away. It didn't matter how many times she saw him; every time was like the first time.

"Hi...how are you feeling?" he asked softly.

"I'm fine, Michael." Her tone was cheerful, trying to lighten the mood. "Agnes told me I just needed to eat. Why are you standing so far away?"

MICHAEL'S EYES POOLED WITH WATER. As he released a sigh of relief, his shoulders relaxed and his hammering heart went back to its normal rhythm knowing all Claudia needed was food and that she was out of danger. If anything were to happen to her, he didn't know what he would do. "I...I don't know." He chuckled and moved closer, but he knew why he was keeping his distance. He was afraid he would break down in front of her. Lowering himself to her, he laced his hand through her hair and kissed her tenderly on her lips.

After almost losing her to Aliah, he had promised himself he would cherish every second, every minute, every day they had together, because it was easy to take life for granted. Telling and showing her how much he loved her was one thing he would never fail to do, and if he overdid it, he didn't care because life was unpredictable. There was no guarantee they would be together forever.

"Can we go home now?" she asked, caressing his cheeks.

Michael closed his eyes, taking in her touch. "Anything you want." He opened his eyes to speak. "You scared the life out of me. Please don't ever do that again." He took her hands in his and kissed each finger, one by one.

"I'M SO SORRY I SCARED you." Claudia's heart felt heavy all of a sudden. Looking at his distraught expression, she could imagine Michael reliving the terrible incident when he'd waited for her at Island of Eden. Not knowing if she would wake up from the healing crystal must have been agonizing, and seeing her like this must have brought back heart-wrenching memories.

"Before we go, would you mind stopping by the fountain? Alexa Rose wants to see you."

"Sure." Claudia sat up, but before she could plant her feet on the ground, Michael pulled her into his embrace and carried her out of Agnes's room. Resting her head on his chest, she draped her arms around his strong neck.

"I have two feet. I can walk," Claudia giggled.

Michael chuckled lightly. "I know, but I'd much rather have you in my arms."

Out by the fountain, Alexa Rose stared below her to the water that sparkled like diamonds. As it twinkled with beaming golden hues, it was blinding to the eyes when looked at from a precise angle. The fine powder of death crystals was hidden in the water, guarded by the watchers that stood majestically around them. It was amazing how the light that shone like the sun gave no warmth, but produced a constant radiant glow to all of Halo City.

Alexa Rose turned upon hearing their footsteps. "Claudia!" She ran toward Claudia as Michael gently lowered her to stand. Alexa Rose's long, curly hair bounced with her running steps. She wore a beautiful white dress accented with pink ribbon around her waist, making her look like a living doll.

"I've missed you," Claudia greeted and gave her a tight squeeze.

Alexa Rose's admiring eyes shifted to the butterfly necklace on Claudia's neck when she released her. "It sparkles like the water."

Then she changed the subject. "Are you okay? Michael was really worried about you."

Claudia couldn't resist running her hands through Alexa Rose's soft, curly hair as she spoke. "I'm fine. It was nothing and you shouldn't worry."

"That's what I told Michael. Grownups worry way too much. He says I shouldn't worry because I'm too little to worry like a grownup."

Claudia nodded to agree and looked tenderly upon Alexa Rose. "Michael is right. You shouldn't worry too much."

"Michael says he's always right," Alexa Rose giggled.

"That's right," Michael reminded. "Have I ever been wrong?"

"I'm not sure. I'm too little to really understand."

Michael chuckled. "It doesn't matter. I'm always right." He winked.

"But Davin says he's always right too, so how can two people always be right? What if one person says this and the other person says that? How will I know?" Alexa Rose shrugged her shoulders, challenging Michael.

"So...Davin told you that?" Michael laughed out loud. "If he ever tells you that again, tell him Michael is always right."

"But he said that too. He said if you said that, he was right." Alexa Rose giggled. "You two make me laugh. You two act like children."

"I have to agree with you there," Claudia said lightly.

Michael frowned with his lips pouting out. He looked so adorable, Claudia couldn't help but melt into his expression. She wanted to go to him and kiss him, but she had to contain herself in front of Alexa Rose.

"Speaking of which, where are Davin, Caleb, and Vivian?" Claudia asked.

"They're on a mission with the venators. They are sweeping the town to make sure there are no existing demons," Michael informed. "Well...I hate to say goodbye, Alexa Rose, but we need to get going."

"Where are you going? Can't you stay here for a bit?" She pouted.

"Remember what I told you earlier?" Michael winked.

"Oh yeah...the secret." She nodded to confirm. "I can't wait."

"What secret?" Claudia tilted her head toward Michael, slightly glaring at him.

"A secret isn't a secret if it's told." Alex Rose beamed a mischievous smile.

"Alright then, I guess I'll have to wait." Claudia bent low and gave Alexa Rose a warm hug.

Just as Claudia released her hug, Alexa Rose pulled her in again and whispered in her ear so Michael wouldn't hear. "I know your secret."

Claudia caught Alexa Rose's eyes. "You do?" How could she know this? Agnes wouldn't have told a child, and she had promised not to tell a soul.

"Don't worry. I won't tell. I can feel them," Alexa Rose whispered again. "Only children...I meant angel children...can feel this special kind of energy."

"Thanks." Claudia's face felt warm and so did the rest of her body. Without warning, she felt dizzy and queasy. Michael steadied her when she planted her hand on his arm. "I'll catch you later, Alexa Rose."

Holding onto Claudia, Michael gave Alexa Rose a high five, a gesture he had learned from Davin. "I'd better take Claudia home."

"What would Davin say? Okie dokie."

Michael enclosed Claudia with his wings, smiling at Alexa Rose.

"See you when I see you," Alexa Rose said sadly.

Claudia and Michael became translucent and disappeared.

CHAPTER 3

AFTER EATING AND GETTING HER energy back, as instructed by Michael, Claudia slipped into a creamy long dress and matching high heels he had bought for her. To Claudia, it looked like an elegant, simple wedding dress. Strapless and form fitting at the top, it flowed out towards the bottom with a small train. With light makeup and her hair straight, she was all set to go.

Sitting alone in her room with her door opened wide, she watched the candlelight dance to the gentle breeze as she waited for Michael's return. As the scent of jasmine filled the room, she gazed at the picture of her adopted mom Ava and Gamma that she had placed on the nightstand. It broke her heart every time she looked at it, but the pain lessened knowing Gamma was in Heaven and Ava had her life back.

Michael had promised he would be back in ten minutes, but it seemed like hours, especially when Claudia was so worried about how he would react to her news. There was no reason to fear. Knowing Michael, he would welcome her pregnancy, but then again, she wasn't sure, only because they hadn't discussed the topic before it happened. Actually, they hadn't thought they needed to. Having a normal human life was out of the question, at least the having children part.

"Hey, beautiful."

Claudia jumped, startled by his sudden appearance, and turned to the sound of his voice. Michael wore a tuxedo and his hair was combed back. Looking debonair, he took her breath away, and heat ignited in her body at the sight of him. "Hey, handsome."

Grinning shyly as he peered down to his shoes, Michael blushed. Pacing toward her with a beaming smile, one hand was behind his back. When he stood in front of her, he revealed a bouquet of red roses. "Davin told me once red roses represent love. I hope you like them."

"Like them? I love them," she squealed, and took them from him. "Thank you." Inhaling the smell of the sweet divine roses, she gently brushed the silk-like petals between her fingers. "You know...these petals almost feel as smooth as your wings."

"Do they?" Michael's brows perked up. "I never knew. But for me, they feel almost as soft as your skin...and I mean all parts of you."

Claudia felt hot from his words, and she was sure her cheeks were just as red as the roses. All she could do was smile and look away shyly.

Michael placed both of his hands on her cheeks and forced her to look at him. "I could just stand here and stare at you forever, but I have other plans for us. Will you be my date tonight?"

"No."

"No?" Michael looked baffled.

"I meant...I'll be your date every night." She took several steps back and placed the roses on her bed.

"Much better." Without her permission, he swept her off her feet, making her gasp in surprise, and stood by the edge on their floor level.

"You know I can walk, don't you?"

"Yes, I know." He chuckled. "But I'd much rather have you in my arms and do this."

Before Claudia could mutter a word, Michael flashed his wings open and elevated into the night sky. Though she knew she was safe in his hold, she closed her eyes and looped her arms tightly around his neck.

"Open your eyes, Claudia. Just breathe and fly with me. You know I'll never let you go."

And so she did. She opened her eyes to see the most amazing sight. No matter how many times she had flown with him, the novelty never wore off. What he shared with her was always special and unique.

Soaring across the universe, the stars dazzled like crystals in the sky. There were so many she felt overwhelmed, but soon after, a sense of serenity consumed her. It was so peaceful and quiet that she had forgotten all her worries. "It's breathtaking." Her eyes were wide with wonderment, taking in the miracles of their existence and their purpose.

Claudia recalled Austin telling her a myth about the stars. When they first met, he had said they were human's souls only because he didn't want Claudia to think he was crazy. Later, when she knew Earth angels existed, he explained that the stars were Earth angels' souls.

Earth angels were special because they were the ones that lived among humans and had a deeper connection with them. When an Earth angel passed away, their souls were split into two; one part went to a special place in Beyond. The other part turned into a star in the sky, and stayed there as a reminder to humans that there were greater beings watching out for them. It was a reminder for humans, when all hope was lost, that there was a light at the end of the tunnel and that they were not alone.

"Yes...breathtaking, but I'd much rather look at one star I'm holding in my arms right now. She is the only one that makes my eyes sparkle and makes me feel alive. And did I tell you how perfect you look tonight?"

"Oh, Michael," Claudia gushed, feeling a warm glow in her heart.

Then Michael spiraled downward and took her to the location of their date night. As usual, he brought her down so her back was toward what he wanted to show her. Unfurling his wings, they retracted to a place near his shoulder blades without any evidence of their existence. "Turn around, Claudia." With his hands on her waist, he guided her.

Claudia's mouth dropped and her eyes welled up with tears, taking in the beauty of the scenery. Weeping willow trees stood in front of her, their graceful and refined sweeping branches curled out and forward like an open crown. Each strand of branches was filled with drooping lavender. The unique flowers reminded Claudia of caterpillars...very hairy looking close up, but spectacular when looked at as a whole. The trees were adorned with white lights, and candles were placed throughout, illuminating the darkness. It was enchanting and magical, and she could do nothing but stand there, spellbound by the moment.

"Michael, you decorated this place all by yourself?"

"Yes," he said proudly, guiding her body toward him after he gave her enough time to soak it all in.

"You never cease to amaze me," she muttered as a teardrop trickled down her cheek.

"Don't cry, my love." He kissed the back of her hands and wiped the droplet of water that fell from her eyes. "Walk with me." As he led her further in, they were completed enclosed by the weeping willows and glittering lights. She was even more awe struck being at the center of it all. On the ground was the blue picnic blanket they'd sat on several occasions before. On top of the blanket were flickering candle lights, a crystal bowl filled with chocolate covered strawberries, and to her surprise, an iPad.

"You have an iPad?" Claudia shrieked in surprise.

"Davin told me I could play music with it. He let me borrow it." Michael lit a shy grin. "Sit down with me." His tone sounded nervous, and Michael was never nervous.

Claudia sat next to him while he held both of her hands close to his heart. With his eyes sparkling with love and adoration, he spoke. "I brought you here for a reason. Though I know you know we could never have a normal life together, I want to give you all the possibility and everything that I can offer from who I am. Claudia, before you, my life was a starless night, so dark and empty. But when you came into my world, you lit a blazing light into my heart. It made me spark alive. You make me want to be a better being. I am who I am because of you. I want to take care of you. I will honor you, protect you, cherish you, and spend the rest of my life showing you how much you mean to me. Will you let me be the one you will spend the rest of your life with?"

Claudia felt overwhelmed with Michael's loving words, and happy tears streamed down her face. She knew Michael loved her with all his heart and soul, but to hear it in this romantic place was beyond her dreams. As always, Michael wiped her tears, but this time Claudia saw his eyes well up too. They sparkled, reflected by the glistening lights surrounding them. She had so much to say, so she cleared her throat in hopes that it would help her clear her thoughts too.

"Michael, before you I never knew such love could exist. It is so rare and one of a kind that I feel blessed that you have chosen me. You have always been there for me, constantly. Our love is like the ocean. I will be right there beside you through the smooth sailing, but most of all, I will ride the stormy waves with you when things get rough. I promise to be there for you as you have been for me, and I will love you with every beat of my heart, and even if my heart stops beating, I'll love you still. Yes, you are the one I want to spend the rest of my life with."

Michael fumbled through his front pocket, took out something, knelt down on one knee, and held Claudia's left hand in his.

Claudia inhaled sharply. "Michael, what are you doing?"

Gazing into her eyes with a huge irresistible smile, that smile that he did so well to make Claudia crumble underneath him, he slipped a ring on her finger. "Will you be my wife for eternity?"

She had imagined this scene many times before, and though she had been sure it would never happen, here they were. Happy tears poured down her cheeks and her eyes shifted to her ring. A shiny, clear crystal heart shone brightly against the light that was looped around with a silver band. "Yes," she managed to mutter. Her lips quivered and her words were barely audible.

"I have nothing to give you but my heart. I hold no wealth nor valuable possessions, but what I give to you, I give you unequivocally, and that is all my love. I give you all of me. I surrender to you...completely."

Claudia was motionless except her eyes, which moved to set on Michael's. "It's beautiful, Michael." She paused. "You just gave me the one thing I want most...and that is you."

"I made this from the same crystal I used to make the butterfly necklace you are wearing now; however, it won't warn you of fallen nearby because I've added just enough to make it sparkle." Michael continued. "It symbolizes my love for you, and no matter what you do or where you go, my love for you will follow. It grows with each passing day."

Michael released her hands, stood up, pulled her into his embrace, and whispered into her ears. "With every breath I take, with every beat of my heart, I will love you for eternity, and even in death, I'll love you still."

There were no words exchanged after that. Claudia melted into his hold and settled in for a long passionate kiss, but soon after, she released herself. A heavy burden hung over her like a plague. Before it ate her alive, she needed to tell him. "I need to tell you something. I don't know how to say it."

"Claudia, you know you can tell me anything, don't you?"

Claudia nodded as tears threatened to fall. For some unknown reason she panicked, worried that Michael would disapprove. After their tender exchange of what was like marriage vows, she knew he would be there for her. Whether it was due to hormonal changes or uncertainty of how Michael would feel, she couldn't help feeling emotional. And for some unknown reason, she became afraid for her unborn children.

Michael waited patiently until he couldn't handle it anymore. "Claudia, what is it, my love? Did I do something wrong?"

Unable to stop her tears, she shook her head and tried to speak. "I...I...I'm pregnant," she blurted, and shot her eyes down.

Michael furrowed his brows in confusion and placed his hand on her shoulder. "I think I heard you correctly, but I'm not sure. Did you say you were...um...pregnant?"

"Yes," she nodded. "I'm sorry."

Michael was speechless at first, seeming to take in the news. Finally he spoke. "Oh...no...you don't need to be sorry. Why are you sorry? It takes two loving people to create a miracle, and indeed it is a miracle. I'm a little shocked. No...I take that back. I'm *really* shocked, but happy beyond words." Michael lifted her chin and forced her to look up at him. "This was the reason you fainted, wasn't it?"

"Yes."

"Why didn't you tell me then?"

"I needed time to myself, and I wanted to tell you when we were alone."

"Now I understand why you've seemed distant. Your thoughts and your heart were heavy with the news. Did you think I would disapprove?"

"No...yes...I mean...I wasn't sure how you would feel."

"You were probably worried about the forbidden part too, right?"

Claudia dropped her eyes to the ground, feeling bad for doubting him. "Yes," she said hesitantly.

"I don't care what they think. If I did, I wouldn't be here with you. The only person's opinion that I care about is standing right in front of me. I need to know. How do you feel, Claudia?"

Claudia peered up, feeling like a brick had been lifted off her shoulders now that Michael knew. "I feel blessed to carry lives we've created out of love. Having our babies would be a dream come true, especially since we can't have a 'normal' life. It would be the closest thing to having one."

"Just so you understand, I feel exactly the same." Michael paused, arching his brows, comprehension dawning in his eyes. "Did you say...lives?"

"Umm...yes. We are having twins."

"Wow! I never thought I would be a father, but now I will be a father of two."

"Are we ready for this?" Her tone and eyes were uncertain.

"We are never ready for anything that happens in life. We grab the happiness that comes our way. And this is one that I will cherish...well...two. I'm going to be a father of two. Whoo hoo!" Michael bellowed. His joyful laugher echoed throughout the woods and beyond.

Claudia beamed a relieved smile. She felt she could breathe again. All this time she had worried about nothing, but for her, preparing for the worst was better than not being prepared at all.

Michael held her hands close to his heart again. "Under the power invested in me, I pronounce us husband and wife and soon to be parents. Though angels can't get married, under the stars we are. You are mine and I am yours, for eternity."

Then with a snap of his fingers, countless butterflies fluttered out of the willow branches in swarms and danced around them in circles. Claudia's eyes grew with amazement and she smiled as she felt the light soft breeze that tickled her. Then as fast as they had come, they disappeared into the night. Recalling how Michael had made butterflies appear for her on their first date, she was overwhelmed with the blissful emotion that wrapped around her heart

"Oh, Michael," Claudia gushed. "You make me so happy. Everything about tonight is so perfect, but I don't think Davin, Caleb, and Vivian will be happy to hear that you and I got married under the stars by ourselves."

"They will understand. I'm not about to share you for the most important event of our lives. If they want to have a party like humans do, then that is fine with me. But tonight, you are mine and mine alone. Dance with me." With a flicker from his fingers, the music from the iPad sang. Michael pulled Claudia to his chest, heart to heart, cheek to cheek, as they swayed blissfully around the picnic blanket.

"Mrs. Michael," Michael chuckled lightly. "Since I don't have a last name to pass down to you and our family, I think Mrs. Michael sounds perfect, don't you?"

"I like the sound of that, Mr. Michael," Claudia giggled, looking pleased.

"Mrs. Claudia Michael," Michael whispered in her ear, giving her hot pleasurable sensations down her spine. "I love you." Michael planted a soft lingering kiss, then continued trailing them down her neck, shoulder, down her arm, to the tips of her fingertips.

Standing there, feeling weak at the knees, she wanted to grab him, kiss him back, but contained herself. "Michael." She could hardly say his name. "I love you more."

After their song ended, he led her down to the picnic blanket. Michael leaned his back against the trunk of the tree and pulled Claudia between his legs with her back leaning against his chest. Wrapping his arms around her waist, he kissed her cheeks multiple times. Listening to love songs Davin had downloaded and feeding each other chocolate covered strawberries, they enjoyed the view under the shimmering night sky where the stars burst with their lustrous glow. As the warm breeze brushed against them, their hearts and souls were full.

"It's time to go." Carefully, Michael helped Claudia to stand and flashed his wings, wrapped them around Claudia, and floated in midair.

"Where are we going?"

Michael twitched his brows playfully, then he gave a wicked grin. "I'm taking you to bed. Not to sleep...to consummate our marriage vows, all night long."

CHAPTER 4

"WHAT A LOVELY VIEW," DAVIN said sarcastically with a roll of his eyes. Walking down the severely cracked sidewalk, the roads looked like they had massive spider veins. They were raised out of the ground in every direction he could see, as if an earthquake had cut through the area. All the stores and houses were burned down in the small town of Springfield, where they stood. Black ashes covered the city and continued to fall like light rain.

"These poor humans...their lives were stripped away," Vivian remarked, stepping over the debris.

"I don't think anyone could have survived this," Caleb said, shaking his head. His eyes looked anguished. "We can thank Claudia for her bravery."

"Amen to that," Elissa mumbled, walking beside Caleb.

At Austin's request, the alkins and selected venators—Elissa, Gracie, and Michelle—had been sent on a mission to search for survivors. Since policemen and firemen were geared up from head to toe and already on the scene, Austin's team searched toward the west and tried to remain hidden from them.

The masks worn by the humans indicated how toxic the atmosphere was, but for the angels, there was no need for them. Though they could smell the stench of the burnt wood and other debris, it was impossible for the contaminated air to affect them the way it did the humans.

"Do you think we'll encounter any demons?" Gracie asked, gazing at the damaged houses along the block. When it came down to it, material things didn't matter, especially when the humans' lives were taken from them. No price could ever match what was most precious—life.

"I don't think so, Gracie," Michelle answered. "I believe when Aliah was killed, the demons he created went to Hell with him."

As they advanced further west, they saw the same thing repeatedly—burnt down buildings and black ashes floating in the direction of the wind that carried it. Suddenly, Davin halted and gestured for everyone else to do the same. "Did you hear that?"

"Hear what?" Vivian scanned the perimeter.

"It's a deep groaning sound, coming from there." Davin pointed to a small liquor store to his right.

"I thought you said all the demons were dead?" Michelle whispered to Gracie, willed her bow, and held it close to her.

"Don't be a wimp. It's probably an animal," Gracie whispered back.

Davin turned to them. "Shhh...we're going in. Follow me."

Before Michelle and Gracie could protest, Davin cracked the already broken glass double door open and stepped inside. Stepping over the unrecognizable debris in front of him, he slowly crept along, stepping where he could safely plant his feet as the group followed closely behind him. The thick blanket of black ash prevented the sun from seeping through, but enough hazy light beamed through the tall shattered glass windows and the crumbled ceiling for them to have some visibility. Looking intently at an object, Davin bent down, ruffled the debris off to the side, and picked it up. "Hey...it's a bag of chips." His face beamed with delight as if he had found a treasure. "Now if we could just find some salsa."

Vivian poked Davin on his arm and glared at him as she scolded. "Will you stop thinking about food and find out where the noise you heard came from?"

Davin frowned, narrowing his eyes at her. "Fine." With one hand he held his sword, and with the other, he held the bag of chips. Finding nothing while searching the building, the only place left to look was behind the cash register, but it was enclosed by a pile of debris—broken shelves, wood, and cement.

"Caleb...you go and take a look," Davin directed.

"What?" he snapped. "Why me? You're the leader."

"I'm holding my precious bag of chips, that's why. And plus, who's going to protect all the pretty ladies?"

"No thanks. I'd much rather protect myself," Vivian scoffed.

"I wasn't thinking about you."

Vivian scowled at him.

"Not Gracie and I. We'd like Davin to protect us," Michelle said, giving Davin a flirtatious smile.

Davin blushed and lightly chuckled, enjoying the compliment. "Hey, Michelle...did you see any salsa?"

"I'll look for some." Michelle winked.

"For heaven's sake!" Elissa roared. "I'll go back and check. I'd rather die than watch you guys all gushing over each other." With her bow in position, she jumped over the counter, with Caleb close behind her.

"It's dark down there," Elissa informed, teeter totting, balancing herself to keep from falling.

"We can't see anything from up here," Caleb said. "We may have to go down to get a better look. There's a huge hole...looks like someone was desperate and needed to dig themselves into a barricade. I wouldn't mind, but I'm not sure if I can handle the rotting wood smell. It stinks worse than the outside air."

"Forget it, Caleb. I don't think that's a good idea," Davin advised. "Let's tell Katherine first. We don't know what we'd be facing down there, but—"

Before Davin could finish, something that looked like a massive black cloth flew out.

"It's a fallen!" Gracie shouted with fear in her tone, her bow already in front of her and ready to shoot.

The fallen moved erratically, hopping from one pile of debris to another. Flapping frantically with one wing, the other broken one was bent in an awkward position. Her black dress was tattered and worn, and just like her wing, was torn and ripped unevenly. The group ducked low, trying to shoot her without shooting their friends.

"Don't shoot her!" Davin instructed. "We need to find out where she came from and why she's here."

With Davin's instruction, the group scattered and gave her plenty of room to steady herself.

"We come in peace." Vivian's tone was calm and steady. "We won't harm you. Please tell us your name." She handed her sword to Caleb and carefully took several steps toward her. "It's okay. See...?" She extended her arms. "I have no weapon. Tell me what happened to you."

The frightened fallen stumbled back and accidently trapped herself into a corner. Throwing up her arms in warning, she emitted loud shrieking sounds out of her mouth that made everyone cover their ears. Through her fast movements, the strands of her dirty black hair that had covered her face revealed her striking violet, evil eyes. Even with her face covered with grime, the alkins and the venators were surprised to see that she was very attractive. After Aden's death, the fallen had retreated to their hiding places, so they were stunned to see one, especially alone.

After her shrieks the fallen was silent, staring and seemingly studying the angels that surrounded her.

"Why are you here?" Vivian asked again, holding up her hand in a gesture of peace.

"I...I had come to warn a friend. I must have come at the tail end of a war." Her voice was sweet and tender, but they knew better than to trust her. They had been warned never to turn their backs on or trust fallen under any circumstances, even if they appeared beautiful and friendly, for evil would always remain evil and faithful to their master. The fallen had no other choice, for their souls were condemned and they would never be forgiven, unlike the humans.

"Did you come by yourself?" Caleb asked, looking around for other evil entities.

"Yes, I've come alone. I was surprised to see these...demons. They are not friendly creatures. They have no morals or respect for their kind."

Davin let out a quick laugh and shook his head. "Geez...really? Do they sound familiar to you?"

"Hush," Vivian scorned.

Davin frowned and gave her an apologetic look.

The fallen continued. "When I got here, there were massive numbers of them. Most of them fled to the mountains as if they were instructed to go there, but a group of them stayed behind. They broke my wing when I tried to escape. Unable to fly, I hid here. I had to dig further in to bury myself from the fire. Next thing I knew, they flared up and turned into ashes."

"There hasn't been any of Aden's group of fallen since Aden," Davin scowled, recalling all the trouble Aden had caused. "For your information, if you didn't know, Aden is dead. And where were all the cowards when the world was on the brink of destruction? You could've at least fought alongside us and redeemed your souls."

"You very well know our souls cannot be saved. And we are very aware that Aden is dead, but his followers are seeking revenge. I've come to warn Michael. Do you know him?"

"Michael?!" Davin's fingers curled into a tight ball and his body shook in anger. "Michael is no longer a fallen. He will have nothing to do with you."

"I'm a friend of his—"

"No you're not!" Davin bellowed angrily. "Michael has no fallen friends." With lightning bolt speed, his hands wrapped around the fallen's neck. "Why are you really here? Tell me now before I break your neck, you piece of—"

"Davin!" Vivian shouted. "Control your temper or we will get nowhere with this one."

Knowing Vivian was right, Davin backed away, looking upset with himself that he had lost control. The fallen coughed relentlessly, releasing her pain and letting the oxygen flow through her body. When she was breathing normally, she glared at Davin in discontent and started to maneuver her way to a part of the wall that looked like it had been punched out and was just big enough for her body to slide through.

"Like I said before, I'm here to warn Michael. They want revenge and they will stop at nothing to get their way. I'm not here to represent them. I'm here for Michael. After this, I will go in hiding in fear for my life, for they already know I will warn him."

"And how do they know this?" Caleb asked.

"They found out I was eavesdropping. Fortunately, I was able to escape. Michael saved my life once, so I must repay him. You may look upon fallen as evil creatures—"

"You got that right," Davin interrupted before she could finish.

She scowled at him again. "But we believe a life for a life just as an eye for an eye. So now that I've warned him, I'm free."

"Whoopie...big deal." Davin twirled his finger up in the air in a circular motion. "Michael saved your life and you repay him with a warning. How is that fair? Make sure you save his life if that is ever needed...now that is a life for a life. Your version is a life for 'give him a warning and flee so I won't get my butt whipped by my master.'"

"By all means...this is all I can do for now." Her tone was low, sounding sorrowful.

"Tell me this...who is after Michael?" Elissa asked, recalling the day she was face to face with Michael. She had felt small beneath him. He was gorgeous in every way...she had to wipe that thought out of her mind to concentrate on what was happening now.

"I do not know the specifics, but there is a rumor of revenge being sought upon him."

"Liar! You're not telling the whole truth," Davin said with fire behind his eyes and tone.

"Take it as you will." The fallen spread her black wings to open as much as she could. Wincing in pain, she soared away through the part of the wall that was missing, but dropped to the ground after some distance.

"You let her get away. Why?" Gracie looked astounded.

"She's already dead," Vivian said remorsefully, watching through the broken wall as she tried to take flight again.

Gracie and Michelle were once fallen themselves, but lucky for them, they were half angel and half human. They were more than happy that Katherine had forgiven them, and that they were able to redeem their souls. Being half human gave them the chance for salvation and forgiveness.

Looking flabbergasted, Elissa took a few steps toward Davin. She was fairly new to all the history since she had only recently became a venator. "What's the difference between a fallen and a demon?"

"Demons are created by evil dead spirits," Davin explained. "They take over humans' souls, bodies, and minds, like the ones we fought recently. Though they were humans, they had super strength and powers that were transferred to them by the spirits. Fallen, on the other hand, like her, were angels from the beginning. They were given free will to stay in Heaven or fall with Lucifer. Some fallen were created by Aden. They are called nephilim, half human and half angel. He procreated to build his army in hopes of taking over Crossroads. But that was a while ago."

"We'd better get going. We need to warn Michael," Caleb said in a hurry.

"I agree, but let's not tell him in front of Claudia," Davin said with a heavy heart. Michael and Claudia had just found some peace, and now this. "We will be the ones to tell him, and please...." He gazed upon each of the venators' eyes. "Do not tell anyone what you've heard. We need to gather more information before we bring this up to the Twelve."

With a nod of agreement from everyone, they returned to Nubilus City.

CHAPTER 5

AUSTIN SAT COMFORTABLY ON KATHERINE'S leather office chair at Grand View Hotel. Reclining, he looked up at the high ceiling and gazed upon the sparkling crystal chandelier In a way it reminded him of stars, and he wondered if Claudia was looking at the stars or if she was somewhere beyond. He didn't want to think of her, but when he spent time alone he couldn't help himself. He wondered if she missed him as much as he missed her.

"Whatever," Austin mumbled as Katherine walked in.

Elegantly poised, Katherine wore a fuchsia dress that hit just above her knees, with cream color heels. Pearls adorned her neck, ears, and her right wrist. Though her left middle finger looked bare without her turquoise healing crystal ring she usually wore, Austin knew she would rather have the empty feeling from a missing ring instead of missing her son.

Austin could clearly recall that dreadful day when he thought his life would end at Aliah's hand. Luckily for him, his mother was by his side and had placed the healing crystal on his wound. Since the crystal could be used only once, it had dissolved inside his body; therefore, the ring was gone forever.

"What's whatever?" Katherine asked, gesturing for Austin to get out of her chair.

"Nothing." Austin swirled to the right and jumped off as Katherine came around to the left of the desk.

"Since we don't have any important issues at hand, why don't you make yourself useful and help me plan a party?" Katherine snapped her fingers and the computer powered on. After clicking away on the keyboard, she turned her screen toward Austin and showed him the Grand room settled on the highest floor of the Grand View Hotel.

"What do you want me to do?" Austin asked, feeling bored already. Planning a party was not his thing; going to one was a whole different story.

"The party is for you and the venators. It is set for next week. The invitations were already sent out."

Austin's brows perked up. "Really? How come I didn't get one?"

"I sent you one first. It's probably in the mess you created in your room at Island of Eden. I've never seen it like that before."

Austin shot his eyes down and turned away. "Don't ask. I don't want to talk about it right now...maybe ever." His tone was low and uncaring. His shoulders drooped as if a ton of bricks had settled on them. Every word spoken took a great effort, and the reminder of why his room was a mess made the room spin.

"I wasn't going to. Though I have a hunch the reasons behind..."

Austin shook his head and caught his mother's eyes. "Don't even finish that sentence. Let's talk about the party instead."

"About the party...."

"What is the reason for it?"

"To celebrate life. To celebrate victory."

"So...everyone is invited...like Jeremiah?"

"No. I'm not inviting the Twelve. It would be an uncomfortable setting for everyone else. After all, the party isn't for the Twelve."

"Then the venators and the alkins?"

Katherine paused, seemingly gathering her thoughts. "Austin, you'll have to face her sooner or later. You can't just run away or hide from her forever. Claudia made her decision and there is nothing you can do. Honestly, you knew my plans for you from the beginning. Perhaps it's my fault. I never thought she was your type...I mean, that you would fall for her. You were never the serious type. I would have never appointed you as her guardian angel if I'd even had the slightest clue this would happen."

Austin turned his back to her, ready to saunter out the door. With a heavy sigh, he placed his hand on the doorknob. "I'll help you with the party, but I don't know if I'll be there. And...yeah...you should have never appointed me as her guardian angel."

"You don't mean that."

"Maybe I do and maybe I don't. I just don't want to feel anything right now." His eyes still gazed on the doorknob, unable to look at Katherine in fear that if he did, he may break down in front of her. He had to be strong. Talking about it only made him feel weak and made him miss her even more. "I'll take care of the drinks. I'm good at that." Then he walked out the door.

AFTER A BRIEF MEETING WITH Katherine, the alkins left to meet with Michael and Claudia, but when they arrived, they were nowhere to be seen. So, they plunked themselves on the sofa on the first level.

"So...where do you think they went?" Davin asked, leaning against the wooden wall, munching on chips. "I like how they make this crunchy sound in your mouth." Holding another piece he planned to shove into his mouth, he chuckled giddily like a little boy.

"That's nice." Vivian ignored Davin and turned the page of a fashion magazine she shared with Caleb.

Caleb pointed to a picture. "Maybe I should wear that."

Vivian nodded in agreement. "Yeah...that would look really good on you. We should go window shopping."

"Calvin Klein. We need to find that store."

"For your information," Davin broke in, reaching inside the bag for another chip. "Calvin Klein is the name of the clothes line."

Caleb turned his head away from the magazine to Davin. "Really? And how do you know this?"

"Cause I'm wearing him." He reached over to the back of his shirt, revealing the tag. "See."

"Ahhh...I see," Caleb grinned, finding it amusing.

"He is really famous for his underwear too," Davin continued.

"That's right," Vivian mumbled. "Now I remember. I saw a huge billboard once...somewhere. There was a picture of Calvin and he only had on underwear. I thought it was strange, but I didn't mind looking at his almost naked body." Vivian lit up a smile, slightly blushing.

"I have Calvin underwear on too. You want to see?" Davin started unzipping his pants.

Caleb shot his eyes to the floor and Vivian immediately covered her eyes. "Davin," Vivian raised her voice. "Please. Oh God...no. I believe you. No need to show it."

Davin zipped his pants back up. "Geez, Vivian. I was only going to show you the tag and not my something else."

Caleb chuckled. "Now...that would have been hilarious."

"Shut up. It's bigger than the billboard," Davin chuckled, stuffing more chips into his mouth.

Unexpectedly, Caleb choked and spit out air, seemingly trying to hold in his laughter. "I beg to differ."

Davin glared his eyes at Caleb and frowned. "Find something else to wear. Cause you're not wearing my Calvin."

As they enjoyed the humor between each other, Davin plopped next to Vivian. They kicked up their feet on the center table and relaxed just as Michael and Claudia appeared.

Michael beamed a welcoming grin. "Isn't this a sweet surprise?"

"Claudia!" Davin dropped his bag of chips on the table, jumped out of his seat, passed Michael, wrapped his arms around her waist, and swung her around.

"Good to see you too, Davin," Claudia giggled, straightening her hair and dress. Davin had twirled her so fast she looked like she had been hit by a strong breeze.

After he released her, he turned to Michael, and raised his hand up high. "What's up dude?"

Michael gave Davin a high five as he held tightly unto a stack of books with the other hand.

Davin's eyes went straight to the books. "You're going to read all those? You really have nothing to do."

"No...they're for Claudia. She wanted to go to the bookstore. And what's wrong with reading?"

"Nothing...," Davin chuckled, gazing at the titles. "They're books about yucky romance stuff. Not the kind men would read."

Michael rolled his eyes playfully and turned to greet Vivian and Caleb, who were already in Claudia's arms.

"Better beware," Davin warned. "I've heard the ladies have book boyfriends and they go crazy over them."

"Book boyfriends?" Michael questioned, angling his brows in amusement.

"Yeah...book boyfriends. Claudia might start liking the fake boys more than you."

"No fear brother...I'm the definition and example of a book boyfriend." Michael lifted his head in arrogance.

"Definition of cockiness is more like it," Davin snorted. His shoulders bopped up and down from laughing so hard.

"You'll soon become the definition of a squashed bug if you don't watch what you say," Michael retorted.

Sneering playfully, Michael placed the books on the table, gripped Davin into a choke hold so fast he didn't know what had happened, and rubbed his hair. "Hey...not the hair, dude," Davin murmured under his breath.

"So...WHAT BRINGS YOU HERE?" Michael asked, releasing Davin. "Not that I'm not happy to see you guys."

"We were sent back to a small town called Springfield to see if there were any survivors," Caleb explained carefully, not to disclose any information he promised he wouldn't say.

"Did you find any survivors?" Claudia inquired.

Vivian plopped herself on the sofa and picked up the magazine she was reading. "No...I mean...not where we searched. There were also policemen and firemen searching, but we made sure to stay clear of their path."

"Interesting," Claudia said, headed straight for the wooden coffee table, and placed a chip in her mouth, then another. Then she sat next to Vivian. When she sensed everyone staring at her, she turned to them and smiled. "I see why Davin likes them. Got any salsa, Davin?"

Davin's eyes beamed with excitement. "See...I told you we should have gone to the grocery store to buy salsa. Cause chips go with salsa. They don't get it, Claudia."

Claudia giggled from Davin's cuteness and took another bite.

"Hey," Vivian said suddenly, eyeing Claudia's left hand. "Beautiful ring, Claudia. Did Michael make that for you?" Vivian reached out and held Claudia's hand in hers. "Just stunningly beautiful. I love the heart shape and how they shine just like diamonds. Nice job, Michael...but then again, I only expect perfection from you."

"Thanks," he said, looking proud.

Claudia's heart was escalating as she watched her friends admire her ring. How badly she wanted to tell them they had exchanged vows under the stars, but they hadn't discussed when they would tell them, so she had to dismiss the thought.

Michael cleared his throat to break up the conversation and their stares. "I need a word with Davin. Vivian and Caleb, could you keep Claudia company?" Michael asked with a grin.

"Sure," they agreed, and Davin followed Michael outside.

"YOU'VE PICKED A BEAUTIFUL PLACE to have your happily ever after." Davin gazed at the evergreen trees, taking in the fresh air.

Michael stopped when he thought they were far enough. "Thanks. Claudia and I love it here. I asked you to come out with me so we could talk. I don't mean to be pessimistic, but I can't help the feeling that something will get in the way. I shouldn't think like that, especially since...but—" Michael wanted to tell Davin the good news that Claudia was pregnant, but he couldn't bring himself to tell him, not yet.

"Michael, I have to tell you something." Davin broke in before Michael could finish his words. "I don't know how to tell you this, but when we were in Springfield, we found a fallen. She was actually looking for you. She wanted to warn you that the fallen wanted their revenge for Aden's death."

Michael rooted his eyes on the ground. His mind was reeling to the time he was a fallen. "Did you get her name?"

Davin cracked a nervous laugh. "Uh...that would've been wise, but we were so intent on asking her questions that I...well...kind of forgot. But it doesn't matter. I thought it was best to let you know. It could be nothing."

Michael gazed into Davin's eyes, trying to hide his true feelings. "Please don't say anything to Claudia. I don't want her to worry her. I'm sure everything will be fine."

"I told everyone not to tell Claudia."

"Thanks," Michael said warmly, draping his arms around Davin's shoulders. "You always know what's best for me. I don't know what I would ever do without you."

"Affectionate these days, are we?" Davin pulled him in for a hug and released before Michael had a chance to protest. "I've missed you too. Not that I'm jealous of Claudia taking your time or anything. I just miss those days in Halo City. I'm really happy for you, though."

"Me too, my friend," Michael said, and lightly socked Davin on the arm.

Davin smirked with a lingering sly smile. Without warning, he playfully knocked Michael down and ran as fast as he could. Joyfully, his laughter rang through the woods. "Catch me if you can."

"You're so lucky I wasn't expecting that." Michael stood up, dusted the dirt off his pants, and took off after him.

⁂

THE SILVER MOONLIGHT SEEPED THROUGH the night clouds, casting dimly upon the land. Though the fallens' wings were ebony, at night they seemed even darker and more sinister. Berneal, one of Aden's followers, and Dantanian, one of God's fallen angels since the beginning of time—also known as the angel of many faces—

unfurled their wings when they landed, startling the small forest creatures. Knowing evil was upon them, the creatures scurried away.

Taking pleasure from the gentle breeze that aired their spread out wings, they stood on the edge of a place called "The Cliff." It was a place where the alkins had once encountered Aden and his followers when Claudia went camping.

"Now that Aliah is out of the way, what is our plan for revenge?" Berneal asked, standing with his arms crossed.

"I say we either get Michael on our side again or we get rid of him."

"Get rid of him?" Berneal questioned, his tone indicating it wasn't a good idea.

"If we don't, he'll become a huge problem."

"You can't get rid of Michael."

"And why not?" Dantanian roared with anger. "You think I can't take him?"

"That's not what I meant. You've fought alongside him. You know how he is. His wings are like steel, and he can swing his sword like no one can. He's almost unbeatable. He was known as the angel with the shotgun. Don't you remember?"

"Yes, I remember. I gave him that name. Don't worry. I have a plan. Even a half angel made of steel has a weakness."

"And you know what his is?" Berneal turned to face him and jerked back with fright. His heart pounded against his chest. "You look just like him," he stammered. "I thought you were...don't scare me like that." Berneal took several steps toward him, mesmerized, and examined his face. "You look just like Michael." Only a touch away, he poked Dantanian on the cheek.

"Don't touch me," Dantanian spat, slapping Berneal's hand away from his face. "I'm not called the angel of many faces for nothing."

"Whoa...chill...relax. I know. I've seen your many faces. I was just a little shocked." Berneal paced back to where he had stood a second ago.

"I can't relax until we get Michael on our side or get rid of him."

"I can't figure you out. Either you like him or you hate him?"

"He was Aden's right hand man. Aden treated him like a son...it should've been me. I was the loyal one. Ironically, Michael killed him at the end. I was the one who injured Michael. I could do it again, and this time I won't fail."

"How do we get to him?" Berneal suddenly felt uneasy. He would not only be up against Michael, but his team at Crossroads as well.

"You don't know Michael like I do. He has a soft spot for his friends. We find them first and he'll come to us...this I guarantee." Dantanian gleamed triumphantly as if he had already captured Michael. The thought excited him. When he spotted something from the corner of his eyes, he turned his head and gawked at a baby lizard upon a rock. Without any regards for its life, he stomped on it with his right foot.

The poor creature's body was crushed and its blood painted the rock. "Blood for blood. Life for life. We are not Aden's creations, but God's. We were here first. I will avenge Aden's death. Can you hear me Michael?" He bellowed into the night. His voice echoed through the vast mountains that enclosed them. "You are just a nephilim, only half of an angel. I am a fallen, created long before you were born. I'm coming for you! I'm going to take and destroy everyone you love."

Berneal released his hands that covered his ears, not wanting to hear Dantanian's shout. "I'm sure Michael didn't hear that, but I sure did. So...where is he?"

Dantanian glared at him. He didn't like what Berneal had said. "Last I heard he was up at Crossroads, but now he is somewhere beyond. Like I said before, I already have a plan in motion. Just follow me and don't get in my way. Now...which town shall we visit and make our presence known?"

"That one," Berneal pointed. "The brightest town. There are many people out on a Saturday night."

"Then that town it is." Dantanian unfurled his expansive wings. As he stood there, he took in the night breeze, soared into the darkness, and headed toward the city lights below as Berneal followed behind him. From afar, they looked like a thick, ominous cloud hovering over the land, bringing with them nothing but evil.

CHAPTER 6

VIVIAN SOFTLY KNOCKED ON CLAUDIA'S bedroom door. "Claudia...we're just going to a banquet, not a wedding."

"I'll be right out." Claudia's voice was muffled from the other side.

After receiving invitations, the alkins were excited to attend a celebration in their honor, especially Davin, who loved to party.

Trying dress after dress, Claudia finally picked a long, black, strapless one that clung to her curves comfortably. She wanted to look her best for Michael, but she had a difficult time picking one from all that were hung neatly in her closet. Putting on a dab of light makeup, she kept her hair straight, allowing it to cascade down her back, silky and shiny. She was finally ready to go.

Looking at her profile in the mirror, she placed her hand on her stomach. Though there was a slight bump, only she could tell. Warmth flushed through her heart. She was carrying Michael's children and would soon be the mother of two...now that was something of a miracle, something she had thought was never a possibility. In fact, she was so sure it hadn't even crossed her mind.

Though she was happy beyond words, a part of her was worried. She hadn't had that haunting dream again, but she couldn't stop thinking about it. Perhaps it was the motherly instinct kicking in and she was just being overly protective of her family. Whatever the reason, she had to brush it off for now, because a happy mother made happy children. Another soft knock reverted her back to reality.

"I'm coming." Claudia's voice sang in the air as she took off the butterfly necklace. Though she was hesitant to do so, it didn't match the dress so she decided to leave it behind. After all, she was utterly safe surrounded by the alkins and venators. It was a celebration, and no matter what burdens she carried in her mind, she had to be cheerful and not ruin it for any of her friends.

Claudia cracked the door open and peered out to see Michael's sparkling eyes on her. Without hesitation, he reached for her, took her right hand, and kissed it. "You look delicious," he said, gaping at her from head to toe.

Claudia's cheeks flushed with warmth. "So do you," she said shyly, and turned to her friends. To her surprise, Vivian wore a similar dress, except it was deep purple. From behind, they could pass for twins.

Before Claudia could ask her question, Vivian spoke, "Michael and I went shopping together, remember? I had to buy one for me too...but in a different color, of course." She winked.

"I remember," Claudia smiled, then turned her head to the boys. Davin and Caleb looked dashing in their dark gray suits. They looked like models taken right out of a fashion magazine.

After receiving compliments from Claudia, they flew out of beyond and into a limo, but there was no driver.

"Davin's idea," Michael said, understanding Claudia's puzzled expression.

Claudia looked distressed. "Oh."

Reassuring her, Michael placed his arms around her shoulder. "Don't worry. Davin promised he wouldn't drive the way he flies."

Davin flung the key up in the air while his lips curved into a mischievous grin. After it landed on the palm of his hand, he looked at Claudia and muttered with a cool British accent, "Keep calm and let Davin drive." Then he turned to Michael. "Just breathe and let Michael protect you." He winked, chuckled, and got into the driver's seat.

With a good hardy laugh from everyone, they comfortably took their seats. The window that divided the driver's area and the back where his friends sat immediately started to descend. Davin poked his head through, twitching his brows playfully. "Be still and let Davin take you for the ride of your life."

"Davin!" Michael was losing patience. "Eyes on the road, hands on the steering wheel, and no talking."

"Alright, alright...I was just teasing. Take some humor pills, Michael," he chuckled and started the engine.

Michael seemed a bit on edge lately, but Claudia knew the reasons why. Though Michael was always protective even knowing she could take care of herself, her pregnancy was reason enough for him to be even more so.

It was 10:00 PM when they headed for the Grand View Hotel. The cloudless night sky was dazzled with sparkling diamonds, but it was dim compared to the lights adorning the hotel.

"Looks so beautiful." Vivian's eyes glistened, taking in the beauty. "Hey, Claudia...do you remember when we first came here to what's his name's birthday party?"

"Ryan," Davin reminded.

"We were so excited. Little did we know back then this place belonged to Katherine," Caleb muttered, peering up to find the watchers standing in their statue forms. "I see the watchers."

"I remember clearly," Michael scowled. "You came without my knowledge, putting Claudia in danger. Let's not ever do that again because—"

"Michael, it was my fault," Claudia intervened.

"It was all of our fault," Caleb jumped in.

"Maybe more his." Vivian pointed to Davin, reaching over to sock him on his shoulder playfully.

"No way...it was Claudia's fault." Davin pointed his finger over his shoulder, but keeping his eyes on the roads. "She taunted me with dancing and girls. Such a bad influence." He purposely peered into the rear view mirror so everyone could see his rolling eyes and a flash of his goofy grin.

"Keep your eyes on the road, Davin," Michael said sternly. Holding Claudia's hand tenderly, he gently brushed the heart on her ring.

Davin pulled the limo to the front of the hotel to valet park. After stepping out of the car, Davin tossed the key to the parking attendant. "Keep calm, I'll be back," he said, trying to sound like Arnold Schwarzenegger.

Vivian laughed and shook her head. "Be quiet and don't say a word." Vivian linked arms with Davin and tugged him along.

The group headed toward the hotel, and the bellman opened the glass double doors to the main lobby. Same as before, the crystal chandelier hung from the high ceiling and paintings adorned the walls, but the décor was different since the last time they were there.

On their way to the elevator, Davin stopped at the oil painting of Katherine. "I can't believe someone so beautiful could be Austin's mother."

Vivian peered up and glued her eyes to the painting. "Austin is a good looking guy. If we were both human, I would consider him."

"Whatever." Davin shrugged his shoulders and led the way to the elevator.

Hearing their conversation about Austin, Claudia suddenly felt a twinge in the pit of her stomach. It had been a while since she'd seen him. She knew he would be there, but the reality hadn't hit her until she heard his name. Feeling the elevator speed up to the thirty-eighth floor, her stomach dropped the same way it had when she realized she would have to face Austin again.

The first thing Claudia saw when she entered was the tall ice sculptures of angels with their wings expanded. Glimmering from the reflected spotlights above, they looked crystal clear, beautiful and pristine but icy cold to touch. Then she hesitantly looked across the room to the glass wall, recalling how just looking at the city below had made her stomach churn from her fear of heights.

The tables were covered with white linen cloths, and on top were various wild flowers in small crystal vases. Twinkling lights decoratively hung across the room from one end to the other. Towards the back, a live band filled the air with soft instrumental music, wrapping her with serenity.

"Welcome," Katherine greeted, giving Claudia a hug and a kiss before the alkins. As always, she was dressed elegantly from head to toe, with matching diamond pendant and earrings and a black dress that flowed down to her ankles.

"Good evening Katherine," Michael said. He was the last one to greet her. "Thank you for the invitation. This was a fantastic idea."

"I agree. I'm glad you're all here and I'm glad I thought of it," she smiled proudly with a laugh. "We need to celebrate our victory, honor those who fought bravely and those we will miss. Now... enjoy the drinks and appetizers...and pretend to be humans, or the waitress and waiter will think we are odd. They will be leaving before I make my speech. Humans always have drinks and food at their celebrations. Stay as long as you like, but I will be leaving after my speech." With that she went to greet the others.

"I'm going over there," Vivian said, pointing to a flowing chocolate fountain.

"Wait for me." Caleb sped after her.

"I think I see chips and salsa. See you when I see you. I'll meet you at the dance floor. Don't...." Davin couldn't get there fast enough. His words were lost when he took off.

Michael looked at Claudia. "We're finally alone." He gripped her hand tightly and led the way into the center of the room. "Let's find our table."

As they looked for their table, they waved to greet the venators clustered in small groups throughout the room. After searching for their nameplates, table after table, they finally found them. Pulling out Claudia's chair for her like a perfect gentleman, Michael sat down next to her. Leaning in, he looped his arm around her shoulders, then moved it quickly, thinking it may be inappropriate to display such affection, especially when it was frowned upon. But he couldn't help it. It felt so natural and so right...but not tonight. So, he grabbed her hand underneath the linen cloth where no one could see his fingers lacing through hers.

Knowing Austin was there somewhere, Claudia swept the room carefully. What would their first encounter be like? What should she say? Would he even acknowledge her? As those thoughts circulated through her mind, she spotted him across the room surrounded by females. Claudia chuckled inwardly, wondering what he was saying to them to make them giggle like schoolgirls.

Seeing him well and happy made her feel less guilty. Perhaps it wouldn't be so awkward after all. Then she focused her attention on the five members of the band, one female and four males. The female had a lovely, smooth voice.

When the singer pointed her hand upward, Claudia looked up to the ceiling, and vividly recalled when Aden and his followers had come through the opening. Michael had killed Aden by stabbing him with the death crystal sword, the sword that had belonged to Aden. Her thoughts were broken when Katherine spoke into a microphone from the center of the room.

"Good evening and welcome everyone. I've gathered all of us together to celebrate each and every one of you. Without your devotion and love, this world would have been taken over by evil. As hard as we all fought, we have one person to thank whole-heartedly. Though she will never admit it, because of her courage and her sacrifice, we are here. Claudia...please stand."

Claudia didn't know what to do except to stand. She never imagined Katherine would give her such honor, even though she was the one who had saved them from apocalypse. She never wanted this kind of attention, and if she had known of Katherine's plan, she may not have attended. The audience applauded loudly, filling the room with cheers, and all Claudia could do was smile proudly, but feel humbled by the reaction from her peers.

When she thought the applause was almost over, Michael stood up, and one by one, everyone else stood up too for a standing ovation, which made Claudia's face even redder. "Thank you," she said, but her voice was inaudible due to the applause that continued to build. She raised her hand like a princess to acknowledge and thank them. Finally, when the cheers died down, she settled back into her seat, and Katherine continued her speech.

"We've also gathered here to honor our brothers and sisters who have passed on. We will miss them, but they will never be forgotten. Please give them a moment of silence as we close our eyes and say a prayer for them."

The room was very still for a minute until Katherine spoke again. "Thank you all for coming. I will be leaving soon but stay as long as you like. As the young ones would say...let's party the night away! I'm sure you will, but please leave before sunrise."

Joyful laughter filled the room and the music started again.

CHAPTER 7

THE SOFT INSTRUMENTAL MUSIC CHANGED to a faster beat. "Oh yeah," Davin cheered. "Time for the party to rock and roll. Come on Vivian, let's go."

"I'm not going anywhere with you. You're like my brother. That's just gross. Go ask Holly. Better yet, ask Michelle and Gracie. They'll say yes to you."

"Fine." It didn't take much to persuade Michelle and Gracie, and the three were the first ones on the dance floor.

"Shall we?" Michael asked Claudia, offering his hand.

"Sure."

Weaving through the tables and crowds, Michael led her to the floor. As always, he held her closely and protectively even when not in danger. After a few rounds of fast beats, the music changed to a slower tempo. "My kind of dance," he murmured, pulling her into his embrace. "I get to hold you in my arms, feel your heart beat against mine, and breathe in nothing but your scent that drives me wild."

Claudia could do nothing but give him a shy smile, the smile that warmed Michael's heart, the smile that said "I feel the same." As they continued to sway with their bodies pressed together, they were interrupted by a female voice. "Excuse me...may I cut in?"

Claudia looked startled. Who would dare to cut in? Surprised by this brave voice, Claudia pulled back and set her eyes on her. She was a tad taller with luscious red hair falling below her shoulders. This stranger was striking, but Claudia had nothing to fear. Not wanting to be rude, she winked at Michael. "Sure."

Michael gave her a "don't you leave my side" look as Claudia walked away, smiling. Cautious not to trip in her high heels, she focused on the floor and took small steps as she headed to her table. Unexpectedly, someone grabbed her by the waist and swung her around. Thinking it was Davin, she didn't fight him and placed her arms tightly around his neck. Once in his arms, she knew who it was and her heart stopped. She froze, afraid to show too much affection, and at the same time too little of it.

"Not so fast. You owe me a dance."

"Hello, Austin. You're looking well. I didn't think you would ever speak to me again," she said with a lively tone.

Guiding her to the dance floor but away from Michael, he placed his hands comfortably around her as they swayed to the soft melody. "You look stunning as always."

"Thank you. You look nice too," Claudia said sweetly.

Austin gave a heartfelt warm grin. His cheeks flushed a bit too. "I didn't want to wear this suit, but I did it for my mom. So...how have you been? Are you bored yet?"

"Bored? Tonight is perfect. It was sweet of your mom to have this celebration in honor of everyone."

"Yeah...it was. I helped."

Claudia arched her brows, giving him a sideways glance. "You did?"

"I'm not the party planner type of guy—rather the party goer—but she needed my advice."

"Well, I think both of you did a fantastic job."

His lips curved into a proud smile without a word.

"So...how do you like your new position?" Claudia asked, trying to have a friendly conversation.

"I hate it."

"What?" Claudia's pitch shot up. "Why?"

"Because...I'd much rather be at Island of Eden with you." Austin's words were slow in coming. His eyes burned into hers, letting her know how much he missed her.

Not knowing what to say, all she could muster was one word. "Austin...." She dropped her eyes from his.

Austin referred back to her last comment. "You're right. Tonight is perfect, but I think you could use a new date." His tone became light again and back to being the same flirtatious Austin.

"Austin," Claudia scolded. "Be nice. Michael is my only date."

Just then a young venator stood in front of them. "Excuse me...may I cut in?" he said politely.

Surprised to see someone there, Claudia turned her head in the direction of the voice and saw a stranger grinning from ear to ear at her.

"No, thanks," Austin snapped and looked away.

Claudia narrowed her eyes at Austin, gesturing for him to behave and releasing her hold on him. Then she turned to the new guy. "Sure."

"Nope...no can do." Austin swung Claudia around into the crowd of dancers again.

"I told you to be nice. And he wasn't asking you."

"You should know by now I'm not nice. I don't have to be if I don't want to be."

"You act like a child."

Austin swung her out. "So I've been told. Shhh...no more talking. I'm enjoying my dance."

Claudia shook her head and rolled her eyes. She was just happy he wasn't mad at her. When Austin's hand guided her back into his hold, she searched for Michael.

"Michael is over there with his female companion." Austin pointed his finger toward them when he noted Claudia looking for him. "Looks like they're getting along just fine."

Looking in the direction Austin had pointed, Claudia was sure Michael had caught her eyes, but he didn't smile or acknowledge her. His face was stoic, now looking past her. What troubled her the most was the worried look on his face. Wondering if Michael was looking for someone toward the back, she looked too, but there was no one there. Instead of heading straight for Michael, she decided to wait.

As the bass started pumping harder and the music pounded to their hearts, awakening them, the dance floor once again was filled with the venators.

When the alkins surrounded Claudia, Austin let go of her. "Thanks for the dance." He gave her a peck on her cheek and left the dance floor. Davin glared at Austin until he was lost to the crowd.

"I'm going to go sit." Claudia suddenly felt parched.

"We'll go with you," Davin said, placing his hands on Claudia's back and being more protective than usual. Vivian led the way as Caleb paced to the right of Claudia. The way they enclosed her as they approached their seats made her feel uncomfortable. She could sense something was up.

After they were situated in their seats, Claudia saw Michael heading toward her with a beaming smile and his eyes sparkling only for her. He held a plate in one hand and glass of water in the other.

"Hey, beautiful. Did I tell you how beautiful you look tonight?" Michael sat. "Here you go. Just in case you're hungry." After placing a plate in front of her, he draped his arm over her shoulder and pulled her in tightly.

"You only told me I was beautiful like a thousand times. Probably not enough." Claudia giggled while picking up a strawberry with the tips of her fingers.

"Since you're counting, then I'll tell you a million times more." Michael gave her a quick kiss on her lips.

"I hope you didn't say the same thing to the girl at the bar?" she teased with a jealous tone, and gulped down her glass of water.

"Jealous are we? Remember my dear, you're the one who left me."

"True. I was being nice. I can't help it if I have a good looking boyfriend and every girl wants to have a dance with him." She nudged his shoulder. "So...what were you two talking about?"

Michael leaned in and whispered, "Husband, not boyfriend." He winked.

Claudia's eyes twinkled, recalling that special night and repeated, "Husband, not boyfriend." She turned to her friends, wondering if they were listening to their conversation, but they were unusually quiet. Their eyes swept the room, searching for something or someone. When she drifted her eyes to Michael, he was doing the same.

"Michael, what are you looking at or for?" Claudia tried to follow their eyes, but they moved too swiftly.

Michael arched his brows in confusion. "Claudia...didn't you hear me? I spoke to you in your mind."

"No." She was flabbergasted. "When?"

"When I was at the bar. I told you there were fallen in the room...uninvited, of course."

"Fallen?" Claudia reached for her necklace, then recalled she had taken it off. No wonder she had no idea. There was no necklace to warn her.

"Yes. My dance partner, the one you left me with, was one of them. Knowing they don't come alone, I told Davin, Caleb, and Vivian to be on the lookout and find you."

"I didn't hear you. I mean my mind didn't. Are you sure you did?"

"Yes. Let's try again."

"Okay." Claudia looked straight ahead, anticipating his words. Nothing.

She turned to Michael with a worried look. "Did you say something?"

"Yes."

"Darn. Why can't I hear you?"

"I don't know."

"What did you say?"

"I'd like to take you home right now and kiss you all over." He twitched his brows.

"Michael!" Claudia jerked. Her tone went up an octave and she covered her mouth when she realized how loud she'd said his name. She didn't mean to, but he'd said it in front of their friends. Not only that, his hand had found its way inside her dress underneath the table. She leaned closer, liking this kind of attention, and gave him a playful scolding glare. "Bad Michael."

Michael slowly curled his lips into that irresistible smile, looking intently into her eyes. "I can be naughty Michael if you'd like."

"I don't see anything odd and ugly," Vivian said suddenly, unaware she was breaking into their flirtatious conversation.

"Have you seen yourself lately?" Davin teased.

Caleb busted out laughing.

"Hey...you are...." Unable to finish her sentence, Vivian laughed out loud too. "But seriously." Vivian turned to Michael. "I think they left with what's her name."

"Who was she and what did she tell you, Michael?" Claudia asked, feeling frustrated from not being able to hear his thoughts.

MICHAEL DIDN'T ANSWER HER QUESTION. He didn't want to worry her, especially since she was pregnant. How could he tell her that the woman had come to warn him of dangers in the near future? This news would have to wait until he could investigate further. Meanwhile, he swore to himself he wouldn't let anyone harm his beloved and his unborn children. "No need to worry. Some fallen are not that evil. I would never trust one, but they are good on keeping their promise or paying their debts. She came to warn me that the fallen angels have come out of their hiding now that Aliah is no longer a threat. There is no need to worry. Fallen have been roaming on Earth since the beginning of time."

"Were they afraid of Aliah?" Claudia asked.

"I guess you can say that. Though they are of the same evil, demons are humans that have been taken over by spirits of the dead. Fallen are angels created by God, or created by Aden and his followers. Which one is worse, I don't know, but they don't mix well. I guess that's a good thing. But it also depends on the leader. Even fallen have their own politics."

"Did you know her from your past?"

"Yes, though I didn't recognize her at first."

"Why did they come here?"

"She guessed I would be here. Remember, they don't know I'm somewhere beyond. They think I'm at Crossroads."

"How did they get into the party? Surely Katherine would have known."

"They came as the waitress and waiter. They were in disguise at first and I guess they'd changed to proper attire to blend in."

"How many of them were here?"

"I think three."

"You know you could've told me too. I can help." Claudia paused, rethinking her thoughts. "Right...I couldn't hear you." She frowned. Though she was worried at first, she felt better knowing they couldn't find their home. It wasn't so much she was worried for herself, it was more for her unborn children. And what puzzled her the most was the fact the she couldn't hear Michael's thoughts.

"Wanna get out of here?" Michael asked. "Let's go home. Maybe we can bring what humans call the 'after party' to our place. What do you think?"

Claudia liked the sound of that. The word "home" rang pleasantly in her ears. Her worries immediately disappeared with the smile she gave to Michael as an answer.

"Wanna come?" Claudia asked her alkin friends.

"I never say no to a party, especially an after party." Davin was already out of his seat. "Let me steal...I mean borrow...some chips and salsa, since it seems as though nobody else is eating them."

After they agreed, they said their goodbyes and headed home.

CHAPTER 8

"WHAT HAPPENED HERE?" BERNEAL WAS stunned to see a town that looked so inviting from a distance look like it had been through a war.

"Aliah and his demons," Dantanian grimaced. "It's a good thing we were in hiding. We got to miss all the fun...which was a good thing. I would never fight alongside him. Actually, we wouldn't even have had a chance to do so. He'd have just killed us on the spot."

"I'm guessing the good angels won the war, but how?" Berneal asked, easily hopping over a smashed car.

"Who knows? Who cares? Aliah is dead. It leaves us a clear path to cause more problems. Look, over there. Lots of lights. Lots of lights mean people. Looks like a bar."

Before Berneal had a chance to gaze in the direction Dantanian had pointed, Dantanian was already at the entrance.

Without a care, Dantanian kicked the door open. The bar wasn't filled with people as he had hoped it would be. More people present meant more to torture. Upon Dantanian's entrance, followed by Berneal, the bartender scowled at their rude demeanor, but didn't say a word and kept to his business. Even the customers looked the other way.

There were couples drinking at their tables off to the side and several middle-aged men sitting at the bar. But what caught Dantanian's eyes was a female sitting alone. Dressed in a crimson strapless short cocktail dress, her long slender legs were crossed one over the other. Seemingly in deep thought, the tip of her finger circled the rim of her glass.

Crinkling his nose, Dantanian could smell the scent of her floral perfume. While Berneal plopped himself at the bar, Dantanian sauntered toward her. As if they were lovers, he swiftly turned her stool around and conquered her lips without her permission.

Pushing him away in disgust, she spit on the ground and wiped her mouth with the back of her hand in repulsion. "What the hell was that for?"

"Is that a way to greet me? I was happy to see you. You've come alone. How brave of you."

"You think I'm scared of you? I'm not crazy enough to bring my group so that you can slaughter them without reason."

Dantanian chuckled, amused. "I have a bad habit, don't I? Sorry about your friend. I had to get your attention. He was easily... breakable. With an effortless twist of my hand, I broke his neck. What a shame...too bad he was born so frail." He was enjoying her reaction to his words way too much.

Her eyes were blazing with anger and her fist curled into a tight ball. "Enough! I don't need to hear your sick details. You're a monster. You are truly a fallen."

Knowing she knew he could inflict pain on her, and knowing he had power over her pleased him greatly. "I have a reputation to maintain. It's so much fun that way. But why are you here? Why aren't you looking for Michael?"

"I've already found him. Why do you think I'm dressed like this?" She snarled, darting at his eyes with a bold glare.

"Hmm...I like what you're wearing. Did Michael?" His hand ran up her smooth legs. She whacked him hard before it reached further.

Hissing, he withdrew his hand.

"Don't go there!" she snapped. "Michael is history." She stared blankly. "Well...it was never there. He never took interest. I don't want to talk about it. He knows we're out of hiding."

"He was your friend once. Is this going to be a problem?" He laced his hand through her hair.

She pulled back. "No. I'm doing this for the sole purpose that you'll leave my group alone." She turned her stool to face away from him.

"Raven, don't turn your back on me!" he roared angrily, swinging her stool back to him, looking squarely into her eyes. "Aden is gone so I'm in charge now. Not Michael or anyone else. Got that? You need to continue our plan or you might as well go into hiding yourself. I will hunt you down and kill you with my bare hands if you don't do what I say." He leaned in closer and whispered. "And you know how I love to torture, pleasant or not." He twirled his tongue on the base of her ear. "Let's get away from here. Come with me and I'll help you forget Michael." He pulled her into his chest.

Raven shoved him with all her strength, bruising his ego. "You're not even one fourth of the being that Michael is. I would never give you the pleasure of being with me."

Anger burst out of Dantanian's eyes. Surprising Raven, he backhanded her across the face. Her body flew off the stool, crashing against the bar. Wincing, with both hands on her cheek, she submissively coiled, unable to look him in the eyes.

"Michael would never treat me like this no matter how angry he was," she whimpered.

He glared at her. "Michael...Michael...Michael...I'm beginning to hate the sound of his name. Don't you forget who's the boss." He shuffled toward Berneal and sat adjacent to him.

"Please, we don't want any trouble here," the bartender said carefully, giving a quick glance to Dantanian, seeming afraid to look at him any longer than necessary. "More than half the town is gone. Many loved ones, family, and friends are dead. We are trying to rebuild ourselves from the mess."

"Do you think I care, you filthy worthless human? You should be bowing down to me. Pretty soon, the fallen will be the ones to fear. Now give me a drink."

With a heavy sigh, the bartender shook his head and disregarded Dantanian's words. Fallen? What did he know of them? Most likely, he was thinking Dantanian was out of his mind and needed psychological help. Reluctantly, he slid the mug of beer across the counter to him.

"I'll have what he's drinking." Berneal pointed to the guy next to him, who was slumped over. He looked like he was out of it.

"Cheeee," the guy slurred, raising his glass.

"Don't talk to me. Don't even look at me," Berneal snared, pushed the guy off his stool, and snatched his mug. The guy collapsed on the floor with a loud thump, alerting the other customers to look their way. Too drunk to even notice where he was, he continued to lay there.

"So...who should we play with first?" Dantanian turned to the couples who looked too scared to move. With the mug in his hand, he turned to Berneal and clunked his to cheer. "To capturing Michael and his friends."

After chugging down his drink, Dantanian stood up. Sensing Raven by the door, he spoke without turning to her. "Find me when you've captured one of his dear friends. I'll be waiting, but I'm already running out of patience. When that patience is gone, every day that passes and I don't hear from you, I will find one of your precious friends. One life a day. You know I'm good on my words."

With one hand on the door, she shuddered in fear and anger. "Don't worry. You know I'm good with mine, but I need some time. They're not easy to track," she replied wearily.

"Fine. I'll give you some time, then a life for a day begins. You'd better warn your friends," Dantanian snickered, enjoying intimidating her. Then he turned his attention to the couples at the tables with a wicked grin.

AT THE AFTER PARTY, CLAUDIA, Vivian, and Caleb lazily lounged on the sofa, munching on the chips and salsa Davin had insisted on bringing, while Davin and Michael excused themselves to a private conversation.

"It's so peaceful. I can see why you built your home here," Davin said, walking near the edge of the stream. Though it was dark, there were plenty of lights dangling from the nearby trees that only lit up when the sun went down. "Do you miss being at Crossroads?"

"The only thing I miss about Crossroads is our time together. Of course, I wouldn't change a thing right now. I can't believe the Twelve is allowing us to stay here, where we can almost live like humans."

"Odd, isn't it? Though I have a feeling it's because they are scared of what Claudia could do to them," Davin chuckled. "She can seriously kick their butts." Davin picked up a pebble and darted it across the water.

"True, but you know she's not like that at all. Even with all that power and even knowing she could make anyone do anything she wanted, she is very humble and gentle."

"I know. It's one of the qualities we all love about her."

Michael smiled in agreement and his face became serious. "I'm worried."

Davin shot his eyes to Michael. "You would never say that to me unless it was serious. What's going on? Why are you worried?"

Michael picked up a pebble and threw it across the water like Davin, only further. "The girl that was at the party, her name is Raven. You didn't get a chance to see her since she took off after she spoke to me. She is a leader of a group of fallen. There are many groups, but the one to fear most was Aden's. I'm sure they've broken up since he's no longer around. Raven told me the fallen came out of hiding."

Seeing what Michael did with his stone, Davin scowled. "I wish I had seen her face so at least I'd know what she looked like. Okay...so what does this mean? They've been in and out of hiding before." Davin picked up a thicker and bigger stone and tossed it, rippling it across the water further than Michael's. With a triumphant expression painted on his face, he challenged Michael with a dorky grin.

Taking up his challenge, Michael picked up a stone just as big as Davin's. "The fallen go way back before even our time. There is one to fear by the name of Dantanian. I'm ashamed to say this, but he and I were like...how should I say...like you and me. I learned so much from him. We were a fabulous team of evil beings. This may sound strange, but he was like a brother to me. The other fallen feared us."

Davin narrowed his eyes at him. "You're not the same being you were, so forget about it. So, this Raven chick came to tell you that the fallen is out of hiding, and that's it?"

"Chick?"

"You know...not the chicken chick, but the female chick."

Michael let out a small chuckle. "I know what it means. Sometimes I just don't know when to use it without sounding stupid."

"Oh...don't worry. I'll tell you when you sound stupid," Davin nodded with a crooked smile.

"I'm sure you will. You've been talking more like the humans. I'm learning so much from you." With a twirl and in fast motion speed, Michael threw the stone. It bounced multiple times and clearly passed Davin's mark again. "Beat that." Tuning back to the subject, he continued. "No...that was not all. She told me Dantanian wanted me back. If I don't join him, there will be consequences."

"What?! No way! You—" Davin started to protest.

"Don't worry. I would never even consider it. I have too much to lose. Like you said, I'm not the same being. I was thinking perhaps I can persuade him to turn a new leaf."

Davin cupped a rock in his hand, tossing it as if he was holding a hot potato, strategizing. "Don't even bother. A fallen is always a fallen."

"Like me, right?" Michael said lightly.

"No. I didn't mean you. Don't twist my words."

"I know. I'm just messing with you since you're about to throw that pretty, big rock. It's too big."

"Oh yeah? Watch me." Davin prepared himself. Twisting his body like a professional baseball player, he lifted his leg and swung his arm back to get ready. "So...what's so special about this Dantanian?"

Michael paused and waited for the right moment. Waiting... waiting...wait for it...and then..., "He can change his face."

Upon hearing Michael's words, the arm that was half way in motion curved inward and caused the rock to go just a short distance. "Damn. You said that right on cue and on purpose." He turned with a roll of his eyes. "Did I hear you right? Did you say he could change his face? What the f—?"

"Watch thy mouth before I clean it up with soap." Michael shook his head and fingers. "You can talk like humans, but don't learn the unnecessary slang."

Michael's words went through one ear and out the other. Davin was fascinated by what Dantanian could do. "Seriously? He can change his face?"

"Yup...he could look like me if he wanted, except you could tell since he's a little shorter than I am...that's if we were standing side by side. But not by much."

"My turn again since you purposely messed me up." Davin picked up the same size rock and threw it again. "Darn it. It sank."

"I told you it was too big."

"So...he can change his face to look like mine. We could be twins?" Davin asked, still in disbelief.

"Yup."

"I'm sure he'd look better with my face on him," Davin snorted, patting his face. "This handsome face."

"So...do you guys always talk about how good looking you are when you're not around me?" Claudia said, stepping out from the darkness behind a tree.

"Claudia," Davin greeted in surprise. "Nah...of course not."

"Cause I can tell you both how handsome you are anytime and anywhere." She approached closer, gluing her eyes to Michaels.

Davin blushed. "Umm...sure."

Walking directly to Michael, Claudia crushed her lips on his while she disregarded Davin standing there. Placing her arms around his neck, she bounced off the ground, wrapped her legs around his waist, and anchored them while her lips were still locked on his. "I've missed you. You've been gone way too long."

"I missed you more." Michael kissed her back.

"Gross. Just pretend I'm not here, Claudia. Where's Vivian and Caleb?"

"Gone," Claudia managed to say in between making out with Michael. "Michael, take my breath away."

"I will." Michael's grand and majestic wings shot open. In slow motion, he curled his wings and wrapped them around her.

"You guys just took my breath away in a disgusting way. Okay...awkward. Going now. I know when I'm not wanted. See you when...I see you...next time...hello?" Getting no response from either of them, Davin took off.

CHAPTER 9

"AUSTIN? WHAT ARE YOU DOING here?" Holly ran down the hall and gave him a warm, tight hug.

Holding on to Holly longer than usual, Austin released her. "I miss my room...don't you?"

"Yeah. I actually came by to get some stuff. I guess I use that as an excuse to come by here when I get a chance. So what brings you to Island of Eden?"

"I came by to get a few things too. I left the dagger Claudia used on Aliah somewhere...unless she took it."

"I'll help you look for it if you want. I don't have anything to do today," Holly offered, her eyes pleading for his company.

Austin placed his arm around her shoulder. "Come on, old friend. But I have to warn you, it's a little messy."

"I doubt that. Your room is never out of place."

"It is now." Austin cradled her into his hold as they glided into his room.

When they entered, Holly dropped her jaw. "What happened?" She was absolutely astonished. Austin's room looked like it had been ransacked. The covers were thrown off the bed. Clothes were scattered on the floor, and all the drawers were opened. Even the sliding glass door that opened to the cliff was completely splattered in black paint. She couldn't even see the ocean. It was not how Austin kept his room.

Austin shrugged his shoulders. "What? You've never been in a guy's room before?"

Holly scoffed and lightly socked Austin's arm. "Of course... you're a guy." She paused and realized he meant other guys besides him. "I meant...don't ask me those questions."

"Why? We've known each other for ages. You can tell me anything. That's one topic we've never talked about." Austin plopped on the unmade bed and leaned his back against the headboard. His legs were crossed and his arms were behind his neck for support.

Holly continued to gaze around the room, shaking her finger, giving him a "don't even go there" look. "I'm changing the subject. Seriously...your room has never been messy like this before...ever. What happened?"

Austin arched his brows. "Would you believe me if I told you I had one hell of a sex ride in here?"

Holly cringed and shook her head. "Gross. I told you not to go there."

"I'm just kidding." Austin was very amused by how Holly was reacting to the subject.

Holly stepped over a pile of T-shirts on the floor and sat on the edge of the bed. "Good. Cause as much as you like to pretend you're like, this badass dude, you're not. You have a huge heart. You're the best friend anyone can have."

"Yeah...that's the problem. I'm everyone's best friend." His tone was low and sarcastic.

The sudden change in Austin's tone made Holly tune into his heart. "Look...I know how you feel. Let her go. There are many

Claudias out there. And why am I even saying this?" Holly lightly punched his arm. "You're like, one of the Twelve."

"What? Just because I'm one of them I have to stop sleeping around?"

Holly cringed again and covered her face with the palms of her hands. "Don't go there, okay. I don't want to know."

"You don't think Jeremiah doesn't—"

Grimacing, she shot her eyes at him. "Stop." Holly covered Austin's mouth. "Now, that's so wrong."

Austin gently lowered her hand. "Okay...you're right. I feel bad for the—"

"Shhh...enough." Holly's brows perked with curiosity. "So...I'm guessing Claudia and you never—"

"Now that's off limits." Austin's tone suddenly changed. Sighing heavily, he closed his eyes, then opened them with a goofy grin.

"Sorry," Holly said sheepishly.

"No sweat. What's it like being in charge of all those curators?"

"They're pretty cool. They get the humans...you know what I mean? And plus, I get to live among the humans."

"Yeah...that part is cool, unlike the curators...they're so stiff. I think we should change our roles."

"No way," Holly giggled.

"It's strange, isn't it?"

"What?"

"We were just venators. Our responsibility was to hunt the demons, and now...the world is in our hands."

Holly nodded. "Watch out, world. Austin and I are taking over."

"Is that a good or a bad thing?"

"I hope, good. I believe in you, Austin."

"Thanks." He lit a shy grin. "Sometimes I wish I could turn the clock back...you know...to when Patrick was around. The three of us had so much fun. You know what I mean? Not a care in the world, the three of us at Island of Eden...it was crazy fun back then."

Suddenly, Holly got nostalgic. Her eyes became glassy while she focused on her fingernails. "So...you do think of Patrick often?"

"Yeah, I do." Austin's tone became soft. "Don't you?"

"When I'm alone and when something reminds me of what he used to say or do." She cocked her head with a smile.

Without warning, Austin pulled Holly next to him, cuddling her. "I know what you mean. I do the same. You know I'm always here for you, don't ya? You're my best friend."

"I know. I love you as if you were my real brother. You know that, don't ya?"

"I know."

"Just don't tell anyone I'm a softy, okay? I have a reputation to uphold."

"Me too. As long as you don't tell anyone my room was messy."

"Deal. You didn't answer my question. Your room has never been this crazy messy. As cool as you are, some parts of you are very particular. So, what happened?"

Austin's chest rose and fell. He was silent, taking in deep breaths. Finally, he spoke. "I was upset."

"Upset is a tame word for whatever stormed into this room."

"I'm going to say one word and nothing more."

"Okay, spit it out. What's the word?"

"Claudia."

Holly exhaled a puff of air. "I knew it," she said softly. "But why did you paint the window black like that?"

Austin snuggled into Holly and was quiet for a few seconds too long. "I can't...look...at the...stars. They remind me of...her. I want to see nothing. I want to feel nothing."

With every word spoken, Holly felt the depth of his pain. There were no words to be said after that. Austin held onto her tightly, needing her comfort, her friendship, needing her to understand his pain as one teardrop escaped from the corner of his eye.

RAVEN SAT ON A WOODEN bench, looking out into the sunrise. The glowing light had just started to peep through the darkness, stretching and yawning, bringing a hopeful new day. Though fallen angels couldn't feel any sort of temperature, she could imagine the warmth that would have touched her cheeks and wrapped around her body.

If only she had made the right decision centuries ago and sided with the good instead of evil...but there was no use dwelling on the past. What was done was done and there was no going back. She could never get her soul back even if she begged for mercy, or even if she saved a thousand lives, but there was one life that was worth more to her than the others.

She would do just about anything to bring her friend back from the dead. Drake had been her best friend. If only she had been there to save him. If only she had gone with him. Drake and his men had scouted the outskirts of town. After what could have been the apocalypse, he thought it was best to ensure the demons were no longer a threat. But they ran into someone more dangerous, more sinister, more heartless than a demon—Dantanian.

Along with Michael, Dantanian had once led their group, but after Michael took Aden's life, the fallen had scrambled throughout the land. Some joined Dantanian, but the others hid within the mountains. Drake and Raven had regrouped the lost souls and taken them into the home they'd built.

"Raven, you're back. What do you plan to do?" a male voice asked, swinging the screen door to open. He walked out and sat beside her. His cheeks pinched, indenting into dimples, while producing a warm, comforting smile as he set his eyes on her.

"Hey, Stan." Raven welcomed him with a small smile, sliding over to give him room. Exhaling a deep breath, she released some of her anxiety. "I don't know. I mean...all I know is that I need to do whatever I can to keep our family safe, right?" Her tone sounded uncertain.

"Yes, but what does Dantanian want you to do?"

Raven twisted her head back to the sunrise and wished she was the sun, which held no worries and no pain. "I have to turn Michael in."

Dead silence.

After clearing his throat, looking pale as the white peonies surrounding them, he spoke, "Michael? Why him? He's like, impossible to even...we might as well say goodbye to each other right now."

"Don't say that, Stan. I need time. I need to figure out how I can trick his friends. I just need one."

"How much time?"

"What?"

"Come on, Raven. Don't play dumb with me. Dantanian didn't give you all the time in the world. How much time do you have?"

Raven turned away from him, unable to look him in the eye knowing he would most likely have a heart attack when she gave him the answer. "He really didn't give me a time span, which really translates to now."

"What?!" Stan stood up. He looked intense. "What the...?" He circled her with both of his hands on his forehead. "Are you kidding me? Our lives are at stake. He already killed Drake just to show us he can. How are we going to...? We don't even know where to look."

"I might have an idea, but I need your help."

Stan stood still and relaxed his shoulders. "Of course...anything you need."

"Actually, it's not going to be easy, so I'll need some extra help from the others as well."

"Fine," he agreed, and settled calmly next to Raven again. "They'll understand once they know what's at stake."

"What is really at stake here? Once we make our move, we'll be at war again."

"You're not going soft on Michael, are you? I know he saved your life once, but that was ages ago."

"A debt is a debt. Someday, if he makes it out of this, I will repay him, but I need to take care of us. Michael can hold his own. I'm not sure we can stand up against Dantanian. Berneal, on the other hand, is his puppet. I'm not afraid of him. But, this is the only way, right?"

"You sound so unsure."

"I'm sure. It's just that when I saw him again...well...many of us had taken a liking to him, but he never looked twice. He was a perfect gentleman. He always had a good heart even when he fought with the wrong side. It was inevitable that someday he would leave the group. His conscience was far greater and more honorable than any one of ours."

"I know you may not want to hear this, but the rumor has it that he's taken."

"Well...I'm not surprised. Who wouldn't take him? Anyway, don't worry. I don't care. I only care about our family."

"If you can't handle yourself, then I think it would be best if one of us took over."

Raven flashed her eyes in anger, feeling offended. "Haven't I always taken care of our family? I won't let us down."

"Very well. Fair enough. When do we start the search?"

"Soon. I know they are scouting the towns for survivors. I just need to talk to them and get an idea of who is closest to Michael, then I'll know what to do. We just need to get lucky and pick the right town. I'm only taking a few with me. Get a group together. I need them to snoop around to find more information about the alkins if possible, and tell the rest to go deep into the woods and hide. I'll be right behind you when I can get away."

CHAPTER 10

CLAUDIA RUBBED HER EYES, THEN opened them to find an open book resting on her chest. She sat upright when the aroma of food shot through her nostrils, giving her hunger pangs. Swinging her legs over the side of the bed, she placed her feet on the floor to get something to eat. Just then Michael appeared, holding a tray.

"Hungry?" Michael paced toward her, set the tray on a table, and lifted Claudia's legs back into the bed. After releasing the legs of the tray to stand in place over her, he placed several pillows behind her back for support.

"Yes, I'm starving. Thank you." Picking up a pair of chopsticks, she didn't know what to eat first. In front of her was a plate of kung pao chicken, chow mein, vegetables, and steamed rice. When she took a bite of the chicken, she wanted to gulp the whole plate down her throat. After she took another, she stopped. Where were her manners? "Michael, eat with me."

Michael crawled onto the bed and snuggled beside her. "I'm fine. You need to eat. You're eating for three now. I'll enjoy watching you eat, that will be enough for me."

Thinking of her babies, she ate while giving Michael a bite of her food between her bites. "One for you." Michael graciously opened his mouth. "And three for me and our children," Claudia mumbled, stuffing food into her mouth.

After clearing her plate, Claudia picked up the book she was reading before she fell asleep and showed it to Michael.

"*What To Expect When You're Expecting.* Hmmm...catchy title, but I don't think that will help too much since your pregnancy isn't quite normal," Michael said carefully. "I'm wondering if we should speak to Katherine. Do you agree?"

"I agree, but not now, okay? I'd like to wait."

"Sure, anything you want." He kissed her forehead. "Anything I can do to help? I'm good at giving kisses, massages, and anything to do with giving Mrs. Michael pleasure." He cocked his brows with a tantalizing gaze.

Claudia placed the book by her side, swung her legs, and straddled over him. "The book says that a pregnant woman's hormones increase, especially the ones that got her pregnant. How about that?"

Using his angel strength and speed, Michael flipped Claudia over. With their positions switched, he pinned her arms. He was now the one straddling her. "How interesting. Remember, I'm the one who offered. Name your price, Mrs. Michael: a kiss, a massage, or just plain pleasure."

Claudia paused, looking deeply into his eyes without answering. She was enjoying the moment of exchanging loving and wanting gazes, but was suddenly reminded of the fact she couldn't hear his thoughts, so she tried to reach into his mind.

"So...what's it going to be?"

"I think I deserve all three, Mr. Michael. Didn't you hear me? I was speaking into your mind."

"No, I didn't."

"I thought what happened at the party was just a one day fluke, but it's not. Why is this happening?"

Michael cuddled Claudia into his arms when their playful mood had been broken. "I don't know. We really need to talk to Katherine about this," Michael suggested.

Claudia released a heavy sigh. "Okay."

"Hey...." Michael noted Claudia's facial expression, long and worried. Gently lifting her chin, he matched her eyes. "You're fine. Your body is changing. It's probably temporary. You don't need to hear my thoughts to know how much I love you."

"I know. It's just that I feel...I feel—"

"Normal?"

"Yes," Claudia admitted.

Michael laced his fingers through hers and kissed her knuckles. "You started off being normal, but normal is not what you are... remember that."

"There's nothing wrong with being normal. I just want to make sure we're all safe." If she suffered a temporary loss of her powers, she wouldn't be able to defend those she loved, especially her unborn babies. That thought alone frightened her the most.

"That's why I'm here. I'll always be here, to protect you, to love you, to kiss you...." He leaned over and kissed her tenderly on her cheek. "To kiss you here." He kissed her nose. "And here," he whispered, brushing her lips. "Also right here." He softly sucked her neck.

Claudia moaned, enjoying his caresses, almost forgetting her worries. Without warning, she shuddered lightly. Her stomach started to cramp while her muscles tightened with a sharp pang. The delicious meal she'd just engulfed flowed back up her throat. Feeling like she was car sick, the nauseating feeling kicked in strong and fast. "I think I'm going to throw up."

Michael stopped and looked at Claudia in surprise. "What did you say?"

Claudia pushed Michael's chest, forcing him to move aside, and ran to the restroom. Hugging the porcelain toilet, she opened her mouth and released. Seeing the color of the food she just ate, she grimaced and flushed the toilet. Watching her butterfly necklace dangling under her chin, she moved it to the side. After the incident with the fallen, and especially since her powers were diminishing quickly, she made sure it was always on her. Soon after, she threw up again, then seconds later, more streamed out of her mouth.

"Ugh," she groaned, wiping her mouth with the back of her hand. Weak and cold, Claudia rolled into a ball, afraid to leave just in case there was more to let out.

Michael kneeled down, cradled Claudia into his hold, and wrapped his wings around her for warmth. "You're shivering." He touched her cheeks. "Let me take you back to bed."

"No," she said weakly, wiping the tears that had appeared when she vomited. "I want to throw up again."

"Is this what you call morning sickness? Is that what's happening? I read several chapters when you took a nap."

Claudia gazed at Michael and gave him a "you're so wonderful" smile. "Yes. I believe so."

Michael brushed Claudia's hair away from her face. "I wish I could take your place. I'd rather it was me suffering. I hate to see you this way."

"Don't worry, Michael. I'll be okay. Hopefully it won't last too long."

"Our babies are giving us trouble already, huh?" he joked, trying to lighten the mood. "I hope they're nothing like Davin, at least the giving us trouble part."

Exhausted, unable to say a word, she managed to give him a smile and nuzzled into his arms and wings where she always felt comforted...her serenity...her home.

DAVIN CAREFULLY AND SLOWLY PUSHED the broken glass double door, trying not to make a sound. When he gave it a little tug, the remaining glass toppled over and shattered to pieces on the ground.

"I thought you told us to keep our noise level down," Vivian whispered harshly, looking irritated. "You've now told whatever is in there that we're here."

Davin dropped his mouth, wanting to say something, but he knew Vivian was right. But it wasn't his fault the window had decided to break. "Woman...not my fault," he whispered back, gesturing for the rest of the team to pass through.

"Woman?" Vivian scoffed with a light giggle, obviously thrown off by Davin's comment.

Dark and gloomy, the warehouse stunk of burnt wood and dead flesh. Walking further in, they could see how high the ceiling was from the starlight that seeped through the chunk of missing roof. Multiple rows of wooden crates lined the floor. Some were stacked as high as the ceiling, while some were standing alone and placed at the sides. Huddling together in a tight circle, they cautiously advanced with soft steps as their sword or bow glowed, illuminating just enough to see their immediate surroundings.

"What's inside the crates?" Vivian asked, examining the crates to her side.

"Drugs, machine guns, or antiques," Davin answered.

"And how do you know this?"

"I watch a lot of movies." Davin winked as if he was right, leaving Vivian to wonder if he was joking or being serious.

Suddenly there was soft yelp. Davin turned to the sound and eyed Michelle looking like she had just seen a ghost. Michelle was standing in front of a corpse whose body was burnt to nothing but organs. Michelle grimaced from the sight, shook her head in sorrow, and clung to Gracie for comfort.

"Look straight ahead," Caleb suggested.

There were dead humans on the floor, looking like zombies, some with their limbs torn off. Whatever horrific condition they were in, they were once God's creations, and had been killed by the demons, or they were demons themselves, killed by some other evil.

Elissa turned her head for a second and bumped into Vivian. "Sorry, I didn't know we'd stopped. I swear I thought I saw one shut her eyes."

"Ooooh, zombies. They're alive. Look, there's one behind you," Davin pointed. Though seeing dead humans was nothing to laugh about, Davin couldn't resist using the opportunity to do what Davin did best—irritate the heck out of his friends.

"What!?" Elissa jumped and looked behind her. When she realized she'd been had, she scowled with a huff and crossed her arms. "Not funny. My heart just dropped to the floor."

"Then you'd be just like them," Gracie giggled. "Sorry, I just had to say that."

"Shhh," Vivian hushed them with a serious expression. "Did you see that?"

"No, they were too busy making fun of me," Elissa grunted.

Something in the form of a dark shadow flashed by Davin's field of vision. "There it goes. I saw it. It definitely had wings. A bat out of hell...maybe Batman," he chuckled to himself. "Follow me."

Cautiously they matched Davin's steps. With their backs against the crates, Davin's heart pounded out of his chest. Pacing cautiously, he turned the corner and jumped into place with his sword up for defense—nothing. With a deep sigh, he released his anxiety and quickly continued.

"This way," Vivian directed, running the opposite direction.

"Vivian, stop!" Davin yelled, but she had already sprinted forward. Heading to the last row of crates, she turned the corner and was out of sight. As usual, Caleb was on her tail.

The group followed behind Davin until he suddenly halted. Caleb's arms were up in surrender and his sword was on the floor, and Vivian was in the hands of a fallen, so Davin took caution. There were five of them. Scowling, Davin recognized three of the male fallen. "I remember you guys from the party. You weren't invited there, and you're certainly not invited here."

"You want your friend alive? Back off," the female demanded.

Knowing he had no choice for Vivian's sake, he put his sword down. Instructed by Davin, the rest of the venators did the same. "We've come in peace. We're here to search for demon's activities, not fallen. How about you leave us alone and we'll leave you alone?"

"I've come to give Michael a warning," a female fallen said.

Davin eyed the fallen arms that were tightly wrapped around Vivian's chest while the other held the dagger beside her neck. "What is your message?"

"Tell him to give himself up to Dantanian or else there will be consequences."

"Really? You guys think you can take on Michael, the alkins, the venators, the Twelve, the watchers, and crazy Austin? And I forgot to mention the Earth angels. And...did you ever meet Holly? Now she is a piece of work. She's so crazy—"

"Enough! I got your point. This isn't my fight. Please, many lives are at stake. I will release her when you promise me you'll keep your word. You must tell him."

"And what if I don't promise?"

The fallen pricked Vivian's neck with the dagger. No blood seeped out. Seeing no blood indicated that Vivian was an alkin. Alkins didn't bleed; however, they did feel pain just like the rest of the angels. When the cut got deeper and longer, Vivian yelped in pain.

"Stop!" Davin demanded, seeing Vivian's eyes full of fear. "I'll tell Michael. Where is he to meet you and what's your name?"

"Tell him to meet Raven at the old mountains. He'll know what I'm talking about. He was one of us before, if you'd forgotten."

Davin wanted to grab her neck with his bare hands and choke her to death, but he had to contain himself, especially since Vivian was still in her possession. "Let her go. I'll tell Michael when I see him," he gritted through his teeth with his jaws clenched.

"Don't wait too long." Raven shoved Vivian into Davin's arms and flashed her wings to open. Five sets of black wings soared through the broken ceiling.

Holding Vivian in his arms, Davin teased. "Why, Vivian. I always knew you had the hots for me."

Vivian pushed Davin, making him stumble back a couple of steps. "Gross. Shut up. So what do we do?" Seeing the coast was clear, Vivian placed her hand on her cut that had already started to heal, and picked up her sword from the ground. "What are we going to tell Michael?"

"Nothing. Absolutely nothing." Davin locked eyes with the other venators. "You didn't hear anything...got that?" he ordered.

With a nod from them, he relaxed and picked up his sword.

"Are you sure?" Vivian disagreed, second-guessing his judgment. "You heard what she said."

Davin started pacing forward. "Yes, I heard what she said. He already knows Dantanian wants him, but I don't need to tell him to go to the old mountain just yet. I'll eventually tell him. I'm not going to make him worry for nothing. Let's check the rest of this crappy place and move on to the next town."

CHAPTER 11

Michael held Claudia's hand as they walked through the colossal door. "Here we are, back again. Alexa Rose will be surprised," Michael muttered.

"I feel like a princess every time I come here." Claudia's eyes glistened at the beauty of Halo City.

After planting a kiss on the back of her hand, Michael twirled her and pulled her to his chest. "That you are, my love."

"Michael! Claudia!" Alexa Rose called, running toward them, leaping into Michael's arms. Lifting her up into the air, he twirled her once while she laughed. Afterward, Alexa Rose gently draped her arms around Claudia's waist.

Hearing the sound of a child's laughter, Claudia couldn't wait to hear the laughter of her own children.

"What brings both of you back again? I mean...I'm so happy to see you both." Peering up at Claudia with a wink, then to Michael, Alexa Rose waited for a response.

"Oh, nothing special. Just visiting," Michael smiled.

"Don't be silly, Michael. I know why you're here. I've known since the last visit."

"Really?" Michael looked astounded. "How come I'm always the last one to know?" he pouted, making Alexa Rose giggle. "How about I read a story? Go gather your friends and I'll meet you at the fountain. I need to meet with Agnes first. I'm not sure how long that will take."

"Sure." Alexa Rose bounced cheerfully and skipped out the door.

"Shall we?" Michael asked.

Instead of answering, Claudia gave a mischievous grin. "See you when I see you." She dashed out the door, leaving behind a breeze. Usually, no matter how fast she sped, her vision was clear; however, this time everything looked blurry, causing her to slow down. Feeling like she was on an extremely fast rollercoaster ride, her stomach dropped. Wanting to vomit, she stopped and casually paced forward, not wanting to worry Michael.

Michael beat her to the door. "You've lost your touch, Mrs. Michael." With a smirk, he leaned against the door with his arms crossed, looking dreamy.

Claudia lost her thought as the feeling of queasiness died down, but not completely. "I gotta let you win...sometimes."

Michael yanked her to his chest. "Only if you're the prize."

"Come in Michael," Agnes said from the other side of the door. "Or what the humans would say, get a room."

Embarrassed, he shrugged his shoulders and chuckled like a little boy who'd been caught being naughty. Michael swung the door open. "Agnes, we were just—"

"Michael...please, spare me the details. I'm not here to judge. My virgin ears won't be able to handle it," she joked.

With a nervous chuckle, Michael kept quiet.

"Claudia, why don't you lay on my bed?" Agnes patted the bed. "Angels don't sleep. We use the bed to rest. And yes, we do get tired once in a while. It's also a great relaxation therapy."

Inhaling a deep breath, Claudia spread across the mattress. Exhaling a worried sigh, she waited anxiously. Not being herself lately, she was concerned that something might be wrong with her babies. But when Michael held her hand and lovingly looked into her eyes, she began to relax. Escaping into the world of Michael, she knew that everything would be just fine. It had to be.

Agnes placed both of her hands over Claudia's stomach. Like a mechanical scanner, her hands glowed as if taking an X-ray. "The twins are doing well, with strong heartbeats. They've grown so much since the last time I saw them."

"You can feel their heartbeats?" Claudia said in surprise.

"Yes...here." Hand over hand, Agnes placed Claudia's to the location. "Humans wouldn't be able to feel this, but you can."

Silence.

"I can feel it," Claudia expressed with excitement as her eyes twinkled with joy. Then Agnes guided the other hand to feel the second. Claudia laughed with glee. It filled her soul with bliss...the kind of feeling only a mother to be could feel. There were no words...it was simply pure ecstasy. "Here, Michael." Claudia guided Michael's hands.

With excitement, he waited, and there it was. Knowing and feeling was a whole different story. "I...I...wow! I never knew that I could. It's my first time."

"I hope it is," Claudia lifted her brows, giving him a playful attitude.

"I mean...of course it is." Michael peered up, catching Claudia's eyes. They were glassy, illuminated with tears of joy.

Claudia smiled, never taking her eyes off him. "Thank you, Agnes."

The examination had been completed and Claudia and Michael couldn't be happier from the good news. Claudia wondered who the babies would look like, about the color of their eyes and hair, and what they would be like. And if they took after Michael, would they have wings?

"Would you like to know the sex of your children?" Agnes asked.

"Claudia and I spoke about this. We'd like for it to be a surprise."

"Very well." Agnes smiled. "Have you thought of names?"

"Yes," Michael nodded. "Kind of. We are still thinking about it."

"I understand. Once you give it, there's no going back," Agnes reminded. "Claudia and Michael, your names were chosen by your parents. As for me...I picked mine. Sometimes I wonder why I picked it."

"I think your name suits you well. It's elegant and beautiful," Claudia stated, sitting upright with Michael's help. It was the first time Claudia had seen Agnes blush.

"Thank you. Now...you are set to go. The next time I see you both, I'll be holding them in my arms. Angel pregnancy, though rare, is fast, unlike humans. It'll pass before you know it. You two need to prepare. Nursery, breastfeeding or bottle-feeding, diapers, and so much more, I can't name them all. Have you visited Katherine yet?"

"I'm reading a book about it," Claudia said.

"Good. Books are good, but I suggest you speak to Katherine since it's pretty much like being pregnant as a human, but maybe she can be more helpful since she'd been through it as an angel. This would also be a great way to tell her. The news will spread. I would've wanted you to tell me in person, and knowing Katherine, since she's seen you grow up, it would mean a lot to her. She was Gamma's best friend, after all."

"Yes, you're right. It's just that...."

Sensing Claudia's concern, she pulled her into her embrace. "We're not here to judge, my child. We're here to help and guide you to your destiny. I understand your dilemma. Fear not. It will all work out. You just need hope."

With loving words from Agnes, Claudia felt like a brick had been lifted off her chest. She had expressed some of her worries about being pregnant to Michael, but he never knew to what extent they had burdened her. It was bad enough they were crossing the line by having a forbidden relationship. But there was nothing she wouldn't do to ensure they would be together. Perhaps that was why the Twelve let it be so...they knew they couldn't control them. Such a strong love was rare. It was a one in a million epic kind of love, because angels didn't fall in love the way they had. It was simply meant to be.

CHAPTER 12

CRYING OUT LOUD LIKE TARZAN, Davin swung on a long rope across to the first level from the other side. He plopped right in front of Claudia, startling her as she held flowers in her hands. "Me Tarzan, you Jane." He pointed to Caleb and Vivian on the other side. "They monkeys," Davin chuckled. "I've always wanted to do that. That was so much fun," Davin said with exhilaration.

Claudia laughed out loud as Vivian and Caleb raced across the bridge.

"Monkeys? I heard that." Caleb punched Davin on his arm. "You're the monkey."

Then silence. Claudia felt three pair of eyes staring at her. It had been a couple of weeks since they'd last seen each other. The alkins had continued their missions with the venators to search for survivors and help the small town to get back on its feet after all that had happened.

Davin gawked at Claudia, who was wearing a mid-thigh summer dress with hues of orange and purple. "Claudia...you're... kind of...fat," Davin mumbled, arching his brows in confusion.

Vivian slapped Davin on the back. "You don't ever say that to anyone, especially females."

Davin slapped his mouth, giving Claudia an apologetic look.

"It's okay. Michael and I are...happily surprised," she said, rubbing her hands over her belly, which had gotten bigger, as Davin gazed at it. Though she had been told she would show quickly, she could hardly believe it herself. Her face glowed and her smile radiated with a look of bliss.

They continued to gawk intently in disbelief until Michael snapped them out of their trance when he appeared. "Hey...you're back?" Seeing Davin's disapproving look, Michael raked his hair back. "Umm...we were going to tell you guys—"

"You don't need to tell us. You can clearly see," Davin sounded unhappy. "You could've waited. We were planning a wedding."

Vivian nudged Davin. "Great, now you've told them our plan."

Claudia gaped between Davin and Vivian. "You do know that a wedding requires the man asking the woman before the wedding part happens, right?" Though Michael and Claudia had a private ceremony on their own, she didn't want to tell them.

"That's what I've been trying to tell them," Caleb said, throwing up his hands. "Thanks for clarifying it, because according to them, it's a group decision." He turned to his friends. "Do you believe me now?"

Claudia couldn't help but giggle. They were so cute. She had forgotten there were many things they didn't know, especially when it came to traditions.

"Davin and Caleb, both of you are going to be uncles," Claudia smiled. "And Vivian will be an aunt."

Davin curved his lips from ear to ear, releasing his anger, seemingly taking in the news. "I am? Uncle Davin. I like the sound of that. So...does this mean we need to keep this information from the Twelve?"

"I'm not sure…I mean…we're not sure. Let's just keep this under the radar for now," Michael suggested, placing his arms around Claudia, giving her a kiss on the forehead to let her know everything would be fine.

"I think that'd be a good idea for now, especially since we think…." Claudia blinked.

"Yes…?" Davin waited, anticipating her words.

Claudia held out two fingers.

They gasped in surprise.

"Two?" Davin gulped. "Did…you…say…two? Because two is more than one."

Claudia and Michael didn't answer. They just smiled and nodded.

"Two?" Davin shook his head. "Double trouble…yikes." Then he fainted.

HOLDING AN IMPASSIVE GAZE, AUSTIN stared at the paintings of the Twelve hanging on the wall and recalled the day when he had brought Claudia to the meeting room at Island of Eden. He could vividly picture the star struck expression on her face when she saw the paintings. How inquisitive she had been about their world, and now she was a part of it.

He also recalled teaching her how to shoot the bow he'd given her for Christmas. With a fiery look in her eyes, she was steadfast to learn. Awed by her determination, he knew the reasons behind it. Fearing for her life and tired of running, she wanted to fight back.

How he missed those days when her laughter filled the house. Now he was there, bored out of his mind as he sat at the round table for the monthly meeting with the Twelve and Holly.

"What are your thoughts, Austin?" Jeremiah asked. His eyes pierced intently at him in a disapproving manner.

Returning to the present, Austin shot his eyes to Holly with a look only those two could understand, hoping somehow she could rescue him since he had no clue what they were talking about.

"You know, Jeremiah, Austin has no opinions about the fallen," Holly interceded, taking in Austin's look. "I mean...they haven't given any indication they want to take over. Aden has been gone for some time now. Perhaps they'll just disappear, live among humans and forget about...us." She let out a soft fake laugh.

"Are you Austin's keeper?" Jeremiah sneered. "The boy has a mouth. I'd like to hear his thoughts."

You don't want to hear my thoughts, old fart, Austin thought. Oh, God, he couldn't believe he'd repeated Davin's words. He had a choice...to bow down to Jeremiah and be respectful, or spit in his face and be rude. He chose the latter. "Holly is my keeper, didn't you know?" He winked at Holly, who returned the look with wide eyes, seemingly wondering what on Earth he was going to say after she'd just saved him. "And yes, I do have a mouth, a very kissable mouth, some women might say."

"Augustine," Katherine huffed sharply, kicking her son underneath the table. "Mind your manners." Katherine gave the others an apologetic look.

Jeremiah gave him a repulsed expression and turned to Katherine. "You need to keep your son in line."

Katherine's lips protruded as she tried to contain herself, but to no avail. "Jeremiah, I suggest you watch your mouth first. I will contain my son, but you need to contain your choice of words."

Jeremiah scowled, seemingly knowing he would not win this argument. "The new generation of venators has no respect for the elders."

"Maybe the old generation has an old way of thinking and needs to get with the new generation," Austin rebutted.

Jeremiah's brows rose to their peek and his face looked like he was about to explode.

"Anyway...." Holly interrupted before things got out of hand, shaking her head for being in the middle of this awkward conversation. "The Earth angels have already voted. We've decided to wait to see if the fallen strike first instead of searching for them. We don't want to start a war that may never have begun in the first place."

"This is what I agree with," Elizabeth said.

"Me, too," Jonah seconded.

"Does anyone oppose? Please speak your mind." Sitting up tall and looking like a true leader, Austin's tone became serious.

The room was silent.

"Okay, then," Austin continued. "Since we...."

Jeremiah raised his right hand. "I do, but I know nothing will happen since I'm the only one opposing."

"I understand your concern," Phillip stated. "But you are jumping to conclusions. You are assuming the fallen are ready to attack without any evidence. As far as we know, they're still in hiding."

"We call this...paranoia," Austin commented matter of factly, giving his mischievous grin.

"Paranoia?" Jeremiah scoffed. "Hardly an understatement. You all can do whatever you like. I'll be sending my watchers to observe the fallen, if any dare to come out of hiding. Don't ever say I didn't tell you so."

Taking in Jeremiah's words, Austin spoke. "I like that idea. Let's observe and send out our watchers. Let me know which part of the Earth you'll be sending them to so we don't overlap their location. Perhaps Holly and I can go with them." He winked at Holly.

Jeremiah looked pleased, but wouldn't dare to show even a twitch of a smile.

"Sounds like we have a plan. Holly and Austin, I would like a word with you two. Meeting adjourned." Katherine pounded the gavel on the table for formality, remaining seated as she watched everyone leave. Austin and Holly remained behind, looking like children who were ready to be scolded. The room was still until the door closed behind them.

"Is this about Claudia?" Katherine snapped and rooted her eyes on him.

"What?" Austin was surprised at Katherine's words. "Why did you bring her up? She has nothing to do with whatever you are talking about. What are you talking about?"

Holly zoomed her eyes on the table, seemingly uncomfortable by the topic of this conversation.

"You want to go out in the field so you can see her. Isn't that right?"

"No!" His tone went up an octave higher, then quickly lowered. "I was once a venator. I miss the thrill of the adventures. I don't see why I can't do both."

Katherine released a heavy sigh and relaxed back in her chair. "The Twelve and the curators do not go out in the field, normally, but if you feel the need, I suppose it will be fine. I trust your judgment. I have a strange feeling something is coming our way. Perhaps it is paranoia." Katherine chuckled lightly. "Aden's followers were ruthless. They know the venators will be on search missions. They may be lurking about and taking advantage of the ruined towns."

"See." Austin threw up his hands. "They could use all the help we can offer, and who better to go...than Holly and me, two of your finest."

Katherine reverted her attention to Holly. "Holly, do you feel the same?"

Sheepishly shrugging her shoulders, she answered, "Yes. I can do both."

"Very well. Be careful and report back to me." With that, Katherine stood up and stared at the two of them, most likely wondering if she'd made the right decision, and glided out the door.

Reclining in his chair with his feet on the table, Austin curved his lips into a wicked grin. "You know I always get my way."

Crossing her arms, Holly leaned forward. "I'm not stupid. I know this is about Claudia, because why would you even want to be near Davin, your favorite friend?"

"Okay...I'll admit it...partially," he replied with a soft tone. "I miss her."

"Why put yourself through that torture? Why, Austin? Why for the love of God? You live for pain, don't you?"

Austin frowned. "You know why...because even though she belongs to someone else and even though my heart will painfully bleed from her absence, the gratification, the high I get from even a glimpse of her is worth the torment afterward. It swallows me into a blissful moment and spits me back out with a punch in the gut. Anyway, you may think I'm crazy, but it's because you've never known real love. Unless you've been there, it's impossible for you to understand. It's the love that stays with you no matter how hard you try to deny it. Don't worry. I'm letting her go. I have to. One day at a time."

"Wow! You sound like you should be in a romantic novel, movie, or something," Holly teased, seemingly trying to lighten the mood.

"Shut up." Austin perked up with a grin. "You're going to think I'm even crazier...I kind of miss Davin."

"Yup...you've gone overboard. This new job of yours has made you all fluffy and sensitive."

"I can be all fluffy and sensitive in bed," he winked.

"Gross. I told you that subject was off limits."

"I just love to see you cringe," Austin laughed, amused by Holly's reaction. "Anyway, I didn't say I miss him like a friend. I miss torturing him."

"Oh good, cause for a second there I thought...oh never mind. Let's stop talking and get our butts in the field like the good old days." Holly stood up with an excited glow in her eyes.

"Do you know which town venators were headed to?" Austin asked, walking out the door with Holly.

"Nope. Don't have a clue. Didn't you give them the mission?"

"Just finding out if you knew. Then I'll lead. I can't wait to see the look on Davin's face," Austin chuckled, thinking about how he was going to greet him. With a wicked smile, he sauntered toward the cliff with Holly.

The wind softly brushed against his wings, and if he allowed, he wouldn't have to use any of his own effort to float in the air. He would be carried away with the breeze. Watching the waves crash against the huge boulders below, somehow they looked different, more beautiful and peaceful than before. He realized he had taken the view for granted. Now that he didn't have this view on a daily basis, he missed it.

He also recalled the day when Claudia had accidently fallen off the cliff. Chuckling to himself, he remembered how she had thought he was a demon or a fallen. She was so determined not to give him her soul that she would've jumped to her own death. How innocent and naïve she was about their world. Those were the good old days.

"Shall we?" Holly asked, slowly unfurling her wings, leaning her head back and enjoying the breeze. If she was human, she would've felt the warmth the sun graciously gave to the land.

"I'll meet you at Nubilus City." Austin took flight first, gliding over the vast ocean, then flipping over. With his back toward the water, his arms and legs were spread out without a care in the world.

"Show off," Holly mumbled to herself. When she caught up to him, she flipped over and soared in the same position with him. They looked like two white birds, gliding gracefully across the breathtaking sky, sometimes blending with the puffy white clouds.

CHAPTER 13

STANDING ON THE TOP OF the hill, Davin carefully scanned below to their next destination. "It doesn't look like anyone could've survived there. Looks like a giant gopher had a field day."

Patches of the ground had been sucked underneath and the fire had destroyed most of the houses. The thick black smoke still lingered, looking like the smoke coming out of the chimneys. Though it was near the end of summer, it seemed as though winter had stayed awhile as the ashes and the dying fire produced a heavy blanket over the town and prevented the sun from penetrating.

It was a huge contrast from where they stood. Plush greenery spread for miles while various wild flowers gave beauty to the land. The branches of the trees were full and fruitful. It was like Heaven, while the town was like Hell.

"Another hopeless town, whatever's left of it," Vivian sighed sorrowfully.

Caleb stepped forward for a better view. "Let's find out."

"Ready?" Davin asked the venators, looking from left to right.

"Ready," they said in accord, their eyes on the same view.

With a nod, Davin jumped first. "Whoo hoo!"

One after the other, they leapt. With a flash of their wings, they soared side by side. From below they looked like an enormous white parachute gliding to its destination. It was a glorious sight, something pure, something good, something from out of this world. With a thud they landed gracefully, but on a hill of unidentifiable debris. Though the smoke would have been harsh on human lungs, it did not bother the venators; however, the sour, foul odor did.

"What puked on this part of the Earth?" Davin coughed, wanting to vomit.

"You mean the awful smell that smells like you when you make me mad?" Vivian teased.

"Funny, I kind of thought it smelled like you." Willing his sword, Davin cautiously set foot on top of a flattened car.

"Be careful," Caleb uttered.

"What did you say?" Gracie asked, taking a step behind Davin. Suddenly, she sunk into the debris underneath her feet. Stunned by the incident, everyone huddled to see the deep cut of the Earth where Gracie had disappeared.

"Gracie!" Michelle shouted, concerned for her friend. She didn't have to worry too long. Like a shooting star, Gracie shot out and landed next to Michelle.

"That was a close call," Gracie shuddered.

Michelle yanked Gracie into her hold. "Don't scare me like that. Stay close to me. Maybe we can hover instead of using our feet?"

"No," Davin said sternly, pacing forward. "You know the rule...no angelic powers are used unless necessary...just in case humans are around."

Michelle rolled her eyes. "Fine. La de da da," she mumbled, making funny faces behind Davin's back, making Gracie laugh.

Davin turned to them and twitched his brows humorously. "Be aware, Davin knows everything. I heard that and saw that." Then he turned and walked straight ahead. He was almost certain he'd seen a shadowy figure of an angel. "Shhh...something wicked is here. It went this way." He led them into an abandoned, broken down house.

With his sword ready by his side, Davin crept in first. He pushed the front door that was already ajar. Instead of swinging in the direction he wanted, the door dropped to the floor with a big bang. It happened so fast they didn't have a chance to react. The uplifted massive dust and ashes brushed past them.

"Not again, Davin," Vivian coughed, waving her hand, trying to settle the dust. "Whatever you were looking for knows you're here now. Good going."

"Hey, it's not my fault I'm so strong."

"Hardly."

Davin turned to face Vivian, wanting to say something clever, but instead he laughed out loud.

"What's so funny?" Vivian started busting up too seeing Davin's face. He looked like he had taken a bath in ink with his clothes on. He was covered with black ashes from head to toe. By the sound of Davin's laughter, Vivian could imagine how she looked. Then everyone started chuckling, but soon after resumed their positions and became serious again when they heard the sound of a window crashing from the second floor.

"What the heck was that?" Davin stammered, leading his group to the sound. Though it was daylight, the sun was unable to shine through. It looked as though it was dusk. Holding their lit weapons by their sides, their light guided the way. The living room had been trashed. Every single piece of furniture and accessories were flipped over and burnt. As if someone had socked the wall with a hammer, random holes marked the walls.

Striding over shattered glasses, broken picture frames, melted candles, and other kinds of what was now junk, Davin led them up the stairs. With the sound of the wooden stairs creaking, step by step, they reached the top.

Davin had done this many times before, but the anticipation of what he would find made his heart hammer faster every step of the way. Exhaling a deep breath, he treaded down the empty hallway and turned the corner. When he heard the creaking sound of the floor from a room down the hall, he knew which room the noise had come from.

Cautiously they moved forward. The bedroom door was slightly ajar. It wasn't opened wide enough to see who or what could be on the other side, so Davin kicked the door with all his strength. It shot open, only to slam back in his face.

Vivian looked at him. "Duh."

"Shut up. I can't help it that I'm strong." He was just glad it didn't break like the other two doors or he would definitely have looked like a dork, but which was worse? He shook his head and laugh inwardly at himself. He had no luck with doors.

Peering in, Davin saw the shattered windows first, most likely where the sound had come from...the broken pieces were scattered on the floor. With a crunch from his footsteps, Austin appeared out of the shadows. "Austin? What the heck are you doing here? We thought you were a fallen. And have you heard of the door?"

"Not the kind that smacks back in your face," Austin smirked.

Davin perked his lips with "you got me there" look.

"Anyway, is this how you greet one of the Twelve?" Austin crossed his arms, piercing his eyes at him.

Then Holly stepped in front. "Or the master of the curators?"

Silent...silent...stunned...Davin open his lips to speak, then closed them and lifted his brows in confusion.

"Nah...just kidding," Holly giggled.

Silence.

"Hello," Austin said, waving his hand. "We were just joking."

Michelle and Gracie rushed pass Davin, almost knocking him over, and hugged Holly.

"Dang, girlfriend, 1 thought you were serious," Michelle grumbled. "I thought you totally became a snob."

"Hey, don't grab me too tight," Holly said, releasing. "And 1 am a snob. Don't you forget it," she smiled.

Caleb, Vivian, and Davin waved to greet them.

"So, what brings you both to this heavenly place?" Davin asked, relaxing.

"Austin missed you, Davin," Holly teased, watching Davin's eyes pop open.

Austin coughed purposely while giving Holly the evil eye. "She meant I'm here to make sure everything is going as planned. So, how's the mission?"

Davin had never liked Austin because of the love triangle between Austin, Michael, and Claudia. Take Claudia out of the equation and the scenario would have been different. He could actually picture them being friends. Now that Austin was one of the Twelve and his boss, he knew he needed to give him a new level of respect. "Mission is going okay, considering how awful the towns look. We haven't found any survivors, though."

"The chances of that will be slim to none...at least in the towns you've been scouting. The other groups of venators have found survivors, but they were sent to the cities. The demons, if there were any left, or the fallen would most likely hide in small towns. Have you seen any fallen?"

"Nope," Davin said quickly before anyone else had a chance to speak. He didn't want Austin to know the fallen wanted Michael.

"That's good news. Jeremiah thinks since Aliah is out of the picture, the fallen will come out of hiding and retaliate. Anyway, Holly and 1 will be joining you on some of the missions."

"Greaaa...." Davin wanted to say great, but he stopped himself. An unexpected excitement rose within him, but he didn't want to express it. "Okay, but just don't break any windows."

"Fine, if you don't break any doors," Austin said, seemingly trying to hold in his laughter.

"Deal."

"WELCOME, CLAUDIA," KATHERINE GREETED HER with open arms. "Have a seat." She pointed to the leather sofa in her office. "How have you been?"

Surprisingly, Katherine was dressed casually. Nonetheless, she looked stunning in jeans and a cream ruffled shirt. Sitting stiffly, Claudia twiddled her thumbs, feeling edgy, and wondered how she would break the news. She felt like an unwed teenager telling her mom she was pregnant. Well...she was, but this wasn't a normal situation. Nothing about her and her life was normal. This would've never happened in her normal life. She'd always had a good head on her shoulders, and had always exercised good judgment...almost.

"I've come to tell you...well...I'll just get straight to the point. I know how these things happen, but it was never planned. I didn't even think angels could...I mean...I know they can, but I didn't think it would happen to me." Claudia cleared her throat.

"Claudia, going around about is not helping. Do not fear. I'm here to help you, not to judge you. But I think I know what you're going to say. Seeing you wearing that tacky long dress that is twice your size and the way you were walking is an indication of what I'm thinking you're going to tell me. I'm not surprised. No. I take it back...I am surprised that it happened so soon, but I figured it would happen eventually...possibly. Accidents do happen with humans, and it can with angels, but...you know what I mean."

"So...you know I'm pregnant?" Claudia peered up to look at Katherine with wide eyes.

Katherine nodded. "Sorry for asking this question, but do you know who the father is?"

"Yes...of course. It's Michael."

"I'm sorry to ask, but I had to know. How long has it been?"

"Almost two months. Agnes was the first to know. I asked her to keep it a secret until I was ready to inform the Twelve. I've passed the vomiting stage and I'm showing...really showing. I can feel them moving inside my body." Claudia's eyes glistened with joy. "It's the neatest feeling. I can't describe the feelings in words."

"I understand," Katherine smiled. "I had Austin, remember?"

"Yes. It's one of the reasons why I'm here. I'm not sure what to do."

Katherine closed the gap between them and sat on the sofa next to Claudia, looking at her like a mother would a daughter. "Looks like you're doing everything right." Katherine extended her hand close to Claudia's stomach. "May I?"

With a nod from Claudia, Katherine stroked her hand in a circular motion over her belly. Katherine jumped slightly, smiling. "I felt a kick. You are a strong one." She giggled. "Wait...do you know you are carrying twins?" Looking stunned, she dropped her hand. "Yes. It's no wonder you are twice the size I was. Claudia, I don't know how far you think you are, but compared to human babies undergoing nine months of incubation, your babies will have only three. Your dress covered you up; I couldn't tell, but now I see that you're due pretty soon, especially since you're carrying twins. They may speed up the delivery. Did Agnes inform you of all this?"

"Yes."

"Good."

"I have another question. Will you help me deliver my babies?" Claudia asked hesitantly. She didn't know why she was nervous to ask such a question. Perhaps it was the fact that Katherine was Austin's mother.

"Of course. Let's deliver them at Halo City. It's much safer and quieter over there. I suggest you go there in a couple of weeks and rest until they are ready to enter our world."

Claudia nodded.

"Do you have any questions for me?"

"The only thing that I'm concerned about...which I wanted to ask you...well...Michael and I use to be able to mentally communicate with each other, but for some reason, I can't now. I feel as though my strength and speed are not what they used to be. I don't feel like myself."

"I see. It's quite normal. Your body is functioning like a human's body. Your babies are also taking your energy. I also felt the loss of my angel powers when I was pregnant. I promise it'll all come back after the delivery, but it will take some time. For this reason, you need to be cautious. You should hide your pregnancy as long as you can. We don't want this news to get out."

"I understand." Claudia suddenly felt like she was letting Katherine down. With her powers limited, she was of no use. She would be just plain Claudia.

Claudia stood up. "Thank you for your time. I'm sure you have many things to attend to."

Guiding Claudia to the door, Katherine gave her a warm hug. Releasing her, they stood face to face. "Fear not, my child. You will soon be back to yourself. Please don't wander off alone. Stay home, and only go to the places of Beyond."

"Yes. More than anything in this world, I want my babies to be safe."

"To be honest with you, I can't wait to see them. It's such a blessing to be pregnant and to see the miracle of life being born right in front of your eyes. There will be unwanted whispers from some of the Twelve. You know that, don't you?"

"I know. I feel like somehow this is all wrong, like I've done something horrible, but it should be something to celebrate."

"This is a part of being an angel I do not like, especially since I'm a woman. Maybe someday it will change, but for now, you need to understand it is still forbidden."

"I understand." Claudia tipped her head low, feeling embarrassed.

"Claudia, this is a happy moment in your life. Don't let anyone take this away from you. I for one will be on your side. I wish Gamma could've been here."

"I'm not sure about that."

"She would've approved. She was one of the angels who stood by my side during my pregnancy. I'll never forget that. And I'll be there for you."

"Thank you," Claudia said, releasing a burden off her chest. Having Katherine's blessing meant the world to her. It was as if Gamma had blessed her too.

"By the way...," Katherine started to say. "Have you chosen any names?"

"We have a couple of girl's names in mind, but we're not sure of names if the twins end up being boys."

"Michael should be hearing the information I'm about to tell you from one of us, but whatever." Katherine waved her hand. "Perhaps it will be easier if he hears it from you. His father's name was Zachariah. I thought you two may want to know." Katherine winked.

"Thank you. I'll let him know. I'm sure he'll be happy to know a name he can pass on that will mean something special for him."

"Now...please wear something more to your liking and not this...what looks like a pillow case," Katherine grimaced, then laughed. "I know you wore it to hide your pregnancy, but still."

Claudia giggled, feeling a whole lot better than when she'd come in.

CHAPTER 14

"SURPRISE!" THE THREE OF THEM shouted.

Claudia looked at Michael, then to her friends. Her mouth opened to speak, but there were no words. Emotionally overwhelmed by the ambiance of their first level home, her eyes were glassy with tears.

Streamers of pink and blue ribbons were laced from wall to wall. The same two colors of balloons filled their ceiling, and the curly ribbons tied at the ends streamed downward. Several huge banners that read, "Congratulations" were taped to the wall.

On the back table was a cake in the shape of a baby's bib, along with matching paper plates, cups, and napkins. Adjacent to it was a bowl of punch, and next to that was chips and salsa.

"Wow! You did all this for us?" Claudia asked with both of her hands on her cheeks, still unbelieving.

"Michael was in on the plan too, since he had to get you out of here for a while," Vivian explained. "And just so you know, Michael told us about your private wedding ceremony, which we're not too happy about, but we understand. That explained the ring on your finger."

"Not happy," Davin pouted.

"Double not happy," Caleb seconded.

"I'm so sorry," Claudia mumbled sheepishly.

"No need to apologize, Claudia." Vivian held her tightly. "We understand. Michael is Michael...romantic and all. We thought he was sweet; we just wish we could've been there too. But at least we can do this for you."

Releasing Vivian's hold, she smiled. "Thank you. I'm completely surprised and grateful."

Davin placed himself in front of Claudia, mesmerized by her bump that was much bigger than the last time he had seen her. "My, how big your belly has become."

"I know. They're growing so fast. And I can hardly walk or move. I can't wait." Claudia rubbed her stomach in a circular motion. "Come here for a group hug." She gestured with her hands.

Vivian, Caleb, and Davin pulled Claudia into the center, and Claudia pulled Michael alongside her.

"Urgh...I don't need a hug." Michael rolled his eyes.

"Even Superman needs a hug from his friends," Claudia murmured.

Claudia couldn't stop marveling at the decorations. In the corner of the room, she spotted a huge wrapped package and wondered what it was for. "I think we should keep it like this for a while, don't you think so, Michael?"

"Anything you want." Michael planted a kiss on her forehead. "Let's cut the cake."

After it was cut, they sat on the sofa holding paper plates of sliced cake.

"Mmmm...this is sooo good," Claudia said. "I don't remember loving sugar this much."

"Lucky for you, you can actually taste it. It tastes like paper to me...not that I've eaten paper before," Davin explained.

"I'm surprised, Davin. I would've thought you were the paper eating type," Caleb teased.

"Only if you put salsa on it," Davin replied with an expressionless face. It was difficult to tell if he was joking.

"Serious?" Vivian questioned, looking flabbergasted.

"I'm just joking...geesh."

"I wouldn't put anything past you," Vivian giggled, shoving a bite into her mouth. "Anyway, when the little ones come, you'll have to watch your manners. According to one of Claudia's books—and I've taken a peek—they learn from your actions. You may want to keep them away from Davin until they are like...eighteen."

"Hey...I'm not that bad."

Claudia giggled from their conversation. "I was just wondering if you knew something I didn't know. I mean...you put up pink and blue. What if I have twin boys or twin girls?"

The three of them froze and looked at each other like they had made a terrible mistake. "Umm...is this called a baby shower?" Davin asked, sounding uncertain.

"Yes," Claudia replied, smiling, trying to hold in her laughter, already anticipating Davin saying something really cute or asking a funny question.

"And you can only give birth to a boy or a girl...nothing in between...right?"

"What kind of question is that?" Vivian almost spit out her cake.

Davin shrugged his shoulders, chuckling. "I'm just saying. So...pink for girls and blue for boys...right?"

"Right?" Claudia confirmed.

"Well...according to the search engine...." Davin chuckled nervously, then looked as though he was deep in thought. "Ummm ...maybe I didn't read the part about what color to use when we don't know the sex of the baby. So...do you know?"

"No, we want it to be a surprise." Michael graciously took a bite from Claudia's fork, then grimaced. "You're right, it does taste like paper, though I'm not sure what paper tastes like. I'm just using Davin's words. But I'm sure humans find this very tasteful and satisfying."

"Do you have names picked out?" Caleb asked, playing with the frosting, scooping it into a pile with his fork. "They look like Crossroads clouds."

"Yeah they do," Michael snorted, agreeing with Caleb. "We have a few picked out, but we're not a hundred percent sure." Michael looked at Claudia to confirm.

Stuffing chips into his mouth, Davin garbled, "If it's a boy, you can name him Davin."

"So kids can make fun of him?" Vivian teased. "No way."

With a huff of his breath, Davin flicked some salsa at her. "Nothing's wrong with my name, Viv."

Vivian ducked. The salsa splattered on Caleb's cheek. "Grrr! Thanks!"

"Before you have a food fight, I want to ask you some questions," Michael said. His relaxed composure changed. He sat up straight as if to be all business. "Have you seen any fallen on your missions? I mean, besides the one you told me about earlier?"

Silence.

"Nope, nada, zip, none," Davin said finally, unable to look Michael in the eyes.

Michael turned to the others. "Caleb, Vivian, have you?"

"Nope, and the rest of what Davin said," Caleb replied.

"Strange. Raven warned me at the party that the fallen would be coming out of their hiding. I would've at least expected that you would've encountered more of them. Not even one, after the one you told me about?"

Davin shook his head. Then he changed the subject. "It's present time."

"Presents?" Claudia ears perked up.

Davin paced to the corner and uncovered the wrap with one fast yank. "Ta dah. Boxes of diapers. And you're going to use tons of them."

"Awww...." Claudia gushed with teary eyes. Looking at the boxes of diapers reminded her of how soon their babies would arrive. "Thank you so much." Uncontrollable tears streamed down her face. "You don't know how much this means to me. Gamma, Ava, and Patty are no longer a part of my life. I wish they were here to celebrate this with me."

Water dampened her cheeks even more. She didn't mean to cry so much in front of her friends. It was supposed to be a happy occasion and not a crying session. "I'm so sorry. It's the change in hormones," she explained, wiping her tears.

Though Claudia was already in Michael's hold, Davin rushed to her side and pulled her away and into his embrace. "My turn. Share, Superman." Turning his attention to Claudia, he spoke. "We understand. It's okay to cry. We're your family too. We'll always be here for you."

Lifting her face up for air, she looked at her friends. "Thank you. All of you mean so much to me. I can't wait for our babies to be born, and to grow up with a wonderful auntie and uncles by their side. You are my family, and I'll always be here for you too."

Suddenly Davin jumped back and stared at Claudia's belly. "Whoa. What was that? Did...did that come from the babies?"

Claudia giggled, nodding her head. "Yes. He or she really likes you."

"Really? I can tell this one is a fighter." Davin closed the distance he'd created from jerking back. "Holy Moses."

In awe, with Claudia's permission the three of them sat and stared with one hand resting on Claudia's belly.

Caleb twitched when he felt a kick. "That was awesome."

"Awww," Vivian gushed. "I think I feel his or her bottom or head. I can't tell."

Davin bent down to the level of Claudia's stomach and spoke. "Hello there, babies. This is your Uncle Davin. What you are feeling are the hands of your auntie and uncles that can't wait to play with you."

Claudia looked up and caught Michael's smile. She noted how happy he looked. Michael could do nothing but beam as he watched his friends enjoy and witness the miracle of life.

After their friends left, Michael and Claudia continued to rest on the sofa.

"How are we feeling tonight?" Claudia asked, nuzzling on Michael's chest.

"I should be asking you that question," he said, rubbing Claudia's belly. "Finally, my turn."

"They're so calm when you do it."

"Really?" Michael gloated with pride. "That's because they know I'm their daddy. I hope I'll be a good one. I'm not sure how to be one. I don't remember anything about my parents. You learn from what you observe. And you already know how I feel about my father. I'd rather pretend he didn't exist at all. He didn't care enough to want me. Being one of the Twelve, he could've done something...I suppose."

"Michael, you don't have any memory of that past. You don't know for sure. Don't hate him. You will only hurt yourself."

Michael nodded solemnly, seeming to be somewhere else. Then his eyes flickered back to Claudia's. "How can I be a good father when I don't know what it means to be one?"

Out of his embrace, Claudia turned to him. "You follow your heart. How do you know how to be a good boyfriend or husband?"

"True. I'm fantastic, aren't I?" Michael smirked.

"More than fantastic, Mr. Michael." Claudia nodded. "Just as you are a great husband, you will be a wonderful father. I feel it. I know it."

With his hands, Michael gingerly caressed Claudia's cheek and looked at her with loving eyes. "You're going to be a wonderful mommy, Mrs. Michael."

Molding into his touch, Claudia closed her eyes and kissed Michael's hand that was still on her cheek. "I hope so," she mouthed under her breath.

"Would you like to get away from here just for the day?"

"I'll go where you go."

"Good answer." Without warning, Michael straddled her over him. His eyes were filled with yearning and wanting.

"Careful now. You don't want me to break my water on top of you."

"I can't help it. Even though you are big and heavy, you're still the same sexy."

"Hey...who you calling big and heavy?" Claudia giggled. "I'll take the sexy part though."

"Hmmm...I think you're feeling hot. I read that pregnant woman get hot easily. Perhaps you should unbutton a few buttons," Michael mumbled, tracing her collarbone with his finger.

"Are you trying to seduce me? And...and you read my book?" Claudia's eyes grew wide with surprise.

"I actually have one of my own. I didn't want anyone to see it so I hid it. I needed to understand what you were going through. And yes, I'm trying to seduce you, but I'm pretty sure it just worked."

"Oh, Michael. You had me at 'I read your book.'" Surprising Michael, Claudia leaned in for a passionate kiss.

Michael pulled back. "Whoa. Hold on. I don't want wham, bam, thank you sir. I want it slow, lingering, take your time sir. Let's start by eating some cake first."

"What?" Claudia giggled, arching her brows in confusion.

Michael reached behind Claudia and sat back in his place. With his fingertip, he dotted frosting all over Claudia's face.

"Michael?" Her tone was slow and flirty.

"Shhh...don't talk. Just enjoy." He licked the frosting from her forehead, her nose, her cheeks, and trailed his tongue down her neck, to her collarbone and lower. "You feeling hot, Mrs. Michael?"

"Yes, very hot." Claudia started to unbutton her blouse.

Placing his hands over hers, he stopped her from moving further. "Don't bother. I've already done it in super speed mode."

Claudia peered down, and sure enough, they were all unbuttoned. As Michael continued to lick frosting off her, Claudia yelped a little pleasurable cry.

"Would you like some cake too?" Michael asked, trailing kisses up her neck, then to her ears to nibble.

"Yeeessss." Claudia had no idea what he'd just asked. She had already floated off the ground, unable to process the overwhelming pleasure sensations that had made her lose all her self-control.

Slowly, Michael placed a small piece of cake in front of her. Opening her mouth, she took it. "Cake never tasted this delicious before."

"Let me try." Michael crushed his mouth into hers, kissing, tasting, and sucking. "Yes, you're right, it's never tasted this good before. How about I try eating Claudia cake from different parts of your body now?"

"Whatever you like, husband. I'm all yours."

CHAPTER 15

"YOU RANG, MOTHER DEAR?" AUSTIN appeared in front of the open door to Katherine's office. He tossed an apple up in the air and took a bite after it fell into the palm of his hand.

"That's not the forbidden apple, is it?"

"Well...it's not forbidden anymore," he chuckled. "It's quite delicious. You should try one," he mumbled with his mouth full.

"No thanks. Come sit. I have something to tell you."

Austin sauntered to the sofa. Crossing his legs, he leaned back comfortably while taking another bite. "Is this about how Holly and I can't be out in the field? Because I really think—"

"No, it's not." Katherine paced back and forth, seeming to think about something, and then stopped. Looking weary, she focused her eyes on his. "Austin, I don't know how to tell you this. Not that it really matters. I'd rather have you hear it from someone who cares about you than from someone else."

"Mom. Please, just say it."

Katherine inhaled and exhaled deeply. "Claudia is pregnant."

"Say what? Did you say she was...?"

Katherine nodded without a word, trying to read Austin's facial expression.

Austin looked away.

Giving Austin time to digest the news, Katherine finally spoke. "Like I said, I wanted you to hear it from me. Say something, Austin."

Austin's face was pale, showing no emotions. "She told you?"

"Yes."

"She didn't tell—" Austin looked out the window blankly.

"Only because she knew how you would feel."

"How I would feel? Great. Now she cares how I feel? I'm happy for them." His tone was flat and low. "I mean...very poor timing though, don't you think? Didn't you tell me once that when you were pregnant with me, your powers were limited? Claudia is half-human. What does this mean for her?"

"Her powers are diminishing. After she gives birth her powers will be restored, but I don't know how long that will take. It could be months, weeks, or days. I don't know. This is the first time."

Austin tossed the half-eaten apple into the small trash bin next to Katherine's desk. "I suddenly lost my appetite." He paused and uncrossed his legs. "Then...she is of no use to the angels. If something were to happen...well...it's not like we can't handle a war without her. It's a good thing Holly and I are back in the field. So is that is all you needed to tell me? I should be on my way. I'm meeting the venators." He arched his brows, giving a cunning grin as he stood.

"Yes, that is all. I feel much better now that you are aware of it. You've taken the news much better than I expected."

Austin's eyes widened with curiosity. "What did you think I would do or say?"

"I'm not sure. I underestimated your patience."

"I have changed... grown up a bit, I suppose. I'm now one of the Twelve, after all."

"Yes, you are. I'm very proud of you, son. I don't tell you that often, but I am. The human side of you makes you vulnerable, able to understand human emotions better than us, yet the angel side of you gives you the power you need to protect God's creation. You have the best of both beings."

"I don't know if I would agree with you. Sometimes I want to be one sided. I'm stuck in two worlds...not one or the other."

"I'm sorry you feel that way. It is the reason why I look the other way sometimes and let you have more freedom than I should allow."

"Hmmm...maybe you shouldn't."

"In the human world you would be considered an adult. In the angel world, you are one of our leaders. You make your own decisions. I've always trusted you. I trust you still."

"I know." Austin paced over to Katherine and gave her a warm hug. "I haven't hugged you in a while." After giving her a kiss on the cheek, he spread his wings. "This is the best part of being an angel. I have the whole world under my wings."

"Yes, you do," Katherine beamed a proud smile.

Austin gazed up to the ceiling as if searching for words, then back to Katherine. "I blame Gamma."

"What do you mean?"

"Gamma kept Claudia from me, didn't she?"

"It isn't what you think, Austin."

"It doesn't matter anymore. Destiny took a turn not in my favor. It's ironic how she tried to keep Claudia from our world, and yet she is the one who saved it. She was the only one who could. Imagine what it would be like if she wasn't around."

"Life is full of surprises. Just because Gamma kept Claudia away from you doesn't mean you two would have ended up together. And for the record, she didn't keep her away from you. Remember, she wanted you to be her guardian angel."

"Yeah, I know, but she found one by herself in her dreams." Austin shrugged his shoulders.

"Exactly. Life leads us to our destiny no matter how we try to make it in our favor. Sometimes it works and sometimes it doesn't. Like humans would say, just roll with it."

Austin chuckled. "I guess you're right."

"I'm always right," she winked. "Where are you off to?"

"They're moving on to the next town and I'm late."

"Be careful. No matter how old you are or the status you hold, you are my son first. I'm here if you need me."

"I know." He let out a soft sigh. "Thanks for letting me know. I'm sure Claudia would have told me if I'd had the chance to see her...I guess. It doesn't matter anyhow. Gotta go. See you at the next meeting." With a smile, he vanished.

CHAPTER 16

"WHERE ARE WE GOING?" CLAUDIA asked, standing on the bridge that connected the first level of the house to the other side. Feeling the extra weight on her body, she wanted to sit. Not only was it getting closer to her due date, she was getting uncomfortably bigger, and it was getting difficult to do her daily routine activities without Michael's help.

"It's a surprise." Michael uncurled his wings, expanding gloriously toward the sky. The light seeped between the top layers of them, looking like the sunrise peeking over the clouds.

Claudia paused and stood there watching, unable to peel her eyes off him. He stood tall and beautiful, and all she could think was the word "mine." Before she could blink again, Michael swept her off her feet, and they were gliding with the wind.

Soaking in the warmth of the sun and enjoying the beauty of the land beneath her, she welcomed the breeze in Michael's hold as they flew across the heavenly sky. Gently, he spiraled downward to land. When he opened his wings, Claudia's feet pushed down on the greens beneath her. Marveling at the mountains and the various colors of wild flowers around her, she felt a sudden gush of the cool fall breeze. Tucked in Michael's embrace, she was comfortable, but out of his hold, she shivered and noted that fall had kicked in.

"How do you know of this place?" Claudia's eyes roamed as far as she could see.

Michael went around the trunk of a large tree and came back with a blue blanket and a picnic basket Claudia had seen before. "I used to come here often way before I knew you." He threw the picnic blanket into the air, letting it settle on the grass. Then he lay out plates, cups, and utensils. "Have a seat."

"When? How?" Claudia asked, wondering when he'd had the time to set this up without her knowing.

"Early this morning. You know it doesn't take me long to travel by myself. And...I had help from my friends."

"Davin, Caleb, and Vivian?"

"Of course."

"Michael, you are simply the best," Claudia gushed. Sitting on the blanket, she patiently waited. "And so are our friends."

"Yup. They sure are. They will make great baby sitters one day soon. Hungry?"

"Starving is more like it," Claudia grumbled. "This is probably the once in a life time where I get to eat as much as I want and get as fat as I want."

"Well, my love, eat away." Michael placed a club sandwich and strawberries on her plate.

After they ate, Michael leaned his back against the trunk of the tree and Claudia lay with her head on his lap. Patches of puffy clouds adorned the backing of the blue above her. Watching the clouds slowly drift, she felt so small compared to the grandeur of the sky. Closing her eyes, she listened to the sounds of Mother Nature around her, the whistle of the wind brushing her face, and the leaves dancing in the wind.

"This is so wonderful. Just you and me. Sometimes I can't believe this is real," Claudia said with her eyes still closed.

"I know what you mean. I feel the same." Michael idly caressed her hair. "Can you hear my thoughts?"

"No," she sighed, opening her eyes. "I hope it comes back after I give birth. And as you already know, I've lost the ability to move in fast speed now. I definitely don't have my inner light. This is the most frightening part. I can't do anything...well...I can still use my bow if needed."

"I'm here, Claudia. I'll always be here to protect you and our children."

"I know, Michael."

"I've also brought you here for another reason."

Claudia blinked her eyes, her lips curved into a huge smile. "Michael, what do you have up your wings?"

"Up my wings?" he chuckled. "Now that is a new expression for the angels."

After helping Claudia sit upright, Michael reached into the picnic basket and took out a cupcake. Covered with pink frosting, 3D lilac butterflies decorated the top. "Happy Birthday." His face glowed with excitement.

"Happy Birthday? Is it October already?" Claudia's eyes glistened with joy. "Michael?"

"October twenty sixth, to be exact. This brings back the memories of when you were just a human, back to the days when we first fell in love. Well actually, I loved you first. And though angels don't celebrate birthdays—one reason being that we don't know our dates of birth—I do know yours, and because of that, we should celebrate it."

Claudia was speechless as she tried to blink her tears back, but it wasn't working. She recalled the days when Gamma, her mom, Patty, and her school friends would make her birthday special. Gamma was gone and she had stopped appearing in her dreams.

Not that she slept that often, except recently because of changes in her body due to her pregnancy. And her mom, Patty, and her school friends had no memories of her. It was as if she never existed in their lives...ever.

Those thoughts brought sad, hurtful tears, but at the same time, here she was with an angel of her dreams. The angel she never imagined she would find love with. This angel in front of her was something of a miracle, and being who she was, she felt blessed to be near him, with him, and to be loved by him.

"Michael," she managed to mumble his name as a tear escaped from the corner of her eye.

Michael caught the drop before it fell to the ground and ran his thumb to wipe away the remaining ones. "I'll always catch your tears. Don't cry, my love. It's a happy occasion."

Claudia peered up to his sparkling, irresistible eyes that she had become lost in so many times. "These are happy tears, Michael. You're so good to me. It doesn't seem fair that we celebrate mine and never yours."

"Don't you know by now my life revolves around you? You are the center of my life, my world, my existence. You loving me back and us being together is everything I could wish for. And now, what a blessing it is to have two miracles coming soon. I don't know how I'll ever thank you for everything you've given me."

Michael's sweet words touched Claudia deeply. He was thanking her for everything they shared when she should be the one thanking him, but Michael was that way. He never lacked for words or appreciation, and he knew how to show those feelings. She knew how much he loved her, but hearing his loving words reached deeply within her and consumed her soul with warmth and happiness.

"Michael, as much as you thank me, I should be the one thanking you for always being there for me from the start. You've shown your love multiple times, and even put my life over yours.

So thank you for everything you do for me, even remembering my birthday and making me feel special."

"That you are, my love. No more thanking each other. Let's enjoy this happy celebration." With a snap of his fingers, Michael lit a white candle that was already on the cupcake. After he sang "Happy Birthday," Claudia made a wish and blew out the candle. Giving one bite to Claudia first, he took one too.

"Delicious," Claudia said, taking another bite.

"Vivian helped me order this cupcake." Michael winked. "I don't know much about decorating. I only know how to eat them off your body."

Claudia felt heat rise to her cheeks, recalling the night when he had. "I have to say, you do know how to eat your cake very well."

"I can eat Claudia cake or cupcake anytime," he said playfully, reaching inside his jeans pocket and pulling out a necklace. Dangling in front of her was a sterling silver chain that held the word "eternity" in place. "I had this made for you. Vivian hunted down a jewelry maker, and she helped me with the design too. She wanted to tell Davin and Caleb, but I knew you would feel uncomfortable celebrating with everyone since none of us celebrate our birthdays, so I told her it would be just between the two of us. She wasn't happy about it, but she understood. And I didn't know what to get you...and...I wanted to get you something different. Eternity is how long I will love you."

"Oh, Michael." There were no words to describe how Claudia felt, and she knew that if she tried, she wouldn't be able to. She was overwhelmed and her hormones were already affecting her. All she could do was extend her arms over Michael's shoulders and pull him in to her. "I love you. Thank you so much."

After she released him, Michael took off her butterfly necklace and placed it in his jeans pocket for safekeeping. Then he hooked the new necklace around her neck. "Beautiful."

"It sure is," Claudia smiled, brushing her hand over the calligraphy inscription.

"I was taking about my wife, not the necklace," he stated.

Claudia blushed again. It didn't matter how many times Michael told her she was beautiful, it was as if he had told her for the very first time. Everything was always new and heartfelt when with him.

"Would you like to head back home?"

"No. Could we lay here for a bit? I'm so tired and my back aches. I just want to rest a bit."

"Sure, whatever you want."

AFTER CLAUDIA LAY ON THE blanket, Michael bunched the corner of the blanket to support her neck. Standing up to stretch, he cautiously scanned the perimeter. He could've sworn he'd seen a flash of something just up ahead. Did he make a mistake bringing Claudia here? Could the fallen possible still linger about this place, even knowing Aden was dead?

With lightning bolt speed he dashed from tree to tree, always keeping one eye on Claudia and making sure not to go too far from her. If there was a fallen lurking about, he wanted to lure him or her away.

Unexpectedly, Claudia's butterfly necklace that was tucked inside his jean pocket started to vibrate. Now he knew for sure that a fallen was nearby. When he heard the shuffling sound of the leaves, he jolted sideways. Seeing the same shadow, he went around to the opposite side of the same tree in hopes of surprising the visitor.

"Who are you and what do you want?" Michael's tone was harsh and demanding, holding his sword in front of him.

"It's me," a female voice said. Her long black cape swayed with the breeze when she stepped out of the shadows from behind a grand tree. When she lowered the hood of her cape, her red luscious hair unraveled and cascaded down her shoulders.

"Raven?" Michael dropped his sword by his side.

"From the sound of your tone, you're not here to give yourself up. I guess your friend didn't tell you."

"What are you talking about?" Michael arched his brows. His eyes narrowed at her from her nonsense talk.

"No use in explaining. You have no idea."

Confused with her rambling, he raised his tone. "Have you been spying on me?"

"I actually live near these mountains with some friends."

"You've made this place your home even after Aden's death? I didn't think anyone would stick around. I mean...after all, this was our favorite place to regroup. I've been surveying this area for a while for fallen and I've seen none." Michael had been scouting any chance he had without Claudia knowing. He didn't want to worry her, so he would sneak off when she took a nap.

"No one really comes around here. It's like it's almost forbidden. If you want to search for fallen, you've come to the wrong place. You need to be searching where your friends have been. Like I told you at the party, some fallen want to be left alone and others are regrouping with Dantanian and Berneal."

"Are you sure? How do you know this?"

"He asked me to join him."

"And have you?" Michael gripped his sword tighter.

Raven eye's dropped to his sword. "No, but you know what will happen. You're damned if you do and you're damned if you don't. I suggest you find him and get rid of him before he starts a war."

Michael laughed out loud. "His army can't defeat the alkins and the venators."

"He thinks he can if he has you by his side."

"It will never happen. I'm an alkin and I always will be one. Next time you see him, give him my message. Tell him if he tries anything, I will personally see to it he joins Aden forever."

With yearning eyes, she swayed gracefully toward him. Reaching out her hands, Michael knew she wanted to touch him, but when he backed away, she dropped them.

"Is it her?" Raven gestured with her eyes, looking toward the direction where Claudia was sleeping.

Michael's eyes widened, full of fear and anger. "Don't you dare threaten me. Leave her out of this."

Raven retreated a step with her hands up. "Fair enough. Don't ever say I didn't warn you. There will be war heading your way if you don't stop him now."

"If he needs me to win a war, then he has already lost. I've spent too much time here. I suggest you hide or go far away until things die down if you are in that much fear of him."

"Easier said than done."

"Your choice, but if it comes down to it, where will you stand?"

"I pick the winning side. See you around, Michael." With that she flapped her wings and soared away.

CHAPTER 17

THE POLLUTED SMOKY AIR FINALLY lifted, allowing the sun to shine upon the land. It was evident how badly the town had been hit. Though it was a town, it was bigger than the others they'd previously scouted.

"You know, I'm kind of tired of seeing the same thing over and over," Vivian said, walking down the paved road.

"Yeah, I kind of agree with you there, Vivian. There are no survivors," Caleb muttered, looking down at his feet, seeming to be very careful with his steps.

"I know what you mean. They've either escaped or the demons got to them," Holly explained, directing the venators with her hand.

Getting ready to enter a broken down hotel, they cautiously moved without a sound. Their bows were ready as they stood to the left and right of Holly. Holly turned to Davin. "Are you sure you want to go in there?"

"I saw something through the broken wall. I think we should check out this building. You and I can even check out a room." He raised his brows.

"Gross. You did not just say that to me," Holly grimaced.

"Nope." He lit an innocent grin. "I gotta stop hanging out with Michael and Claudia," he mumbled to himself, shaking his head. A part of him had wanted to know what she'd say, because he always got a kick out of how she'd respond to an awkward question. Holly may have seemed tough on the outside, but he knew she'd put up a wall to protect her shyness and her soft heart. Regardless, Davin was always trying to make others laugh. There was joy in laughter, and he loved to see it radiate out of peoples' hearts. He extended his hand, gesturing for Holly to walk in first.

"After you," Holly said.

"Nah, uh, no way. I've had bad luck with the doors. I have a better idea." Davin peered up. "Jump." So he did.

A huge chunk of the third story structure was demolished, as if a giant cannon ball had gone through it. As Davin waited for his friends, he noted he was standing on a wooden plank. Though it was daytime, it was dim inside. With his sword lit, he could see the damage underneath him. The debris was burnt and unidentifiable.

Above him, he could see many levels of floors that had been plunged through by some force of nature. The planks that held the foundation together were visible on each floor, unevenly spread out. From below, it looked like a maze.

Gingerly, he tiptoed forward on the long plank to the other side. If he were human, this would've been an impossible task, especially since the plank was narrow and thin. If he fell, he knew he could stop his fall, so not an ounce of fear pricked him. It was easily done.

"Did you see anything odd?" Davin whispered, now standing on torn carpet, what was left of it. Pacing the floor, which got narrower by the steps, his back was now against the wall.

"Nope...just you," Caleb snorted, following Davin's steps.

"Watch it. You might have an accident, my dear friend," Davin sneered playfully.

"Not if you have one first, my not so dear friend." Caleb chuckled lightly.

Davin gave him the evil, yet sort of friendly eye. "Don't talk like humans do. Just keep your eyes open."

"You two stop talking. We're at a dead-end. Davin can only concentrate on one thing at a time," Vivian said, placing her hands on her hips. "So boss, what do we do now?"

Ignoring Vivian's question, Davin leaped to the plank in front. He turned to his friends, gesturing for them to follow him. Caleb jumped and almost lost his balance as he teeter tottered back and forth. Peering sideways, noting Caleb swinging, Davin gripped his shirt to steady him.

"Thanks," Caleb said.

Before Davin could reply, he saw a flash of something cross his vision. "Did you see that shadow?" Davin's eyes followed the movements from left to right, then up.

"Where?" Caleb asked, looking every way possible.

"There." Holly's eyes followed Davin's line of gaze. The shadow grew larger, looking as if the being was growing. Unexpectedly, the one giant shadow multiplied right before their eyes and split into countless ones, who then disappeared as fast as they had come.

"There!" Davin pointed to the ceiling. Soaring from plank to plank, he reached higher and higher.

"Davin, wait!" Holly shouted, trying to catch up to his speed. "It could be a trap."

Sure enough, as the team sped up the planks behind Davin, they halted when something shot downward. Without warning, a broken bed frame, half of a sofa, a leg from a desk, and pieces of unidentified objects plummeted, breaking the planks from different directions. Without a place to plant their feet, they expanded their wings to steady themselves.

As the team continued to fly upward, they flew from side to side, dodging the objects that were being thrown toward them. It was pandemonium as the team scattered. Suddenly, soaring down toward them was a massive blanket of something dark, something evil. The shadow stretched to its full capacity and broke apart individually.

"Fallen!" Davin shouted, gripping his sword. Too focused on the one coming toward him, he failed to see the one to his side that rammed into him. Davin's forefront slammed against something solid. His left cheek practically imprinted on the wall. Dazed, he quickly turned and ducked a swipe. Using the wall to his advantage, he pushed off with his hands and used the momentum from the force to kick the fallen's face to the sky.

From Davin's view, he could clearly see they were outnumbered. Taken by surprise that the fallen surrounded him, he took a second to compose himself before he jumped back into the action as air rushed frantically in and out of him. All he could see were the fast movements of black and white and silvery lights that shot out from the venators' bows. The ear splitting sound of metal upon metal and the flapping from the wings snapped him back to what he needed to do at that moment...to duck from the sword that was inches away from his heart.

"Davin! Caleb!" Vivian yelled, swinging her sword from left to right, fighting two fallen at once. "This is totally not fair." She closed her wings and dropped, confusing the fallen that were beside her. When she plunged downward, her foot contacted a fallen's head and caused him to be pushed out of the way. Somehow, Vivian ended up floating in front of Holly.

"Thanks," Holly said, confused. "Let's get out of here. Where's Davin?"

Just when she opened her mouth, someone soared toward them. "Hello ladies," Davin winked, then became serious. "Let's make a circle."

Holly understood. They had talked about this tactic before, but they never had the need to use it. She pursed her lips, placed her index finger and thumb in her mouth, and blew as loud as she could. The vision of white wings charged toward her like a dart with white feathers, leaving the black in midair without any opponents.

The venators gathered to make a complete circle, glowing like a huge halo with their swords and bows ready in their hands. Pointing their bows upward, their silver lights flashed like lightning, creating an incredible light show. Some bolts hit the fallen dead on, but the ones that escaped retaliated and soared hastily downward to the venators.

"Hold!" Davin commanded. "Wait...wait...wait for my signal. Here they come. Hold. Steady...and...now!"

With a flash from their wings and holding hands, they spun to the right. Faster. Faster. Faster they spun, creating a massive tunnel of wind. Just before the fallen could reach them, they were blasted by the speed of the air. The tornado-like wind pushed them back to the ceiling with incredible speed.

Unable to control the direction, some fallen flew into a broken plank, only to have it puncture their body, killing them. The ones that survived aimlessly blasted skyward like cannon balls, breaking more of the structure of the building.

The rubble from the impact dropped like heavy rain. "Break away," Davin yelled. With a speedy whoosh, they broke the circle and backed away as far as they could, pressing their backs against the walls. The wreckage collided with the debris that was already piled on the first floor, elevating the remains and uplifting massive smoky dust that engulfed them. When it had settled, Davin took a moment to release the panic and fright that he had pushed aside when the adrenaline and the will to survive took over.

"Everyone okay?" Davin's tone was loud as he searched for Caleb and Vivian. When he spotted them, he heaved a sigh of relief.

One by one, he called out their names and made sure everyone was accounted for. "Let's go home."

THE DECISION WASN'T A DIFFICULT one. After their private marriage ceremony, Claudia had moved to Michael's floor and Claudia's floor became the nursery. Michael spent hours making two cribs from the surrounding trees. How she loved watching Michael doing carpentry. He was so natural and knowledgeable. If he was a human, living a normal life, she could see him making things with his hands. Perhaps he would've been a carpenter, designer, painter, or even a jewelry maker.

"Claudia, should I move this bed here or there?" Michael pointed.

"How about placing them against the wall, adjacent to each other?" Claudia directed. "The dresser, the rug, and the diaper tables are perfect where they are. I like where the pile of diaper boxes is located in the corner. Their clothes are already folded in the dresser. I think we're all set."

Holding hands, they sauntered to the back of the room together to get a full view. Exhaling a deep breath of relief for getting the room ready on time, Claudia also exhaled from the realization their lives would never be the same.

"We did great, don't you think?" Michael asked, placing his arms around Claudia's waist.

"I believe it was all you, husband. You're quite good with your hands. Is this how you get all your muscles?" Claudia giggled, running her hands up the curves of his arms and down his chest.

Michael twitched his brows playfully. "Maybe. Would you like for me to show you?"

"I would want you to, but...." Claudia paused. She suddenly felt something wet trickling down her thighs as if she was urinating without even knowing that she was. Strange. She had no urge or sensation. Then it suddenly dawned on her. "I think my water broke."

"You don't want me to...huh?"

"Michael, my water broke." Though her tone was calm, she started to panic. Her breath got caught in her throat.

"Okay...I'll fix it...but where is it broken?" Michael looked confused, looking around the room.

Claudia pointed. "Michael, look down."

Water pooled around them.

"Um...Claudia, did you urinate in your pants or...is that...it can't be. I think your water broke." He sounded nervous.

"Yes...I tried to tell you that. You need to get me to Agnes."

"Sorry, hun. I didn't understand." Michael started pacing around the room, talking to himself as if he was mumbling a list of things.

Claudia waddled to him, feeling uncomfortable from the wetness, not to mention the difficulty she was having walking across the room. "Michael." She gripped his arms, making him stop. "What are you doing?"

"I'm reading the book in my mind...what to do when water breaks. Photographic memory."

"You don't need to think right now. Just get me to Agnes... okay?" She spoke with a stern tone. "Then you need to let Katherine know. Also, don't forget to get ahold of Davin, Vivian, and Caleb. We'll never hear the end of it if we don't let them know."

With a nod, he finally understood what he needed to do. With a deep ginormous intake of breath, Michael unfurled his wings and covered Claudia completely. "This is it. It's happening."

CHAPTER 18

A S CLAUDIA LAY ON AGNES'S bed, she was filled with anxiety, excitement, and many mixed emotions. Her stomach muscles tightened then released as the contractions increased by the minute. Though she had read about this, feeling it was a whole different story. Oh...the pain...and more pain...but a pain with a purpose, she kept repeating to herself to help her endure it.

"I'm right here, Claudia." Agnes reached for her hand and placed the other over Claudia's belly. "Don't worry. Everything will be alright. They are ready to meet their mommy. Do you feel any pain?"

"Yes." Claudia jumped at the chance to let her know. "It feels like I'm having menstrual cramps, but worse...a lot worse."

"The pain you're feeling right now is nothing compared to what human moms feel during labor," Katherine said as she walked in. "This is nothing, my dear; however, Agnes can tame the pain." Katherine smiled at Agnes and extended her arms for a hug and a kiss on her cheek. "It's good to see you."

"Same here, my friend." Agnes released the hug and turned to Claudia. "I can help so you won't feel any pain." She reached for her.

"No!" Claudia said, louder than she had anticipated as she grabbed Agnes's wrist and let go. "I mean...I want to feel what it's like to be in labor. I want to feel what human moms feel."

"Very well, Claudia. Just let me know if you need my help."

With a quick smile and a nod, Claudia bent her legs and held onto her belly. The pain had increased, worse than it was a second ago. She could feel the pressure and the intensity of the urge to push. Recalling what she'd read in the book, she inhaled and exhaled with deep breaths, but it was difficult when all she felt was the throbbing that travelled from the tips of her toes, up her legs and past her stomach. She thought her body was going to break in two.

"Claudia, you're dilated. This is a good sign," Agnes said with elation.

Under normal circumstances Claudia would've felt uncomfortable, but at this point, she didn't care if she was naked in front of them. In fact, she only heard parts of Agnes's words. She was overwhelmed with what was happening and the pain...oh, the pain was taking over her mind. Losing control of her breathing, losing control of her thoughts, she was just thinking about asking Agnes for help when Michael walked in.

"Katherine, Agnes," Michael quickly greeted them first, then turned to Claudia. "Sorry, my love. Davin, Vivian, and Caleb were a bit hard to find, but they're waiting outside."

Katherine moved over for Michael. He held Claudia's right hand to his chest, looking lovingly into her eyes with a look of concern. "Why is she in so much pain?"

"Claudia wants to go through the human emotions," Katherine explained. "She only needs to say one word and we can make this experience a lot easier for her. Keep in mind Claudia...even the human moms get epidural shots to ease their pain."

"Claudia?" Michael looked at her, waiting for an answer, pleading with his eyes to ask Agnes for help.

Claudia didn't reply. The pain had taken over again. Pulling her hand away from Michael, she shifted sideways. Taking shorter breaths, she cradled her belly with a look of extreme discomfort.

"Claudia, look at me," Michael demanded.

"No. I can do this," Claudia managed to let the words escape her mouth. Her nails dug deeply into the mattress and tightly wrung the sheet beneath her.

Michael took her hand again. "Please. I don't like to see you like this, especially when it can be avoided."

"Please...I want this." Claudia's tone said it all. It was final.

Michael sighed heavily, surrendering. "Okay...I'm here with you every step of the way." He kissed the back of her hand and wiped the small bubbles of sweat on her forehead.

"You can push now," Agnes said excitedly.

Squeezing tightly onto Michael's hand, she propped to an angle and pushed. "Aaaaaagh," she groaned. A few seconds later, she pushed again, then again. Burning sensations ran up her thighs to her chest. Though she felt a partial release, her body felt as if it was still on fire. With the feeling of her hips expanding, she could feel her baby exiting her womb, but not all the way.

Suddenly, panic took over; she didn't know if she could do this. Her blood was pounding in her ears and her heart rate had escalated so fast she could hardly breathe. Should she have taken Agnes's offer?

"Look at me, Claudia," Michael said sternly, seemingly sensing Claudia's worries. "Breathe, Claudia. I'm right here. You can do this. Breathe with me."

Hearing the voice that pulled her out of her trance many times before, the voice that easily got her attention, as if his voice was the epidural to ease her pain, she shifted her eyes to his. Using Michael's beautiful, radiant eyes as her focal point, she felt nothing but peace and comfort. Staring at them always helped her escape into a place where only they existed. And that was all she needed as she pushed. Today was the day their world would change forever... not just their lives, but everyone else they loved too.

"Almost there, Claudia. I can see a head," Katherine beamed an exhilarated smile. Her hand was positioned, ready for the babies.

"One more big push," Michael said, smiling as excitement rose in his tone.

The strong urge to push took over her body and she let it guide her. With one strong forceful effort, giving all she could give, she tightened her stomach muscles, inhaled a deep breath, and... pushed.

"It's a boy," Katherine cried, wrapping him inside a blue blanket and passing him to Agnes. "Claudia, you have one more. You're doing great."

"Michael," Claudia muttered, looking drained. Sticky wetness clung all over her body. It felt like she had just put on her clothing without drying herself after the shower. Sweat trickled from the sides of her temples and her body trembled from exhaustion, but she didn't care. This was a special moment she would always remember...every detail of what she went through in bringing her newborns into the world. With one last push, still holding onto Michael's eyes, she collapsed.

"It's a girl," Katherine gloated, wrapping her in a pink blanket. "They're so beautiful."

Katherine and Agnes carefully placed the wrapped babies into Michael's arms. Looking at them, his eyes pooled with joyful tears. "We have a son and a daughter," he said to Claudia. "Welcome to our world, little ones. Mommy and Daddy love you both very much."

Tears streamed down Claudia's cheeks as she looked at her babies for the very first time. Though she was extremely fatigued, the pure joy of seeing her newborns was difficult to put into words. She had imagined what they would look like, but she'd never imagined this. From their heads full of hair, to their tiny curled fingers, to their wrinkled feet, in her eyes, they were perfect in every way.

At that moment she fell in love with the two beautiful beings, and the feeling took her breath away. She needed them just as much as they needed her. Somehow she felt different. She wasn't the same Claudia anymore. She was not just a wife, she was a mother now with a big responsibility, whether she was ready for it or not. But as long as Michael was by her side, she knew anything was possible. How they'd come this far together was implausible...a miracle.

With soft "awwws," Davin, Vivian, and Caleb entered. "Oh my goodness, they are beautiful!" Vivian gushed, swiping the one with the blue blanket away from Michael while Davin held the baby with the pink blanket.

"She's so small," Davin gloated. "Look at her tiny nose and those tiny lips. She looks like a doll."

"Have you decided on their names, or shall we call them baby blue and baby pink?" Agnes giggled.

"Claudia and I had many discussions regarding names. We chose their names for a specific reason. Our son's name is Zachary. He's named after my father, Zachariah." Michael turned to Katherine and mouthed, "Thank you." Then he turned to the others. "We thought Zachary was a more up to date name. Our daughter's name is Lucia. She is name after Claudia's grandmother, Lucy," Michael explained, holding Claudia's hand.

"Well, as much as I hoped Zachary would be called Davin, I understand the reason behind it. It just means you'll have to have more children and name the next son after me." Davin flashed a goofy grin.

As the laughter rang in the air, Claudia cleared her throat. "Does the mother get to hold her babies?"

Immediately, Vivian and Davin placed them in her arms. They all stood and watched the interaction between them. Claudia could say nothing. Her eyes said the words she wanted to express. She kissed them one by one on their foreheads and nuzzled them carefully into her cheeks. "I love how they smell...so sweet and divine."

"Okay." Caleb leaned in. "I've been waiting patiently. Can I hold them now?"

"Sure, Caleb. You can hold them both." Claudia released them to him. "But they will need to eat real soon."

Caleb looked anxious, positioning them in his arms. "I need to hold them as long as I can. Phillip and Margaret are coming." Then Davin, Vivian, Agnes, and Katherine quickly surrounded him.

Michael took this moment and kissed Claudia on her lips. "How are you feeling?"

"I'm tired, but never happier."

"I didn't like you in pain like that, but you did great."

"Never underestimate a woman in labor," Claudia giggled. "The pain can make you do just about anything."

"I could see that. I would never want to be in a woman's shoes giving birth. If I were human, you would have definitely pulled my hand off from squeezing so tightly. I could only imagine the pain that I don't ever want to feel. You are very brave, my love."

"I'm glad it was only half the pain I would've really felt. I'm glad I did. I want to remember every moment, the pain and all."

Michael leaned over and swept the damp hair away from her face, then kissed her lips softly again. With each word carefully spoken, with each ginger stroke to her cheek, he said, "I...love...you. I...love...us."

CHAPTER 19

A WEEK LATER, ZACHARY AND Lucia were taken to their nursery. Davin, Vivian, and Caleb couldn't get enough of them. They spent most of their time there when they were not on missions.

Claudia recovered quickly and was able to breast feed much better now than she could days ago. Though she preferred breast-feeding directly from her breast, she would sometimes pump just so Michael could feed them from a bottle.

Their days were the same...feeding, napping, and diapering the twins...but they made sure to have quality time for just the two of them when they could.

Michael couldn't get enough of holding them. When Claudia took her mini naps, he would stare at his little ones and sing to them while they slept in his embrace.

The sun has set and so must you.
Close your eyes and welcome the moon.
Don't you fright and don't you frown
For when you wake I'll be around.

Don't be scared my precious ones
For angels keep you safe and sound.
So fly away to your wonderland.
Dream all that your hearts can.
In your dreams you can be
Whatever you want to be.
In your dreams you can make
All your wishes come true.
So close your eyes my little ones
For today's work is done.
Rest your little sleepy heads
For tomorrow is a brand new day.

"THEY'RE FINALLY DOWN FOR A nap." Michael plopped next to Claudia in bed, who had just woken up from a mini nap.

Claudia had awakened to Michael's beautiful voice and song, and her heart had melted. Planting a kiss on Michael's cheek, she peered up to him. "You're a wonderful father and a fantastic husband." Then she placed her head on his chest, hearing his heart pump with slow, steady, blissful beats.

"I couldn't be happier." Michael brushed her cheeks with his knuckles.

"Me too," Claudia said, releasing a happy sigh. With Michael and her babies by her side, healthy and safe, she couldn't ask for anything more. She was beyond grateful.

With her arms and legs entangled around him, she enjoyed the peace and quiet. There were no words to exchange. She felt it in her mind, heart, and soul. They'd come so far and had been through so much together that to be there right where they were was blessing enough.

"How are you feeling?" Michael turned to his side, pulling her into his chest.

"I'm feeling great. You've asked me that question every day." Her hand laced through his hair. "I'm really fine. Don't worry so much."

"Okay, but I'll ask you that question a thousand times more if I must. Are you feeling any different?"

"Are you trying to ask me if my power has come back? Is there something you need to tell me?"

"No. I'm just wondering because you haven't heard what I've been trying to say in your mind."

Claudia hadn't thought about her powers until now. She knew they would eventually come back, but hearing the tone from Michael's question had her mind swimming with worried thoughts. "I guess it will take some time," she mumbled, feeling disappointed.

"Claudia, I didn't ask to make you feel bad. I just wanted to know because I've been trying to tell you something, but I guess it's not working."

She didn't know if her hormones were doing crazy things to her emotions or she was just simply upset Michael had brought it up. She didn't want to cause a fight or bring up something she was only assuming. After all, she really couldn't read Michael's thoughts. Knowing he always had only good intentions, she let it go. "What did you say?"

"That...I love you."

What could she say after that? The heat that crawled to the surface was quickly extinguished. Draping her arms around Michael's neck, she pulled him in and kissed him all over his face.

"Gross. Good to see things haven't changed...or maybe not." Davin walked in, holding Lucia upright, showing the diaper he'd just put on her. "Look what I did," he said proudly. "Zachary is sleeping in Vivian's arms and Caleb is in the nursery."

Claudia giggled softly, trying to contain the laughter that was growing inside her. Michael closed one eye and narrowed the other at the diaper. "You did a great job, Davin, but...it's kind of... backward."

Davin turned Lucia toward him and looked behind her. "Ha ha," Davin laughed nervously. "I'll be right back." He sped toward the nursery.

"It's a good thing we have so much help," Claudia giggled.

Michael shook his head with a big grin on his face. "We sure do. They're wonderful, even Davin."

"I heard that," Davin said out loud. "Be careful, Michael. I may accidently put a diaper on you. Maybe on your face, with poop and all."

"I heard that," Michael said, appearing at the nursery, making Davin jerk back from his sudden appearance. Claudia stood right beside Michael, greeting them with a smile.

Davin held Lucia in front of him. "Whoa...watch it Superman. I'm holding a deadly weapon. It will spit and poop on you if you don't back off."

"Are you using my child as your shield?" Michael stepped forward with an authoritative tone.

Davin shrugged his shoulders, pulling Lucia into his hold. "I would never." He pouted and backed away.

"I'm just joking, Davin. Thanks for being here," Michael said quickly after hearing Davin's upset tone.

"Got ya. I'm joking too." Davin gave a mischievous grin. Then turned his attention to Lucia. "You're beautiful. You look just like your mommy...and...not your daddy."

"Awww...thanks Davin." Claudia looped her arms around him, peered into Lucia's eyes, then to Zachary's, who was in Vivian's arms.

"I can stare at them all day and night. And they smell so sweet," Vivian gushed, inhaling their scent. "You gave us the best presents.

I love being an auntie. I never knew it could be like this. Knowing and holding them in your arms is a whole different feeling. But, unfortunately we can't stay too long today. We're heading to another town, to a city this time, requested by us."

"Be careful," Michael said, setting his eyes on his friends. "I'm sure everything will be fine. I don't want to worry you, but the fallen are out there, as you already know. Most likely they are observing, trying to figure out their tactics. If you ever run into fallen by the names of Dantanian or Berneal, run. Don't even bother to fight back. They are ruthless, dangerous, and will show no mercy. Do you understand?"

"Okay," Caleb said. "Your words were scary enough. We'll run...or fly...or whatever."

"I'm serious," Michael warned again.

"Got it," Vivian said, cuddling Zachary, kissing him on his cheeks. "I can't get enough of him. He smells like Heaven."

"Does Heaven have a scent?" Davin smirked, placing Lucia back into her crib.

Vivian threw an evil eye at him. "You know what I meant."

"I did. Just messing with ya." Then he turned to Michael. "I have to say, you did a fantastic job with this place."

Michael looked proud. "For my family, I'll do anything."

"Awww...thanks, Michael. I could use a few things." Davin patted Michael on the back.

Michael narrowed his eyes at him, letting him know he was irritated with that smack.

"Or not...." Davin sheepishly looked away.

Claudia stood there listening, watching the humor between them. How quickly time flew by. It seemed like just yesterday when she'd first met them. Now, she knew them so well, as if they were her own brothers and sisters. They were her family now, but never did a day go by when she didn't think of her human family and friends. She made a mental note to visit them soon, even though they wouldn't recognize her. It didn't matter. She just needed to see them to make sure they were safe and happy.

CHAPTER 20

"ARE YOU SURE THIS IS the right location?" Davin peered up at the sign that flashed "Salsa" while passing through the entrance. His eyes twinkled with excitement, drinking in the atmosphere. "It's a restaurant and there are real humans in here." He paused. His nose twitched, tickled with the smell of chips and salsa. Then his lips curled up into a blissful grin.

It was indeed crowded and all the tables were taken from what Davin could see. Red linen covered the tops of the round tables, but the booths off to the side had none. Davin's eyes drifted to the lady standing in front behind a podium.

"How many in your party, sir?" the hostess asked politely.

Ignoring the lady who was waiting for his response, he turned to Vivian and whispered. "Are you sure this is the place? It doesn't look like a place where fallen or demons would hang out."

"Holly said come to this location. 848 Blooms Street. It's the right address."

Caleb went out the door and came back in. "Yup, it's the right address."

"Would you like to be seated?" the lady asked, looking confused.

"What do we say?" Vivian whispered, looking panicked.

Never having been at a restaurant like this before, the setting was unfamiliar to them and Davin didn't know what to do. Sure, they'd been to bars and formal occasions where there was human contact, but not a place like this. Then it suddenly hit him.

With an "I got this" smug grin, Davin stepped forward. "Sure. We are looking for our friends. Their names are Holly and Austin, and I don't know if Michelle and Gracie will be here."

"Oh, yes. They are already here seated at their table." She retreated several steps and pointed toward the back. "If you follow the restroom sign toward the back, you'll see them."

"Cool, thanks." Davin shrugged his shoulders and looped his arms around his buddies. "Well...shall we stand here all night and look like dorks or shall we find our friends?"

"Dorks?" Vivian questioned.

"If you don't know what a dork is, then you are one. Come on. And don't take out your swords. People will call the cops," he whispered in Vivian's ears, sensing her tension and uneasiness. "Just act natural. Keep calm and follow Davin."

With a soft shove on their backs, Davin led the way. Weaving through the tables, he grinned widely and enjoyed the interaction with humans as if he was one. "They're so nice and friendly." He waved to the people sitting at their tables to the left and right of him, as if he was walking down a parade route and he was the show. Tugging Vivian and Caleb—who were as stiff as boards, seemingly wondering if the humans knew who they were—across the room, he continued to follow the bathroom sign.

Davin couldn't have been happier when he saw Holly, Michelle, Gracie, and Austin waving, already sitting at a table toward the back. He was getting tired of tugging the two dorks who had worn fake nervous smiles the whole time, but finally loosened up when they saw familiar faces. After the greeting, they took their seats and

Vivian jumped in with her questions. "Why are we here? I thought we were supposed to look for fallen and demons?"

Austin cleared his throat. "By your requests, I thought you guys might want to have a little fun. I've been hearing complaints about how you see the same thing over and over on your missions," Austin explained, taking a sip of his drink. "So, I thought you could use a friendly atmosphere to take the drag out of your mind. Unless you prefer to go back."

There was no need to explain further. Davin interrupted, kicking Vivian who was sitting next to him. "We were just surprised to see such a fun place. We were expecting...you know, the usual...debris, junk, and more debris and junk," Davin said lightly.

"I thought this was a good idea," Holly added, looking like she was bored already. "You know...so that we can get to know each other better." She grimaced at the thought. "We can sit and...umm ...what's that word? Oh yeah...talk."

"We're only together when we're killing something, but I'd like to get to know you better too. Don't you think it was a great idea?" Michelle twisted her lips into a flirty smile at Davin, waiting for a response.

"Oh...yeah...I guess...I mean...sure." That was all Vivian could say, watching Davin doing googly eyes back to Michelle.

Austin purposely let out a cough again. "Look...I know things have been weird or awkward...or whatever word you want to use...you know...us being venators and you guys being alkins, and Michael, Claudia and I...umm...anyway, we need to have a fresh start, especially since we'll be seeing each other more...often."

"We thought being at a restaurant...." Gracie's tone lowered. "With humans, almost surrounded by normalcy, would be good for us...you know, so we won't kill each other."

"Gracie," Holly's pitch went up a notch.

Gracie shot an apologetic look. "I mean...I'm not thinking of killing any of you. Maybe I should keep my mouth shut."

Austin took a sip of his drink again. "Anyway. We can try to talk about normal stuff, and not think so much about what we do best...killing fallen and demons, and irritating the heck out of each other."

Holly slapped Austin's arm.

"What?" He glared. "I'm just saying."

"From here on, we only use nice words," Holly demanded, catching everyone's eyes in agreement.

Davin, Vivian, and Caleb looked at each other, wondering what the heck this was about, but they played along. Before things got awkward, the waitress came with bowls of chips, salsa, and guacamole and placed them on the table. Without a second to lose, Davin plastered a lustful grin on his face. "My favorite. What is this place?"

"It's a restaurant called Salsa. We knew you like chips and salsa so we picked this place," Holly informed him, and pushed the bowls Davin's way. "Eat up."

"Thanks. I saw them on every table." Davin reached over, dipped a chip in the salsa bowl, and shoved it into his mouth. "You guys know how to make me happy. I think we're going to be best buddies."

Austin raised his brows in amusement. "See...I can be nice. I would've brought you chips and salsa a long time ago if I had known that's all it took."

"I don't think I would've liked you back then either way, but you're alright," Davin said, chewing and swallowing. He picked up another chip. "I know it tastes like nothing to us, but I like the texture. That I can feel." He paused. "Look at the humans." Everyone eyes followed Davin's gaze. "It must taste really good. Everyone is eating them and they look so happy."

Everyone's face turned soft as they gazed at the humans they'd been protecting all their lives. Seeing a baby reminded Davin of Zachary and Lucia, and he couldn't wait to hold them in his arms.

"Being a human seems great and all, but I'd rather be me." Davin turned his head to face his friends.

"I have to agree with you there," Austin seconded.

"Really?"

"Yup."

"Wow...I think we can actually be friends."

"I might actually like you," Austin chuckled, dipping a piece of chip in the salsa bowl.

"Okay. Let's stop there. I think we used all the nice words we can find." Davin looked puzzled. There was a part of him that actually had forgotten he was talking to Austin and realized that they could actually be friends. He didn't know if he liked the feeling so he put a stop to the friendly conversation.

After they ordered their food—which took a long time because the alkins were trying to figure out what tamales, burritos, and tacos would taste like or even look like since there were no pictures on the menus—they finally ordered. When the food came, they each took a bite, tasting, describing, dissecting, and enjoying themselves with the new type of cuisine.

As they ate, they joked about what kind of jobs they would've had if they were human, and even made up stories about their fake families. They also chatted about their war wounds, but they had no scars to prove their stories were true. Sometimes the conversation shifted. The girls talked about fashion and going shopping, while the guys talked about their favorite drinks, sports, and cars.

Lots of food and drinks filled their tables as laughter rang around them. Time flew by without a care in the world. The topic of Michael, Claudia, and the twins never came to the forefront. They were enjoying each other's company and having conversations that were long overdue.

RAVEN SAT IN THE OPPOSITE corner of Salsa, hiding behind a menu, waiting for a friend. Little did the venators and alkins know a fallen sat just a few tables away from them, easily blending with the human crowd. Having eavesdropped on Holly and Austin's conversation when she had last seen them at one of the broken down buildings, Raven had followed them to Salsa.

The alkins and venators were busy talking among themselves and having a great time, and had let their guard down. She knew they were confident that no fallen would be there, because fallen were "insane beings." They would be the first to strike when seeing a good angel among them, and no fallen would be crazy enough to show themselves among humans...except for the ones that could tame themselves, like Raven's group and a few others that had come out of hiding recently at Raven's request.

"Thanks for meeting me here, James," she whispered, hiding her face behind the menu.

"You look beautiful as always." He kissed her cheek, breathed in her scent, brushed his face into her lavish, striking red hair, and sat across from her. "You said it was important."

"I think I know which one to capture." Raven peeked over the top of the menu and shifted her body to the right to get a clear view of her. "We need to kick back and not show ourselves anymore. If they think we are no longer around, perhaps they'll let their guard down, and that is when we make our move."

"Are you sure you want to stir up trouble?" James placed his menu down, staring at the chips and salsa already on the table, grimacing. "How can they eat this stuff?"

"Suppose to taste good. Humans like them. You see them on all the tables. I see that alkin, called Davin, eating it up like it's choco-late. Anyway, I have no choice. Do I want to do this? The answer is no. But if I don't, our lives are at stake, and that is one risk I'm not willing to take. I've already spoken to Michael, and he has dismissed my warning. I told him I would fight with the winning team. Right now, I'm betting on Dantanian."

"If that's what you want, then we'll help you. I see your point. We have no alternative plan."

"We're stuck in the middle, my friend. We kind of have no choice. Dantanian's army is growing. He's reaching out and searching for all the fallen he can summon. He only asked me for one thing, and if I do his favor, he'll leave us alone."

The waitress stopped by and placed several plates of food on the table.

"Thanks." Raven smiled at the waitress who smiled back and left. "Oh. I took the liberty of ordering so we can blend in. I ordered whatever I saw first."

"That's fine. It's not like I'm going to eat this stuff." James crossed his arms on the table, leaning in. "Do you really believe him? Can Dantanian's words be trusted?"

"I have before."

"He's the worst kind there is. He's made from God, not angels. He has no remorse, no sympathy, no compassion for anyone except for himself."

Raven blinked her eyes in agreement, realizing the full depth of her troubles. "I have to say, you've described him to the tee. But again, I have no choice. I also brought you here for another reason. Last time I was lucky enough to get close to them to know they were meeting here. I need to know when the ladies are planning to go out together and where. You have supersonic hearing. I need you to hone in on their conversation."

"That's what I do best." He tuned out Raven and concentrated on the tables nearby.

While Raven picked at the food with her fork, James sat silently, looking stoic for some time. After more food playing, Raven tapped her feet on the floor as she waited as patiently as she could. James finally looked up with a sly smile. "Got it. Next week. What do I get in return for the information?" His tone was playful.

Raven was not in the mood for his flirting. In fact, even if she wanted to flirt, it certainly wouldn't be with him. Now Michael, on the other hand, was a different story. She recalled the unexpected encounter with him in the mountains, and how he could make heat crawl deliciously through every inch of her. She didn't understand the hold he had on her. With just one look from him, she would do just about anything for him, but she had to be strong. It wasn't just her life in danger; it was her whole team's life at stake...practically in her hands.

With a look of disgust in her eyes, she raised a brow. "You get to live."

CHAPTER 21

"DID YOU MISS UNCLE DAVIN?" he cooed as soon as he walked into the nursery.

"Hardly," Michael joked, snuggling the twins in his arms. "Maybe they missed Auntie Vivian and Uncle Caleb though."

"Ya...I missed you too, Michael," Davin slapped him across his back, the kind of slap Michael disliked. Davin knew it and knowingly did it to irritate him.

"So...what have you been up to lately?" Michael asked, watching the babies being lifted out of his arms by Vivian and Caleb.

"I'm not telling," Davin frowned, not seeming to like Michael's unfriendly greeting.

"We've been hanging out with Austin and his friends," Vivian muttered, making silly faces at Lucia.

"Some people don't know when to stay quiet," Davin huffed.

"Really? With Austin and his friends?" Michael sounded surprised.

"Do I hear a hint of jealousy in your tone, brother?" Davin's ears perked up.

"Hardly."

"Umm...that seems to be your favorite word today." Davin crossed his arms.

"It's been a long week. The twins are not sleeping on the same schedule. Claudia feels like she's a cow, pumping milk all the time. All they do is sleep, eat, and need diaper changing and baths... and...." Michael plopped on the sofa looking drained, not from lack of sleep—he didn't need it—but more from all the work of taking care of twins.

"How about you and Claudia take a break?" Vivian suggested. "Go have fun. We'll watch the twins. Take as long as you want."

Michael's eyes got big, like he'd just been given an energy drug. "Not a bad idea. We'll go as soon as she finishes pumping." Then he turned to Davin. "You and Austin, huh?"

"Yes. Austin and me. We are like frenemies."

"Like what?"

"You know. He's a friend and an enemy all packaged into one. I made up that word...I think...or maybe I heard it somewhere, but I'm pretty sure I invented the word."

"Only you would come up with a word like that."

Davin scowled. "You're just jealous."

"Nope. So, you guys are not looking for fallen anymore? Shouldn't you be scouting?"

"We haven't seen one in a while," Caleb explained. "I think they've stopped whatever they had in mind."

Michael stood up, paced back and forth, and stopped to kiss the twins on their cheeks. "If I know Dantanian, he's up to no good. Something is happening. He's planning something. I also saw Raven. Oh...now I know why I'm mad." Michael glared at his friends. His eyes darkened and anger oozed out of him.

Everyone froze. Davin gulped in fear. Michael was rarely mad at them. Sure, he joked about being mad, but when he said the word "mad" and looked the way he did...well, he simply was.

"Put my babies down in their crib," Michael said with a steady, low tone.

Caleb and Vivian scrambled, startled by Michael's sudden demanding tone, and carefully placed them in the nearest one. When he had their full attention, he spoke. "I ran into Raven last week. Sound familiar? You know, she's this tall." He raised his hand to about Vivian's height. "With red hair." He gawked at them one by one. "She thought I was giving myself up to Dantanian. Hmmm ...I wonder how she got that idea?"

Davin let out a nervous laugh. "You see, she found us first and told us to give you this information, but I thought it was better you didn't know."

Michael steamed toward Davin and stood right in front of him. His muscles were tight, and if fire could have blazed out of his body, it would have. "Davin. Such critical information as you are telling me right now, I need to know. Don't hide anything from me. My family's lives are at stake. You are all at stake. When I say family, you are all part of it. I told you Dantanian is a dangerous being. He's one of the original fallen. Do you understand what that means?"

They were speechless, obviously sorry for not telling him in the first place. They could do nothing but nod their heads.

"I don't think you do. He will kill just for pleasure. I know. I used to be one of them." His head was low. Trying to forget his past was impossible now when he had just admitted he was once just as evil as Dantanian.

"I'm sorry." Davin placed his hand on Michael's shoulder. "It won't ever happen again."

Michael's hand covered his face as he sat back down on the sofa. Fear he had never known before took him over. He had the lives of his wife and children to consider over his own, and the "what ifs" circulated in his head. Not only that, he had never wanted his friends to know how evil he had been back then. He had buried that guilt soon after he found his love, but now it was crawling its way back up to the surface. What would they think of him if they ever found out how ruthless he was?

"Michael. We're sorry." Vivian kneeled beside him, trying to push up his shoulders to look at him, but he wouldn't budge.

Finally, he gripped Vivian's wrist and a small, deep smile formed on Michael's lips. "It's okay. I just don't want anything to happen to anyone because of me. You have to promise me that no matter what the Twelve and the Earth angels decide, you will keep your ears and eyes open. Dantanian is coming for me, and all I can think right now is how I'm going to protect all of you and my own family." There was fear in his tone. They had never seen Michael this way before, so vulnerable and expressive with his feelings.

"I can protect you."

With the ring of her voice Michael loved to hear, the sound that had touched his heart many times before, he peered up, wondering how much she'd heard. Jolting up, he produced a wide grin.

"Hello, Claudia," everyone cheered, but the greeting wasn't like the other times before.

"Why do we look so down?" she asked, hugging her friends one by one with a kiss on their cheek. "I haven't seen you in a while."

"They were with their frenemies." Michael quoted by using two fingers—index and middle—wiggling them in midair.

"Frenemies?" Claudia giggled lightly, seemingly amused by the word. "Oh, don't mind Michael. He's just grouchy. The twins are taking a lot of our time, not that we mind. We love doing it. And I'm not complaining. We just didn't realize all the work that was involved. You know what they say...'you don't know until you've experienced it'... or was it 'you don't know until you're in it.' Anyway, I'm happy to see you here."

"They're growing up so fast. They look bigger than the last time we saw them," Vivian said, picking up Lucia, who was closest to her.

Michael sauntered to Claudia with a look of affection and desire. "Speaking of which, they've offered to babysit so you and I can have some time together."

"Really?" Claudia squealed, placing her arms around Michael's waist. Michael took her hand and kissed it softly.

"Yup...go right ahead. Take your time. Have your date day or date night or whatever you call it. It's still day time, so I guess it's a date day," Davin rambled.

"We'll be back before the sun goes down. They've already been fed, and extra bottles of milk are all ready," Michael said, peering down at Claudia. He was excited just to be alone with her. "Where would you like to go?"

"To the bookstore first. I need to know when they can eat solid food and what to feed them." Claudia opened a drawer, took out her butterfly necklace that was inside a small box, and placed it on the diaper table. "I know we are safe here, but just in case. If you see it change colors, please don't hesitate and take them straight to Crossroads."

"I see you're wearing the new necklace," Vivian winked, gazing at it.

"Yes, thank you," Claudia said shyly, recalling Michael telling her how Vivian helped him with the design. She had meant to thank her earlier, but she had forgotten. In a way she felt bad that they hadn't celebrated her birthday with their friends, but she thought it was unfair to always celebrate hers and not theirs. Since it seemed that Vivian understood, she brushed off the guilty feeling.

"It's beautiful, and don't worry so much," Vivian smiled.

"Keep calm, the alkins are here," Davin reassured her with a wink. "Don't worry, Claudia. They will be more than fine."

And she knew they would be safe in their care. With a nod, she snuggled into Michael's expanded wings that awaited her. "My favorite place to be," she said.

Gingerly, taking his time, he engulfed her completely. Holding onto her eyes, he gave a devious grin. "Now...you're mine."

"Oh, gross. Go away," Davin said, chuckling.

"Don't worry. On our way now," Michael said, never taking his eyes off Claudia's, drinking her in, keeping her under his spell. "Don't put the diaper on backwards on my daughter, or I'll make you wear one."

With that they were gone, leaving their friends behind as Michael and Claudia's laughter surrounded them, echoing into the woods until it was no longer heard.

"Make sure to poop and spit up on your dad, Zach," Davin cooed, making Caleb and Vivian chuckle out loud.

"I heard that, and his name is Zachary."

Davin jerked back, startled by Michael's words suddenly ringing in his head. "I hate it when he does that," he said to his friends.

"I heard that too."

"Ugh. Just go away," Davin said, chuckling. "How I love your dad," he said to Zachary.

CHAPTER 22

T HE SMELL OF THE FRESH pages whiffed through Claudia's nose when they entered the bookstore. It was the biggest bookstore she had ever known. With three flights of stairs, they had every sort of book she could possibly want or need. The last time she was there, she had actually snuck away without Michael and purchased the book about what to expect when she was pregnant without him knowing. He had never questioned how she got it, because the last time they had come together, she had bought so many books.

Hand in hand, Michael led the way to the young adult section. As always, it didn't matter where they were, he was always guarding her with his arms. It wasn't as crowded as it was the last time they were there. In fact, it was pretty deserted. They passed by the front desk, smiling back at the lady who had bright eyes for Michael. Yeah...that was irritating, but then again, Claudia was used to it. She couldn't blame the ladies...he was way too beautiful for their eyes. She didn't mind it though; he was hers and hers alone.

Slowly pacing down the aisle, Claudia jumped her eyes from cover to cover. Pulling one off the shelf, she read the synopsis of the story, only to put it back down. Then she opened another that caught her eye and skimmed through the pages. "I can really get high on books," she giggled, shivering from the pleasure they produced from their smell and the possibility of the story she could fall in love with.

"How about this one?" Michael placed a book in front of her view. "The cover looks pretty. The girl is kind of hot."

"What?" Claudia peered up with a snap.

"Jealous are we? I got your attention, didn't I? You were kind of paying more attention to the books than me." Michael gave a wicked grin, carefully shelved the book back into its space, and placed his hands on her waist. Peering down in her eyes, his body pressed into hers. "You're not looking for a book boyfriend, are ya?" His tone was low and playfully challenging.

"Now who's the jealous one?" Claudia's finger traced his lips. Michael slightly turned his head and teasingly licked and nipped her finger. "No, I don't have a book boyfriend, 'cause only a real boyfriend could make me do what I just did, Mr. Michael. You made me wet."

Michael looked at her smugly, fire burning in his eyes. "Hmmm ...I like the sound of that. Are you trying to seduce me, Mrs. Michael?"

Claudia giggled. Her husband was hot all right, and he could make her do just about anything, but she hadn't meant what he thought she'd meant. Claudia's eyes fell to her breasts as Michael's eyes followed. "I meant my milk is leaking."

"What happened?"

"You kind of made me...." She pulled him closer and whispered a hot breath into his ears. "Excited."

"I can do that?" The sudden revelation of what he could do created a huge illuminated spark in his eyes. He slid his fingers between her breasts, taking a peek. "I see. Hello, there."

Claudia lightly smacked his hand away. "Hey...no peeking, especially in the library. And no talking to them."

Still holding her, Michael nuzzled into the space between her head and shoulder and started to nibble gingerly.

"Michael...we're at the bookstore," Claudia whispered, trying to sound stern, but it wasn't working. She melted into his teasing and got lost in his tender kisses that did all sorts of crazy stuff to her body.

Michael pulled back and supported Claudia on her weak knees as she looked lazily into his eyes with a slow smile. "I think I'm ready to go home. Milk is seeping out, drenching the pads inside the bra."

He lit a devilish grin again. "I'm amazing."

"That you are, no doubt about it. But before we go, I need to get a book about feeding...you know...the reason why we came in the first place. But I'll hurry. My hands have a mind of their own." Claudia's hand ran over his hard ripped chest that had captured her attention the first time he took off his shirt for her with a good intention...not to show off, of course.

"Hurry," he winked. "I want to see them pour."

Claudia felt the heat rise to her face again. His words were tantalizing, making her feel hot all over. Now milk had leaked through to her shirt.

AFTER BUYING THE BOOKS SHE needed, they flew home. Their alkin friends stuck around for a little while and left. With the twins bathed, fed, and changed, they were finally down for the night. Michael and Claudia collapsed on their bed, snuggling and entangling their bodies into one.

"Did you hear that?" Michael said all of a sudden.

Claudia turned toward him, propping her head with her fist underneath her chin. "Hear what?"

"You're still not connecting with me," he stated glumly with a concerned look in his eyes. "Sorry. I didn't mean it that way. I just miss when we could. I'm sure it will happen soon."

"Yeah," Claudia said, peering down disappointedly. "I'm still the normal me."

Michael pulled her chin up, forcing her to gaze into his eyes. "Hey...I love the normal you, and soon enough you'll get your powers back."

"I'm kind of useless, and I can't do anything to help...you know, if we got attacked by the fallen or something."

Michael slowly ran his hand down the side of her face, over her shoulders, and lowered to her waist, feeling every angle, every curve. "Have you heard of the angel named Michael? I've heard he's pretty good at protecting his loved ones."

"Really?" Claudia giggled.

"I heard he's pretty hot."

"Really?"

"I heard he's awesome."

"Really?"

"I heard he only has the hots for a particular amazing, beautiful, normal human girl."

"She's so lucky. I think I'd like to meet him. Maybe he'll like me instead."

"You can meet him now."

Before she had a chance to reply, he pressed his lips on hers. First it was soft and tender, taking his time, enjoying the taste of her. Then it intensified as his hands explored her body. He pulled away only to move up, nibbling as his hot breath brushed against her ears to whisper, "I promised you I would make your milk pour, and I never back out on my promises."

Michael could feel Claudia shudder in his arms from the excitement and the anticipation of what was to come. Knowingly, he teased her more with his kisses while he unbuttoned her sweater and the rest of her clothing at high speed. He felt her pull and tug his shoulders, wanting more of him, but he wasn't going to give in right away. He wanted to take his time, giving her pleasure they hadn't had time to share.

Without warning, he shot her arms straight up and pinned them there so she was unable to move. If she had her powers back, she would have been able to almost match his strength, but right now she couldn't. "I got you where I want you." His tone was hot and heavy, and his eyes darkened with intent. He moved to her mouth again and slowly trailed kisses down her exposed flesh.

With one hand at the small nape of her neck, the other around her waist, his body pressed into her. The world around them completely stopped: no fears, no worries, just the two of them sharing and giving their love for each another. Their bodies twisted and entangled, and he took in her scent, her touch, and her love. Though his love for her grew deeper with every new day, he made sweet love to her as if it was the very first time.

"Michael," she yelped a soft cry of pleasure, making him even more excited. How he loved to hear the sound of her voice, the voice he held dear to his heart. It was what gave him strength.

With a flash of his wings, he wrapped them around her. As his wings brushed her bare skin, it produced a different kind of sensation that added to his pleasure. In his arms, she felt so warm, soft, and fragile underneath him. Looking into her eyes, he recalled the Claudia who once was when she had no powers, the Claudia he fell in love with at the Crossroads.

After he released his hold on her, he draped his long leg over her hip and embraced her tightly with all of him. Looking into her eyes, with a long lingering kiss to her forehead, he mouthed without a sound. "I love you."

Claudia returned the smile and the sweet words he loved to hear sang out of her mouth. "I love you more." As their eyes were transfixed onto each other as if they could read into their souls, a soft cry startled their silence.

"I think Lucia is up," Michael said with a soft sigh.

"Sounds more like Zachary's cry to me."

Then another cry sang in symphony.

"Looks like we won't be able to find out who cried first," Michael chuckled.

"At least they waited. Good timing though." Claudia winked and dressed herself while Michael lay there and watched. "Hey...." She realized he hadn't moved and darted an evil eye at him.

"I'm taking in my view, and how...I...love...my view." Michael stood up and had already magically dressed.

Claudia crossed her arms and stood her ground, trying to look tough. "You just wait till I get my powers back."

Suddenly, Michael snatched Claudia, draped her over his shoulders, and flew up to the nursery. "Put me down. I will not be man handled," she giggled.

"I'm not a man. I'm more than a man," he smirked, placing her down gently with a kiss.

That he was, but he couldn't wait till Claudia got her powers back. Not so much for him, but for her and the twins' safety. If ever something went wrong and he couldn't be there to protect them, he knew he would lose them forever, and that frightened him more than anything he had ever known before. It was worse than fear.

Until the threat was gone, he knew they were not safe. But he didn't know how bad the threat was. Knowing Dantanian, and if the rumor was not just a rumor, then there was more to fear. He would be very cautious, but knowing Dantanian didn't know of their place, he knew they were safe for now.

CHAPTER 23

"I HAVEN'T DONE THIS IN such a long time," Vivian gushed, walking down the center of the indoor mall, looking at the stores to the left and right of her. "Do you do this often?"

"The last time we were out together shopping was actually with Claudia," Michelle explained. "You know...before...when she couldn't remember...poor thing looked so lost and confused."

"Yeah, I bet she did," Vivian said softly, feeling bad for what Michael and Claudia had been through. Michael was like a brother to her, and seeing him without hope and all battered up had tormented her too.

"Anyway," Holly cheered, breaking Vivian out of her thoughts. "Let's go shopping."

The local mall was big with two levels. There were so many women's clothing stores that they didn't know which one to go to first. Finally they decided to enter whichever store was on the right. Walking in, their eyes lit up like children who had just walked inside a candy store. They glanced at all the racks of clothing in front of them, admiring how big the place was. There were several customers toward the back, but they didn't care. They were overly excited to be there, especially Vivian, who mostly window-shopped at Fashion Wear, where Claudia used to work. Though she had gone shopping with Michael for Claudia, it wasn't the same experience as hanging out with just the girls.

"Hello and welcome," the sales lady greeted. "If you need anything, just let me know."

After returning her smile, they speed walked straight down the aisle.

"Okay, ladies. Get what you want and let's meet at the dressing room," Holly directed. She dug into her purse, took out something square and small, and flashed it in the air. "Get whatever you want. I have Austin's credit card." Her tone went up an octave.

Michelle and Gracie's eyes grew wide, showing their perfect white teeth.

Vivian giggled. "Does Austin know?"

"Oh...he'll know. Don't worry. He has tons of money." Holly smirked. "He won't mind. I've got him under control." Her brows twitched, making everyone laugh again.

After some time had passed, Vivian's arms were draped with layers of clothing, mostly jeans and T-shirts and some dresses. The sales lady came by to help her. "Would you like for me to put those in the dressing room?"

"Sure," Vivian smiled. Empty arms meant more clothes to drape over them.

"I'm going in," Holly announced. Michelle and Gracie followed her. "Are you coming?" she asked Vivian.

"I'll be right there."

Vivian turned and headed for the rack of clothes that had caught her eye when she first walked in. When she glanced around, she noted she was the only customer around. Not knowing how many people usually went shopping on a weekday, she didn't think much of it until she heard a voice.

"Hello, Vivian," she said.

A frightful tingling sensation punched her in the gut. Michael had warned them that fallen would be out and about, but she didn't think they would actually be in a mall, where tons of people hung out. When she turned, she saw the lady with the red hair that had nicked her neck before, and standing beside her were several men that were twice her size, looking down on her with "I can crush you" looks.

Swallowing a lump of fear, she tried not to show it and acted casual, but her heart was pumping a mile a minute. "Hello. Your name is Raven, right?"

"You have a good memory. But then again, I did hurt you a little. Feeling better?" she snickered with a devilish grin.

"What do you want?" Vivian's tone was angry, trying to sound brave. "My friends are waiting for me."

"I'm sure they are, but you didn't know they had company, did you?" Raven turned her head. "Oh...here they come now."

Vivian twisted her head to see her friends in the arms of fallen. Blades were held across their necks and their arms were held behind their backs.

"They were waiting in the dressing room," Raven continued. "I'm sure your friends were quite surprised. You didn't know we were here shopping too? What a coincidence, don't you think?" Raven smiled triumphantly.

"What do you want?" Holly huffed, twisting her body from her captive's hold. "We didn't do anything. You mess with us, you'll be starting a war. Do you even know who I am?"

Raven sauntered to Holly and looked squarely into her eyes. With a slow, steady tone she said, "I...really...don't...care."

"Oh yeah...really? You're going to find out now." Holly took the opportunity to knee her in the gut with all her might, and elbowed the fallen who held her captive right where it counted. Watching Raven fall back from Holly's punch, Vivian and the rest took out their weapons. The fallen did the same as they whipped out their black wings.

Vivian ducked a blow, swung, missed, and sliced a rack in half. The shirts slid off and layer upon layer blanketed the floor. Jabbing her sword into a shirt, she tossed one right after another to the fallen who came for her. Some of the shirts flew to his right when he swatted them away, but he missed the ones that came even faster. When his face was covered over with several items, Vivian stabbed the sword into his gut, pulled it out, and slid it across his neck with one stroke. With a poof of black smoke and ashes, he disappeared.

Quickly she scanned the store to find her friends. Seeing silver lightning like bolts flashing, she spotted them at the other end. She had forgotten how beautiful the lights looked, and seeing three different flashes meant three friends were still alive.

The store was a complete mess, looking like a tornado had hit it. Racks and shelves were broken in halves. Most of the clothes were on the ground and torn. The walls had lightning marks across them that tore into the structure, visibly showing wood and plaster.

Wondering where Raven was, she cautiously turned in every direction, but there was no sign of her or any other fallen besides the ones her friends were fighting. Strange. She'd only killed one...she knew there were more. Had they escaped? She was just about to dash toward her friends when she felt the wind knocked out her. It was quick, but she felt a throbbing pain in her head and shoulders. Then everything went dark.

"OUR TIME HAS COME, MY brothers and sister." Standing next to Berneal, Dantanian's voice was loud, projecting out into the crowd of fallen. "The demons are gone and they are no longer a threat to us. Now the door has opened, giving us an opportunity to take back what is ours." The loudness of the crowd cheering sounded like the roaring of thunder.

He could have easily floated as he spoke, but decided to stand on a boulder with Berneal instead to show unity. As his eyes lay upon the vast numbers of his comrades, he could see nothing but the black from their wings, smell nothing but pure evil, and he sensed the victory that was almost in his hands.

"What is our plan of victory, Dantanian?" one questioned. The voice carried deep within the middle of the crowd.

"We'll get Michael to join us!" Berneal shouted.

Loud murmurs spread with a rippling effect, getting louder by the second.

"Hear us out!" Dantanian raised his hand to silence them. "Michael knows everything about our enemies. Aden, Michael, and I had a plan, a plan that was executed before the initial attack. He lost his memories, but I assure you, I'll make him remember."

"Are you talking about Michael? Zachariah's son?" another one asked.

"Yes, I am," Dantanian said proudly. "He was like a brother to me, but he will do as I ask or he shall die along with the rest."

"We've been hiding ever since the war ended. We are fine and happy. Why now?" one asked from the left side of the crowd.

Dantanian was getting irritated by the questions thrown at him, as if he was incapable of getting his way. "Don't underestimate the power of darkness. Everything has its own time, and I say the time for us is now."

"And how are you going to get Michael to be on our side? He's been with them for so long."

"I assure you, I know his weak spot. It's already started. Next time we meet, it will be to win. If you are not with me and will not fight alongside me, you may leave now."

"You're giving us a choice?"

Dantanian produced a smug grin. "Yes. If anyone dares." His tone was wicked, challenging.

"I won't fight alongside you," one said, breaking out from the crowd, walking toward Dantanian. "You're all crazy. You'll be fighting against the venators, alkins, the Twelve, Earth angels, and the watchers. There is no way in hell we'll win this war. I'd rather live than die trying to start a war that ended when Aden died. Who is with me?"

Dantanian's eyes brewed with fire. His whole body shuddered with volcanic anger, ready to erupt. "Come here, my friend. Stand beside me. You can have your turn to speak. Let's see how this will play out. After all, we've become a fallen so we may have freedom of speech and will."

The fallen who dared to speak out against the war flew to stand next to Dantanian. "What I'm saying is that they have left us alone for all these years. We are comfortable. We have peace."

The crowded started to cheer, agreeing with the speaker. This is not what Dantanian wanted. He had been certain he would have their support. He had to stop the speaker before he lost his army of fallen, which he needed in hopes to win the war.

Dantanian turned to face the fallen who had spoken out. "I'll give you peace." His hand penetrated his rib cage so fast the speaker had no idea what had happened to him, and neither did the crowd. With a twist of his hand, Dantanian pulled out his heart. With a look of surprise, the speaker fell to his knees and tumbled off the boulder.

Hearing the loud gasps from the crowd, Dantanian raised the heart and let the blood seep down his arm. "This is what will happen if you are against me. Don't betray me." Then he squeezed it, letting the crimson red liquid drip down like rain. "I tell you now, we will take over Crossroads."

"You're so sure of yourself," one bellowed from the back.

"That's because step one and two of my plan have already been successful."

"What is that?"

"To find Aden's golden cuffs and to capture an alkin." Dantanian's eyes grew dark. His wings expanded to their fullest as he lay back his head and looked up to the belly of the clouds. Silence filled the air so that even the whispers of the wind, the ruffles of the leaves on the trees, and God's creatures that scurried away in fright could not be heard. The world around them was muted, and the dead silence said it all.

CHAPTER 24

HOLLY'S HEART POUNDED OUT OF her chest so hard and fast that it was difficult to breathe. Her whole body ached. That had only happened once before...when she'd lost Patrick. Oh God...did she care for Vivian? Yes...she did, but she didn't want to. Caring meant pain and heartbreak came with it. But she had to snap out of it. There was nothing she could say, but there was one thing she could do.

"Davin!" she bellowed desperately, frantically running down the hall of Nubilus City. She opened the double door to the training room. "Where's Davin?"

The venators stopped what they were doing and froze in place, startled by her tone of alarm. One pointed and said, "He's not here. He's with Caleb in the garden."

Holly ran out into the garden. It was always breathtaking and serene out there. Looking out into the vastness of nothing but puffy cotton ball clouds, the kind of clouds you could sit on and sail away to a peaceful place, she lost herself for a second. Shaking her head, she recalled why she was there. "Davin! Are you out here?"

"Did you miss me already?" Davin said cheerfully from behind her.

Holly jerked forward from the sudden voice that brushed the back of her neck. She turned, heaving, eyes pooling with water. Placing both hands on his shoulders with a sympathetic and alarmed look, she locked his eyes, but was unable to speak.

"Holly? I like you too, but this is kind of awkward, don't you think?" Davin teased, chuckling, seemingly unable to avoid the opportunity to say something to irritate her.

Ignoring Davin, she asked, "Where's Caleb?"

"I'm here. What's wrong?" He was now beside them with a look of concern.

"It's Vivian."

Her words and tone said it all. Davin's face turned pale, the smile became a serious thin line, and his body tightened with dread.

"Well, well, well." Dantanian circled around Vivian.

She pierced her eyes at him with a look of hatred, trying to look just as cold as him, but he mocked her instead.

"You won't be giving me that look once I'm done with you."

"You promised you wouldn't hurt her," Raven said, standing behind her with one hand tightly gripped on Vivian's arm.

"You going soft on me?"

"I brought her here, didn't I?"

Dantanian flashed an angry look at Raven. "Just to be clear, she is my prisoner now. I do what I want with her."

Vivian scanned the perimeter with her peripheral vision, trying not to be obvious. There were two exit doors, but she had to get there first. Noting she was at a warehouse they had been to before, she could vividly see the blueprint of this place since they had searched every corner of it. She had to think fast and do something quickly. "My friends will be coming for you," she spat, giving him the evilest look.

"Oh, you have no idea how I'm counting on it." Dantanian's face beamed with excitement. Extending his hand, he trailed his fingers down Vivian's cheek. "Such a pretty face. It's too bad I'll have to kill you."

With the word "kill" drilling in her mind, adrenaline rushed through her body. After yanking her arm back from Raven's hold, she took flight to the first exit, only to get stopped by several fallen that came out of the dark shadows. How could she have missed them? Without a second to lose, she sped to the other exit, only to be stopped by more fallen.

"Where do you think you're going?" a fallen slithered. "Let me introduce myself. They call me Berneal."

Vivian gasped, recalling the name Michael had mentioned. Retreating her steps and keeping her eyes on all the fallen, she realized this was not a win situation. She would have to bear what was to come.

Fear gripped her and she felt so alone. Never had she been in a situation like this before. Her friends had always surrounded her. Trembling inside, her heart pumped erratically and she had never known fear like she was experiencing now. Would today be her last day to live? As she held unto the faces of her friends that meant the world to her—Davin, Caleb, Michael, Claudia, and even the twins—she had to suck it up and be brave.

Berneal's sinister laughter broke Vivian out of her thoughts. "You think it'll be that easy to escape here?"

Stepping backwards, she bumped into a body. When she turned, Dantanian was right in her face. Gripping the nape of her neck, he yanked her into him for a lustful kiss so fast she had no idea it was coming. Somehow managing to pull away from him, she swiped her mouth with one long stroke, and then slapped him across the face. Looking squarely into his eyes, she held her ground.

"You like it hard and rough, don't you?" he sneered, holding on to her burning gaze. "Take her to our hide out and put the golden cuffs on her," he ordered Berneal. "And go gather the other groups of fallen who are waiting for us." Then he turned to Raven. "What are you waiting for? Go bring the other one." He paused. "No...wait. I have an idea. Oh...this will be really good. I'm coming with you."

WITHOUT STRATEGIZING, DAVIN AND CALEB frantically went from town to town where they had previously encountered the fallen, painstakingly searching for Vivian, but to no avail. When they were just about to give up and go to Michael for help, Raven stood in front of them.

With lightning bolt speed, Davin went for her, but suddenly stopped in his tracks, thinking it could be a trap. "Where is she?" he shouted angrily. "What have you done with her?"

"I didn't do anything, but I'll tell you where I saw her last."

"Why should we believe you?" Caleb retorted.

"Because I've come alone. It seemed like the right thing to do."

"Since when do you care about doing the right thing?" Davin growled.

"Suit yourself." She flashed her black wings to open, ready to take flight.

Contemplating whether to believe her, Davin decided to take a chance. Though there was a chance this could be a trap, he needed to get to Vivian, and fast. If by chance he could rescue her and he didn't go, he would never forgive himself. "Wait! Stop! Where is she?"

"Go to the small town east of Springfield called Pinewood. She's locked up in a cage, inside an abandoned office building. There are several of them. Go to the first one you see. Don't bother getting the rest of your friends. If you hurry and go now, you can save her before he comes back."

"Who?" Caleb asked.

"Dantanian."

There it was. The shiver Davin hadn't felt in a long time painfully blasted through his gut. Though he had never met him in person, from Michael's description of him, the name alone gave him a dreadful feeling. He could feel the evil surrounding him, crawling up his skin.

He imagined how frightened Vivian must be feeling. Needing to get to her as soon as possible, he didn't think about the possible consequences that could be waiting for them. It didn't matter anyway. There was no time to think, no time to plan. Saving Vivian was all that was on his mind. She meant the world to him, and he would do anything to save her.

Reaching their destination, Davin spotted the first building. Just like Raven had described the town, it was gloomy, cold, and deserted. Not a soul lived in this town...at least, not anyone with a soul. Holding up his sword, Davin cautiously placed his hand on the door as Caleb followed closely behind. Then he stopped. Recalling the times he had broken the other doors, he decided not to take the chance.

Peering up to see an empty space where a window should have been, he leapt and steadied himself to get a better view. Sure enough, he saw a body curled up into a ball inside a cage.

He jumped down without a sound and placed his back flat against the wall. With his sword in front, he instructed Caleb to stay behind to be on the lookout. When the coast was clear, he tiptoed toward the cage as he continued to scan the perimeter. "Vivian," he whispered.

The female turned around, revealing someone who looked like Vivian, but Davin was uncertain. "Vivian?" he questioned, carefully examining the female and the cage. Long steel bars he could easily bend stood between them. When he was certain it was her, he spoke. "I'll get you out."

When she peered up, Davin noted the left side of her cheek was bluish gray. Impossible! Alkins didn't bruise. They healed quickly. In fact, they healed fasted than the venators. But when he saw the golden cuffs on her wrists, he knew the reason why, and his heart dropped even more.

Inspecting her from head to toe, he trembled with volcanic anger and sympathy, for she didn't look like the Vivian he knew. Her mangled hair covered the side of her face and she looked worn and battered, like she had been through hell. There were slits in her jeans and T-shirt, as if she had been slashed with a whip. And to make matters worse, there were bloodstains on them.

Whimpering sounds quietly floated out of her mouth when she tried to smile back. Wincing, she wobbled to him, holding onto the bar for support. Though her eyes beamed with happiness, they were dulled and somber.

His hand over hers, she felt cold as he tried to comfort her. After letting go of her hand, with all his strength, he bent the bars to open. "I'll kill the person who did this to you. I swear it," Davin sneered through his clenched jaws. Carefully, he helped her out. Elated to see her, he embraced her with all of his love. "You're safe. Let's get you home."

"Wait," she said, extending her arms. "How about these?"

Davin held both of her hands and rubbed them gently. It pained him deeply to see these on her. "We'll get Claudia to unlock them."

"Or maybe they can be transferred to you." Her tone had suddenly changed and her voice sent a chill to his spine, for it sounded like a man's voice.

Wondering if he'd heard correctly, he looked up at her and froze. He no longer saw Vivian's face, but that of a man he had never seen before. Davin stumbled back in astonishment, only to find both of his wrists glowing. "Shit," he mumbled under his breath.

"Let me introduce myself," Dantanian snickered, walking in circles around Davin.

"No need. I know who you are...or were...because pretty soon you'll be dead."

Dantanian laughed out loud. "I've heard about you, Davin. You're funny. I need to laugh once in a while. I think I'll make you part of my team."

"Then you'll be waiting forever...oh wait. Did I forget to mention, perhaps you don't have to wait that long 'cause you'll be dead soon?"

"I like your humor, but your humor won't save your friends."

Speaking of friends, Davin looked around, hoping Caleb had escaped, but his hopes were short lived. Surrounded by a group of fallen, Caleb's hands were cuffed too.

"I wasn't expecting to catch two today, but what a treat," Dantanian gloated.

"Why don't you just save yourself some time and uncuff me so I can kill you myself?" Davin roared.

Dantanian flashed himself right in front of Davin's face. "Don't play with my patience. You are just a means to the completion of my plan. I can and will get rid of you if you don't cooperate. I suggest you watch your mouth and give me respect." He expanded his ominous dark wings. They were just as grand as Michael's.

Davin pierced his eyes into his in anger. "Your dirty wings don't scare me, and your breath stinks like baby's poop." Suddenly Davin felt a harsh sting on his face. Though the pain lasted for a few seconds, it was long enough for him to know Dantanian had punched him. Then everything went dark.

CHAPTER 25

"SETTLE DOWN!" JEREMIAH TRIED TO tame the voices that erupted when Holly told them about the fallen and how they had captured Vivian. When the crowd didn't settle, he stood up and raised his hands. When all was quiet again, he turned to Holly. "Do you have proof?"

"Do I have proof?" Holly flashed an "are you kidding look." "You think I'm lying?" She couldn't believe he was asking a stupid question. Davin was right. He was an old fart. The more she got to know him during the meetings, the more she wondered how in the world he became one of the Twelve. Then again, there was always someone like him in a group.

"Must I repeat myself?" He rolled his eyes.

If he was going to play that game then so was she. "Did I see her disappear right in front of my eyes? The answer is no. But when Michelle, Gracie, and I kicked ass...I mean...got rid of the ones we were fighting, there was no sign of Vivian. She wouldn't just take off."

"And why not?" Jeremiah continued with his idiotic questions. "Maybe she went to find her alkin friends."

Hello...because we had shopping to do. "She would've stayed to make sure we were okay." With that, Holly realized she was really gone. Perhaps one of the fallen or Raven had killed her. What happened when an alkin died? Did they turn into ashes and get blown away like the fallen? She didn't know. She was a venator, and when a venator died, their body remained.

Suddenly the round table looked ginormous. The walls were pushed back further. Swimming in her mind was a vision of Vivian and Patrick. Vivian was dead, and Holly could do nothing to bring her back...just like Patrick. How could she have let this happen? They were careless. No...they were having fun. Stupid fun. They had acted like humans instead of angels, and now this was their price to pay.

"We have not seen Vivian," Phillip said in a hurry. There was concern in his tone.

"Perhaps we should seek Davin and Caleb, or even Michael and Claudia. She could be with them as far as we know," Margaret said hopefully.

"I think we should get a group together and search for Vivian," Austin said in his authoritative tone. "At the same time, we can scout for fallen. If what Holly says is right, then they are scheming to start a war."

"We will do no such thing. There is no need. You think that a group of fallen is brave enough to come our way? They know their agreement. Live in peace, leave us alone, and they can roam the Earth freely," Elizabeth reminded.

"But...but...what if they've captured her? What if she needs us?" Holly's tone was soft. She could feel her lips quivering and there was wetness in her eyes. Blinking, she spoke in anger. "Sure, if it were one of you, I bet you would've been searching by now. Just because she's an alkin, you'll let her be. A life is a life."

"Holly," Katherine said, placing her hand gently on hers. "We can't just go. We need a plan. If she has been captured, they will ask for something in return. If we don't hear from them soon...well...I don't want to think about that...let's just hope they contact us."

Holly wanted to scream and tell them they were all fools. Just because they had an agreement didn't meant the fallen would stick to it, especially if they were being forced to pick a side or die. "Fine. I'll wait a little bit until my patience runs out. If we don't hear from them, I'm going on my own. Anyone who wants to help me, thank you, and if you don't...well then, that is your choice."

She really wanted to say screw you, but she knew better. They probably wouldn't understand anyhow, except for Austin and Davin. Oh God, how she missed Davin right now. After the meeting she would search for him. Mostly likely he was with Caleb and they were searching for Vivian, trying to scout any information about her whereabouts.

Without a doubt, she would help him. But this was bad. Perhaps it was all the bonding, going out together, trying different types of food and going shopping. Whatever had happened over the course of the last month, she had grown to like them as her own family. It was a wonderful feeling to care, but it was something she really didn't want that had crept up on her all of a sudden and wrapped around her heart, making her soft...fuzzy...and...yup...she did care. She really did care.

WHEN DAVIN AND CALEB WERE nowhere to be found, Holly flew to Michael's place. Only having been there a couple of times, she wasn't sure if she would be welcomed back. Timidly, she flew to the first level. The other few times, she had been there during the night, but seeing this place in daylight definitely described what paradise would look like.

With endless tall trees reaching to the sky, bundles of vibrant wild flowers, and a flowing peaceful stream that seemed never ending, she saw why Michael had chosen this place. As her eyes set upon layers of wood, she wondered how in the world Michael had managed to build such beauty with his own hands. Thinking of Michael, when she took one step back, she ran into a hard body. With a gulp, she turned.

"Uh...hey Michael," she said shyly. She never looked at him this way because of Austin, but now that war was over...dang! He was too gorgeous for his own good. Not to mention that body.

"Holly? What brings you here? I mean...I'm glad you're here to visit," Michael rambled, seemingly uncomfortable by her sudden appearance, but she soon found out why.

A soft cry permeated the air, giving her chills down her spine. They weren't frightened chills, more like surprised ones. She looked up because she knew the sound had come from one of the floors above her. "Michael? Is that what I think it is?"

"Follow me," he sighed. He didn't even open up his wings... totally not fair...he was strong that way. He just bolted straight up like an arrow and landed on the highest plank. There she saw Claudia holding not one, but two babies in her arms, and they were absolutely beautiful.

With tiny bodies and tiny everything she observed, all she could do was marvel at the miracles in front of her eyes. She never knew Claudia was pregnant. But then again, they hadn't seen each other in a while...a long five month while, if she was counting human time.

"Say hello to your Auntie Holly," Claudia said, walking toward her.

"Auntie?" Holly muttered under her breath. Holly held her hands up, backed away, bumped into Michael again, and peered up.

"Must you stand behind me?" she snorted. Then she turned to Claudia. "I've never held babies before. I may drop them. I don't want to be responsible for that, or them, or babies."

"It's okay. I'll help you," Claudia smiled, looking happier than she'd ever seen her.

And suddenly, one was in her arms. Her body was tense and her hands shuddered slightly underneath the infant. "You're holding Zachary," Claudia said. "I'm holding Lucia."

"A boy and a girl. What a perfect combination. You've kept them hidden?" Holly asked, unable to peel her eyes off Zachary, who peered back at her. Round and big, his eyes reminded her of Michael's. Involuntarily, Zachary grasped Holly's finger that was on its way to his cheek. He gripped tightly, pulling it to his mouth.

"Wow...little guy. I'm not food." Holly laughed as her worries disappeared.

"It's almost feeding time," Michael explained.

"They're beautiful. This little guy looks like you Michael, and Lucia looks like Claudia," Holly gushed.

She couldn't believe such sweet words escaped out of her mouth, but then again, she was holding a glorious miracle in her hands. This feeling was alien to her, but was wrapping around her heart and soul. She withered blissfully, as if she had taken a happy drug and she never wanted to let go.

Michael comfortably settled himself on the sofa. Stretching his long legs on the coffee table, he tucked his arms behind his head for support, and there he sat looking so dreamy and sexy that Holly had to turn away while taking deep breaths. What was wrong with her? Perhaps it was Austin's fault from all that talk about sex.

"Did you come alone? Where is the rest of your group?" Michael asked.

Holly popped her eyes to Michael, then glanced at Claudia. Suddenly, her eyes were filled with fear and sadness. She swallowed a lump of guilt and her eyes stung again. Gaping back between them, she didn't know how to break the news.

"What is it, Holly?" Claudia asked, sensing Holly's uneasiness.

"It's Vivian, and I think Davin and Caleb too."

Holly explained the details of their shopping excursion and what had happened afterward. She even told them about the meeting she'd had with the Twelve. The only clear detail she could give was that one of the fallen went by the name of Raven. Besides giving a few locations of the places they had encountered the fallen, she couldn't give them much to go on.

"You did the right thing by letting us know." Michael stood up. His eyes were dark and worried. "But I'm afraid this is my fault."

Holly and Claudia flashed their eyes at him.

"Why would you say that?" Claudia asked, placing Lucia into Holly's arms. Holly seemed uncomfortable holding two, but she quickly adjusted.

Michael explained how Davin's group had run into Raven and what she'd said, about him running into her in the mountains during Claudia's birthday celebration, and about Dantanian wanting Michael on his side.

After discussing their plan, Claudia agreed to take the twins and stay at Crossroads, and Holly agreed to escort them there. Meanwhile, Michael would scout the towns Holly had mentioned, but promised not to do anything on his own.

Claudia looped her arms tightly around Michael's neck. "Michael, please be careful," she urged. She promised herself she wouldn't shed a tear, but it was uncontrollable. They were making their way to the surface, and her haunting dreams suddenly became something to fear.

Michael pulled back and wiped the tears flowing down her cheeks. "Claudia, I'll be back. I'll be back for you and I'll be back for our children. Nothing means more to me than our family. I will be extremely careful. I will not take them on my own. Our family is my sole purpose for living."

Claudia replied with a smile, but her heart was breaking. If she had her powers back, she could go with him. She could stand by her husband and fight alongside him. At least she would have had peace of mind. At least she would know he was safe.

"I love you...I love us." Michael beamed the smile he did so well, mixed with playfulness and hotness.

"Have I told you, you could probably make any woman do what you wanted simply by smiling?" She tried to lighten the mood.

"Really? But I don't care about other women, Mrs. Michael. I only care about you."

Claudia gushed. "Only me," she repeated, then silence filled the air between them, prolonging the inevitable. "I know you should get going. Time is precious." Her hand gripped tightly onto Michael's arm, but she knew he couldn't feel how tightly she was holding onto him. This was proof. Her powers were still buried deep within her. Frustration and anger erupted through her veins. She wanted to scream, but she knew that wouldn't bring her powers back.

Having their children was worth it all, but it was really bad timing. Knowing he needed to go and he wouldn't leave until she let go, she loosened her grip, one finger at a time. "I love you," she said, holding onto him with her eyes. "Come back to me." Her lips quivered and her pulse raced with anxiety.

Michael exhaled a deep breath and dipped Claudia back, the way he always did when they danced. "I swear to you, I'll come back. I'm never letting you go. I'm never letting our family go."

Feeling herself in an upright position, she felt every word to her heart. Finding his eyes again, she noted they were glassy and she saw the worried look in them, which made her heart ache even more. Closing her eyes, she ran her hands from the top of his forehead, curving over his eyebrows, down to his nose, brushing across his supple lips, and along his strong jaw line, memorizing his face, memorizing his smell, memorizing how it felt to be in his arms, memorizing...him.

"I'm just going to scout and then I'll be back."

"Bring our friends back."

"I will," he said with conviction.

After Claudia nodded, their bodies collided and his lips crushed hers. In desperation and unsure of their future, their love for each other poured through their kisses. Michael broke away and caressed his cheek to hers. He held her tightly, so tightly she thought he would break her, but she didn't care. She didn't know what the future held, but she couldn't let negative thoughts get in the way either.

Thinking of Vivian, Davin, and Caleb, she hesitantly pulled away. It took a great amount of effort to do so, but she had to let go. "Go...before I don't let you." But soon after, she couldn't help herself. She wrung his shirt with her fingers in desperation. "I love you," she mouthed, afraid to let the words escape her lips. It felt like she was saying it for the last time.

Michael gingerly peeled her grip and kissed each of her knuckles. "Multiply my love by infinity and take it to the depths of forever, and you still have only a glimpse of how I feel for you. I...love...you...more." He gave her one last kiss to her lips. Turning to the twins, who were still in Holly's arms, he placed a long soft kiss on each of their foreheads, sighed heavily, and promised to return. Then, he flashed his wings.

Tears streamed down Claudia's face as she watched her love soar away. His glorious, beautiful wings were fully expanded in the shape of a huge white heart. How she loved being wrapped inside them. When he was out of her vision, she turned to Holly, who was now standing on the bridge, cuddling Claudia's babies in her arms.

"Ready?" Holly asked.

"Yes. We can go now."

"Don't worry. He'll be back."

Claudia smiled, wiping away the last evidence of her tears, but she sensed something heading their way...danger...evil...death.

CHAPTER 26

CLAUDIA AND THE TWINS WERE warmly welcomed by all the Calkins at the Crossroads. Though eventually the news would spread and the angel community would hear about it, she didn't expect the secret to be out this soon. Phillip, Margaret, and Agnes made sure Claudia and the twins were settled comfortably in Michael's room. Everything was perfect, but it felt so empty and lonely without Michael there.

Looking around, she saw the unfinished paintings of her that Michael had started, but stopped when she had lost her memories. On the table were the tools he had used to make her necklace and perhaps the wedding ring on her finger. Being in his room helped ease her mind somewhat, but she couldn't keep her pulse from racing, making her unable to breathe comfortably.

Looking out onto the fountain from the large window, she could see the children gathered around playing games, laughing with no worries in the world. How great it was to be a child, and she couldn't wait for her children to play like them. Hearing the sound of soft cute baby noises from the twins, she turned her head to the bed where they lay.

As she watched the interaction between them, she couldn't believe she was a wife and a mother. Everything up to now seemed like a dream, and though a year had gone by, it seemed a lot longer considering all that she had been through in a short amount of time. Twisting the ring on her finger, she brushed the heart shaped crystal with her right thumb and reached for the butterfly necklace that was crystal clear. She had worn it knowing there was a possibility of facing the fallen. "Come back to me, Michael," she muttered under her breath. "Hurry."

Until he came back, she wouldn't be able to breathe, and the only thing that kept her glued together was the twins. She had to be strong, if not for herself, then for their children.

"Claudia," a voice said by the door.

Startled, Claudia whipped around to see Katherine. "Come in."

Claudia always admired how, whatever the occasion, Katherine was always dressed elegantly. She decided that when she stopped breastfeeding she would pay more attention to her appearance and wear the nice clothes Vivian and Michael had bought for her.

Katherine went to the twins first. "They are lovely. They are bigger than the last time I saw them. You're feeding them quite well," she smiled.

When Claudia met her at the bed, Katherine reached out and gave her a warm hug. "I came by because I wanted to explain what is happening. Most of the Twelve believe we shouldn't start anything without any clear evidence. We have nothing to go by. Do you understand what I mean?"

Claudia didn't answer. She just stared and waited for her to continue.

"We have no proof Vivian was captured. I know she hasn't been around, but we can't just use that and start a war."

"But she would never just take off without telling one of us." Claudia's tone was louder than she wanted, but she couldn't help it. Feeling frustrated, she took it out on Katherine. "In fact, she was always around. This is her home. We are her family."

"I know, but unfortunately, even angels have political issues. We've made a deal with the fallen, and we can't break that unless it's absolute necessary. Vivian being missing isn't a reason."

"Did you know Davin and Caleb are missing too?"

Katherine paused for a moment. "I didn't know."

"They went to look for Vivian and never returned," Claudia's tone was desperate. "Michael took off hoping to find something that would lead us to them. How about those reasons? Are they enough?"

Katherine had lost the glow on her face she had come in with. Her face held no expression, and her body was taut. "Tell Michael to come see me when he comes back."

"I will, but I have a problem."

Katherine looked at her with concern. "What is it?"

"I don't have my powers back," she sighed heavily. "I can't do anything. I'm useless. What if...?"

"Claudia, I don't know what to tell you. You and I are different. The good thing is that we are not fighting against one of God's first angels. Then I would be greatly concerned because you are the only one that could defeat him, but we are talking about fallen."

"I know, but I guess I don't know much about them. I only remember how scared I was when I was chased by them."

"That was when you were a human. If there was a fallen in front of you, you could have flicked him off the living by just a small amount of your light."

"That's the problem. I don't have any of my light."

Katherine tried not to show it, but Claudia could read through the worried emotions behind her eyes. "Stay here. You and your children will be safe. I'll send extra watchers to guard Crossroads, but I assure you, they can't pass here unless—"

Zachary started wailing, forcing them out of their conversation. Claudia picked him up and positioned him into a feeding hold. She lifted her shirt, clicked her bra open from the front, and guided him to feed. "He's been eating so much. He's draining all my energy." Claudia paused… there was that sentence, "draining all my energy."

Katherine and Claudia shot looks into each other's eyes, and found the answer they were looking for.

"Claudia, I didn't breast feed Austin. My powers came back quickly. Perhaps you should stop and see if that will work. Things that make your body relate to being a human, such as being pregnant and breast feeding, will hinder you from returning to what you once were."

"I'll try." A spark lit in Claudia's eyes as hope returned. She wanted to do right by her babies, but she needed to be back on her feet, not as a mother, but as herself.

"You must remember not to overdo it. When your powers come back, you may lack control and the intensity of it. And don't forget, you must fight back with love and never with anger, hatred, or vengeance. Love is the key. Love is powerful. Be careful." With that, Katherine excused herself.

Claudia held her babies and breastfed them for the last time. How she would miss the motherly bonding, but there were other things she could do. Ending breastfeeding didn't mean it was the end of the world, but there was a possibility that other things could end. And if she could stop them, she had to do what was best for all.

MICHAEL SEARCHED HIGH AND LOW, in building after building and town after town. Then he recalled when he'd come across Raven. She had asked him if he was there to surrender. And that was where he was headed, back to the mountain, back to her home.

Carefully, he spiraled down to the wooden cabin he was sure was her place of residence. Since there was no other around, it had to be. Placing his back against the wood planks, he chuckled thinking what a crummy job they'd done on the construction. He could have done so much better.

Snapping his mind back to why he was there, he peeked into the window, only to see an empty place. Then he walked in through the front door.

Two large sofas and a wooden table were set in the middle of the living space. Other than that, it was pretty much bare. Sensing someone near, he whipped around with his sword in front of his chest. Sure enough, he saw Raven by the door that was already open.

"Hello, Michael," she greeted calmly, as if she had expected him to come.

"I'm going to ask you this once, Raven. Where are they?"

"Oh...you mean Vivian, Davin, and Caleb?"

Michael sighed heavily. Though he had hoped they were not in Dantanian's possession, Raven confirming what he feared made it a thousand times worse. At this point his words were lacking because his heart was breaking. "Yes," was all he could say.

"Don't worry, Michael. I made a deal with Dantanian. He isn't allowed to touch them until he finishes his deal with you. I can't say they are well, but at least they are alive. I warned you. You should have taken him out while you had the chance. Now you'll have to face the consequences of ignoring me."

Raven was right...at least they were alive. That was all that mattered to him. "Take me to Dantanian. I want to negotiate with him." Though he had promised Claudia he wouldn't take matters into his own hands, he had no time to waste. Seeing that Raven was willing to take him now, he had to go before she changed her mind. With her, there was never consistency. He only hoped Dantanian would listen, but even knowing it was a slim chance, he had to go. If something were to happen to his friends because he took the time to beg the Twelve for their help, he would never forgive himself.

"Gladly...follow me."

"Before we go, tell me, why are you on his side? This isn't you."

"You left me no choice. If I don't help him, then he'll take what I have left. And you know very well we live forever, and forever is a very long time to grieve the ones we've lost. Sorry, I rather it be you than me."

"You know you'll be breaking your contract with the Twelve. At least if you help us now, you will be pardoned."

"Like I said before, I side with the winning team. Right now, I'm betting on Dantanian."

"We'll see about that. You had your chance."

Their wings unfurled, letting the wind lift them up to flight. They had been comfortable at Beyond where the weather was perfect, so Michael hadn't realized the weather had changed. The clouds were dark grey, looking like it was going to rain. As they passed through the thick belly of the clouds, they landed at a town he had never been to before.

The town was small, away from other towns, with few houses and a large building that looked like an abandoned warehouse. It was deadly silent. Only the whispers of wind and the rustling of the leaves could be heard. No cars and no people roamed the street. Michael knew instantly that this was where Dantanian had been hiding.

Raven pushed the colossal steel door that was slightly ajar to open fully, walked in, and closed it behind Michael. The windows located near the high ceiling allowed the light to penetrate, but it wasn't enough, making the room appear dim.

Michael's footsteps echoed and his heartbeat matched them. Glancing around, he was surprised he wasn't surrounded by Dantanian's group of fallen the minute he'd entered. Where were they hiding? As he continued to follow Raven, the anticipation of finding his friends was crawling up his skin. "Where are they?" he asked impatiently.

Raven didn't need to answer. From out of the shadows behind one of the crates appeared Dantanian. "Hello, Michael. We meet again."

"I'm here to negotiate. Let my friends go; they have nothing to do with you. I'll make sure the Twelve and venators won't hunt you down after they find out what you've done. This war is between you and me and no one else."

"What? No hello after all these years?" His tone was friendly, but sinister.

Michael ignored his question again. "Where's Berneal?"

"Obviously Berneal isn't here, and he doesn't make the decisions. I'm the one in charge," he raged, then his tone became cordial. "I'm not in the mood to negotiate. I have bigger and better plans. But let me start by telling you how good you look. Because the last time I saw you...you were near death." Dantanian eyed Michael, examining him from head to toe. "Hmmm...funny...I don't think you're all that hot. Raven seems to think you are though."

"Shut up!" Raven snapped. "Get on with it."

Michael didn't say a word. His jaw was tight, his vision narrowed at his target, his fist ready to whip out his sword.

"I have one thing to say to you, Michael. It's really simple. Join me, or die with your friends."

Michael laughed out loud. "I dare you to try."

Dantanian's eyes pulsed with anger, looking like he was ready to explode. Without warning, he soared across the empty space between them and knocked Michael off balance. Michael flew through the air for several feet, but managed to somersault and land gracefully on his feet.

Several fallen who were standing on tall crates along the walls darted after him, but Michael was faster and stronger. With his sword, he slashed one's neck, pivoted to the right, turned, and plunged his sword through a second one's gut. The third one came for him from behind, but Michael waited until the precise moment to duck, flip over him, and slit him across his chest. As always when destroying fallen, they turned into black ashes and disappeared.

With a roar, Dantanian charged. Sparks flew like lightning when their swords collided, and the power with which they struck sounded like thunder. They moved in an angry tango from one crate to another. Michael struck but missed, and his sword went through a crate and lodged itself. Dantanian took advantage of the opportunity and kicked Michael in the stomach. Michael was forcefully pushed backward and tried to stop his motion by planting his feet on the ground, but as the momentum continued, he skidded as if he was on ice.

When he finally stopped, he jumped on top of a crate, followed shortly by Dantanian. Searching for his sword, he tried to locate the crate where it was stuck, but Dantanian stood in his way. "Looking for this?" He sneered.

Michael stood frozen at first, but instead of showing his alarm he confidently folded his arms across his chest and glared at Dantanian. "You need two swords to fight me? How pathetic."

Dantanian, aroused in anger, took Michael's bait. He charged Michael full force with both swords. At the right moment, Michael unfurled his wings and used them like swords. They hopped from one crate onto another as their weapons collided.

"Smell my feet," Michael said, thinking that it was something Davin would say. How he missed his friend. His strength, power, and speed came from his determination to bring his friends back home. There was nothing he wouldn't do to get them back.

When Michael's feet contacted Dantanian's face, he was sent flying toward the ceiling like a rag doll and lost his grip on both swords in midair. With one graceful jump, Michael captured both of them while keeping one eye on his enemy. When Dantanian's body crashed to the ground, both swords were immediately pointed to his chest. "Tell Raven to let them go before I have your head," Michael roared.

"You might want to think about that," Dantanian snickered, still flat on his back. "Raven has no idea."

With his sword held steady, Michael turned to Raven, who stood there watching the whole time, not helping one or the other. "I don't know where they are," she stated.

Michael flashed his eyes back to Dantanian and pierced the sword even more.

Dantanian flashed a wicked grin. "Okay...I'll take you to them. If you insist."

CHAPTER 27

Following Dantanian, Michael leapt down, turned the corner, and came upon another crate, much larger than the ones he had been standing on. His heart broke when he looked inside. Vivian, Caleb, and Davin were bound with golden cuffs, their arms over their heads and their feet barely touching the ground. Their mouths were gagged so they couldn't speak, but the looks in their eyes ripped Michael's heart into shreds. Several fallen were in the cage with them, with menacing grins on their faces and swords in their hands.

"Well...here they are, but I'm afraid you can't take them. You know what the golden cuffs do, don't you?"

Michael kept quiet. Fear had taken over, and he didn't know what to do.

"Shall we remind you?" Dantanian moved closer to the cage.

"No!" Michael snapped, contemplating his next move. How were they going to escape this one? "Where did you get the golden cuffs?" Michael's voice was low, already feeling defeated. He could see Claudia and their babies in his mind.

"Oh, believe me, I've searched for those things for decades. And lo and behold, all these years Aden had a handful of them hidden safely where he used to reside. I had to find them of course...it wasn't like he kept them out in the open. But you see, he had a soft spot for you, so he would never use them on you. That was his weak spot, and his weak spot was what got him killed."

"Let them go. I'll trade you...them for me," Michael said wearily. He couldn't stand to see his friends like this. It wasn't even their fight. They were just a means to an end.

Dantanian advanced toward Davin, gesturing for Michael to enter. "This one talks too much."

When Michael got a closer view of their faces he was furious, and his eyes burned with anger. Grayish blue patches marked their faces...someone had beaten them. His fingers gripped tightly inside the palm of his hands and his body trembled with disgust. "You hit them? What are you, an animal?" Michael roared.

"Funny," Dantanian said calmly. He turned to his fellow fallen and took his dagger. "That was done to the fallen, not to me of course. We are just returning the favor. Aren't we boys?"

The group of fallen by his side cheered with grunting sounds.

"They had nothing to do with the war. Let them go," Michael demanded with a forceful tone. The two swords that had been by Michael's sides were now at Dantanian's chest, but it was too late; Dantanian's dagger was pointed at Davin's arm.

"Let me remind you what the golden cuffs can do." Dantanian ran the blade down Davin's bicep, not for long, but just enough to make him bleed and wince in pain.

Davin's eyes were wide, seemingly scared to see red liquid trickling down his arm.

"Stop!" Michael yelled. "That's enough!"

Keeping his eyes on Michael, Dantanian's tongue ran across the blade, licking the blood with one swipe. "Angel's blood sure tastes delicious. The Royal Council did a great job creating the golden cuffs. Too bad they can be used on any angels. Even alkins can bleed now. That's the beauty of them. They make you vulnerable, like humans. You see Michael, there is no deal. I have you right where I want you."

Dantanian gestured to the fallen, who were already standing behind the alkins, each with one arm resting on an alkin's shoulders while the other hand held a dagger in front of their hearts. Meanwhile, one fallen carried a golden cuff and stood behind Michael. Michael nervously looked around him, calculating all the fallens' moves.

"Either you cooperate and let me place those on you, or we drive the daggers into your friends' hearts," Dantanian said, leaning against the wall, seemingly enjoying the defeated look in Michael's eyes.

Michael thought about every option, but there were none. No way would he let his friends die so he could go home. And Dantanian had known all along how he could get to him with Raven's help. Speaking of which, Raven was nowhere in sight.

The muffled sounds of the alkins' voices forced Michael to look at them again. He knew without hearing their words that they were telling him not to do it. But there was no choice...this was the way it had to be.

When he made up his mind, he extended both of his arms outward with his head held high. Dantanian cuffed him and pulled him next to Davin to anchor him. Michael's arms were straight up, just like his friends, but since he was taller, his feet were planted on the ground.

"You know what? I'm not such a bad guy. I'll take out the gags from your friends' mouths so the four of you can say your last goodbyes." Dantanian removed the gags from Caleb, Vivian, and then Davin.

"You no good, rotten, douche bag, stinky shit that smells like babies' barf," Davin spit.

"You see what I mean?" Dantanian sneered. "This one has a mouth. You can deal with him."

Michael didn't respond. As far as he was concerned, he felt exactly the same as Davin. And it sounded a lot funnier coming out of his mouth. "What do you want? You're going to keep us here forever?" Michael hissed.

"No. I was hoping I didn't have to. Like I said before, the four of you can join me or die. It's very simple." Dantanian took a side step in front of Michael. "What say you, my brother?"

"He's not your brother!" Davin screeched.

Dantanian ignored Davin and kept his eyes rooted to Michael's. "One way or another, I'll have you by my side. Now that you have the golden cuffs on, I can brain wash you to do what I want. You know that, don't you? So, you do it the easy way or the hard way. Let me know. You have a couple of days to decide." He turned to the fallen. "Keep an eye on them. I'll be back soon. I think I need to search for a beautiful young lady named Claudia. What belongs to Michael belongs to me."

Michael darted his eyes to him with hatred. He knew Claudia was safe. Dantanian would never find her. Unless....

Dantanian swung around after taking several steps. "Oh...by the way...." He punched Michael in the gut. "That was for...what did you say before you kicked me in my face? Smell my feet?"

The pain rippled from his stomach to the rest of his body. His body curled inward, trying to sooth the hurt. It really sucked to be able to feel human pain. When Dantanian was gone, he left his sinister laughter trailing behind him.

Michael turned to his friends. "I'm so sorry. I didn't mean to get you in the middle of this."

"It's not your fault, Michael," Vivian said softly, her words sounding hoarse. When she peered up to him, she produced soft whimpering sounds.

Michael closed his eyes tightly, taking in Vivian's pain. "Vivian," Michael gulped a string of tears down his throat. He couldn't cry in front of them. They needed him to be strong, to be their leader, as he always had been. But seeing them like this...there were no words to describe it. "Are you okay? I mean, I know you are very bruised. I can see it on your faces. Did he do anything else to you?"

Drops of tears fell from Vivian's eyes. "He tried, but I'm a pretty good fighter. I gave him several good punches, especially right where it hurt him the most." Her words were slow, seemingly needing to use great effort to speak.

"That's a good girl," Michael said. "How about you, Caleb?"

"I feel sore all over." Caleb groaned. "I think...he may have broken my ribs. Our arms have been tied up for so long, I can't feel them."

"I'm so sorry," Michael said wearily, shaking his head. The guilt was hitting him really hard. "He gave you bruises, didn't he? What information was he trying to get out of you?"

Silence...silence...silence.

"It's okay. Please tell me," Michael continued.

"He wanted to know where you lived," Vivian replied softly. "He wanted to know who Claudia was. I guess there were rumors about her. When they go hiding, they really go hiding, don't they?"

"I guess. All I know is that they stay clear of demons created by Aliah," Michael replied. "So...he tried to get information by hitting you because you wouldn't talk."

Silence.

Michael sighed heavily. No answer from Vivian was a confirmed yes. He knew she knew how guilty he would feel, but it didn't matter; guilt already consumed his heart and soul to the point it was draining him. Then there was a pause...a long pause. Michael cleared his throat. "Davin."

"Yes...Michael." His tone was hardly audible.

"It's good to see you, my friend. It's good to see you too...Vivian...Caleb. I thought...well...I didn't know if...." Another pause. "If I would ever see you guys again." There was a quiver in his tone.

"I knew you would come for us, but at the same time I was hoping you wouldn't," Vivian sighed.

"I feel the same, Michael," Caleb said.

There was dead silence again as Davin said nothing. Michael heard small sobs and saw teardrops fall to the ground, creating a small pool of water. It was strange to see Davin cry. He had never seen him shed a tear...ever...at least not in front of him. Even when he had thought Claudia was dead, he'd never displayed his emotions around Michael.

"We were really...scared. I didn't think...I would ever see you again." Davin managed to speak as his words trembled out of his mouth. "I especially didn't want to see you here...like this. Why did you come? I mean...we would rather see you live your life with Claudia. And you're a father now. Our deaths would be for a good reason. And now you're...." Davin sniffed and shifted his suddenly twinkling eyes to Michael. "Claudia. She could get us out of here. She is the only other person that could." His tone was hopeful.

Michael exhaled a heavy, disappointed sigh. "I'm afraid she can't. Her body thinks it's human again. It started when she became pregnant. It hasn't come back yet. I didn't tell you guys because it really wasn't relevant...but...." He sighed again.

"Oh...." Davin sounded shocked.

"Then...there is no...hope," Caleb mumbled.

"I thought we would live...forever...together," Vivian whispered. "Claudia...."

It didn't matter what he said or how he explained it, the outcome was the same...Claudia couldn't be their hero. But he would rather know that his family was safe. It was all that mattered to him. As the images of their faces danced in his mind, he only thought about the happy times. There had to be a way out. He just needed time to think. Two days was surely enough time.

"Don't give up hope," Michael said. "Let's put our minds together and think."

"We can't do anything unless these things come off us." Davin yanked hard, producing a loud clunking sound from the metal. Then he grunted. "That stinking hurt. I really feel bad for the humans."

"Quiet down there!" a fallen yelled, banging his sword loudly as if it would startle them.

"Come here and make me, you worthless burger," Davin bellowed.

"Don't, Davin," Vivian pleaded. "He'll inflict more pain."

Sure enough, one fallen stood in front of Davin, giving him a challenging stare. "What did you say?"

Davin stared back. With a steady, cool tone, he said, "I said... kiss...my...butt."

The fallen's eyes grew wide, pressing his face into Davin's.

"Instead of staring at my beautiful face, why don't you take the cuffs off me and let's fight like real angels? I may even let you take the first swing," Davin dared.

The fallen looked up, seemingly thinking about Davin's proposal. "You think I'm stupid?" He turned and unexpectedly rammed his fist into Michael's gut.

With the loud groaning sound from Michael, trying to put the pain aside, he glared intently and kicked the fallen in his chest, but the fallen only stumbled a few steps. The fallen started to laugh, seemingly amused how someone so powerful as Michael could do no harm to him. "You're all lucky I'm supposed to keep you alive," he spat and retreated, keeping his eyes on them.

"What's your name?" Michael gritted through his teeth in anger.

"It's Keith. And don't you forget it," he gloated with his head held high.

"When this is over, I'm going to personally thank you for giving me the anger to tear your sorry little wings off your body," Michael sneered. His tone sounded more evil than Dantanian's. "Or...you can let us go, and I'll make sure we keep you alive...Keith."

Keith shivered from Michael's words at first, but then he started to laugh...a wimpy laugh. Then he jumped back up to the others.

Michael turned to Davin. "Please...don't talk. I really missed you, but let's not ruin it."

"Sorry, I'll keep my mouth shut." Davin let out a small weak chuckle, seeming to enjoy the humor between them even in their worst possible situation. "But one question."

"What?"

"You really told Dantanian to smell your feet?"

"I guess I missed you so much that I thought of what you might've said if you were in my situation."

Davin's shed another tear. "You're the bomb, Michael. That was awesome. You're sounding just like me."

"I don't know if I should be proud of that."

Davin let out a small soft chuckle again. "Hey, Michael."

"I told you not to talk anymore. I need to think."

"Okay...but...I missed you...more."

Those words tugged so deeply at Michael's heart that it hurt, but it was a different kind of hurt. It was the kind that told him how much his friends meant to him, and how much he missed his family.

It was getting dark. The sun had gone home for the day. It meant another day without his precious family, another day Claudia would worry.

Under normal circumstances, they wouldn't be able to feel the cold fall breeze, but they did tonight, for their bodies were more like humans than angels. As Michael's body trembled from the cold, he tried to block the awful feeling that stung through his whole body. This only confirmed that he never wanted to be a human again, even though he'd wanted to be many times before he met the love of his existence.

In the huge warehouse, inside the big crate, inside a metal cage, four lights glowed in the darkness. The light that held them captive gave no warmth, no hope...only dread, death, and darkness. Michael began to realize there was nothing he could do. He would never see his family again. In the darkness he could let his guard down. He could privately shed tears as he thought about his family and the friends who would have to die alongside him because of his past. As his tears fell to the ground, he closed his eyes to float away to his happy place, in the arms of his beloved.

CHAPTER 28

I T WAS NIGHTTIME. CLAUDIA WAS sure of it, even though light shone upon Halo City. But then again, there was always light there; there was no sun, and no sense of time. The twins sleeping was the only indication it was nighttime.

Michael should have been back by now, and having heard no word from him filled Claudia's body with desperate anxiety. Pacing back and forth in Michael's room, her blood pressure escalated with every moment he didn't return. Where could he be? He'd promised he would return instead of taking them on his own, but would he? No...she trusted his promise; he wouldn't do anything to affect this family. She was absolute sure of it.

Trying to calm her nerves, she sat on the bed and watched the twins sleep for the night. Gazing at them caused a reaction in her breasts, and she could feel liquid leaking out of them. Her breasts were hard as rocks since she'd stopped breastfeeding. It had only been a day, but she missed the bond between them during feeding time.

Though she knew she should wait for Michael at the Crossroads, she wanted to talk to Holly to get more details. Knowing Katherine would stop by soon, she thought about asking her to take her to Holly or to have Holly come to her. As these thoughts circulated in her mind, a soft knock broke her thoughts.

Expecting Agnes or Margaret, Claudia stood up. "Come in."

The door cracked opened and Austin walked in. "Hello, Mommy." He gave a warm "I miss you" kind of a smile.

"Austin?" Claudia was unexpectedly surprised. She was so stunned she didn't know if she should give him a hug or just a smile, but whatever she intended to do, it didn't matter. Austin swooped in and embraced her tightly, longer than usual, and let go.

"You look great for someone who recently gave birth...but then again, you always look great," he grinned.

Claudia blushed. "Thanks. What brings you here?"

"I heard you were in town so I stopped by to see you." He shifted his eyes to the bed. "And...and...them." He stared at the twins with no apparent emotions.

Claudia pointed. "This is Zachary and this is Lucia." Claudia looked at Austin from her peripheral vision. He had a peaceful, impassive expression.

"They're sleeping. They look like angels," he said softly, looking as if he was in a trance. "I see what Holly has been saying."

Was this when she should say "thank you," or should she just smile? It didn't matter...she was glad he was there. She could talk to him instead of Holly. "Austin, do you know what's going on?"

Austin broke away and turned to Claudia. "I do, but there is nothing I can do about it. It's a group decision, and I can't just do what I want. I have to follow the rules. I'm bound by their trust, bound by the laws that have kept the Twelve together since long before I was born."

"Since when do you play by anyone else's rules beside your own?" Claudia snapped.

Ignoring Claudia's question, Austin looked around and seemed to realize he was in Michael's room for the first time. He saw many things that were too personal, and suddenly the large room became way too small. "Since...I became what you wanted me to be."

"That's not fair."

Austin looked at her. "You know what else is not fair?" He didn't give her a chance to answer. "It's destiny, and your grandmother had a hand in shaping it."

"What?" Claudia blinked in surprise. "What are you talking about?"

"Nothing."

Claudia poked Austin on the chest with anger in her eyes. "You don't get to say that word...you hear me? So...spit it out."

Austin sighed heavily as he stared into space, looking deep in thought. "Your grandmother took you away from me. You don't remember, but you and I used to hang out when we were young." His eyes glowed with the memories of the past. "You let me hold your hand. You even let me kiss you, and you enjoyed it." His eyes drank her in. "We had a connection, but your grandmother stopped it all." Then his eyes became soft. "I understand why she did it. I really do, but it just doesn't seem—"

"I know Austin. I remember everything."

He tilted his head and his eyes grew wider with bewilderment. "What?"

"When I died and got my memories back...well...I didn't get my memories back because I died, I got them back because I gave my memories to Aliah, and then he gave them back to me when he died."

"Okay...okay...I get the point."

Claudia lifted an eyebrow at him. "Rudeness won't get your answer any faster." She crossed her arms.

He held his hand up as if to surrender. "Okay...I'm sorry."

"Anyway...I remember us...when we were kids."

Austin's eyes lit up again.

"I remember how sweet you were. I remember how Katherine, Gamma, you, and I spent our days at Nubilus City. And I remember how you would steal kisses," she blushed. "But we were kids Austin. We went our separate ways because that was how it was supposed to be. Life happened. We grow, we hurt, we love, we change, we make mistakes, and we learn from them. But it doesn't matter Austin...I love Michael."

"I...know." Austin raked his hair back. "I just needed to blame this on...someone. I guess I was holding onto the past. When Gamma took you away from me and she wouldn't let me in your life, I was...I felt...pain. It took me awhile to get over it...over you. Then, as luck would have it, I ran into you again and I fell in...anyway...you know the rest."

Claudia's eyes became somber. "I'm sorry, but I'm glad we got this out of the way. Maybe we can be friends now. But right now I need to go find Michael. He promised to be back, but he's not. Something is wrong. I'm going to ask Agnes to watch the twins while I go search."

Claudia grabbed a red sweater that was on the bed and shoved her arms into the sleeves. Before she could reach the door, Austin swung her around. "Where do you think you're going? Are you nuts? Holly told me you didn't have your powers back. You are a human in every way. Do you realize that?"

Looking at Austin's hand on her arm, she yanked it away. "I know, but no one else is helping and I'm not going to beg. I need to find my husband. I know he's in trouble. I feel it in my gut."

"Husband?" Austin backed away, looking flabbergasted.

And there again was that hurt look on his face. Claudia looked away, unable to look him in the eyes. After a long pause that filled the room with utter silence, Austin spoke again.

"Give him another day or two. Did he tell you how long he would be gone?"

Claudia looked back with a blank expression. She thought about what Austin said. He was right. Michael hadn't said he would be back the same day. In fact, he hadn't given her any timeframe, so what was she supposed to do? But something was wrong, and that desperate feeling was slowly getting stronger, taking over her mind.

"Anyway, until you get your powers back, you can't go anyway. I'll lock you up if I have to," Austin said sternly, gripping her arm again.

"You can't stop me," Claudia gritted through her teeth in annoyance. There was no way anyone would stop her from looking for Michael and her alkin friends. They needed her...she could feel it to the depths of her soul. And she definitely didn't like the threat Austin held over her, though she knew he meant well.

"I mean it, Claudia. Think of the little ones. They need their mother." He gestured to them with his head.

"Let go, Austin. I don't need you to tell me what they need. I'm not going to do something stupid."

He squeezed her arm. "No...not until you promise me."

There were no thoughts of anger, just pure irritation, but that was enough. She reclaimed her arm with a forceful yank. Something inside Claudia sparked when Austin moved in to capture her again. Extending her hand outward, ready for him, her hand landed on his chest. A dim light glowed and Austin flew back, not far, but just enough.

Stunned, Claudia froze in place. Her eyes set on Austin, who was spread out on the floor, then her eyes shifted to her dim glowing hand. A satisfied grin marked her face. How she had missed her powers. "Welcome back," she muttered under her breath. Then she reached for Austin and offered him her hand. "I'm so sorry. Are you okay?"

"Don't touch me," he said lightly, standing up. "I guess you're getting your light back. I know where you're headed. Don't do anything stupid. Unless the fallen start a full blown war, I can't say the Twelve will help."

"I don't need their help," Claudia huffed, but she understood. She understood the politics that she would never follow or agree with as long as she lived. A life was a life. To her, they were her family, they were her everything, and there was nothing she wouldn't do to get them back.

CHAPTER 29

"TIME'S UP." DANTANIAN CLAPPED HIS hands loudly to get their attention.

Michael snapped his head up from the sound that startled him. Had two days gone by? Thinking of Claudia and the twins, his eyes were closed so he could imagine they were with him. It was the only way he could comfort himself from the treacherous cold. His body was sore and his arms, still tied up, felt utterly numb. The golden cuffs were draining him, making him weaker by the day. He could feel only half the strength he'd had coming in. If he felt this bad, he wondered how his friends had held up for this long.

Davin growled. "Go away. We've got another day. You said three, not two."

Dantanian sauntered toward him and stopped when his chest touched his. "I know what I said. One day early doesn't matter, 'cause you're going to die if Michael doesn't cooperate."

"Get your body off me. I'm not your type." Davin spit on his face and rammed his chest on his, but bounced back when Dantanian remained in place.

"You fail to remember, your body is now in human form," Dantanian roared, giving Davin a good punch in the face.

Red liquid squirted out of Davin's mouth when his head shot to the left. "Is that all you got, fart face?"

"Stop it, Davin," Vivian said weakly.

The sounds of Dantanian's steps echoed dangerously inside the crate as he paced toward Vivian. Peering down on her, he raked his eyes on her from head to toe, then wrapped his arms around her waist. "I almost forgot about this one. You don't look as attractive with the bruises on your face, but it won't stop me from doing what I'm thinking of doing to you. Being tied up can be a lot of fun," he snickered, running his hand along the curves of her body.

"Don't touch her," Michael said in a commanding tone.

Dantanian was in Michael's face in less then one second, glowing in triumph. "Your time is up. What's it going to be?" When Michael didn't respond, Dantanian spoke again. "Let me give you an incentive. If you give yourself to me, I'll let your friends live, but they will remain here until the war is over to ensure you won't turn your back on me. So what say you, Michael?"

Michael didn't say a word. He pierced his eyes to Dantanian with so much hatred that his face blazed with heat. The golden cuffs rattled, making rapid metal upon metal sounds, shaking the whole cage, matching his anger, matching the rhythm of his body shaking.

Dantanian's face beamed mischievously and his eyes were darker than death. His tone was harsh and evil. "So be it. I'm going to make you remember how ruthless you once were. I'm going to bring that Michael back. And I'm going to enjoy giving you pain beyond anything you've imagined."

Before Michael had a chance to utter a word, Dantanian placed both of his hands over Michael's head. Within an instant, Michael jolted upright, his eyes shot open, and his body shook uncontrollably as if he had been electrocuted.

"Stop...stop...stop!" Vivian screamed, drawing out all the energy she had left.

Davin and Caleb yanked the golden cuffs, trying to release themselves even knowing there was nothing they could do.

Dantanian stopped. "With pain comes gain."

Michael would have collapsed to the hard floor if not for the restraints holding him in place. Feeling the weight of his heavy body, he thought his arms would detach from the sockets. His face was pale and his whole body throbbed with excruciating raw pain. But no scream escaped from his throat. He would not give Dantanian the satisfaction, and he would not show any emotions. Not wanting to remember and unwilling to be that angel from the past, he would fight him with everything he had left.

Dantanian did it again...again...again. "Don't fight me. You're only making it harder for yourself. Let me enter. Let...me...in."

Michael could do nothing now, especially when his body was more like a human's under the influence of the golden cuffs. No matter how hard he tried to fight Dantanian, he could only take so much. He didn't give up, but his body did.

When the sound of Dantanian's voice stopped, he sluggishly looked up and saw three overlapping images of Dantanian. Though Dantanian's lips were moving, blurring in and out, the sounds coming out of his mouth were muted. The world around Michael stopped. When blinking to clear his vision did not work, he closed his eyes to the darkness, and slipped into a world where he had once lived.

"AHHH...MY SONS HAVE COME back," Aden said joyfully, opening his arms.

In accord, Michael and Dantanian dropped to their knees and bowed.

"Stand up my sons, and tell me about your adventure. Have you found more fallen to join our side?"

They both stood, side by side, looking proud of what they'd accomplished.

"Michael and I have been keeping count of how many we have each killed or pulled to our side."

"And how is his score?" Aden asked.

"Almost as good as mine." Dantanian playful socked Michael on the arm.

Michael pulled Dantanian into a choke hold and ruffled his hair. "You mean...better."

Dantanian back kicked, swiped Michael's leg, and tried to flip him over, but Michael was stronger and faster. Instead, Michael pinned him to the floor.

Dantanian let out a small chuckle, feeling winded by Michael's strength. "Whoo...easy there brother."

Michael extended his arm to help him up. "I learned from the best," he grinned, peering up to Aden, who was beaming with pride.

"There is still more to learn from me," Aden said. "I have not taught you everything yet...but soon."

Suddenly, Dantanian's face changed. He looked like one of the fallen. Michael chuckled. "Why not change your face into something more appealing to my eyes?"

Dantanian chuckled out loud and changed his face back to his own. "They don't call me the angel of many faces for nothing."

"NO...." MICHAEL SHOOK HIS HEAD. His vision was unsteady, shifting from clear to blurry, as Dantanian gloated wickedly in front of him.

Then his eyes fluttered as he desperately tried to keep them open, but they were too heavy. Uncontrollably, his eyelids shut and he started to drift again.

"I saw what you saw," Dantanian said victoriously. "You're starting to remember. We'll start again in the morning. Sweet dreams, brother."

CHAPTER 30

"Claudia," Michael muttered under his breath.

Standing in the mist of clouds, she appeared in a long white flowing dress that clung to her body from the warm breeze. He could smell her scent in the wind, filling his heart with love and peace. As he watched her from afar, he waited patiently as she came for him.

She was breathtakingly beautiful as she glided toward him, smiling, whispering his name. How he had missed her, that face, that smile. Ready to embrace her, he stretched his arms open and enclosed her in them, only to find his arms wrapped around himself instead. Letting out a long gasp from the brush of her warmth, he knew it was her, but why couldn't he hold her? Like a spirit, she had passed right through him. What had happened? She was right there...he'd seen her with his own eyes.

It was a joke, a sick joke, but wait...was he dreaming? He turned to search for her. When he found her, he could see her looking all around, but not at him. "Michael, where are you?"

"Claudia!" he called. He decided that if she couldn't find him then he would go to her, but he couldn't move. His feet seemed glued to where he stood. Tugging, shaking, and jerking didn't help either. What was happening to him? How was this possible? "Claudia, I'm here!" No matter how loud he called for her, he was not in her line of vision.

Claudia continued to frantically search for him, but she could not find him. "Michael, where are you?" she asked again. "Where are Davin, Caleb, and Vivian?"

With those words, Michael started to regain his senses, and realized it was definitely a dream. But alkins didn't dream. They couldn't, unless their body was in human form. As he started to remember where he was, he whispered, "I'm in a small town." Not knowing why he had said those words since it was just a dream, he panicked when Claudia started to disappear.

"No," he managed to breathe softly out of his mouth. Feeling a sharp sting whip across his face, he woke up to see Dantanian's face in his.

"Having a nightmare, Michael?" he snickered.

"I owe you a slap in the face and everything else you did to us," Michael said softly with anger in his eyes. With the loss of energy, he had no strength to speak as harshly as he'd wanted to. Not knowing how long he had been under Dantanian's spell, he turned to Davin to his left, and Vivian and Caleb to his right. They looked just as bad as he felt. Their breathing was heavy as their chests rose and fell with effort. They were slowly dying, and he didn't know what to do.

"You won't be saying that soon," Dantanian hissed, staring down on him. "I'm running out of patience. Since you won't tell me where Claudia is, I'm just going to speed this along." Then he placed his hand on Michael's head again.

"Kneel down before me," Dantanian demanded, pointing his sword at his chest.

The young boy trembled in fear. "Please...I swear I didn't—"

"Shut up!" Dantanian glared at him. "You dare to insult my intelligence?"

The boy shook his head vigorously. "No, no, no...I would ne—"

The boy never saw it coming. Upon hearing the key word "intelligence," Michael followed Dantanian's order. With one smooth slice across the boy's neck from Michael's sword, he was decapitated. The eyes of the crowd followed the head, which tumbled several feet.

"Who is next?" Dantanian bellowed. "Join us or die!"

"We'll never join you!" one cried out.

"We'd rather die!" shouted another.

"So be it," Dantanian said slyly, glaring victoriously at Michael. "The one who kills the most wins."

"You're on." Michael accepted the challenge as if killing was a sport with no regard for life. With a flash of his massive wings, he twirled them like an airplane propeller. Made strong like steel, he used his wings and sword to kill quickly and precisely with one strike so he could win the bet.

Dantanian was just as deadly, but he could not match Michael's skill, which was the reason why Aden favored Michael...but it didn't matter. Together they were better, more deadly, and more fearsome than any other evil beings that existed.

When there was no one left to kill, Michael swept his eyes over the vast markings of black ashes on the ground. There was no doubt about it. Clearly he had killed more than Dantanian. Standing tall with his arms crossed, he held an arrogant stance. "What do I win?"

"Dang, Michael," Dantanian squealed happily. "You just keep getting better. You're like an angel with a shot gun."

"I have a purpose."

"And what is that purpose?"

"The same purpose we all share. To get our freedom so we can live among the humans."

"Ahhh...a good purpose. Come on, my brother." Dantanian draped his arm around Michael's shoulders. "Let's go celebrate."

MICHAEL INHALED A DEEP GASP as if he had just come up for air after being under water too long. Guilt was written all over his face. Though he had always recalled killing the innocents, he hadn't remembered how cold he was. He had truly been an evil being, and though he had learned to forgive himself with Claudia's love, it was all crashing back again, tearing his heart apart, piece by piece.

"Oh...how I wish your friends could see what you once were," Dantanian said. "They would really get a kick out of that." He leaned closer. "Do you think they would feel the same about the almighty Michael knowing what I know? I think not. But then again, you did grow a conscience. That's what got you in trouble in the first place."

"Having a conscience is what defines us...the difference between nephilim and fallen angels," Michael gritted through his teeth.

"You're wrong. I do have one. Just not that kind you wish I had." Dantanian turned to Michael's friends and paced from one to another. "They look so damaged, tortured...almost dead."

Then without looking back, he started to proceed out of the crate. With a sudden turn, he looked at Michael. "By the way...

Raven has been searching for Claudia. I'm sure I'll get a chance to meet her soon. I'll be back for more enjoyable sessions."

DANTANIAN STOOD OVER MICHAEL, KNOWING he was in a state of slumber. *Perhaps he is dreaming again*, Dantanian thought. Tilting his head to the side, he watched Michael's body twitch as he spoke a few words out loud. Getting Michael to remember was a huge gain, and as soon as he regained all his memory, he would again become the dark angel he once was. "Ready for some more fun? I'm baaack."

MICHAEL AND HIS FRIENDS GATHERED near the mountain to strategize for their next attack. Holding a long branch and bent down on his knees, he made a big circle on the bald spot where the grass was dead. He used the letter "X" to represent themselves, and the letter "O" to represent their enemies. They'd already won many battles using similar strategies, so this was a quick refresher meeting. Seeing admiration and adoration in their eyes as he spoke, he smiled inwardly knowing how much they respected him as a leader.

When approaching sounds of footsteps echoed nearby, he glanced past the trees. Seeing Aden, Dantanian, and a few others he didn't recognize, he stood up to greet them and gestured his men to do the same.

"I see you are preparing for the next attack," Aden said proudly, clasping his hands in front of him and gazing at the faces among the crowd.

"We are waiting on your location, Aden," Michael said, breaking his observation.

"Good." Then Aden turned to those behind him. "Let me introduce... Berneal, Trinity, Raven, and Rachel."

Michael nodded to Berneal to greet him. Gloating, he could feel the ladies' burning desire when they looked at him, but it didn't faze him. He was used to it.

"They will be joining you on your next mission," Aden continued. "We are headed to a small town called Mellow Creek. I was told a group of fallen are hiding in that town among the humans. Show them no mercy and kill everyone there. The news will travel quickly afterward and no one will aid any of those who escape our group."

"We don't touch the humans," Michael directed to his group.

"Kill them all," Aden retorted.

"Surely you don't mean the women and children."

"The fallen have already broken the rules. They are not to mingle with the humans. Do I need to be more specific? Kill them all. Is there something wrong with what I'm asking you to do, Michael?" Aden took several challenging steps toward him.

"Why don't I lead the group, Aden?" Dantanian suggested.

"No. I'll carry the order," Michael said, but there was an uncertainty in his tone.

CHAPTER 31

CLAUDIA AND HOLLY SPLIT UP the search. Though it wasn't safe to do so, it was the fastest way. Claudia searched high and low and all through the towns Holly mentioned, but still there was no sign of the alkins. Just as she was about to leave the last town, she sensed a presence. Though her powers were not fully restored, sensing a presence was one power that had never left her.

Hearing the quick flapping of wings, she moved to the sound, but she wasn't fast enough to find the source. As swiftly as she could, she whipped around, but ended up going around in circles until she'd had enough. Whoever it was, he or she was toying with her.

"Stop it!" Claudia yelled.

The noise stopped. It was silent...so quiet that she could hear every sound around her: the creaking of the broken door, the banging of metals, and the debris on the street rolling like tumbleweeds carried away down the street by the hard breeze. Being in the shelters at the Crossroads, she had forgotten how cold it was. But it wasn't as bad as the last time when she was with

Michael at the picnic site. This was one indication her powers were slowly returning. Nonetheless, she was shivering from the cold.

Her red sweater wasn't enough to keep her warm. Not only that, the cold nipped her nostrils and stung down to the tips of her toes. As she hugged herself for warmth, she waited to see what would appear in front of her. But when her butterfly necklace shook and turned black, she was certain she would be facing a fallen.

Then out of the shadows appeared a woman. Her spread out dark wings gave Claudia chills down her spine. Was it from the sudden cold breeze that struck her again, or was it from the mysterious fallen in front of her? Under normal circumstances she would have had nothing to fear, but her powers hadn't returned completely. Her mind eased when she recognized the woman from the party.

"What do you want?" Claudia asked. Pressing her fingers inside the palms of her hands, she was preparing herself to will her bow if needed.

"Something you want."

"We don't want the same thing. How could someone like you want the—?"

"It's Michael."

"Is he okay?" Claudia's body started to shudder. Her vision was temporarily blinded by the sudden tears in her eyes, and her lips quivered as she swallowed a frightful hard lump down her throat, afraid to hear the answer.

"Yes."

The tremble went away only to be replaced by anxiety. "Do you know where he is?"

"Yes, but before I tell you, you must hear me out."

"Why should I listen to you?" Claudia spat. "You are a fallen." She looked at her wings again.

"Because I know where he is and you don't."

"Okay...." She sighed. "I'll listen."

"When I take you to him, he may not be the Michael you knew and loved. Dantanian is making him remember his past, the past that was erased from his mind by one of the Twelve. It shouldn't affect him, but Dantanian is also brain washing him, making him think he is that fallen angel."

Claudia couldn't believe what she was hearing. How was this possible? Should she have stopped him from going? But they had no choice. His friends were missing. "Are his friends with him?"

"Yes...but I'm afraid they may already be...dead."

Hearing this terrible news, her heart dropped and she lost her breath. This wasn't possible. "What do you mean?"

"They were bound by golden cuffs. Angels can't be held by them for too long. Their bodies turn into human form so they can feel every pain in their nerves, bones, and muscles. And they are unable to heal. Knowing you would be searching for them, Dantanian asked me to find you and bring you to him."

"So you're really standing before me to take me as hostage and not to save Michael?"

"Both, I'm afraid. You have one advantage over Dantanian, because he doesn't know who you really are...meaning the extent of your powers. You see...we are able to roam the Earth, but we are not allowed to have human contact. When Aden died, we went into hiding. We remained hidden when Aliah was free. Because of our deal with the Twelve, we were also Aliah's enemies ...meaning Aliah's demons would have killed us on sight. Despite what we have done in the past, because we are fallen we will never have salvation. We can't ask for forgiveness. I'm only trying to protect the ones I care about just as you are. We are no different."

"You're wrong!" Claudia bellowed in anger, but she understood. In a way, they were the same, at least in this situation. There wasn't anything Claudia wouldn't do to save her loved ones.

"I'm sorry you feel that way, but I had no choice. I don't expect you to understand. But before I take you to them, you must promise me one thing."

"What?"

"When Dantanian heard of you, he had the fallen search for any information they could find about you. What type of powers you had, what your weakness were."

"What did they find?"

"Not much, but from what little information they could gather, you have no powers. Is this true?"

"And how did they come up with this conclusion?"

"You would have saved your friends already."

Claudia could feel her muscles tightening and guilt consuming her, causing her to feel weaker. Had she had her powers, she would've already helped them, and perhaps none of this would've gone this far. It didn't matter. She had to stop thinking of "what ifs." At this point, she just had to get to them even if she didn't have her powers back. She had enough powers...some...a little...maybe... not enough. She gave a heavy sigh.

Raven enclosed her wings to disappear. "You can't save Michael, can you?" Her tone became soft and worried.

Claudia didn't respond. She didn't want to hear anything negative, nor did she want to tell her how her body was changing. It was none of her business, and it certainly didn't concern her. She wasn't going to have a one on one discussion with her as if she was a good friend.

"Before I take you, you need to promise me one thing," Raven asked politely.

"What do you want me to promise you?"

"If by some miracle you get Michael out of the golden cuffs, he'll need to recover. I can help you. All I ask in return is that you leave us out of this war. My group of friends and I are not to be hunted. I may have aided Dantanian, but I had no choice. He would have slaughtered everyone I loved. Certainly you can understand that. I want amnesty. I want you to promise me this."

Having no choice and not knowing if her words were good enough to hold a deal such as this, she had to do it. And though her mind told her to get help, her heart told her otherwise. She was running out of time, and at this point, knowing what she knew, every second counted. The longer she waited, the possibility of them being dead was greater. "Okay. I promise."

CHAPTER 32

"MICHAEL? VIVIAN? CALEB?" DAVIN WHISPERED, opening his eyes, wondering how long he had been unconscious. His voice was hoarse, hardly audible, and his body felt disjointed and numb. Exhausting almost all of his energy, it was extremely difficult to even breathe a word out of his mouth.

"I'm here," Michael said feebly.

"I'm here," Vivian sniffed.

"I'm still holding on," Caleb whispered.

From the corner of Davin's eyes, he could see his friends slumped over like rag dolls, and his heart ached for them.

Unable to remember what he had said before or how many times he'd said it, he didn't care. Even if his words would be the last he breathed, the last energy he could manage to summon from his mouth, he had to say it. "I love you guys...for eternity. You'll always be in my heart." His lips quivered as tears fell from his eyes, and each word spoken cut painfully though his heart.

"Don't talk...like that," Vivian started to sob, but she had no tears left. She had let them all out watching Michael go through the horrid sessions with Dantanian.

"Don't forget our good times together...all our laughter...what we've been through," Davin continued.

Sorrowful sighs echoed after a pause.

"I never thanked you, Davin." Michael slowly twisted his head to face him.

"There are many things you should thank me for," Davin answered with a weak chuckle.

"That's true, but I want to thank you for being there for me when I first settled in Halo City. You helped me figure things out. You were a huge thorn in my side, but you steered me to the right path."

Davin choked back tears. "That's what friends are for."

"Davin, Caleb, and Vivian...you are the truest friends. I don't know what I would've done without you three."

"From what we've been through together, we are the truest definition of friendship," Davin continued. "And I've also always wanted a motto...you know, like what the three musketeers say...all for one and one for all. I've been thinking about this. How about... together as one?"

"Sounds great," Michael agreed.

"That sounds perfect, Davin," Vivian said somberly.

"I agree," Caleb said wearily.

Davin could hear the sadness in their tones, though they tried to sound cheerful. After a long pause, Michael spoke. "Promise me something."

"Anything," everyone said in accord.

"If I turn...if I'm lost to the darkness...." Michael paused. "You'll have to do everything in your power to stop me, even if it means my death. Do you understand?"

Vivian's tone was desperate. "No, Michael. You have to fight it. Claudia is coming. I can feel it. You have to hold on. It can't end this way."

"Promise me," Michael continued. "I don't know what I will become."

Suddenly, Davin's energy burst just enough to let anger take over as his whole body shook. "I'm going to kill Dantanian!" His words sheared like a sharp razor cut. Then his tone became soft and tender again. "If your soul is dirty and worn, we will cleanse you. If you are too blind to see the light, we will be your eyes. If the sea of evil darkness swallows you up, we will anchor you and won't let you go. We'll fight for you till the very end, till all of our strength and will are spent. Even if we have to fight till our dying breath, we'll never let you go. We're not going to kill you, Michael. How could we?"

"Just hold on and don't let go," Caleb begged.

Michael exhaled lightly and paused. Tears streamed down his face as he listened with a broken heart. "You say that now, but when I plunge my sword to any one of you, you will change your mind. It's okay. I might not remember you. I don't know what will happen. All I know is that I'm starting to remember my past." Michael let out a sorrowful sigh. "Make sure to give...." The space that held his heart was empty. He was beyond agony and he was at the point of losing control of his emotions he'd learned to hide so well. "Tell Claudia, Zachary, and Lucia how much I love them, and that I fought hard to get to them...that I'll always be with them no matter where I go. Promise me that you'll always watch over them." *And even after death, I'll still love you then.*

"You know we always will, but don't talk like that," Caleb said slowly.

"Well...well...well." Dantanian entered, breaking the conversation. "Isn't this cozy and nice? Too bad it won't last long. Time to play, Michael."

Davin could see Michael wither at the sound of Dantanian's voice. This wasn't good at all. He could tell Michael was afraid, and Michael was never afraid. From what he could tell, Dantanian had a hold on him, and whatever he was doing to him was working.

Without a fight this time, Michael inhaled a deep breath, closed his eyes tightly, and prayed. *All those years I was so angry, then you gave me one shot of happiness. Now you're taking it away. Why? Please...if you're not going to let me live then let my friends live. Claudia will lose the only family she's ever known since she could not have contact with her human family. You've already taken everything I could give you...my parents, my human life I can't remember...and now I give you my life. Take it from me if you must, but please don't take my friends'. I will take their places and make up for the sins of my past. Please...I beg you. Don't make my Claudia suffer because of me.*

IN MELLOW CREEK LIVED A group of fallen that had occupied that town. Michael's group had killed most of them. Kneeling on the floor with their hands behind the napes of their necks, a line of fallen awaited the verdict regarding their fates.

"So what shall we do, Michael? Do we pardon them and have them join our party, or kill them all?" Dantanian asked, pointing his sword at their chests as he made his way down the line, piercing his eyes on them with authority.

"Why not ask them to join us?" Trinity said out of the blue, standing face to face with Michael. Batting her beautiful violet eyes at him, she pleaded.

Michael had already made up his mind. He was going to kill them, but when Trinity placed her hand on his chest, he could feel his heart soften. At that moment, he changed his mind and knew he had made the right decision.

"If they want to join our team, let them," Michael said sternly and out loud, letting everyone know he was in command. "Rise," he directed to the fallen kneeling on the ground. "We will take you to our master. Follow my lead."

The new group of fallen stared in awe at Michael's massive wings when he leisurely spread them out to take flight. One by one, they opened theirs too, and all seemed to note how their wings looked puny when compared with those of their new leader.

"Wait!" Dantanian shrieked. "There are to be no survivors."

Michael froze in place and shifted his eyes to the women and children huddled at a distance. They were surrounded by his soldiers of fallen. "Let them be. They have no weapons, nor skills."

"I will take care of them," Berneal snickered, staring toward them with death written in his eyes. "They are mixed breed any way...forbidden."

"You have forgotten your order from Aden," Dantanian reminded.

"They can do no harm," Michael retorted.

"And what shall we tell Aden when you have all these witnesses in front of you? I'm only looking after you, my brother."

Having no choice and feeling the weight of their stares, Michael gave the kill command. Though his heart told him to do otherwise, Dantanian was right. Aden would be furious with him if he did not follow his orders. Would he be willing to go against him? He would not. Aden was like a father to him, and was one person he never wanted to disappoint, but something was happening to Michael. It was a feeling he could not explain, nor did he want it.

MICHAEL'S VISION WAS LIKE A dream or a movie he was watching about his past life. But it was not just observed by him. Dantanian could see everything Michael was remembering. Dantanian was able to connect to his memories, and seemed to be enjoying what he was seeing, but he could not connect to the inner emotions Michael felt, only the ones he expressed outwardly.

Session after session, Michael could feel his mind disconnecting with him. He was clearly remembering so much more than he ever wanted. The clearer and better his memories became, the less he knew of the present Michael. Whatever Dantanian was doing to him, it was working. He would soon be conquered by the darkness.

Whatever evil lived inside him was already emerging. Unknowingly, it had already crept to the surface. He could feel it, taste it, and almost wanted it. But no! He had to fight it. He had to fight for his love, his babies, and his friends. Holding onto hope was all he could do, for every thought was a struggle, every ache was torture, and every step into the darkness was a battle he could not win.

Holding tightly onto every memory of his family, which were quickly fading, was all he could do. Claudia's love for him that was deep as the sea was being overpowered by fear and evil. Soon every thought, every breath, every step he took would not be by his own free will, and his pure heart would be conquered by a dangerous, angry storm.

Feeling Claudia's presence snapped him back to reality, but then he was whipped back to the Michael that was evolving at Dantanian's hand. Against his will he was losing control of the present Michael again. Breathing heavily, his eyes became darker and colder. He could feel something evil growing inside him, growing stronger with each session. As his body became tense and rigid, he growled like a wild untamed animal.

AFTER THEIR MISSION WAS COMPLETED, Aden threw a banquet in honor of them. The celebration wasn't at a fancy restaurant or a classy building...it was held outdoors, high in the mountains where Aden's home was, away from civilization and deeply hidden.

Live music filled the air as they danced, sang, and ate delicious food. Unexpectedly Aden stood up on a boulder holding a wine glass in his hand, looking proudly at his followers. "Soon, my sons and daughters, we will take over Crossroads and you can enjoy this every day."

As loud cheers rang, Aden held up his hand and gestured everyone to quiet down. "Our army has grown tremendously because of your loyalty and your faith in me, and for the cause we all share. Here is to Michael and Dantanian. Without the both of them, we wouldn't have come this far." Aden raised his glass to the sky. "To victory."

"To victory," the crowd cheered, pointing their glasses of wine toward Michael and Dantanian standing just below Aden.

After the cheering, the music continued and everyone dispersed into small groups. Gliding down from the boulder, Aden placed his arms around Dantanian and Michael. "My two sons. When this is over, you two will be sitting beside me, and everyone will bow down to us."

"Aden, I didn't mean to speak of this during our celebration, but how do we even attempt to enter Crossroads when it's nearly impossible for any fallen to go near it?" Dantanian asked.

Aden placed his hands down to his sides. "It's quite all right, Dantanian. I was going to speak of it tonight with the two of you. We are going to start a riot by attacking the humans. This will get the Twelve's attention and start a war." Aden turned to Michael, looking squarely into his eyes. "You will pretend to fight against me and I will drive my sword into you. Don't worry, my son, I won't kill you. We'll play it through just enough so that they will believe you.

You will have to ask for forgiveness, get down on your knees and beg for mercy, and do whatever it takes to have them take you back.

"Once you are in, find out who the gatekeeper is and win his or her friendship. Get the gatekeeper to open the gates to Crossroads, then we are home free. Another way is to find a being with a Holy Soul, but that is almost impossible. It's like finding a diamond in the rough. I know this is easier said than done, but I have faith in you. You have the charisma to win them over. Look at all the women gloating around you right now." Aden paused and waited for Michael to gaze upon the women looking at him as if he was their prize.

"They want a piece of you," Aden continued. "You have that kind of effect on everyone. Use that to your advantage."

"Why can't you send Dantanian?" Michael asked. "I'm sure he would love to go."

"Dantanian was one of God's first angels, making him part of the first group of fallen. No matter how much he pleaded, he would not be forgiven. His soul is already damned, just like mine. I'm not asking you if you want to do this. I'm telling you that this is the way it has to be. You're our only hope."

Michael took in his words and smiled. "I won't let you down."

"I know you won't," Aden said. "Let's not talk about this tonight. It's time to celebrate." Then he walked away, leaving Michael and Dantanian behind.

"May I have a word with you?" a female voice asked.

Michael turned to see a beautiful angel in front of him. "Trinity." When a huge grin marked Michael's face, Dantanian excused himself and paced over to Berneal and Raven.

Trinity closed the space between them and placed her hands on his chest. "You're too beautiful to be evil, you know that?"

Michael blushed with a small grin.

"Could we talk somewhere private?"

Michael didn't have a chance to respond; she was tugging at his shirt, leading him away from the party behind a tree.

"Why did you bring me here?" Michael asked, leaning his back against the tree.

Trinity paused for a moment, just staring at him, drinking him in. The glow from the moon precisely hit his profile, making him look heavenly.

"To talk," she smiled, flirting with her eyes.

"We could've talked at the party."

"I've never met anyone like you before," she continued, trailing both of her hands up to his broad shoulders. "There's so much there." She placed her hand on his heart. "You're confused, aren't you? I can tell you're battling good and evil inside you."

Michael gripped both of her hands, locked them behind her back, and pierced his eyes on hers with anger. "You're wrong. You have no idea what you're talking about."

Peering back with no fear, she retorted, "You're growing a conscience. I can see it in your eyes...I can...."

Before she could finish, afraid others would hear, Michael kissed her. When she kissed back, Michael released her hands. He felt a tug and found his body pressed on hers. It was soft and sweet, and there was a small spark, but it was enough to keep his interest.

Trying not to offend her, he pulled back slowly with his eyes open. Suddenly her face wasn't Trinity's anymore. It belonged to someone he'd never seen before. Unable to look away as if he was spellbound, his eyes were fixated on hers. She was simply beautiful, and *she* took his breath away.

This stranger made his heart race faster than it ever had before. He felt like he was flying through the clouds, as if he had taken a euphoric drug, making him feel alive. He could do nothing but stare.

"Michael," she spoke. "I'm here, my love. I'm here." Those words echoed inside his mind.

Surprised that she spoke as though she knew him, he blinked his eyes and tried to recall who she was.

But before he could put two and two together, the image of her became translucent and disappeared. He was whipped back into reality to the sound of Dantanian's voice. "That's enough. Ahhh... that must be her. How did she get into your mind? You don't need to know her."

When his vision cleared to see Dantanian standing in front of him with a huge grin, Michael smiled back. "Where have you been, my brother, the angel with many faces?"

Then Michael heard a soft heart-wrenching cry from someone next to him. "Noooo!"

CHAPTER 33

"WELCOME TO OUR TEMPORARY HOME, my lady Claudia," a male voice said politely, standing at a distance. Claudia had just stepped out of Raven's hold, anxious to see Michael and her friends, when she felt her necklace vibrate. Scanning the perimeter, she only saw the fallen who had spoken to her at first from the distance, but when her eyes moved to the top of the crates on either side of her, she saw them.

Hundreds of fallen, if not more, were staring down on her. Chills spiked her skin. She not only shivered from the sight of them, but from the freezing cold. Dismissing them, she focused her attention ahead of her, and on the reason she was there. "Take me to Michael," she demanded, walking toward him.

"Let me introduce myself, then maybe your tone will change. My name is Dantanian." He extended his arm to offer his hand to her.

Claudia gasped inwardly when she heard his name. Icy goose bumps chilled her from head to toe, but she would not show he intimidated her, nor did she take his hand in hers. Sizing him up, she caught his eyes and stared boldly into them. "I want to see Michael."

"So beautiful. I see what he sees in you." Dantanian ignored her and reached out to brush her cheek with the back of his knuckles.

His hand had barely touched her skin when she slapped it away. "Don't touch me."

Dantanian's eyes darkened with madness. Without warning, he yanked Claudia so fast she had no idea it was coming. In an instant her back was pinned to him and his arms were around her neck and waist. "Don't be rude to me," he breathed in her ear. "Soon, I'll make you mine...and I believe you won't be needing this anymore." He yanked her butterfly necklace off and placed it in his pocket.

Not only was she furious he had taken her necklace, his words and his body touching hers disgusted her. She tried to pull away, but it was no use. The little power that she had gained was no match for his. "You'll never have me. I'd rather die," she said through her gritted teeth.

"We'll see about that. Brothers share everything." Dantanian released his hold and pointed to a large crate, larger than the ones she had seen coming in. "He's in there."

"Michael," she called. An overwhelming happiness filled her as she ran to the crate. She would be reunited with her husband and her friends. What condition they were in was unknown, but it didn't matter at this point. All that mattered was that they were alive, and that somehow she could negotiate for their safety...she hoped. But when she turned the corner and set her eyes on the whole picture, she froze and her heart stopped beating.

Her heart ached from the dreadful sight. Her body shook, from not only anger, but from the raw pain of seeing them in such a state. Davin, Caleb, and Vivian looked barely alive, hanging on by threads. Their faces were black and blue. But when she moved her eyes to Michael, her face became even paler as the blood drained out of her.

"Michael," she whispered as her lips quivered. The scenario reminded her of the dreams she'd had several times, and how she wished it was just a dream now. He looked so different, as if he had been to hell and back. His eyes were blood red, portraying evil. No expression marked his face, and though he looked straight at her, he didn't smile, nor did he seem to recognize who she was.

Tears pooled in her eyes and her knees felt like they would buckle under her. "What has he done to you?" she whispered, her lips quivering even more. Then she shifted her eyes to her friends, who looked back at her with weak twinkles of hope, but soon after closed their eyes again.

"Please, release them," Claudia begged, keeping her eyes rooted on them. "I'll do anything you say."

"All I want is your powers," Dantanian requested, standing behind her. "I've heard rumors. Though I've yet to see what you can do, it doesn't matter. The rumors speak volumes."

Claudia whipped around. "I can't give you my powers. I can't just transfer them to you."

"That's not what I was told. Didn't you give Aliah your memories?" Dantanian started to pace back and forth. "Is that how you do it?"

"Yes, but that is—"

"Then you can give me your powers."

"And if I don't, what—?"

Dantanian didn't wait for her to finish. With fast motion he took her into the crate. Standing right in front of the alkins with Dantanian's hand over hers, she unwillingly held a sword.

She felt like a puppet while his hand guided hers, pointing the sword to each of her friends, one by one. "Who shall we kill first...this one...that one...or this one?"

Claudia tried to break away, but she couldn't. Somehow fear gripped her so tightly, it had completely taken hold of her and she couldn't call upon even a little bit of her light. Terrified that her power was not enough to save them, she couldn't even bring herself to release the golden cuffs like she could do so easily before.

She had to snap out of it, but seeing them in such horrendous condition and Michael looking like he had been possessed by evil, she felt alone and so afraid. Where was her courage, her strength, and her love for them?

"Who is it going to be?" he said sharply, startling her.

"I can't. I don't know how...please, I need more time...I...," she rambled desperately, unable to think, unable to reason clearly. But it didn't matter. The sword they held together drove into Caleb's stomach.

"Nooo!" She bellowed in horror, watching the sword plunge in further and slide out of him. Her piercing loud painful scream rattled the small windows above. As if bodies had burst through the glass, they exploded and the broken pieces shattered outward like rain. Not only that, her scream rattled the oversized wooden crate, pushed its sides outward, and exposed the cage completely.

Caleb's eyes were wide with shock. He gasped a long, sharp, deep breath as blood soaked his shirt that now looked like a leaking faucet, dripping on the ground. Claudia saw blood...Caleb's blood. Alkins never bled. Horrified, she was immobile at first, then something happened as she set her eyes on her friend who was dying because she wasn't strong enough or was too scared to retrieve her light. She knew he would die if she didn't do something, and knowing she was the only one who could was like a wakeup call.

Something was happening inside her. A tingly powerful sensation started from her feet and blazed upward through her body. She was in agony, and then the heartache caused another sensation...it was anger, hate, and vengeance toward Dantanian. Anger she had never felt before was blistering, growing by the second.

Her fists were tight, her body shuddered, and every inch of her burned. It happened so fast she thought she was going to explode. Feeling her powers coming back, but not sure to what intensity, she laid her eyes on the golden cuffs and sneered the only word that would release them. "Lucian!" she bellowed. Then she shot her eyes angrily at Dantanian and placed her hand on his chest. With one simple touch light glowed out of her hands and he flew across space, knocking the wind out of him.

When all four of the golden cuffs thudded on the ground, the alkins dropped to the floor. Guardedly, she rushed to their sides as the fallen surrounded them. Without the cuffs, Caleb started to heal. Davin and Vivian opened their eyes. Their chests rose and fell with more ease. But Michael was the same. Nothing had changed in him for the better.

Recalling Raven's promise, she searched for her, but she was nowhere to be found just as Claudia had suspected. Dismissing her, she pulled out her bow, walking in circles while guarding them from being attacked. The alkins needed time to heal. How much time, she didn't know, but she had to do something. It didn't matter at this point. Dantanian had staggered toward her while keeping his distance.

"Now I see what the rumors were about, but I'm afraid it's not going to be enough. Where are the venators? Where is your rescue team? They've abandoned you, haven't they? I understand how you feel. I've been treated the same before," Dantanian tried to sound sympathetic.

With her bow pointing at him, she didn't answer. Her eyes shifted from left to right, to the ceiling, over her shoulders, preventing any fallen from attacking her friends or Michael.

"Why don't you put that down? You're not winning this battle, my dear." Dantanian sounded confident, approaching her carefully with his hands in front of his chest.

"What happens if I do?" Claudia was stalling for time. But what was to come next was totally unexpected.

Dantanian fell to his knees with both of his hands high in the air in surrender. He had the most devilish grin smeared on his face. Then he said the words she had not expected to hear from his lips. "Help me, Michael."

Hearing a low growl from the cage, she turned her head to see Michael coming for her with a look to kill. "No," she breathed out of her mouth, and jumped high onto one of the crates nearby. She didn't want to leave her friends, but at the same time, she had no choice. Springing from crate to crate, she went as far back as she could go while Michael tailed behind her.

Claudia leaped down, only to find herself with nowhere to hide or flee. As she retreated, Michael paced towards her. This felt so much like her dream, but in her dream there was never a conclusion. If she could help it, she was going to make this one a happy ending. "Michael. It's me, Claudia. You can fight it. I know you're inside. Zachary and Lucia are waiting for you. Come home with me. Let's go home."

He halted for a second, shook his head, and seemed as though something she had said clicked his memories, but he kept coming for her with his sword.

With two hands in front, she showed him she held no weapon. "Surely you wouldn't hurt a woman, especially one without a weapon, right?" she asked nervously.

Michael showed no indication he was listening.

"Michael, I'm warning you. Stop!" Knowing she would hit the wall if she continued to stagger backward, she bolted a dim flash of light out of her hands at him, hoping to wake him from this trance. Sometimes he dodged the light, and a few times it knocked him sideways, but he kept coming with the sinister look in his eyes.

With her back against the wall and his body inches away from hers, she tried one last attempt to reason with him before she really gave it to him. "Michael, I'm here. I'm here, my love. I love you."

He froze from those words as if somehow they had triggered something inside him. Blinking rapidly, still looking confused, his shoulders relaxed a bit, but Claudia wasn't going to take a chance on whether he was going to snap out of it, especially when she needed to get back to her friends. Having this opportunity, she had to take it.

With both hands on either side of his head, she bolted a flash of just enough light so she wouldn't harm him, hoping it would bring back his memories, and hoping it would be enough. When Michael stumbled to the ground, she escaped and headed toward her alkin friends.

Peering down from one of the crates, she noted her friends were standing with their swords in place, but they still looked weak and fragile. Though Caleb's shirt was drenched with blood, she knew he had healed, and the guilt that had consumed her heart diminished. Scanning the perimeter, she could see that they were completely surrounded by the fallen, the reason why they were still inside the cage. Dantanian hadn't moved from where he stood either. It was as if he was waiting for Michael to return with her held captive.

Not knowing when Michael would come after her, and not knowing if and when Holly would find out where they were, she had no time to waste, especially when Dantanian looked straight at her.

"My, my. You are one tough angel after all. I see that you're the one standing and not Michael. Is he knocked out? Surely you didn't kill your lover? I personally think you would make a great asset to our team. What say you?"

"Claudia," the alkin friends shouted in accord, looking up at her.

Her alkin's faces glowed happily. As if they drew strength from her presence, they stood taller, bolder, and more confident, and they possessed the look of triumph.

"Claudia, what are you waiting for?" Davin yelled.

She didn't know. Though she had her light back somewhat, she didn't know what she was waiting for. Why was she just standing there with her bow in place? Then she knew the answer when she heard the sounds of flapping wings. She didn't have Michael on their side. There was a possibility that she had lost him to the darkness. But she wouldn't give up—ever. She had to somehow bring him back home.

Feeling the breeze from Michael's wings, she shot the first arrow at a fallen near the alkins. Then it was chaotic. Sword upon sword, the slicing, clanking sounds echoed through the warehouse. Wanting to escape from Michael before he reached her, she jumped down next to Davin. With her light shooting from her left hand blasting the fallen coming for her, she shot the silvery bolts from her bow with her right.

"You're badass, Claudia," Davin managed to say while ducking a swing.

"Good to see you too, my friend," Claudia said quickly. "We need to capture Michael. When the venators come—if they come—they'll hurt him. Davin, find Michael. Vivian, Caleb, lets lure the fallen out of the warehouse. Holly can't see us in here."

With Claudia's command, the three of them ran and headed for the sunlight while Davin searched for Michael. But just as they reach the outdoors, Holly, Austin, and the venators appeared with their bows already pointed to the massive group of fallen behind them. Floating with their wings expanded, with Holly and Austin in the middle, they were in a straight-line formation looking glorious and deadly at the same time. It was an awesome moment.

"Duck!" Austin yelled.

And so they did. Hundreds of silvery lights streaked across space in unison. The lights were blindingly breathtaking, mesmerizing, but a deadly sight. Peering up, Claudia felt like she was inside the tunnel of a lightning show. The lights intensified when they hovered over her. As she continued to root her eyes on them, she followed till she saw them blast the fallen into nothing but ashes. With so many blasted all at once, the black ash dispersed like falling snow and was carried away by the strong breeze. The alkins whipped around to fight the remaining fallen that came from behind, and the venators joined them.

CHAPTER 34

STRIKING AND BLOCKING WITH HIS sword, Davin fought bravely with the fallen that surrounded him. With one eye aware of his attackers, the other one was searching for Michael. But he didn't need to look far.

"Let us be. Go find the others. This puny one is mine." Holding a cool expression, Michael directed the fallen that surrounded Davin.

"Who you calling puny, Michael? You're going to get it now," Davin huffed. "I'm not going to kill you. I'm just going to knock some sense into your head." Davin shifted from side to side. Hearing Michael growl, Davin guessed he didn't like what he'd heard.

"You have no idea what I'm going to do with you once you're in my hands. I'm going to eat you alive, spit you back up, and toss you to Dantanian. He'll make you smell his feet."

Davin arched his brow, confused. That wasn't something the evil Michael would say...at least he didn't think so. And the menacing, intimidating look in Michael's eyes was no longer present.

But it didn't matter at this point. Standing there in front of him, ready to attack, was a sure sign Michael wasn't back.

Davin shifted his eyes for a brief second when he heard Dantanian chuckling. He was gloating with his sword by his side. But within the blink of an eye, Dananian was using the sword in battle. Unexpectedly and thankfully, he was attacked by a group of venators. Davin took this opportunity and punched Michael in the face. "Ouch," Davin muttered, shaking his hand. "You're really made of steel, as they say."

Michael's cheek turned to the left, but not his body. It was as if he had been slapped instead. With a fierce look in his eyes, he charged forth. "What was that for?"

Attacking Michael with everything Davin had, his sword swung in every direction it could move. "You may be stronger, but I'm faster. Claudia needs you. We need you. Zachary and Lucia need you. You can't just give up. I'm sick of being here. I want to go home. Do you hear me in that thick skull of yours? Fight!"

"Not fast enough, my friend."

Michael had been dodging his every swing without attacking back. But suddenly, with the twist of Michael's wrist, Davin's sword flung skyward. Before Davin knew it, it landed in Michael's hand and Davin was down flat on his back. The tip of Michael's sword was touching Davin's chest with light pressure. "What part of 'smell Dantanian's feet' did you not get?"

Davin's heart pounded with happy beats and he grinned. "You're back! I thought you were a goner. I mean, we weren't going to kill you. We were going to knock some sense in you. And you're not getting me back for that punch, are you? It was just—"

"Davin, stop talking. I need to find Claudia." He gripped Davin's shirt and pulled him up with one yank.

"How about Dantanian and Berneal?"

"I'll deal with them later, but Claudia thinks...I need to find her."

"This way," Davin directed, then suddenly halted, lost in the moment that Michael was back.

"What are you waiting for?" Michael asked quickly.

Yup...Michael was back. With the biggest, mischievous grin Davin could give, lifting up his sword as if victorious, he bellowed, "Together as one!" It was only for a split second, but he saw the heartfelt smile on Michael's face.

LOOKING OUT TO THE OPEN sky, Michael saw black and white wings every way he turned his head. With the sound of metal colliding upon metal and the silvery lights from the venators' bows, a full blown battle was happening right in front of him. He sliced his way through a few fallen who charged him without much effort. Most of the fallen were no match for Michael's strength and speed.

Searching desperately for his beloved, he flapped his wings high above the ground. He spotted Holly with other venators he didn't recognize, but where was Claudia? When a beam of soft golden light by the window captured the corner of his eye, he knew she was there.

Without thinking of the consequences that might await him on the other side, he burst through the window. The shattered glass pooled beneath his feet and splintered even more when he stepped forward. Dusting the shards that lingered off his clothes, he listened for any sound. "Claudia," Michael called, but he could only hear the sound of his own voice.

Suddenly, from out of the corner, Austin, Vivian, and Claudia appeared with their weapons ready.

"MICHAEL?" CLAUDIA ASKED. "IS IT really you?" Her eyes lit up with hope. Perhaps what she had done with her light had worked on him.

Austin gripped her arm before she could make a dash for it. Yanking away from him, she cautiously paced toward Michael. But instead of going directly to him, she kept her distance.

"It's me, my love." His tone was sweet, but she had to be careful. What if this was a trick?

Just when he finished his words, a body flew through the already broken window. "Claudia, don't believe him, my love. I'm the real Michael."

Austin, Vivian, and Claudia looked mortified at seeing two Michaels.

"What the hell?" Austin shrieked, shifting his bow from one Michael to the other. "He has a twin?"

"Don't shoot," Vivian demanded, placing her hand on Austin's bow. "Michael told us about the fallen that could change his face. He goes by Dantanian...whichever he is."

Either way, which ever was the real Michael was apparently not under the evil spell any longer, and that alone lifted Claudia's spirits. But which one was the real Michael? She didn't have a clue.

"Open your wings," she directed.

When they did, they were both white. Could Dantanian change the color of his wings too? Before she had a chance to respond, the second one attacked the first. Now they were sword fighting.

"*Claudia, run.*" She heard Michael's voice in her mind. Shaken up to hear his voice again, she froze. But which Michael had it come from? Her hand fizzled as light brewed inside her. She had to help, but help whom?

"*Run!*" She heard the first Michael say. Then she knew it was him, but she couldn't run, not when she had found her love again.

She wanted to help, but they were moving too fast, shifting from side to side. If she shot her light, she would hurt her Michael too.

"I'm coming for you," she heard in the chaos of the room, as Vivian and Austin could do nothing but watch and keep their weapons ready.

"Which one?" Austin shouted, looking eager to shoot.

"I don't...." Claudia never got to finish her words. One of the Michaels seized her in his arms and flew out the window.

Landing on top of the roof, she could see the black ashes floating with the wind. Though she could see more of the white wings than black, the battle seemed endless. Spotting Holly on the ground, she saw Caleb and Davin adjacent to Michelle and Gracie on the roof of the building across from where she stood. And Austin, Vivian, and Michael—or was it Dantanian?—were frantically searching for her.

This Michael held her from behind and extended her arm out. "Use your light. I'll guide you. Do it now and shoot him when he comes with all your strength." His tone was demanding and urgent.

There was something terribly wrong with the way he was holding her and asking her to do something Michael would never ask of her. At that moment she knew without a doubt that she was in the hands of Dantanian. His touch, his breath on her face sickened her, and she grimaced at the thought. But no matter how much she loathed his arms around her, she had to follow through.

"If you're the real Michael, then you know how dangerous my light can be."

"Do it!" he shrieked with anger in his tone.

Even with her powers back somewhat, she wasn't strong enough to break away from him, but she knew she could with her light. Closing her eyes, she willed it to come as she spoke. "You have no idea who you're messing with. You've kept my friends and my husband away from me. I'm tired and I want to go home. Hell has no fury like a mother's scorn. Feel my light and burn in hell,

Dantanian." Then light burst from within her, shooting outward to the sky.

As she shuddered, her whole body burned like she was on fire, and she was radiating as brightly as the sun. Dantanian hadn't let go. How was he holding on? But when she heard him cry out from pain, she knew he was holding on till the very end. His wrath and determination to kill Michael kept him going, but there was no way she would let that happen.

As her anger grew, so did her light. Katherine had warned her that if and when her powers came back she had to be extremely careful, for there was a possibility she would not be able to control the intensity of them. Katherine was right, for she had lost control due to all the anger that had built up inside. She had to get that peace and love back.

Glowing like a nuclear bomb, she felt the weight of Dantanian move off her, but she couldn't stop, and she knew if it continued, she would blow up herself. But something was happening to her that was out of her control. It had never happened before, and fear gripped her. Her back muscles felt achingly tight and a burning sensation ripped through them. She needed help. Not knowing if Michael would hear her, she prepared to call for him mentally, but she didn't have to.

Soaring toward her, she saw a beautiful, magnificent angel. His glorious heart-shaped wings blocked everything around her, and all she could see was him. Her light radiated outward and surrounded him. From his presence, her panic diminished, and all she felt was his love, wrapping around her heart and soul, cooling her down. Like a dream, she felt his wings envelope her. As the vision of him faded in and out, she drifted into unconsciousness.

"Michael," she managed to utter softly as she collapsed in his arms. Opening her eyes for a brief second, she saw her husband's face fade all too quickly, but she felt the tender strokes on her face, and heard the words she longed to hear just before she fell into darkness. "I'm right here, my love. I'm never letting you go."

CHAPTER 35

Knowing Claudia would be fine, Michael laid her down and leapt up to find Dantanian. He was spread out on the floor on the other end of the roof. Shaking his head to gather himself, Dantanian staggered, using his own sword for support. "Michael, I'm sorry. Let's make a truce."

His tone was almost believable, but Michael knew better. "Do you have any idea what you've put my friends and me through these past few days?"

Surprisingly, Dantanian placed his sword on the ground and got down on his knees. "I promise to change my ways. Let me go and I will never bother you again."

Letting out a heavy sigh, Michael narrowed his eyes at him. "Why should I believe you?"

"Look at me." Dantanian stood up. His once massive black wings were burnt and seared, as if someone had taken a pair of scissors and randomly cut them.

"You look pathetic." Michael grinned proudly. "Claudia did that to you, and you deserved it. That's what you get for messing with her." He quickly looked over his shoulder to check on her, then turned back to Dantanian. "Just leave and never come back. Now you know...you'll never win. This battle of yours just began, and it's already over. Do you understand?"

Dantanian nodded with his head low.

"You should be lucky that I'm not the angel I used to be, or I would've taken your life now. But I won't since you're begging for peace," Michael said somberly. With a sigh of relief, he turned and walked away.

He had turned for only a few seconds, but that was enough time to see a shadow cast on the ground charging toward him from behind. At the precise moment, Michael turned and swung his sword. It sliced Dantanian across his chest, but that didn't stop him. He kept coming, waving his sword with a fierce look in his eyes. "You don't get to tell me what to do, and you certainly don't get to live while I'm alive!"

Michael blocked his ragged swings, gripped him by the shirt, and flipped him over. Flat on his back, Dantanian tried to get up, but Michael's sword was on his chest. "You stupid fool. I gave you a chance to live, to walk free after all you have done. You were once my brother, and for that bond I was willing to take heat from the Twelve. But now you leave me no choice. You are my prisoner now."

"I'm nobody's prisoner," Dantanian sneered.

What was to come next was utterly unexpected. Dantanian whipped out Claudia's necklace, surprising Michael and giving Dantanian that second he needed to yank Michael's sword out of his grip. As Michael eyed his sword flying upward, he felt a brutal kick in his rib cage. Flying backward across space, he landed with a hard thump. Seeing Dantanian's sword close by, he tumbled and reached for it, but a foot was suddenly planted on his hand, holding him there in place.

"That's my sword, Michael," Dantanian heaved, with Michael's own sword pointing at his neck. "Who is the prisoner now?"

Michael's body shook with anger. His jaw and muscles were tight. "I'm really getting tired of being nice. Now you leave me no choice. Smell my feet for the last time," he gritted through his teeth in a cold and low tone. Extending his right leg, Michael rammed it against Dantanian's jaw. Dantanian flew straight up into the air like a rocket.

Soaring upward beside Dantanian, Michael plunged Dantanian's sword into his chest and watched him burst into ashes. On his way down, Michael snatched the butterfly necklace. "That belongs to my wife." Then he dove down to catch another item. "And that's my sword."

After he landed, he swooped up Claudia and leapt down to where the battle had not ended. Claudia was now in Davin's arms. "Guard her with your life," Michael said to Davin. Dashing to the remaining fallen, he told the venators to back off, and even Austin and Holly did as they were ordered.

"Berneal!" Michael shouted, standing behind him.

Berneal turned and without a second to lose, thrashed his sword at Michael.

After blocking Berneal's swing, with one clear swipe Michael cut through his neck. Then he spotted Keith. "You!" he shouted, pointing directly toward him. "I never back out on my word."

Instead of retaliating, Keith ran and tried to hide among the group of fallen who stood there with their swords up, looking shocked from seeing how Michael had just taken out Berneal.

Weary from all that he had endured, from missing Zachary and Lucia, to wanting Claudia back in his arms, with one whoosh Michael's deadly wings spread out like tiny little knives projecting from each single feather. He spun like an airplane propeller, slicing, dicing, and mutilating anything with black wings till there was nothing left except for the ashes that floated in the air like snowflakes. Peering up to see himself completely surrounded by a tunnel of black dust, he let the adrenaline calm as he heaved with exhaustion.

With his head low, he dropped to his knees. "Forgive me, for I have fought with anger, but it was for love." Then he stood up to see the looks of admiration sparkling in his comrades' eyes. Then his eyes moved to Claudia in Davin's arm. With a feeling of relief that everyone he loved was safe, he lit a huge warm smile.

THE VENATORS RUSHED TOWARD HIM, circling him, staring, as if silently thanking him, but at the same time awestruck.

"Thank you for coming." Michael extended his arm, giving his hand to Holly, then to Austin.

"We would've come either way, but the Twelve finally app-roved," Austin said, letting go of his hand, looking baffled by the handshake Michael had offered.

"Michael," Holly huffed, giving him a little bit of attitude. "Why didn't you do that awesome thing that you did in the first place? What were you waiting for?"

"Oh...sorry." Michael laced his fingers through his hair and looked at Davin with a wink. "What would be the fun in that? And...sorry, but Claudia's safety came first." Michael paced toward Davin, retrieved Claudia from his arms, and kissed her on her lips, though she had no idea what was going on. "I'm right here, my love. Let's go home."

"How about Raven?" Davin asked.

"Let her be. She's not a threat. She was only doing what we were doing...protecting our loved ones."

"Okay, if you say so." Davin watched Michael whip out his wings and take flight.

Holly shrugged her shoulders and shook her head, referring back to how he'd used his wings like a weapon. "Why didn't he—?"

"It drains his energy. He only does it if it's absolutely necessary," Davin explained.

"Oh," she murmured admiringly. "His wings are like—"

"Yup," Davin said proudly before Holly could finish her words. "He's an angel with a shot gun."

"More like an angel with a machine gun."

"True...an angel with a handsome face and a great body," Michelle offered in a dream-like state.

"An angel with a ginormous heart," Vivian added.

"An angel who deserves to be happy," Caleb muttered.

"Let's go home," Davin exclaimed, watching Michael float away. "I really need some chips and salsa right now."

With a chuckle from those who heard him, one by one, with quick flashes from their wings they soared victoriously to the heavenly sky as Davin bellowed, "Together as one!" Surprising, others repeated after him, filling Davin's heart with bliss. They looked like one massive white puffy cloud, gliding, projecting comfort, projecting peace, projecting love across the universe.

HOLDING CLAUDIA, MICHAEL RUSHED TO Halo City with the alkins by his side.

"Michael," Agnes, Margaret, and Phillip called, coming toward him. They still had no idea what the alkins had endured.

"She's fine. Just too much power all at once. I'm taking her to my room."

Phillip nodded and moved aside.

"I'll bring Zachary and Lucia to you," Agnes said.

"Yes, please."

"We'll wait at the fountain, but make sure to let us know when Claudia awakens," Davin urged.

"I will." Michael headed to his room.

Covering Claudia with a light blanket, he waited for his babies. He couldn't wait to hold them in his arms. He was unaware of how much time had passed, but it didn't matter; every day away from them was precious time lost.

Caressing Claudia's hair, he sat on the edge of the bed watching her chest rise and fall. As he took in her beauty, he recalled the agonizing torture he had endured at Dantanian's hand. Though many times before he'd wished he could remember his past, a part of him wished the memories were still buried. But the best way for a being to become a better being was to learn from their past mistakes.

By Dantanian's evil plan, Michael had regained almost all of his memories. He remembered everything, the good and the bad. And the part of his past he most wanted to remember was very clear now. Closing his eyes, he inhaled a heavy, deep breath, and played out the images of his past that led to him parting with Aden...a part of his memories Dantanian never got to witness.

FOLLOWING ADEN TO ONE OF the small towns nearest to the mountainside, Michael soared alongside a group of fallen, whose purpose was to get the Twelve's attention by slaughtering the human beings. With their dark wings spread out side by side against the backing of the daytime sky, they looked like one massive murderous cloud, ready to pound on the land with fury.

Their wings disappeared as they landed, and they strode together in a straight-line formation with an evil purpose, looks of malice emanating from their eyes. From street to street, they massacred every human they encountered on sight. Their swords were drenched with blood, and crimson painted the town.

"Where is your God now?" Aden asked smugly to a man forced down on his knees.

"Where he's always been...in my heart," he said proudly, looking directly at him without an ounce of fear. "I know what you are. You have no heart, nor soul. And one day, it will be your turn to die. So tell me, what will happen to you then?"

"Meet your maker, you worthless human being," Aden said angrily, as if he was offended by his words.

"Unlike you, I have no fear. But I smell fear in every breath that stinks out of your mouth." With those words, he closed his eyes and raised his hands to the sky. "Take me home, and forgive him even though he's already damned."

Just as he finished his words, Aden swiped the sword across his chest and split him into two. Blood streamed from his body and pooled on the ground. As if splashed by paint, drops of his blood spotted the fallen, and some landed on Michael's shirt. Looking down at them, something happened to Michael. He couldn't quite understand what he was feeling, but he knew he didn't want to be there.

Hearing how this human had so much faith even in the hour of his death had affected him deeply. The man had felt every word, had felt his peace, and most of all he had felt his faith. And for unexplainable reasons, Michael wanted to feel the same things. Perhaps it was knowing he was once like the human he admired, or perhaps it was the shock of seeing so much blood. Whatever the reason, it was changing him, and that terrified him.

When he'd killed before, all he saw were black ashes. Seeing blood was a whole different experience, and the sounds of the humans' cries were enough to make him want to flee. These poor creatures of God couldn't protect themselves. Not having the super powerful strength the angels possessed was a human weakness, but killing them for no reason besides their being a means to an end was affecting him in ways he never thought possible.

Had Trinity been right? Was his conscience getting the best of him? He didn't know what to do. All he knew for sure was that he didn't want to continue down this path, especially after today's mission. Realizing he had closed his heart and had been blinded by power, he knew he had lost his faith. He wanted to have it again, to feel what that human had felt, and he knew that if he didn't change, he would never find that faith again. "I think we've done enough damage for one day. There's blood everywhere. The Twelve will surely hear of this," Michael said to Aden.

"If you really want to make a statement, kill them all," Dantanian suggested with a satisfied grin.

"No. It's enough," Michael said sternly, looking into Aden's eyes.

"You're not going soft on me, are you Michael?" Aden stared back at him, like a father examining his child.

"No, of course not." Michael had to think fast and convince Aden somehow, and thought his reply was pretty clever. "We need to leave some witnesses behind so they can tell the Twelve who did this. Wasn't that the purpose? What good is it if the Twelve doesn't know it was our doing?"

Aden turned his head toward the surviving humans, who were hiding, trying to stay out of sight. "You're right. Let's go home."

CHAPTER 36

WHEN MICHAEL RETURNED, THE FIRST thing he did was pull Trinity aside.

"Michael," she greeted, pacing toward him as he came for her. Her eyes gazed on the wound on his arm. "You're hurt."

"This one is very deep. It'll take some time, but I'll be fine." Michael recalled how one human had fought bravely and slit him with a knife. Remembering the face of the man he'd had to kill was eating at him. Guilt clung to his heart, and he didn't know if his memory could erase the look on the man's face before he killed him.

"Here...let me help you." Trinity placed her hand on his cut. A low beam of light glowed from out of her hand. When she let go, there was no trace of his injury.

Michael marveled at what she could do. Taking both of her hands, he looked into her eyes with urgency. "Thank you, but don't ever show anyone what you can do. Do you understand?"

"Why?"

"You need to trust me on this...okay?"

She nodded.

"We need to talk, but not here. Let's talk somewhere private."

They snuck away into the deepest part of the forest. The night clouds had already covered the day sky and the wind was especially harsh, but Michael took no notice. When it seemed as though no fallen were around, he felt safe to talk freely.

"I saw blood...lots of it." His tone was panicky and his chest rose and fell quickly. Though he was peering down to her eyes, he wasn't looking at her. He saw the faces of the ones he'd killed. "They were innocent. They had no weapons. They were no match for us. What have we done? What have I become?"

Trinity placed her arms around Michael to comfort him. "I know. I was there...remember? I knew this was happening. I could see it growing day by day. And if you're not careful, Aden and Dantanian will know too. They will kill you." She let go, placed her hands on his face, and made him look at her. "Do you understand?"

Michael's eyes were deep and somber. "I know. What am I to do?" He paused, pacing back and forth while raking his hair back. "I don't want you in trouble. If anything were to happen to me, they may link you to me. Ahhh! I don't know. You should stay away. I've already—"

"Michael, stop!" She closed the space between them, looking at him with admiration. "Don't you know by now what you mean to me? Didn't our kiss mean anything to you?" Her eyes sparkled with hope.

He cleared his throat, not wanting to answer that question. "I...I...well...women in general like to kiss me."

Trinity arched her brows. It was obviously not the answer she wanted to hear, but she continued regardless. "You may not love me the way I love you, or care half as much as I care for you, but I know there is something there." She placed her hand on his chest and started to tenderly stroke upward. "Let's run away together. This is the only way we can truly be together. I've heard there are places in Beyond. We can build a new life there. You don't have to continue killing. You don't have to answer to Aden and Dantanian. Isn't this what freedom is all about? To be the being you want to be and not what others want you to be?"

Michael closed his eyes, fighting what he wanted to do right at that moment—run away. But Aden was like a father and Dantanian was like a brother to him. Though he was not happy with their actions, it didn't seem right to just leave without explaining. He needed to talk some sense into them, let them know how he felt. That was what families did...or at least he thought it was.

As for Trinity, he would be crazy not to accept this offer from a beautiful angel, but something was missing. When two beings fell in love, their hearts should be like two separate puzzle pieces, that when placed side by side fit perfectly together as one...no doubt about it. But that was not how he felt.

He cared for her, no doubt. She had always been there for him when he needed someone, and he enjoyed her attention and several stolen kisses, but he knew in his heart this wouldn't last. But...he could give this relationship a try, and perhaps in time, he could care for her just as much as she cared for him.

Michael gripped both of her hands together. "In order for us to even start a life at Beyond, we need to make sure we will not be haunted by Aden and Dantanian for the rest of our lives. Do you understand?"

Trinity nodded, beaming with a smile. "I understand. But just so you know, I don't want to be here either. Aden is not the leader I want to follow. He will only bring death and loss. But I would follow you, Michael. You're a great leader. Even though we are fallen, not all fallen are evil. I want to live in peace, away from the humans. I want to be with you."

Michael nodded. "I need to explain to Aden what I want and what I'm willing to do. I won't abandon him, but I will not kill another human being. I don't know how he will react, but I have to do this. It's the only way. With his blessing, we can start a life somewhere Beyond."

Trinity wrapped her arms around him tightly. "I can't wait."

THREE DAYS LATER

"WE'VE BEEN FOUND!" A FALLEN shouted.

With the sound of angry thunder and fierce lightning flashing across the sky, something that resembled a massive white blanket hovered over them and cast a shadow on the ground. As the clouds above tumbled rapidly, thunder roared again, and the whiteness above split into layers and fell like snow.

Watching them drop from the clouds, Michael's heart hammered at an abnormal speed, which had never happened to him before. Even in all the battles he'd fought, never had his heartbeat escalated to this level of stress. But today he felt like a captive, because he now understood he was fighting on the wrong side.

"Michael!" Aden called sharply, snapping him out of his trance. "Remember what I told you to do." Aden's tone was desperate. He too was keeping his eyes on them, looking slightly nervous.

"Aden, for the first time, please listen to me. We're not going to win this battle. We need to escape while we have the chance."

"What are you talking about?" Dantanian raised his voice, suddenly appearing behind Aden. "We fight today."

"Michael, you do what I told you to do," Aden reminded with a demanding tone. "You don't get to change your mind now. The plan has been set in motion. It's really simple. I wound you and you beg for forgiveness. Find the gatekeeper, but most importantly, find out if they have been able to locate the one with a Holy Soul, if there is one. When you find that information, we'll search for that being. That is how we'll get inside the Crossroads. That is the only way. Don't feel intimidated by them, my son. You are faster and stronger than any angel I've ever known. I wanted them to come here so we can fight on familiar ground." Then Aden raised his sword, seeing that the angels above were a lot closer than before, and spoke to his followers. "Today, victory will be ours!"

Just as he finished his words, the angels of light landed and swung their swords in full force without even trying to negotiate. Blinding sparks flew from colliding swords, and though the fallen fought with all the hatred and anger they could summon in their hearts, their skills could not compare with those of the angels, especially when they were outnumbered.

Without a choice, Michael fought back, but he didn't fight back with everything he could give. He just couldn't hurt them.

While blocking a strike, he sidestepped and stood behind Aden. "I can't do this Aden. I'm not going to surrender."

Unexpectedly, Aden flipped over to stand in front of Michael and swung his sword at him. "You will do as I say!"

Michael blocked each of Aden's thrusts. "What are you doing?" Michael shouted, stunned by Aden's sudden outburst toward him. He had always treated him with kindness, with pride, and like a son. But...had it been just a façade all along? Was he just a means to an end? Michael didn't want to rule over Crossroads. He wanted to live among the humans. That was what he was fighting for. And he certainly didn't want to fight face to face against any of the Twelve.

As Aden continued to come at him, he spoke with each angry slice. "You do not back out on me. I'm sending you to Crossroads. You must keep the plan in motion."

Michael was beyond furious. He wasn't going to go easy on him. With a twirl of his sword, he attacked back. "If free will is what we are fighting for, then why do I feel like I don't even have that with you?"

He didn't get a reply. Aden and Michael were forced to separate when several swords suddenly thrust toward them from the sides.

"Look out, Raven!" Michael shouted, and pulled her behind him. Dodging a blow from a watcher, he bent low and punched him hard on his chest, sending him to smack against a nearby tree. Had Michael not intervened, she would have been killed. He twirled to Raven. "Run...we are not going to win this war. Do you understand?"

"Thanks, Michael, for saving my life. I owe you. I'll run with those who want to, and you should do the same." Then she soared out of sight.

"Give yourself up, Aden!" Katherine bellowed, pointing her sword against his chest.

Michael felt torn at that moment. Should he help Aden, or should he allow Katherine to capture him? Even though he had watchers around him, he knew he could take them on. From a distance, he could see Dantanian doing some damage himself.

"You think pointing that sword is going to make me surrender?" Aden laughed out loud.

"Perhaps you will change your mind since there is another one behind you." One of the Twelve was standing behind Aden. He was majestic looking with his alabaster wings fanned out.

"Zachariah," Aden said with a smug grin plastered on his face. "Your timing is so perfect. Perhaps you'll change your mind. If you're here to save your son, you're too late. He's mine. You should've claimed him when you had the chance."

"You know very well that the Royal Council does not allow any contact with our descendants. It...." He stopped. "My son?" He sounded confused, seemingly stunned by this sudden revelation.

"That's right. I have your son." Aden revealed proudly.

"Where...is...my...son?" Each word was accentuated. Each word was spoken with fury, and his eyes were intense with anger.

"He's around...or was around. That's the agony of all this. Perhaps you've already killed him."

"He's alive. I know this. You wouldn't be threatening me otherwise. I shall claim him back."

"He's already been damned. It's too late. He won't want you."

"You don't know the power of love. You never did. That's the reason why no one will ever care about you. Soon, you'll be all alone. Even your followers will abandon you."

His son? Zachariah had a son? As Michael wondered who this son was, he calculated and planned an escape for Trinity and himself. She was there on the battleground, somewhere.

Aden's eyes grew angrier and his face cringed with hatred. His whole body shook while his fist tightened. What he did next was unreasonable and utterly crazy. He charged at Michael. It seemed at first the watchers didn't know what to do. After all, what being in their right mind would attack a person on their own team?

Michael didn't know what to do at first, and he was also unsure of Aden's motive. Sure, Aden's plan was to swipe him across his chest and injure him, but why would the Twelve let a wounded one be taken to Crossroads, since only those with pure souls could enter? He was certain his soul was tainted.

"Stop, Aden!" Michael said out loud. Somehow Dantanian was behind him now, but before he could mutter a word, Dantanian attacked him too. Was this a plan he was not aware of? Now he was fighting two of the people that meant the most to him. It was strange to protect himself, but what happened next was even stranger. Zachariah fought alongside Michael.

"Leave him be. This is not his fight," Zachariah roared as he continued to block and strike Aden.

From the corner of his eyes Michael saw Katherine surrounded by fallen. With a swift leap, he escaped Dantanian and somersaulted over a few watchers to stand beside Katherine. Just in the nick of time, Michael blocked a swing that was meant for her. For some unknown reason, he was helping her. In fear of Michael, the group of fallen retreated.

Katherine ignored Michael and soared to help the watchers. This gave Michael an opportunity to find Trinity.

"Michael, you traitor!" Dantanian stormed, charging with fury in his eyes.

"No!" Trinity bellowed from behind Dantanian.

Suddenly, Dantanian came to an abrupt halt, rotated his arms behind him, and gripped Trinity around her neck. "I'll snap her neck."

"Leave her alone. She is not the one you want," Michael demanded, and dropped his sword, watching Trinity's body twist and turn, struggling to break free.

Through the chaos, from out of nowhere Aden bolted toward Michael. Michael reached for his sword when he saw him coming for him. Somehow Trinity escaped. Dantanian also charged toward him while Zachariah soared behind Aden.

Everything happened so fast. Baffled by the sudden betrayal from the people he'd cared for, and confused by the newfound feeling of having a conscience, Michael froze, unable to decide which side he was fighting for. But it didn't matter.

Dantanian's sword nicked Michael on the chest while he was trying to block Aden's sword. The second strike from Aden, which would have plunged into Michael, went deep into Zachariah's back instead. Zachariah's weight forced Michael to drop to the ground. The sound of Earth pounded in Michael's ears, and the clouds above became blurred.

"I'm sorry," Zachariah whispered faintly, still draped over Michael's body as his tears dotted Michael's cheeks. "I loved your mom so much...but I let her go...let you go. I should have fought for her...for you. If you love, don't ever let her go. I'm so sorry...my son...I...." With a sharp intake of breath, Zachariah had taken his last one.

Aden had known all along that Zachariah was his father and had kept this from him. And the fact that Aden had blurted it out in front of everyone, just when things were not in his favor, proved to Michael that he was just a means to an end to Aden. Michael had killed for him, he had lied for him, he had given his life to him, but Aden had never cared about him.

Gently rolling his father over, Michael struggled to get up. His head was spinning with many questions and uncertainties. Shocked, his body was weak, and any movement was made with much effort. It felt as though his mind and body were not in sync, and everything seemed to move in slow motion.

He had to fight back...fight back for his father who had just saved him. When he stood, he heard Trinity's cry, telling him to duck, but he couldn't move fast enough. His eyes were fixated on the angel in front of him, whose face was that of his father. Then he realized it was Dantanian who stood in front of him...he had tricked him once again.

A loud noise from the sound of two swords colliding echoed in his ears. Trinity blocked the swing that was swung to hit Michael, but she couldn't block the second swing that plunged into Michael's stomach, then to hers. Michael locked his eyes on Dantanian, who had changed his face back to his own, heartbroken by the betrayal of the only brother he'd ever known, and heartbroken that he'd tried to kill Trinity as well.

Falling next to his father, as everything started to blur around him, he saw Dantanian soar away. Tears slipped through Michael's eyes as his fingers crawled through the dirt, needing to touch the man who'd tried to save him, the father he wished he had known before, the angel that shouldn't have died. Just then, Katherine and Phillip entered his line of vision, kneeling down next to him. He blinked in and out of unconsciousness, but he heard their conversation, which broke his heart even more.

"Zachariah's gone." Katherine wept as she cradled him in her arms. "No...no...no...it cannot be," she sobbed in agony.

"He did it to save his son," Phillip said wearily.

"I know," Katherine said softly. "He gave up his life for Michael so his son may have a chance of salvation."

"This is the only way it could be done. There was no other way...a life for a life. We need to get going. Michael looks badly wounded, but I believe he will live. We can now take him to Crossroads. Zachariah would have wanted that. He will know his life was not taken in vain."

"Then I'll take this one with me to Nubilus City...the one they call Trinity. She has a good soul, not a pure one, but we can save her since she's a nephilim. Seems like she has the ability to heal."

"Very well," Phillip said. "Let's keep them apart for now."

"Okay. I suggest you get started on training the alkins. We are not fit for battles. Had it not been for Michael, I would have been....anyway...we should get going."

Those words were the last words Michael heard before he fell into the darkness.

CHAPTER 37

ICHAEL WHIPPED BACK TO REALITY with tears in his eyes. They streamed down faster as he blinked, soaking in the memories of his past. Though he had wished he could remember that dreadful day many times before, in ways he wished he could block the memories again. But he knew that remembering the truth, remembering the heartaches and pain, would help him understand his past and create a better future.

All his life he'd thought his father hadn't cared about him. A part of him had pretended he never had one. The pain of not being wanted was unbearable, and not being able to remember his past confused him greatly, but now he knew the absolute truth. Now he could put the past behind him and move forward with no regret, no pain, no misunderstandings, but with only love and hope.

"I found the one, Father." He choked back the tears while holding Claudia's hand tenderly to his heart. "Till every drop of my blood runs out of my veins, till the last breath that I take, I won't ever let her go. Thank you for giving me a second chance...thank you for loving me from afar...and thank you for giving your life for my salvation. Having my own children...now I understand what a father would do for his own. In my evil past, I was so blinded by darkness and fear that I couldn't see the light. I was utterly lost, but having a second chance, I was found. It's all clear now...it's all clear."

Hearing a soft knock, he quickly wiped the last lingering tears and greeted Agnes and Margaret with a huge smile.

"Zachary, Lucia," he squealed in delight, wrapping them both tightly in his arms. "Thank you both for taking care of them."

"It was our pleasure," Agnes replied. "Sorry it took so long. Davin, Vivian, and Caleb wanted to hold them before I brought them to you."

"Oh...thank you."

"Anytime. We're so happy both of you are safe," Margaret smiled.

"Thank you, me too," Michael grinned shyly.

After they left, Michael closed the door and squeezed the twins gently. "Daddy missed you so much." Inhaling their sweet scent, he kissed them all over their faces. "I see you've both been eating a lot and growing stronger. I'm so sorry I was away, but I'm here now. Mommy and Daddy are here, and we're never letting either of you go." He looked over at Claudia who was still sleeping, and placed the twins on the bed.

Situating the twins in the middle, Michael gently stroked their cheeks and devoured every part of them with his eyes. Touching them meant they were real. It was a physical confirmation that he was back with the family he had missed so much. He needed that reality to ease the pain and to erase the thoughts that had tormented him every day he was away...that he might never see them again.

Then Michael surrendered to Zachary's grip that tightly wrung around his finger, breaking him out of his thoughts. "Whoa...you're so strong, my son," he gushed, grinning from ear to ear. He couldn't peel his eyes off them. He loved them so much, and the thought of never seeing them again reminded him of how precious life was, how precious time was, and how grateful he was to have them in his life, even after all that he had done in the past. He was grateful for second chances.

CLAUDIA COULD HEAR FAINT BABY sounds and the sweet melody of Michael's voice. Where was she? Was this a dream? If it was, she didn't want to wake up. A second ago, she had felt like she was floating, but now she could feel the weight of her body. And though she could feel something soft beneath her, there was a throbbing pain from her head down to her toes, and especially her upper back.

Blinking her eyes to focus, her vision became clear. They set on Michael's beautiful face first. He looked so happy, peering down on the twins. Then she felt a small tiny hand brushing against her cheek. Though she knew it was involuntary, it didn't matter. She loved everything about them.

"Claudia." Michael caught her eyes with another big smile, making her blush, making her feel she could float off the bed. "Welcome back, my love." He leaned over and gave her a long kiss on her lips with his arms reached over the twins, and held the three of them tightly with all of his love.

Tears welled up in Claudia's eyes, realizing that what she saw in front of her wasn't a dream. It was real. They were home and they were safe. Somehow, everything had worked out in the end.

Michael let go and brushed her cheeks. "How are you feeling?"

Slowly, she sat upright and kissed the twins before she spoke. "I'm fine. I feel a little hot and drained. How did...what happened? Is everyone safe?"

As Michael explained most of the details, she couldn't control the tears. She had almost lost her husband, her friends, and even her babies if she never had made it home. But she knew she had to stop thinking and celebrate their victory. Celebrate what was now.

After Michael wiped her tears, he held her hands close to his chest and kissed them. "Claudia, I've been thinking. I don't know if you'll like the idea, but after what we've been through, I think it's best to live in Halo city until the kids are old enough, or maybe just stay here forever. Now, before you disagree, I know how much you love our home, but—"

"Michael. Stop. You're jabbering the way Davin does," she giggled. "I've been thinking the same thing."

"You have?" Michael sounded surprise.

"Yes. I don't see any other way. If it was just you and I, we would be okay. I know our home we built together in Beyond is safe. But when it comes to the safety of our children...well...." Claudia paused. "I'm going to miss it there, but we have to do this."

Michael embraced Claudia. "It's okay. It can be like what humans have, a vacation home. What do you think?"

"I think it's a great plan. Let's go tell Agnes, Margaret, and Phillip."

"They will be very happy to hear this news. We need to stop by the fountain first. Davin, Caleb, and Vivian are waiting for you."

"Okay," Claudia agreed. "Zachary and Lucia fell asleep. It's probably from all the gentle caresses from your hands. Believe me. I know how they feel. Your hands are like magic."

Michael's eyes lit up, wiggling his fingers. "Really?" Then he scooped Claudia into his arms.

"CLAUDIA...YOU'RE BACK!" DAVIN SWUNG her around and then let her go quickly. "Oh...sorry. I know you just got up, or not?"

"It's okay, Davin. You know I don't mind." Then she reached for Vivian and Caleb, who had smiles on their faces.

"Group hug!" Davin said out loud, wrapping his arms around them too.

"I thought we would never see you again." Vivian's voice muffled into Claudia's arm.

"Me too, Vivian." Tears streamed down Claudia's cheeks as vivid images of them tied up pooled to the forefront of her mind. Her heart had ached to see them the way they had been bound by golden cuffs and with bruises on their faces. But that was over now. And these tears were happy tears. They were safe and alive, and that was all that mattered.

Feeling Michael's arms, Claudia peered up and even saw his eyes glisten. Seeing the five of them all cuddled up gave her a sense of overwhelming warmth in her heart. Then there was complete silence as they held each other tightly. Through their tears they would heal, through their tears they would find comfort, and through their tears they knew they were safe and always had each other's backs for life.

Michael broke away first, then the rest followed suit. Wiping her tears, Claudia smiled as she watched her friends.

"So...let's celebrate," Davin cheered. "What say you?" Suddenly Davin covered his mouth.

"What's wrong," Caleb asked.

"That's what Dantanian kept saying over and over to Michael," he gritted through his teeth while his body shook with anger. "I was so tired of hearing it. I can't believe I'm saying it."

"It's okay, Davin," Vivian said with a calm tone. "It's going to take a while to get over what we've been through." Then she placed her arms around him. "Just breathe and let Vivian comfort you."

With her words, they started to laugh.

"I'm going to ask Holly and a few venators to join us...is that okay?" Davin asked, looking at Michael, then to Claudia.

"Sure," Michael said with a smile. "If you're asking me if Austin is invited, your frenemie, that's okay with me."

Claudia laced her fingers through Michael's hair, thanking him silently for understanding and for being the wonderful being he was, who was not jealous, who only found goodness in people, who loved the people around him with all his heart.

As they were about to leave the fountain, Alexa Rose came skipping along with her group of friends. "Why was everyone hugging and...and...." She gazed on everyone's eyes. "Crying?"

"These are happy tears," Davin explained, kneeling down to her.

"Oh, but if you're happy, you don't cry," she said. "And by the way, Michael says he's always right."

Davin stood up and frowned at Michael. "Did he now?" Then his lips curved up. "Right now, Michael can be right. I'm just glad he's home."

Michael looked to his friend with a smile, seemingly feeling the same.

"Run along now, Alexa Rose. It's time for grownups to play." Davin clapped his hands, lighting a goofy grin.

"Grownups don't play," she reminded.

Davin nodded his head in agreement. "Oh yeah...it's time for grownups to do grownup stuff then."

With a kiss from everyone, Alexa Rose bounced along with her friends. As Alexa Rose exited, Katherine entered.

"It's nice to see you all. I'm glad you're all home safely. So...having a party without me?" Katherine winked.

"How did you know?" Davin looked staggered.

"I didn't. I was just saying...but now I do," Katherine giggled. "Don't worry, Davin, I'll bring some chips and salsa."

Davin dropped his jaw. "You like chips and salsa too? My kind of woman." Davin cleared his throat and stiffened. "I mean...not my kind...and I didn't mean woman...I mean...you're an angel...not a woman...but you are a woman...."

Katherine giggled. "You can stop now, Davin. I understand what you mean. I actually came here to speak to Michael."

"Oh," he said quickly, looking relieved.

"Why don't you get the party ready? I'll be right there." Michael kissed Claudia on the forehead. "I know we talked about leaving Zachary and Lucia behind with Agnes, but I want you to bring them. I don't want any time spent without them. I mean...at least for now."

Claudia looked back at Michael with understanding. "I know what you mean. See you soon."

Katherine waited, making sure they were alone before she spoke. "Michael. I've been informed that you have your memories back."

Michael rooted his eyes to his shoes, feeling ashamed of his past. "Yes. I'm not sure to what degree, but I do remember enough."

"Please look at me, Michael." She waited till he did. "I'm not here to judge or blame you for what happened. I just wanted to make sure you're okay." Katherine paused. "I know you. I'm not sure how much you remember, but I wanted you to know your father loved you very much. As you already know, it's forbidden to love a human and produce offspring. It's rare, but it happens. Even angels make mistakes...though, to me, it wasn't a mistake. A small percentage of us will fall in love, and when it happens it completely takes us over, as you already know. "

"I remember pretty much everything from the memories Dantanian wanted me to remember, but I can't remember the before parts, like my childhood."

Katherine let out a soft sigh and continued. "We, the Twelve, decided it was best you didn't remember your past. Aden, whom I'm sure was like a father figure to you, was the one who killed your father. Reliving the memories of your father's death...I think that was just too much to ask anyone to handle. As far as the before part, that was the Royal Councils' doing. Those memories can only be given back by them."

"You're right, Katherine. I can handle it now because my life is filled with so much happiness. My family and my friends' love make me appreciate what I have, and I can forget the past. So, don't worry too much. I can bear it."

"I'm happy to hear that. If you dwell on the past, it will hinder a wonderful future. By the way, you were the reason I wanted to have a child of my own. Of course, I too fell in love with a human."

Michael's face turned slightly warm. "Thank you."

Then it turned even warmer when Katherine placed the palm of her hand on his cheek. "I'm so proud of you, and I know your father is too."

Michael blinked back his tears. "I know that now."

"Well. I won't keep you long. I'm sure they're anxious to get the party started." With a smile, Katherine's long, white, elegant dress swayed with the rhythm of her graceful steps. About half way past the fountain, she turned. "I never got to thank you for saving my life that day. It would have been difficult to explain earlier, especially since you wouldn't have remembered, but now that you do I can say it without sounding crazy. You may see it differently than I do, but because you always had a pure heart, you fought alongside me. You blocked a fallen's swing that was meant for me."

Michael smiled as he watched Katherine leave his sight. Yes...he did remember, and he was happy he had.

CHAPTER 38

THE SILVER MOONLIGHT GLISTENED AGAINST the blackness of night, but the brightness didn't compare to all the candles and white lights hung on the trees that surrounded their five layered home. Along with the soft instrumental music that filled the air, it created an enchanting and magical place to be.

"Austin?" Holly saw a figure near the end of the bridge and ran toward him. "I'm so happy you've come, but are you ready to be here? I mean...."

"I'm fine, Holly," he said with a grin. "Davin invited me to the party, and I thought it would be a good opportunity for me to start healing." Shoving his hands through his pockets, he slightly rocked back and forth. "The past is the past. I'll always care for her, but I've already let go. I've stopped being mad. I've stopped blaming. I'm moving forward."

Holly's heartfelt smile was just as bright as the lights surrounding them. "I'm so proud of you," she grinned, draping her arms around him tightly. "Come on. Let's start the party."

About half way across the bridge, Austin halted. "What's wrong?" Holly asked, looking concerned. "Have you changed your mind?"

"No." His eyes sparkled. "I can see the ocean and the stars from my bedroom now. I've replaced the windows."

Holly looked so proud, squeezing him tighter. "Good for you."

"You know," Austin started to say, pacing forward. "You should come check out my room. I could show you a few things." Twitching his brows, his tone was playful.

Holly smacked him across his arms, blushing. "I told you not to go there."

"Get your mind out of the gutter. I wasn't talking about sex," Austin teased. "But if you want, I could show you that too."

Shaking her head, her face turned red. "Shut up and walk faster."

WHILE MICHAEL WAS WITH KATHERINE, Claudia had the opportunity to speak to Austin. It was the first time Austin had agreed to visit, and Claudia was happy. The fact that Claudia remembered their past and the special times they'd shared during their younger days seemed to help Austin move on...a closure that he'd needed. And being there under the same roof with her and knowing Michael was on his way was an indication that he wanted to be a part of her life, he was finally moving forward, and was becoming more like a friend.

Though Claudia knew it would be difficult for him, she also knew that just like in everything in life that needed healing, it would happen one day at a time. It also seemed as though Austin had finally realized that, though destiny may not be taking the course he had hoped for, it had other greater plans for him that he had not expected, like being the head of the Twelve, and perhaps even greater things in the future. That was the beauty of destiny...it was like an open book. One never knew what adventures one would encounter. One had to live through the pages, good and bad, move forward with an open mind, and let the beauty of the story unfold.

Sitting comfortably on the sofa, Davin cradled Zachary while Austin held Lucia. Vivian, Holly, Caleb, and Claudia sat on the other sofa, eating chips and salsa.

"I could totally get use to eating this," Holly said. "I mean... we've eaten enough of them."

"Next time, could we try a different restaurant? I'm getting tired of these chips," Vivian commented. "Next time, I get to pick."

Davin stopped rocking Zachary in his arms and looked at Vivian as if the words had shocked him. He paused for a second, parted his lips to speak, then closed them. Then he opened them again, seeming unable to make up his mind. Finally he said, defeated, "Okay."

Vivian sat back, sinking into the plush cushions, and thankfully smiled at Davin.

It was nice to see everyone Claudia cared about getting along. Though at times they would bicker, though somewhat playfully, tonight was different. Davin was right. After what they'd been through, not knowing if they would escape from Dantanian's torture with their lives, nothing seemed to matter except that they were there together under the same roof, under the same stars.

Then Michael appeared, leaning against the wall. The radiating lights beamed around him, making him look like a vision from a dream. Claudia sucked in warm air, like she always did when he appeared like that. His appearance captured her eyes and countless butterflies danced blissfully in her stomach.

"Well, look who's back, Zach...I mean Zachary," Davin cheered, shifting Zachary to the curve of his body.

With a warm smile to everyone, Claudia paced toward Michael and embraced him tightly. Through his hug, Claudia could feel his love and how much he'd missed her, though he hadn't been gone that long. Sliding his arms around her shoulder, they leaned back against the wall together, simply enjoying the moment—the bonding of alkins, venators, and their children.

Davin's eyes suddenly widened while rubbing Zachary's back. "Hey...Zachary has two bumps by his shoulder blades. Does that mean he's growing wings?"

"Yes," Michael confirmed proudly. "Lucia has them too."

"Already?" Vivian said, walking toward Lucia, feeling her back. "You're right. I can't wait."

Caleb got off the sofa, headed to Zachary, and rubbed his back too. "Oh boy. Pretty soon, they'll be flying everywhere." Caleb shook his head and sat next to Davin. "They look sleepy."

"Well, it looks like sleep time for them. How about when this party is over, we head on to a night club?" Austin nudged Davin. "I sort of had plans. I told Michelle and Gracie to meet us there."

"Sure. I'm sure Claudia and Michael wouldn't mind some private family bonding time." Davin twitched his brows at Michael.

"Umm...sure," Holly agreed, flipping through a magazine. "I could hang out tonight."

"I'm up for it," Vivian seconded, gazing at the same page with Holly, pointing. "I like that dress."

"Yeah, I'll go," Caleb said. "We haven't been to one in a while. It should be fun since we're not hunting for demons...right?"

"Right. Don't worry...I think," Davin replied. "There will always be demons around, but for tonight, let's pretend they don't exist. Let's just have fun and pretend to be humans. Unless they attack us first, of course...but...."

"Okay," Caleb intervened. "I got your point."

"I'm just saying."

Suddenly, Holly busted out laughing. "What in the world?!" Her eyes were glued to a page in the magazine.

"Oh, no, Davin. No, you didn't." Vivian laughed out loud.

Caleb shot off the sofa to see what the girls were talking about. "Oh, yes, he did." Caleb shook his head and chuckled.

"What happened?" Claudia said, still in Michael's arms.

Holly flipped the magazine so everyone could have a better look. "Meet our newest Calvin Klein model. And his name changed too. It's Davin Klein now."

Laughter rang in the room as tears spotted their eyes from laughing so hard.

"Unbelievable, Davin." Even Michael couldn't stop laughing. "How?"

Davin was blushing red. "Oh...don't worry. It's just this once. I kind of pressed my fingers and changed a few things. You know, like, put my beautiful face over his and put Davin instead of Calvin."

"You are just too darn cute." Holly leaned forward and squeezed Davin's cheeks.

"Yeah...I know." Davin shrugged his shoulders and tilted his glowing, blushing face. "Wait till you see the billboard."

"What?!" Everyone said in accord, laughing out loud again.

"Well...I think you look better than the other model," Holly said, standing up, making Davin blush even more if that was possible. "We should get going while the night is still young."

Michael took Zachary from Davin's arms and Claudia took Lucia from Austin's.

"Before you go, there is something I would like to say." Michael cleared his throat as he laced through his hair with his fingers. "I'm not sure where to begin, so I'll simply start by saying thank you. Thank you for caring, thank you for risking your lives to save us, and thank you for your friendship. Claudia and I will never forget it. You all mean the world to us, though we may not show it at times. Zachary and Lucia are truly blessed to have your love."

"We feel the same, Michael," Holly said sincerely with dampness in her eyes.

The three alkins and Austin beamed warm smiles back.

"Well, are we going to fly there or shall we steal...I mean borrow...a fast car?" Vivian asked out of the blue, breaking the comfortable silence.

Davin's lips curved into a mischievous smile. "Oh, my dear, you should know by now I prefer driving in the human world. I already stole...I mean, I've already borrowed one. It's just waiting for its driver...me."

Vivian giggled. "Fine. One last ride."

"Not so fast," Caleb said slowly, smoothly. "Let Caleb drive, 'cause I've got the keys."

"What? No you don't." Davin patted the pockets of his pants and even shoved his hands inside them. When he came up empty handed, he gave Caleb the evil eye. "No way...but how?"

"Oh...just a trick or two I learned from Davin Klein."

Michael and Claudia gazed into each other's eyes, seemingly thinking the same thing. "Here we go again. Just like the good old days," Claudia giggled.

From a distance, Claudia could hear Austin telling them to hurry, Davin and Caleb still arguing about who got to drive, and Holly and Vivian wanting to check out the Davin Klein billboard.

AFTER SETTLING THE TWINS FOR the night, Michael and Claudia headed to their room. Claudia stood on the edge of the top floor, looking down on the magical place Michael had built for them. Her heart ached knowing tonight was their last night there, but she knew it was the best thing for the safety of their children. After what had happened, there was no other way. Absolute safety was a must.

Feeling a warm body pressed to her back, she let herself go and melted into his arms. "It's breathtaking during the day, but it's magical during the night. I could stay here and just stare forever."

"We can come back. Remember what I said before, this can be our vacation home."

"I know." Claudia nodded with a deep sigh.

"Mrs. Michael, did I tell you how beautiful you look tonight?" Michael spun Claudia around unexpectedly. "Did I tell you how, by just looking at you, you take my breath away?"

"Maybe not enough." She wrapped her arms around him, knowing what he would do next, and sure enough, he leaned in slowly, taking his time, teasing her.

"You're bad, Mr. Michael," she muttered, waiting for his lips to press on hers. "You need to remember I have my speed back." Then with a whoosh of the wind, Claudia zapped herself out of his hold, leaving Michael behind, while his arms folded into empty space.

Michael chuckled. "I guess I deserved that for taking my time."

Claudia ran from tree to tree as fast as her legs would allow. She loved how the cool breeze brushed against her skin, and the rush from the speed that carried her as if she was one with the wind.

"Claudia. I'm right behind you." Michael said in her mind. Claudia turned, but there was no Michael. He had tricked her.

"I'm not where you think I am." She said in his mind. How she had missed talking to him like this. *"You can't trick me."*

"Oh, yes I can," Michael said, standing right behind her, startling her. Before she could move, Michael captured her. "Oh, by the way. I'm much faster when you're my prize." With a flash of his glorious wings that glowed even in the dark, he seized her.

"Before you take me to our favorite place, there is something I need to show you, but I'm a little shy about it, so you'll have to close your eyes and wings."

Michael chuckled while his eyes sparked with amusement. "Close my eyes, huh?"

"Yes. It's my turn to surprise you."

Michael chuckled again while closing his eyes and wings. "My eyes are closed, but you better hurry. I'm not as patient as you. And you...." He paused and quivered slightly. His brows lifted in curiosity. "Claudia...are you covering me up with a blanket?"

"Open your eyes, Michael." Claudia had never seen Michael's eyes that wide before.

"Are these real? I mean...you have wings?" He looked utterly stunned.

Claudia's wings that were already wrapped around Michael ruffled and lightly teased him.

"How? When?" Michael asked, admiring the beauty of her wings and gently stroking them as if he was caressing her delicate skin.

"I think it happened when I was trying to get Dantanian off me on the roof. The intensity of it must have made them appear. I remember feeling my back muscles stretch and ache, but I thought it was due to my power that I couldn't control. When I continuously felt sensation on the same spot, I knew something was happening. And when I had some time alone, I applied myself and concentrated on the area. To my utmost surprise, wings appeared. Michael...I have wings like you! I wanted to show them to you when we got the chance." Claudia started to tear up. It was an amazing feeling, and a miracle she thought would never happen.

"Wait till our children and our friends see them. Not only will they be in shock, they will be ecstatic."

"I know." Claudia looked down shyly, feeling embarrassed and yet at the same time exhilarated.

"Have you flown?"

"No. I wanted my first time to be with you."

Michael held her cheeks in the palms of his hands. "It will be my honor. Gamma had hindered your powers to protect you. But it was just a matter of time. You've become who you were meant to be. You are a descendant of the highest order of angels. There was never a doubt in my mind that someday you would become your true self. Embrace them, my love. Claudia, you are beautiful...they are beautiful, and they are just as big as mine. We match completely." Michael opened his wings and they pressed against hers. As if their wings were hands they feathered, stroked, and felt each other.

Without another word, he soared to the highest part of the universe, a place where it seemed as though time stood still, so quiet, so peaceful, and a place where just the two of them existed—with no worries, no regrets, and not a care in the world.

"Just breathe and fly with me, Claudia." Michael opened just enough for her to peer through. Though she was in his arms, she had just enough room to let her wings take flight. How surreal it was to fly with Michael with her own set of wings. It was magical and everything she imagined it would be.

Looking at her husband, she flashed him a huge grateful smile, for there were no words to describe her feelings. Her facial expression said it all. She was thankful for everyone in her life and for everything she had.

"How about Lucia and Zachary?" Claudia said, concerned.

"Don't worry. They are sound asleep. I can hear their heartbeats."

"You can?"

"I can do a lot of things," Michael winked.

"I know."

Michael's flirtatious expression disappeared to a somber one. "I'm sorry for what I've put you through."

"It's not your fault."

"It was my past."

"The long forgotten past, and so you should forget it too."

Michael embraced her tightly. "I don't know what I ever did to deserve you."

"It's from who you are." She placed her hand on his heart. "It's from right there."

"It came from there because I found you."

"Oh, Michael, take my breath away." She begged with her eyes.

Michael looked surprised by her words. "This would be the first." Then his lips slowly curled to a naughty grin. "As you wish."

In the middle of space, the middle of nowhere, under the stars, he kissed her tenderly. Claudia sucked in air when she felt the soft warmth from his wings, not to mention she discovered she was undressed...and so was Michael, but she didn't mind that part at all.

"I told you I was fast," he moaned while trailing his kisses gingerly down the base of her neck and lower.

While her body arched from the pleasurable sensations, she could see nothing but the stars that completely surrounded them. How enchanting and romantic it was to make love under them. As their bodies moved with the rhythm of the universe, through space, through time, Claudia cried a pleasurable cry, pouring out the emotions buried within.

She had almost lost Michael, she had almost lost her friends, and there was a moment when she thought she would never see her children again. But everything was fine now, and feeling, touching, and making love to the man she loved more than anything in life caused happy tears to stream down her face.

"I surrender to you completely. With all my love, I give you all of me...for eternity," Michael whispered, brushing the curve of the inscription on her necklace and the ring he'd made for her. "And even in death, I'd love you still."

"Michael," she cried his name, bursting with ecstasy, losing control as they shared this loving moment between husband and wife. As they continued to toss and turn through space, they held each other tightly, promising never to let go, promising to keep the ones they loved safe, promising all their love for eternity.

CHAPTER 39

CLAUDIA STOOD ON THE DIRT road where it had all began at the Crossroads. Peering up, she recalled how tall the grass had been and how she couldn't get through. Never did she imagine Halo City would become her place of residence...not only that, she had a husband and two beautiful children.

As her feet shuffled against the pebbled road, she held Lucia upright so she could get a better view. "This is our new home, Lucia." Then she turned to Zachary, who was in the same position but in Michael's arms. "This is your new home, Zachary. From a dream is where it all started. Here is where I met your daddy, and here is where we fell in love."

"But Daddy loved your mommy long before we ever met," Michael said, gazing lovingly into Claudia's eyes. "God made you to save me. And when he created you, he spent more time on you. With every breath, with exact precision, with every hope, and with His love, He made you for me. You are my miracle, and I wouldn't want to be with anyone else, or any*where* else, except right here with you. You are my home. With you and our children is where I belong."

"Oh, Michael." Claudia didn't know what to say. She took all of his love and words to her heart as she looked back at him with the same loving expression.

"And then, the rest was history. And here we are again. I guess we were meant to be here. As long as we're together, and you are all safe, it doesn't matter where we are, right Zachary?" On cue, Zachary made a cute baby sound, as if he understood. "I think he agrees," Michael said, chuckling, kissing him on the cheek.

Then Lucia made the same sound. "I think Lucia agrees with Zachary," Claudia giggled.

"Well...shall we, my love?" Michael asked, parting the tall green grass as he turned to Claudia. Then he froze.

Claudia followed Michael's gaze with her eyes and also became immobile. After realizing who they were looking at, her lips curved into a welcoming, warm smile. At a distance stood Gamma and Zachariah, glowing as if they were the center of the sun. Completely surrounded by light, it radiated out from them. The light pulsed like a beating heart, sometimes blinding them. Somehow Gamma's appearance was different this time, too pure to touch, and Claudia understood.

Claudia was so happy, and she knew Michael felt the same. Gamma hadn't appeared in her dreams for the longest time, but she knew why. Gamma couldn't interfere with her life anymore. After she was saved and reborn from the healing crystal, Gamma's soul had moved on, as if she had stayed behind for that purpose. Whatever the reason, she was glad to see Gamma one last time. It was Zachariah and Gamma's last goodbye to them.

"Gamma," Claudia muttered under her breath. Her lips quivered as happy tears streaked down her face.

"We're here to see you one last time. Everything is right with the world. We are so proud of you and Michael." Though Gamma's

lips were still, Claudia heard Gamma's thoughts in her mind. She had never done this before with her.

"I know, Gamma. I love you."

"I love you too. I see you named your daughter after me. I'm truly honored. Your children are miracles, and they will do great things to help mankind when they are ready, just as Michael and you have."

Upon hearing Michael's name, Claudia peered up to him, and she could tell he was telepathically communicating with his father. How wonderful and fulfilling this must be for Michael. Then she quickly turned back to her grandmother, knowing she would leave soon.

"I miss you very much." Claudia said to Gamma. "The memories of you will forever be in my heart. I will carry your love with me whatever I do and wherever I go."

"As I you. And don't forget, do everything with your heart, with love and not from anger, hatred or vengeance. If you do, the light will always conquer darkness. Love is the most powerful weapon. But you already knew that. I'm sorry this visit is so short, but I must go now.

"I know Gamma."

"Before I go, I want to say a little blessing for your family...May God keep you always, safe and warm. May your life be fulfilled with all that it has to offer, making dreams come true. May your heart be filled with joy, laughter, and love. If darkness ever finds you, may your light be strong enough to let love, hope, and faith guide you out. And may you always be true to yourself, and shine your light and do for others, even if they don't do for you. May your heart be pure, and stay forever young. I love you Claudia. I've always loved you like my own. I'll always be watching over you and your family. I'm so proud of you."

And with those words, like before, with a burst of light, Gamma and Zachariah slowly became translucent, disappearing to the spiritual world of beyond.

Michael idly thumbed Claudia's cheek, wiping her tears away after he had wiped his own. "That was a nice surprise for the both of us...wasn't it?"

"Yes, I agree." And it was. After visiting Patty at Fashion Wear and observing Ava from a distance before they had came to Crossroads, seeing Gamma and having her blessing gave her the most complete feeling. Inhaling a deep satisfying sigh, she gazed upon her two precious children and the husband she never thought was possible.

"Shall we?" Michael asked, parting the grass again.

"Yes," Claudia replied with a smile and conviction in her tone.

CHAPTER 40

FOUR YEARS LATER

"A HHHH...." LUCIA AND ZACHARY SCREAMED in high pitched toddler sounds while holding Vivian's hands on either side as Alexa Rose ran right behind them.

"Run faster," Vivian directed.

"I'm going to get you," Davin roared, running with his back hunched. His arms were extended with his fingers like bear's claws.

"Me too," Caleb chuckled, looking at Davin's hideous monster expression.

"Thank goodness for our uncles and auntie to keep them company." Michael's back rested against the trunk of the tree while holding Claudia in his arms.

"I agree," Claudia giggled, watching them. "I can't believe they're four already." In time, the twins would grow up and no longer play with Alexa Rose. Like the other inhabitants of Beyond, they would continue to grow until they became young adults, and remain that way for eternity. Claudia wondered how Alexa Rose would feel about that. Alexa Rose would always be the perfect little angel and remain at that innocent age because the Twelve had taken her.

"Me either." Michael planted a kiss on Claudia's cheek and pulled her tighter.

Though Davin and Caleb were not running at their normal speed, they were catching up to the twins.

LOOKING OVER HIS SHOULDER, ZACHARY could see that his uncles were closer than before. He knew they would never harm him, but his imagination got the best of him. As his heart pounded against his chest in fear, blood rushed to his head. Blazing with heat, his body felt like it was on fire and something was tearing on his back, penetrating through.

"*Something is happening, Lucia,*" Zachary said to his sister telepathically as he continued to run, still holding onto Vivian's hand. "*It's my back. I can feel something.*"

"*Same thing is happening to me too. It burns,*" Lucia panicked, speaking through her mind. "*I think our wings are growing. Don't be scared. We'll be able to fly like Mommy and Daddy.*"

"*It's happening...I can feel them...oh no!*"

"*Let go of Auntie Vivian's hand,*" Lucia directed in her mind.

It happened so fast. Pain shot through him when it happened and then disappeared, and the next thing he knew, he was hovering above the ground with Lucia. Unsteadily flying side by side, they both beamed with exhilaration, looking into each other's eyes.

"See I told you," Lucia exclaimed, then bumped into her brother in the air. "Sorry...I can't control it."

"Me too," Zachary said excitedly, laughing, trying to steady himself, rocking back and forth.

WITH A JOLT, MICHAEL AND Claudia stood up in amazement. The children looked like two beautiful white baby doves just learning how to fly. It was definitely a moment to remember, just like when they'd started to crawl, when they took their first steps, and when they first spoke.

"They're flying!" Michael shouted from happiness, but he suddenly got worried when he noted they were unable to control the direction or the speed. "They don't know how to control themselves. Catch them!"

Those words left Michael's lips, but he didn't wait for anyone to respond. Soaring toward them, he managed to catch them with his wings, as if his wings were a net.

"Yeah! That was so much fun!" Zachary cheered.

"Let's do it again," Lucia squealed.

"Daddy needs to teach you how to land. I don't want you flying into a tree, let alone a being." Still wrapped in the safety of Michael's wings, he spiraled gently to the ground.

As everyone rushed toward them, Claudia hugged the twins.

"That was awesome," Davin said, chuckling.

"You can fly," Vivian gushed.

"That was fun, Uncle Davin." Zachary looked so proud, flapping his wings, admiring them. "They look just like Mommy's and Daddy's."

"Can you chase us again, Uncle Caleb?" Lucia asked, feeling the softness of her wings.

"First I think you need to figure out how to fold your wings back in," Vivian stated. "And we need to go somewhere, but we'll be back."

"Where're you going?" Alexa Rose asked, holding Lucia's hand.

"We're going to kill...." Davin paused, giving that "oops I said too much" look. "I mean, hunt...I mean—"

"What Uncle Davin meant was that we need to find some friends," Caleb intervened, raising his brows at Davin.

"Yes," Vivian seconded, looking at Claudia and Michael. "We're looking for some special friends, but we'll be back."

"Be careful," Claudia muttered. Every time her alkin friends went hunting for demons, she kept them in her thoughts, and she couldn't rest until they were back home safely. "Give our love to Holly and Austin."

"Sure will." Vivian went down on her knees and kissed Zachary, Lucia, and Alexa Rose on their cheeks. "We'll be back."

Then it was Davin's turn as he patiently waited for Caleb to step aside. "Keep calm, Uncle Davin will be back to play with you again. Oh...by the way, I'll bring you some snacks. You're gonna love chips and salsa."

As laughter rang by the fountain, the three alkins soared away.

10 YEARS LATER

"Did Dad really build that house, Uncle Davin?" Zachary asked.

"With my bare hands," Michael said proudly, ruffling through Zachary's hair, sitting next to him on a small boulder by the stream. Zachary was looking more like his dad and was growing, already reaching Michael's shoulder.

"Not the hair, Dad," Zachary frowned.

Michael chuckled. "That's something your Uncle Davin would say. You're hanging out with him too much."

"No...not enough. And mind you, I helped too, don't forget," Davin reminded, lightly socking Michael on the arm.

Ignoring Davin, Michael caressed Zachary's hair again. "You're growing up too fast."

"How about me, Dad?" Lucia said, sneaking from behind the tree and sitting next to him. Her long brown hair was just past her shoulder blades, and her figure frame resembled Claudia's.

"You too, of course. And you're just as beautiful as your mom." Michael kissed her on the forehead.

The sound of the leaves crushing made everyone turn.

"So, this is where the party is." Caleb smiled and sat next to Lucia.

"Well...don't leave me out," Vivian muttered, sitting next to Caleb.

"And me too." Claudia squeezed between Michael and Davin, but just when she was about to sit, Michael gripped her hips and placed her on his lap.

Sitting by the stream, watching the clear water ripple lightly, produced a peaceful ambiance, filling Claudia's heart. Having her family and friends together was the best thing of all. Occasionally they had visited their vacation home without the twins, but today was their first time there with them. It was a special place where they could pretend to be a normal family.

"So...I was wondering when we could visit the humans," Zachary said. "Don't you think Lucia and I are old enough?"

"Maybe next year," Michael replied.

"Can we attend high school too?" Lucia asked, excited.

"What?!" Michael raised his voice in surprise. "How do you know of high school?"

"Uncle Davin told us," Zachary said, as if it was no big deal.

Michael gave Davin the evil eye, the evil eye that Davin loathed.

Davin chuckled nervously. "You see...Daaaad. These young adult books Claudia bought from the bookstore that is now at the Crossroads library happened to mention the word "high school," so I had to explain it to both of them."

"Oh," Michael arched his brows in suspicion.

"I have to say, Davin is right. I read most of them." Claudia winked at Davin.

"Hmmm...." Michael narrowed his eyes at Claudia with a smile. "Whatever you say, my love."

"Sure...believe Claudia and not me," Davin pouted, pretending to look upset.

"And there is a reason for that," Michael chuckled.

Davin lit up a mischievous grin. "Okay...I see why...but...I'm not all bad."

Zachary stood up. "Uncle Davin, Uncle Caleb, and Auntie Vivian promised to take us swimming at the waterfall. Can we go now?"

"Sure." Caleb stood up and gave Lucia and Vivian a hand.

"Are you guys coming?" Vivian asked Claudia."

Before Claudia could answer, Michael winked at Claudia and spoke for her. "Claudia and I will be right behind you, but we have some things to do first."

"Sure...take your time. You know where to find us." Davin strode forward, following the stream. "Last one there is a rotten egg."

"What's a rotten egg?" Lucia asked, amused.

Davin chuckled. "I'll show you one."

"That's gross, Davin," Vivian remarked.

Michael blanketed Claudia's body tenderly with his wings as he watched them continue on the path. "Look at our five children together."

Claudia giggled. "Five?"

"Okay...maybe three. I'm counting Davin too."

"True, but he makes us young at heart."

"He sure does, and I love him very much, like a brother."

From a distance Michael could hear their conversation with his supersonic hearing.

Zachary: "Do you think Dad would let us observe high school kids so we can learn from them?"

Davin: "I don't know. Maybe we can ask him. But knowing him, he'll probably say no. But maybe I can take you there without him knowing...just maybe. I don't want him getting mad at me."

Michael spoke in Davin's mind. *"I heard that!"*

Davin: "Darn, your dad is listening. I thought he would be making out...I mean...I thought he would be busy."

Michael: *"I heard that too."*

Davin: "Grrr...."

Michael: *"I heard that too."*

Davin: "I meant for you to hear that. Now...out of my head."

Michael: *"Tell Zachary and Lucia that I will seriously think about it after their training is over, and their training is coming to an end soon. They need to hold a venator status first."*

Davin: "Cool."

MICHAEL TUNED OUT DAVIN AND focused on Claudia. "Now, where were we?"

Claudia was flirting with her eyes, sliding her hands along the fine ripped muscles of Michael's chest. "I think you were undressing me with your eyes, Mr. Michael."

"I can do more than that, Mrs. Michael, and it will only take me a second." Cupping her face into the palm of his hands, he tenderly stroked her cheeks, then to the necklace, and traced the words with the tips of his fingers. "I love you, Mrs. Michael, for eternity. Everything that we've been through, even the heartaches, I would do it all over again just to be right here with you and our children. I couldn't ask for anything more. I have more than I've ever dreamed of."

Claudia's heart felt so full—full from his love and full from his words—that it tingled, filling up with so much emotion that she thought it would burst. Without a doubt she felt the same. Melting into his body like it was the first time—because with Michael every time felt like the first time—she spoke from the depths of her heart and soul, "I feel the same, Michael. I love you more, for eternity."

After pressing his lips on hers, he asked, "Ready?"

Claudia proudly, slowly opened up her wings and Michael did the same. As their wings tenderly caressed, they started to enclose each other. With no need for words, they looked loving into each other's eyes, and their wings feathered together. Gently spiraling upward, they kissed under the heavenly blue sky, somewhere beyond, and promised to live each passing day blissfully with love and hope, for every day they had was a blessing. Truly and without a doubt...love and friendship know no boundaries.

THE END

CROSSROADS SAGA READING ORDER:
Crossroads
Between
Beyond
Eternity
Halo City

OTHER BOOKS BY MARY TING:
From Gods

PEN NAME, M. CLARKE:
Something Great
Something Wonderful
Something Forever 8/25/2014
My Clarity (stand-alone) 5/12/2014

KEEP READING FOR TEASERS FROM OTHER MARY TING BOOKS!

(New Adult) *Something Great*—writing as M. Clarke
(Young Adult) *From Gods*

SOMETHING GREAT
BY MARY TING WRITING AS M. CLARKE

CHAPTER 6

LUKE WASN'T THE "PERFECT GENTLEMAN" type of guy. Most men opened the car door for their date, but he never showed that kind of charisma. But what did I know about men, anyway? They were all different, just like us. Was it too much for me to want him to open the door for me?

The restaurant was nice, dimly lit, and not too crowded. White linen tablecloths covered the tables that were adorned with candles on top, giving it a romantic ambiance. I had to give him credit for that. The hostess took us toward the back to a table for two, but the tables were very close together. I had hoped there wouldn't be anyone sitting near us.

The hostess pulled out my chair, and after I sat, she placed the white linen napkin on my lap. "Thank you," I said to her.

"The waiter will be right with you." She smiled and left.

"How was your day?" Luke asked. He had one eye on me and the other eye on the phone. "Sorry...checking an urgent email."

"That's okay. I had a fantastic day actually. I got the job I was talking about." I tried my best to contain my excitement, but he looked at me like he had no idea what I was talking about. I clearly remembered texting him about it the night before. Apparently, he hadn't read the text or had forgotten.

"Yes, of course, I remember," he said slowly and mechanically as his eyes flickered to his phone, then to me. "That's wonderful. What position will you be holding for the company?"

"I'll be going in to talk about that next week."

"I see," he nodded, looking past me, seemingly in deep thought, but not about our conversation.

The waiter came by with the menus. "May I take your orders for your drinks?"

I was just about to ask for a glass of water when Luke broke in. "We'll both have glasses of water, please."

He didn't even ask me what I wanted. I brushed it off, thinking he knew I always ordered water.

"Sure." The waiter left after he told us the specials.

Gazing from top to bottom of the menu, I had a hard time deciding what to order, especially when all I could think of was the need to use the restroom. "Excuse me. I'll be right back. Can you order me the salmon special if the waiter comes back before I do?"

"Sure."

Not knowing exactly where the restroom was, I headed toward the back where restrooms were usually located. This place was like a maze, or I had a very bad sense of direction. Seeing a bar, I thought I'd ask the bartender.

Though there was no one standing behind the bar, I figured the bartender went to get something and would be right back. From where I stood, I could see the waitress and waiters, but I didn't feel like walking in that direction again just to ask a question, so I waited. I could see the pendant on my neck sparkling brilliantly against the mirrored wall. What a great fake diamond!

From the corner of my eye I saw a figure, but dismissed it and shifted my eyes to the right, where they settled on the elusive restroom sign. I was just about to head in that direction when someone spoke to me from behind in a deep, manly voice that sent shivers down my back.

"I'm your prescription. Let me be your new addiction." His words glided like butter, smooth and cool.

Startled, I twitched, and turned my body to his voice. There he was, all six feet of him, peering down on me with that smile that could make me do just about anything. Though there was nothing to laugh about, especially seeing this hottie in front of me, I couldn't help but giggle from his words.

He wore beige casual pants and a black sweater that fit perfectly to the tone of his body. His hair was brushed to the side, showing his nice forehead. Whatever kind of cologne he had on made me want to dive right into his arms...maybe it wasn't the cologne, but just him.

"Pretty cheesy, huh?" he chuckled.

I shyly giggled as I stared down at my shoes. What's wrong with me? Answer him. "Umm...kind of," I smiled as I peered up, only to have him take my breath away again.

"Sorry. I just had to say that. You looked so lost and vulnerable. Did you need some help?"

Great! To him I was just a lost puppy...lost and vulnerable. "I actually found what I was looking for." I was staring into his eyes, melting, feeling myself sinking into him. Snap out of it!

"You certainly did," he said with a playful tone.

Arching my brows in confusion, I thought about what I'd said. From his perspective, my words had been about him.

"We meet again, for the third time."

He was counting?

"You left so abruptly at Café Express, I didn't get to ask you for your name."

"Umm...my name? Oh...my name is Jeanella Mefferd, but you can call me Jenna."

Extending his hand, he waited for me. "I'm Maxwell. But you can call me Max."

Nervously, I placed my hand in his to shake. It was strong, yet gentle...just right, and heat blazed through me from his touch.

"Are you here with someone?"

"Yes." I looked away shyly.

"Are you lost? Do you need some help?"

"Actually, I was looking for the restroom. Since I didn't know where it was I thought I'd ask the bartender, but I guess there isn't one, and I'm on my way to the restroom." I rambled nervously as I slowly pulled my hand back to point in the direction I meant to go. I had just realized we were holding hands during our short conversation. "So...I'd better go."

"I'll walk you there."

What? "Oh...no need. I'm sure I won't get lost." Feeling the heat on my face again, I turned before he could say another word, but it didn't matter what I had said. His hand was gently placed on my back, guiding me to the women's room. I turned my back to the bathroom door to thank him, but he spoke first.

"I think this is my stop," he muttered, looking straight at me. "I'm not wanted in there. What do you think?" He arched his brows, and his tone held a note of challenge.

Huh? He wants to go in with me? I gasped silently, as I was still lost in his eyes. "I think the women in there will throw themselves at you." I couldn't believe I'd said those words. I couldn't take it back. What was I doing, flirting with him?

He seemed to like what he heard. His arms reached out, his muscles flexing as he placed one on each side of me on the wall. With nowhere to go, I was trapped inside the bubble of his arms. He leaned down toward the left side of my face and brushed my hair with his cheek. "You smell...delicious," he whispered. His hot breath shot tingles to places I hadn't expected them.

Out of nervousness and habit, my left index finger flew inside my mouth. Max gave a crooked, naughty grin and slowly took my hand out of my mouth. "Did you know that biting one's finger is an indication one is sexually deprived?" His words came out slowly, playfully, but hot. "I can fix that for you, if you'd like."

He did not just say that to me! I parted my lips for a good comeback, but I couldn't find one. Feeling my chest rise and fall quickly, I tried to control the heated desire. Sure, he'd helped me once, but that didn't mean we were friends, or flirting buddies, or that I would allow him to fix my sexual deprivation. Oh God...can guys tell if you haven't done it in a very long time? This had to stop or else...oh dear...I wanted to take him with me into the restroom.

Needing to put a stop to the heat, I placed my hand on his chest... big mistake. Touching him made the heat worse, and tingles that were already intensifying burst through every inch of me. I had to push him away.

As if he knew what I meant to do, he pulled back, but his eyes did the talking instead. There was no need for words; I felt his hard stare on my body, as if he was undressing me with his gorgeous eyes. His gaze was powerful, as if his eyes were hands; I felt them all over me, completely unraveling me.

Just when I thought I was going to faint, his eyes shifted to mine again. "It was really nice to meet you, Jenna. I'm sure we'll see each other again, real soon. I better let you go. Your someone must be waiting for you. By the way...." There was a pause as he charmed me with his eyes again. "You...took my breath away. If I were your someone, I wouldn't let you out of my sight for even a second, because someone like me will surely try to whisk you away." He winked and left.

Oh no...don't ever wink again. That wink made me shiver even more, let alone his words. I pushed the door with my behind without thinking. Thank goodness there was no one by the door, or I would have knocked a stranger over with the force of my push. Max was right. How long had I been away, but did Luke even care? Oh no...what if he came to find me and he saw...oh no! I quickly took care of business and headed back toward our table.

Wiping Max and his words out of my head, I had to think of an excuse. What would I say if he saw us? How could I explain? Anxiety was rising to the surface, and so was my blood pressure. Just as I turned the corner to our table, I saw that another couple had been seated next to us. I gazed around the room, a little upset. Why would they seat another couple next to us when there were other empty tables around us? I didn't understand.

"Luke, I'm so sorry," I apologized as I sat. "I got lost and then...."

Oh no...Max was sitting adjacent to me, and his beautiful date was sitting across from him. My face felt hot, but my hands felt cold as the blood drained down to my toes. Max having a date was not the issue. Flirting with me when he was on a date was. How wrong was that? He was trouble for sure. In a way I felt guilty, guilty towards Luke, because I had enjoyed it.

"Are you okay?" Luke asked.

Placing my hands on my cheeks, my cold hands soothed them somewhat. "I think I'm coming down with something," I whispered, trying not to attract Max's attention, but who was I kidding? He was not blind or stupid.

"Would you like to go home?" Luke asked, looking concerned.

"I'll be fine, Luke. Maybe I just need something to eat."

When dinner arrived, our conversation was minimal. A part of me kept quiet because of Max. In a way, I was more interested in their conversation, because his date giggled every so often. From what I could tell, she was tall and her dark hair fell to her shoulders. Was this a personal or a business date? I couldn't tell, but why did I care?

Never once did I look his way, and never once did he look my way. Well, truth be told, I did peek with my peripheral vision. I wasn't sure if Max snuck a glance, but Luke looked their way when Max's date was a little bit too loud.

When Luke excused himself to the restroom after he had finished his dinner, Max's date did the same thing. Though there were more couples around us now, I felt as though this place only existed for the two of us. Feeling uncomfortable, I focused on my plate. With my fork, I swirled around what was left of my mashed potatoes. Suddenly, I gasped and turned. I knew it was Max, but the fact that he'd pulled up his chair and bumped his shoulder into mine startled me.

"Hi, again. Ignoring me, aren't you?" he said casually, as if we were good friends.

I turned to him. His face was way too close for my comfort. I had no choice but to gaze into his hypnotic eyes. "Ignoring you? I hardly know you, and you and I each have a date," I snapped. I didn't know where the angry tone was coming from.

"We can fix that."

"We can?" I asked, dumbfounded.

Instead of answering, he tilted his head, with a look as if he remembered something he wanted to say. "I meant to ask you how your hand was earlier, but I got a little...distracted." Max grabbed my right hand and tenderly rubbed the area where the hot coffee had spilled. He'd even remembered which hand it was.

"It's much better. Thank you for asking," I mumbled, fixated on his index finger, stroking the area on my hand. His touch produced a tingling vibration that was slowly waving throughout my body, and I didn't want him to stop, but I managed to pull back without offending him. If I'd let him continue, I would have dived into his arms, and I didn't want to make a fool out of myself.

"Good. I'm glad, but I think your someone is boring. And he doesn't treat you well."

Now, he was being rude and arrogant. "He's just fine. You don't know him."

"True, I don't know him. Maybe your someone is with my someone, and they're making out in the bathroom."

I didn't know why I thought that was funny, but I laughed, a good hardy laugh, the kind of laugh that gives you tears, and he laughed with me. No, I couldn't see what he'd just planted in my mind, but the thought was hilarious. But why? Because I thought that a sweet, non-dangerous type of guy like Luke wouldn't make out with someone like her. Nah...couldn't picture it.

Wiping the little tears that had settled in the corner of my eyes, I looked at Max. His eyes were soft and kind, and he looked at me with the sweetest smile. Neither one of us looked away, as if we were reaching for something deeper. I felt something that I couldn't describe in his gaze, like I had known him all my life. There was a strong, undeniable connection, like two lost souls finally finding each other. Was it the hot, steamy flirtations we shared, or was it the laughter? I didn't know. Whatever it was, I liked the feeling too much. But at the same time, it frightened me deeply, so I looked away.

Just in the nick of time, Max settled back to his table. Luke showed up first. He didn't ask me if I wanted dessert or if I was finished; he'd already paid the bill, and just asked me if I was ready. As usual, he didn't walk with me. I followed behind him. Was someone like Luke—a readable, easy, non-dangerous type of guy—what I wanted? I wasn't sure, but my eyes were opened that night.

Just before Max was out of my sight, I peered over my shoulder. I figured I was safe to look since his date had come back just as I got up, but I was wrong. His piercing eyes were watching me the whole time as I exited, and just before I turned the corner to disappear, he winked at me, leaving me completely unglued.

from gods

BY MARY TING

MASON'S VOICE WAS SWEET AND caring. It was this side of him that made Skylar forget about his rude self. She always knew there was a wonderful side to him. She could just feel it when she first looked into his soulful eyes. "What will you say to them? Won't they be looking for him?"

"I'll figure something out. But that is not the reason I came here. I came to make sure you were okay, and since you weren't answering your text, I thought...actually, I didn't know what to think. I knew Remus went out and when he does, he's out pretty late. I'm actually appalled. I never thought he could...well...he did have anger issues, but that's not an excuse for what he did. I didn't want you to think I left you there so Remus could do what he did, even though I had no idea what he did at first. You didn't think that, did you?"

Skylar couldn't remember if that ever crossed her mind, and since she didn't want to make him feel bad, she shook her head. "No...I didn't."

"Good, because you may think I'm what you would call a 'bad boy,' I would never hurt you physically. I'm not that bad."

Skylar gave a short smile and almost giggled, but stopped when his finger traced the cut on her lower right lip.

"Remus did this to you, didn't he?" For a brief moment he closed his eyes and inhaled a deep breath, as if he was trying to suppress the anger that seemed to have crept up on him. Delicately, he brushed it again. "I'm sorry."

The small gesture of his simple touch drove Skylar into a whirlwind of heated emotions. He was already sitting way too close, and every time she turned her head to speak, all she could do was think impure thoughts. In order to avoid something she might regret doing, she nodded to answer and pulled back, making Mason drop his hand.

"You should smile more often. It makes me smile," he said unexpectedly.

Blushing like she'd never blushed before, she looked away shyly.

"How did you get back home? You didn't fly, did you?"

"Nooo," Skylar took in his teasing. "I...well...kind of...borrowed Remus's car."

"Borrowed, huh? I think it's more like stealing."

Unsure if Mason was joking again by his tone, she tensed up. "I—"

"I think I need to call the cops. Maybe I should call Doug. What do you think, Ms. Rome?" Mason chuckled.

He had called her Ms. Rome the night they met. Skylar couldn't believe his sense of humor tonight. Laughing like a schoolgirl, she held on to the moment. After what had happened just a couple of hours ago, his presence gave her comfort and put her mind and heart at ease.

"If you don't mind, I'm going to drive his car home."

"Yes, of course. The key is on top of the dresser. Then, what about your car?"

"I didn't drive here."

"Then...how did you get here?"

Mason leaned over and whispered, "It's my little secret."

The small breeze from his warm breath in her ear sent tingly awareness all over her. Brushing away the thought of his lips on hers, she tried to focus on other things. Knowing he had super abilities, it didn't surprise her that he ran there. Most likely, he figured out she'd taken Remus's car to get home, so he came to retrieve it.

"It's way past your bedtime, and you have to work tomorrow. I should go." He got up and gave her his hand. The force of his pull made her leap into his arms. Inhaling a small gasp, she immediately drowned in their tangled bodies. In his arms she felt small, but safe for the very first time. From that moment, she knew without a doubt that she could trust him.

Mason finally released Skylar after gazing into her eyes longer than usual. "Umm...I should go now." His eyes scanned her from head to toe as he guided her to her bed. "So...is this what you wear to bed?"

Warmth flushed to her cheeks. She suddenly realized she wasn't wearing a bra, and immediately got into bed and pulled the sheet above her chest.

He gave a mischievous grin, twitching his brows.

"Why?" She examined what she wore...short shorts and a tank top. "What's wrong with what I'm wearing? Should I be wearing something else?"

"Kind of skimpy, don't you think?"

Great! He was back to being himself again. "Kind of skimpy? It's hot," she stated. Suddenly, she felt like she was exposing herself.

"It's hot alright. Wear something longer next time, or else I may not be able to control myself."

Skylar flushed with warmth again. He was actually flirting with her.

"Close your eyes," he said, guiding her lower until her head was on the pillow. Then he sat on the edge of the bed. Flexing his muscles, he pressed his hands on either side of the pillow, and the intensity of the want and need in his eyes as he looked at her left her breathless. His eyes traveled to her lips, then back up to her eyes, and stayed there as he slowly moved to close the distance.

Withering beneath him, Skylar's breath was still caught in her chest. His close proximity aroused every inch of her, and undeniable desire brewed in the energy between them. In anticipation of the sweetness of his lips on hers, the pitter-patter of her heart made her chest rapidly rise and fall. Parting her lips, she was ready for him as he lowered toward her...closer...closer. What seemed to take a great amount of effort from him to turn away, he nuzzled the side of her neck instead.

"Close your eyes." He huffed out a heavy, rough breath, as if he was trying to restrain himself from something he wanted to do. His hot breath brushed against the side of her neck, making her quiver in all the right places.

Frozen in place, Skylar had to gather herself before she could speak from the letdown. "Close my eyes? But, you're still here." Her words barely escaped her lips. Snuggling into her pillow, she tried to shake off the heated daze.

Raking his hair back, he sat up, looking overcome. "Stop talking, Echo, or you're going to the naughty corner." His lips stretched into a smug half grin. Oh...that grin he does so well, frisky and sexy at the same time.

"And if I don't? What are you going to do, spank me? No...are you going to shock me?"

He twitched his brows playfully. "You really want to know? We can do both and see how that feels."

With no comeback, she sank deeper into the mattress, hiding beneath the sheet, secretly thinking how hot but twisted that sounded.

His hand reached over, covering her eyes. "Go to sleep, Echo." His authoritative tone was final, but she was up for the challenge.

"My name isn't Echo, and you're still here," she yawned, feeling extremely lethargic, waiting for his response. When she didn't feel the lightweight over her eyes, she opened them. There was no sign of Mason, or any evidence he had gone out the door.

ABOUT THE AUTHOR

 Author Mary Ting resides in Southern California with her husband and two children. She enjoys oil painting and making jewelry. Writing her first novel, Crossroads Saga, happened by chance. It was a way to grieve the death of her beloved grandmother, and inspired by a dream she once had as a young girl. When she started reading new adult novels, she fell in love with the genre. It was the reason she had to write one-Something Great. Why the pen name, M Clarke? She tours with Magic Johnson Foundation to promote literacy and her children's chapter book-No Bullies Allowed.

Website: www.authormaryting.com
Facebook: Facebook.com/AuthorMaryTing

Twitter: https://twitter.com/MaryTing
Goodreads: Goodreads.com/author/show/7181038.M_Clarke
Goodreads: Goodreads.com/author/show/4388953.Mary_Ting
Pinterest: http://www.pinterest.com/mting888/
Instagram: http://instagram.com/authormaryting
Blog: www.marytingbooks.blogspot.com

Made in the USA
Charleston, SC
29 March 2014